Forever Sunshine

by

Collette Scott

This is a work of fiction. Names, characters and incidents are the products of the author's imagination or are used fictitiously. Any resemblance to actual events, locales, or persons, living or dead, is purely coincidental.

For information address Marimay Publishing, P.O.Box 11821, Tempe, AZ 85284

ISBN: 978-0-615-46254-7
ISBN - 10: 0-61-546254-5
ISBN: 978-1-4524-7424-3 (ebook)

In Loving Memory of

Mary Josephine Brennan, Anne and Frank McKay, and Maylah and Richard Park. Thank you for your acceptance and guidance. Though I wish you were still here in the flesh, I always hear your voices in the wind.

Acknowledgments

No book would ever be written if a writer did not have the time to concentrate. Therefore, my first round of thanks extends to My Girls and Steve. Thank you for giving me the time and space to enter my own little world. This is and always will be for you.

To my editor, Steve: thank you for your critical input. Every writer needs brutal honesty at times, and your time and patience is greatly appreciated.

Thank you Wendy, for your last minute input.

To the Lee family: your enthusiasm and encouragement gave me strength. I love you all and am so glad you're a part of my life.

To Erika: thank you for really lighting the fire beneath me. Best of luck to your projects as well.

To my family and friends: I am so thankful to say that I have too many to list in such a short page. You all know who you are. Thank you for being a part of my life. I truly am blessed to have your support.

Prologue

Doctor Stansfield told me to write down what I was feeling. He said that if I did, perhaps I would begin to heal. Of course, he's never gone through something like this, so how could he truly know if it will help? How could he know how to heal the gaping hole in my chest that used to be my heart? How would he know how badly I ache inside, how tortured my soul feels?

How empty I am.

How could this have happened?

The shadowed forms that came to the door still haunt my dreams. In fact, they even haunt my every thought. I don't think that will ever go away. The pity in their swollen, bloodshot eyes mocks me, and the sounds of their somber words still ring in my ears. I can still hear the puppy barking.

"I'm sorry, Cher, there's been an accident."

An accident?

I knew right away.

I could see it in their eyes. Even though they tried to hide their emotions from me, I could see the despair, shock, and sadness all jumbled like a kaleidoscope on their faces.

Oh, yes, I fought them. I screamed at them to tell me it was a joke. How could it be?

We had spoken not three hours before.

Doctor Stansfield told me that those initial feelings were not unusual. He said that there are stages of loss widely experienced by people and my reactions were common. Initially I suffered from denial and anger. The bargaining was normal, he said.

They had posted several officers to stay with me that first night. To watch over me, they said. Among them were Chuck and Kerri, with pained looks of stunned grief on their faces. They watched me with sorrow in their eyes. I knew they were hurting, too.

Statistics are a sad thing. I think it's a horrible way to commend the life of another. There are statistics for the number of deaths attributed to domestic violence. There are statistics for the number of deaths attributed to cancer. There are statistics for the number of deaths attributed to automobile accidents. Now my family has become connected with a statistic once again, and I hate that. But if we were not a statistic, I probably would not be sitting here now, pouring out my heart to a blank notebook of bright white pages and pale blue lines. I would not know this agony of loss or the pain of this complete sorrow. Then, too, I would not have known the unconditional surrender in the love I received. Nor the joy of the brief time we shared.

Am I a survivor? Can I find the strength to pull through this? Right now I do not think I can. I have lost so much, but inside a part of me understood that there are those who suffer like this every day. Who am I to claim my pain is any worse than another's?

To be a survivor is an amazing thing. I see it every day at Mary's shelter. These strong women give up everything, walk away with nothing but the clothes on their back, and they are able to find their courage and learn to move on, smarter and wiser than before. Will I be able to as well? Am I really as strong as they are?

I think that's why I sit here now. To find out if I am as tough as everyone thinks I am. In despair I shall relive those brief years, and maybe, just maybe, Doctor Stansfield is right. Maybe I will heal at least a portion of my heart. And maybe I will understand that I was blessed in receiving the kind of love many people only dream of. I was one of the lucky few.

Chapter 1

It was a suffocating summer evening when my sister brought her unhappy marriage to my apartment door. Summer in the Valley was similar to winter in the more northern states, where the stifling temperatures caused tempers to flare because most wanted to escape the oven that had become Phoenix. Closed quarters due to the heat trapped people in their homes like the cold up north kept people indoors. The feeling of being trapped sometimes encourages anger, and anger at times spreads to violence. Violence sent Shelly into my arms, and she needed my help.

That single phone call changed my young life forever, shaping it into a form I never would have thought possible. She also brought the man who would be harbinger of that change with her.

At the time I was frightened. Shelly was sobbing when she called me at work, so I did the only thing I could think of. I was still a kid, though I never would have admitted it, and my lack of worldly wisdom shaped the events of that night. See, instead of notifying the police straight away, I drove out to her East Mesa house and brought her and Jacob to my apartment not far from the Arizona State University campus in Tempe.

Despite the distance, we were followed.

"You should've told me sooner," I whispered.

I crouched down in front of the door of my apartment, close enough to hear but safe from the man outside. It had grown dark as the evening progressed, but it was still oppressively hot. The thermometer attached to my windowsill claimed it was still 95 degrees outside. The air retained the oppressiveness of the day, and it was thick and heavy with heat – almost like being in a dryer. Standing out there only seemed to irritate him more.

The coaxing on the other side of my door worsened to an angry howl, and my voice could barely be heard over his demands. More urgent knocking ensued, sending me crawling across the room. Reaching up to the switch on the wall, I shut off the last of the lights in the small living room leaving only a dim orange glow from the streetlights outside. I still was stunned that he had gotten there so quickly.

Blinking several times to adjust to the darkness, I dashed back to Shelly's side. My sister huddled underneath the single window in the living room of my apartment with her knees drawn up to her chest, which was heaving. Of course, mine was, too. Eyes swimming with tears, she frowned at the harshness of my words.

"Tell you what, Cher? That my husband hits me when he gets drunk? That's not something you want to announce to everyone, you know?" Her voice lowered. "It wasn't always like this."

Shelly's voice was rough with tears and hoarse from her cries. Throwing my arm around her shoulders, I noticed that she winced from the pain. With a heavy sigh, I eased my arm away and leaned against the wall. Though I was not sure exactly what had happened that night, I could tell that it was not the first time. She still bore red marks around her shoulders where he had shoved her against the wall and held her there.

"Was he drinking?"

She was slow to answer. "I don't think so."

This Joe was not the man I had known for the past seven years. The man I remembered from Easter, Thanksgiving and Christmas dinners was a charming, friendly guy. Maybe he was a little controlling, but never deliberately mean. I had to admit that I was scared at the sudden change.

"What happened tonight? Why's he freaking out like this?"

She shook her head in confusion. "I don't know. He came home angry... This is the first time I've left the house."

After a few moments, I realized it grew quiet outside again. This was nothing new. Several times already he had stopped his incessant pleas to drink from the brown, paper-bag wrapped bottle in his hand. What I originally thought was spirits ended up being an oversized water bottle, which did not surprise me. I expected that he would have gotten tired of sitting on concrete stairs that still retained the heat of the summer sun. In the summer, one did not sit on any form of pavement. It was just too darn hot.

"Shelly, if you do not open this door right now, there will be serious trouble later."

We exchanged glances on the other side of the door. His voice was ominously calm, and I felt a shiver race down my back. "That's it. I'm calling."

"Cher, no, please..." I ignored my sister's plea and came to my feet. The phone was sitting in the charger on the wall in the kitchen, and I reached for it quickly before Shelly could protest any more. After dialing those precious three numbers, I waited to lodge my complaint.

No sooner had I hung up the phone than the knocking began

again. He was still using the calm tone at the moment, almost in a sing-song pattern that reminded me of a villain in a scary movie. Returning my attention to my sister, I noticed that her fingers strayed to the lock on the door again.

"Don't you do it! Not with Jacob asleep in the other room."

"Is he even asleep now? With all this noise, who knows?"

My eyes narrowed. The lack of concern in her tone made me suspicious. "Has he hurt Jacob before, too?"

She shook her head, wincing at the pain her movement caused. "No," she whispered, "not yet."

"Oh, Shelly, you should've told me sooner."

I pressed my cheek against the cool aluminum of the door. My brother-in-law was making enough noise to wake the whole apartment complex. I hoped management would not evict me for this scene so late at night. While the complex housed mostly ASU students who partied late into the night during the regular semesters, during the summer the place could be as calm as a graveyard. Right now, there were a few people out who sent curious glances towards my place before hurrying to their apartments to lock their doors.

"Shel-ly!"

"Go home, Joe!" I shouted. "I've called the police. Please, just go home now."

"I want my wife! Goddamn it, send her out here... Cheeerrr!"

His voice rose on a wail. I was reminded of a spoiled toddler, whining because he was not getting his way. I had to bite the inside of my cheek to keep my big mouth shut.

When we did not answer, he began to pound on the door with increasing violence. I scooted away again. This time it sounded as though he was kicking the door with both of his booted feet, and I could see it straining under his powerful blows. For a moment I worried that it would not hold.

Shelly grimaced in nervousness and pain. Her eyes were wide and wild – at least one of them was. "Jesus, Cher. He's all out of sorts. Maybe I should just go out and talk to him."

I stared at my sister hard. Even with only light from outside streaming in, I could see her eye swelling rapidly with every long minute that passed. Her fair skin was now turning purple and red in splotches of swollen tissue. Soon she would be sporting a black eye and multiple bruises.

"There's no way I'll let you go out to him while he is acting like this. He needs to cool off. I called the police; they should be here soon. Will you just wait?"

"But he'll kill me if he gets arrested," Shelly whispered, her good eye still glistening with tears.

I shook my head adamantly, totally naïve but brave. How little I knew then. "No, he won't. I called the police, not you. If he wants to blame someone, he can blame me."

As if on cue I saw the flashing lights illuminate the hallway from my bedroom. I sighed with relief and came to my knees. "Wait here," I ordered firmly.

Hurrying down the short hall to my bedroom, I first made sure that Jacob was asleep in my bed. Then I tiptoed to the small window overlooking the parking lot below. With a shaky hand, I reached for the blinds to peek outside. Two white and blue cruisers had stopped, and their red, white, and blue lights illuminated the entire parking lot as well as my small bedroom. It amazed me just how quiet the normally bustling area had grown. Most likely all my neighbors were huddled by their windows watching the Friday night drama unfold.

"Well, they're here," Shelly said with resignation. She stood in the doorway, her face pale with fear. Her voice sounded hollow, and it frightened me more than the red marks covering her neck and shoulders.

"Yes... and the whole complex knows it."

"I'm so sorry, Cher. I shouldn't have involved you in this." She grimaced. "I never should've come here."

"Of course you should've come here. I'd never want to see you hurt. What he did was wrong, and he needs to know that you won't tolerate it," I said bravely, smoothing a lock of Shelly's long brown hair from her face. "I'm your sister. If you can't count on me, who is there?"

As I waited for her to answer, I returned my attention to the activity outside. Already two of the policemen had emerged from their car, one stocky and the other tall and thin, both dressed in the dark uniform of the police department.

My eyes drifted to a third officer, just then climbing out of his vehicle. I did not know why he captured my attention, but I could not drag my gaze away. He seemed to exude self-confidence, and his calm nonchalance was soothing to my frazzled nerves. Though he appeared young, there was authority in his manner. This man, I thought, could help end this tonight.

He carelessly shut the door of his cruiser behind him and ran a hand over his close-cropped hair with a casual indifference before placing on his hat. He was much taller than the other two and lean, with long legs encased in dark uniform slacks and dark boots. I watched as he pulled his flashlight from his duty belt and followed close behind the other officers. They exchanged a few friendly words as they passed by my window.

"No one." At the sound of Shelly's voice, I dropped back down.

Throwing her a grim smile, I nodded my head. "That's right.

We'll get him away from you."

"God, Cher," she said with a shaky laugh. "You make it sound so easy. You have absolutely no idea who you're dealing with."

The ominous sound of her words gave me pause, but I was still so inexperienced that I shrugged it off with a smile. At the time, I had no idea the amount of power one person could hold over another. "Come on. They'll find Joe in a minute."

We shut the door behind us as we left my bedroom in the hopes that Jacob would remain asleep while the police were there. Returning to my front door, we heard Joe descend the concrete stairs and begin talking to the approaching officers. A silent communication passed between us, and we remained silent while we strained to listen. Shelly dropped to her knees by the window to witness the spectacle unfolding below, and I crouched down beside her, pulling a small corner of the silky sheer curtain covering the blinds aside to witness his lies.

"He wouldn't be so bad if he hadn't just lost his job," I heard Shelly say softly.

"You don't have to make excuses for him. I'll help you, Shelly, you know I will."

"But you have to pay tuition for another year and a half. You work yourself so hard for your degree. I couldn't accept your pity."

"It wouldn't be pity, you know that. You're my matronly older sister."

She turned to face me, a wry smile on her face. "I'm only five years older than you. Don't make me sound so ancient."

I grinned at her and reached for her hand. Joining our fingers, I could feel her cool and clammy skin, and I knew she was terrified. The slight trembling in her limbs pierced my heart.

By rights we were not the closest of siblings, but I still felt the familiar bond. Five years older and married by the age of 21, Shelly had not been a major influence in my life. Nevertheless, blood was thicker than water. That was even more important since our parents had decided Arizona was too hot and retired to the wilderness of Montana. We were the only family left, which meant that I had to protect her – especially since her husband would not.

Besides, I adored Jacob.

Darling Jacob was four. A sweet, soft-spoken boy, with black hair and the most striking blue eyes I had ever seen. He had inherited my father's eyes, but the rest of him was pure Joe. Joe was handsome in a rugged sort of way. Tall and heavyset, he had hair as black as night, like his son's, but his eyes were the color of muddy water.

Muddy, like his soul.

I watched him below with growing disbelief. He had advanced upon the wary policemen and held out his hand, his smile wide. The shorter officer nodded his head coolly and began questioning him. For a moment it appeared as though they believed his story – whatever it could have been – but then his partner glanced up at the window where we peered out through the glass. With startled gasps, we both crouched down, and then managed nervous giggles at our childish reaction. Despite our frazzled nerves, our similar reactions brought back memories of our childhood together, and once more I swore to do everything I could to protect them. The righteous anger that filled me made me braver than I should have been, almost to the point of foolishness.

The officers below were still talking. Though their voices were muffled through the thickness of the double-paned glass and hum of my air conditioning, I was able to hear them curtly ask for Joe's explanation and then explain to him that he was disturbing the peace. Nervously peeking one last time, I caught the short one's partner glance our way. The short one and the authoritative one exchanged words, and then they started the ascent. Joe remained behind reluctantly with the short one's partner, watching the other two climb the stairs that led to my door.

I sat back from the window and stared at Shelly. Her gaze flicked between the scene below and my face. I could tell that she was on the verge of caving already, and somehow I knew that was exactly what Joe expected. She was unable to meet my eyes, so I took her hands in mine and spoke firmly. "Maybe you should go check on Jacob, Shelly. I can handle this by myself."

"But…"

"No buts. Remember how scared Jacob was?"

"So?"

"He's too afraid to go home. And if Joe hit you earlier, he's only going to be angrier with you now. He's been outside for ages, probably getting angrier… Please, just go."

I shoved her away just as the first knock came on the door. Despite my ignorance with spousal abuse, I was not that foolish. Tempers were high on this hot, oppressive night. I knew something terrible would happen if they left with him, and I was not going to let that happen. Not while I could stop it.

Even as children, Shelly had never been known as an ambitious child. The daring one in the family had always been me. I was the one who led the way and Shelly followed. Growing up, I was labeled the popular one, the pretty one, the smart one. It seemed strange to me, especially when most psychological studies claimed the firstborn was the over-achiever. Never Shelly. The quiet way she grew up transferred into a soft-spoken adult who married soon after high school. Jacob arrived just two short years later, and Shelly devoted all of her time to her family.

I knew that she had agreed to leave only because I had been so forceful. She wanted to please everyone, and going against Joe was the last thing she wanted to do. However, that night I had promised that I would take care of her and Jacob, and I was determined to fulfill that promise.

With that determination steeling my spine, I returned my attention to the door. To my surprise, my voice trembled slightly when I asked who was there.

"Police, ma'am," came the deliberate reply.

As if I did not already know.

I opened the door a crack, my poised foot preventing more than half my face to show. The stocky officer was staring expectantly at me, waiting for me to let him in. He had a kind face, though at the moment he appeared stern. The crinkle lines around his eyes belied his firm words. "Did you call the police, ma'am?"

"Yes," I said. My voice trembled with nervousness. "He's been at my door all evening, knocking and pounding. I just want him to go away."

Taking an aggressive step toward the stairs, Joe met my level gaze with a scowl. "Officer, my wife and I had an argument earlier today," he called out. "Cher, here, showed up at my house and convinced my wife to take our son and come here. All I want to do is talk to Shelly and make sure she's okay."

"Are you serious?" I asked incredulously.

Any nervousness I had felt was quickly replaced by anger. This Joe I did not know. He was completely foreign to me. All charming and smooth, when just moments ago he was sobbing. I could not comprehend this bizarre behavior.

"Wait a minute!" the second officer commanded as though sensing how close I was to losing my temper. He turned back to Joe.

"Were you banging on the door?"

Joe smiled and bowed his head, looking like a perfect remorseful man. "I didn't mean to scare them. I was just worried."

The transformation taking place held me rooted to the spot. Though I knew that Joe was always charming, I was unable to hide my incredulousness. How could a man cry and sob outside our door for an hour, despite our requests for him to go home, suddenly rise up and smile and shake the hands of the policemen coming to question him?

Talk about bizarre.

"So you were making all the noise here?"

"Yes, sir. I wanted to make sure she was okay, that's all."

"Have you been drinking this evening?"

"Not a drop."

"I want him to go away," I insisted, my voice cracking.

When the officers returned their attention back to me, Joe sent me another warning glance. "I'll go away when I'm sure my wife's okay."

I ignored him. "She's fine and doesn't want to see you right now."

The officers exchanged looks before returning their attention to me. "May we come in, Miss...?"

"Bridwell," I said quickly.

"We'd like to speak to your sister."

"Fine," I said. Standing slightly to the side, I opened the door wide to allow them to pass.

When Shelly entered the room, I was stunned by her appearance. She had applied some of my makeup to her bruises, magnificently covering up her injuries. After sending me a pleading glance, she broke down and sobbed herself. She tried to defend Joe. After he had beat on her and terrified their son, she actually tried to cover for him and claimed that she had fallen and hurt her eye. I was even more surprised and not just a little bit angry to realize that she was so convincing that even I almost believed her.

The two officers were polite and actually spoke amiably. I could sense their stoic resignation as they patiently listened to our version of the story. They collected our licenses and ran us through their system, returning and handing everything back with no indication as to what they were feeling. While I fumed, the tall, authoritative one questioned my sister for her side of the story. He was polite and kindly asked her if she needed medical attention for her eye, to which she quickly refused. I wanted to shout at them to be realistic and realize that she was lying through her teeth.

The shorter, portly man with graying-brown hair broke away and silently wandered around my apartment, looking around for drugs or weapons, or God only knows what. Occasionally he would throw a question my way, asking me to confirm something that was said. I watched Shelly and the authoritative officer, who ignored me completely and focused on my sister. Though he was gentle, his face remained aloof as he spoke to her. I was able to overhear him warning her that Jacob could be removed from the house if they thought he was in any danger. Shelly gasped and turned to me in a sheer panic.

I got his attention when I stepped forward and insisted that he was safe in my apartment. What more could I do?

On two other occasions I was aware of the same officer watching me, perhaps sizing me up, yet when I raised my head defiantly to return the stare he looked away. I can handle my nephew, but I need your help to save my sister, I wanted to scream. Can't you see that he's nuts?

Of course, I should have known that they had much more

experience than I did on battered women and domestic violence. The two officers that had crammed into my tight living room that sultry night had known before I did that the beatings had been going on for longer than that one incident, and there was nothing they could do when she was denying he hit her. It was all in Shelly's hands. When she was ready, they could help her.

Clamping my mouth shut, I listened to Shelly weave her story and went to sulk in the corner of the living room by one of my roommate's potted plants. The best advice they could give was given. The problem lay with Shelly following it. I was going to learn that firsthand.

I was distant, to say the least, and filled with the bitter taste of helplessness and disappointment when they explained to me to tell Joe to go home. If he returned, they could arrest him for trespassing. I had expected so much more from the police that night. I had thought it would be easier.

"That's the best you can do?" I asked furiously.

Smiling grimly, the shorter officer nodded his head. "It's a start."

Frowning angrily, I watched as they returned to their cars. With silent ease, their cars departed from the complex behind an outwardly willing Joe, once more casting the parking lot in the dull orange glow of the lamps outside.

The night had progressed to the witching hour. After spending the entire day at work and then coming home to all the stressful excitement, I was exhausted down to my bones. Therefore, while Shelly went into my roommate's bathroom to soak in the tub, I eagerly prepared for bed. After going through the apartment and checking that every door was locked and every window secure, I climbed under my lightweight covers and listened to the air conditioning hum. I felt safe then, knowing that I had taken the time to slide the locks on the wide windows in the living room and bedrooms and drawn every curtain and blind in my place closed.

It was not long before I became aware that locks would not keep Joe away.

Chapter 2

Dawn was not far away when I heard the hushed voices over the subtle whoosh of the air conditioning. My eyes opened reluctantly while my exhausted mind screamed at me to ignore the sounds. It felt as though I had just gone to bed, and my limbs were heavy as I slowly regained complete consciousness. Then the events of the late night sent my dreams scattering, and I sat up with a gasp.

The voice I had heard in my living room was male, a male who had not been there when I went to bed just a few short hours before.

Throwing back the sheet, I slipped from beneath the covers and peeked out the door. Soft light illuminated the dark room, and I noticed that Jacob was still sleeping on the floor, a tangled heap amid the slippery sleeping bag. Long, spindly legs poked from the dark coverlet, the small toes twitching as he dreamed. He was fine, but Shelly was gone.

I sighed. The sounds of Joe's voice was reaching me clearly now, rising in pitch and tone. The hallway was shrouded in shadows, so I eased my way quietly a few steps to assess what was going on. Even before I reached he living room, I could smell the alcohol. Maybe he had been hitting all of the Mill Avenue or Tempe Marketplace bars after he left my place. What time was last call?

At first I was stunned, but that was quickly replaced with anger. My hot temper flared when I realized it had been Shelly who allowed him into my home stinking of alcohol and angry to boot.

Before I confronted them both, I returned to my room and closed the door solidly behind me. It latched with a click, but I assumed Jacob would not notice. I did not want to frighten my nephew any more than he was already. He had seen enough for one night. While he had probably witnessed scenes like that before, there was no use having him overhear something he did not have to.

Though I had opted for stealth, things in the living room seemed to be escalating quickly. Their voices rose in pitch and intensity. Shelly's pleading did nothing to calm the anger inside of Joe. Even though she was begging him to go home, he continued to berate her for daring to leave him and calling the police.

The threats were violent and hurtful, insulting and controlling. I had never heard someone speak to another person like that in my short life. Sure, I had heard about domestic violence, but the few relationships I had participated in or observed in others always had a modicum of mutual respect. Joe did not respect Shelly. He was cruel in his accusations against her. According to him, she was useless, ugly, fat, whining, and the biggest mistake he had ever made. I was stopped in my tracks, listening in disbelief, wondering how my sister could tolerate this.

Her soft sobbing and murmured apologies seemed to have no effect on him. Nor did it stop his tirade. I heard her whisper at him to shush before he woke me, that she would go home with him if he would just calm down. She said that if I did awaken I would probably call the police again.

That was when he completely snapped.

A loud crash erupted caused me to burst from the shadows, and the scene that greeted me took me completely by surprise. Joe, easily forty pounds larger than Shelly, had grabbed a hold of the back of her neck and was dragging her towards the door. She had apparently reached for the lamp on the end table, and it was on the ground, shattered into large pieces of broken ceramic. The neck of the lamp rested at an awkward angle, held to the base only by the black cord.

"I warned you before about involving others in our family business," he was growling as he dragged her forward.

"Ohmigosh! Joe!" I shrieked. "What are you doing?" Stunned, I could not stop myself from hesitating. Having never been in such a situation, I had no idea what to do.

Joe continued, not realizing I was there. "You made things worse tonight by coming here. You need to be taught who's in charge here."

The room seemed to waver as though lit by a candle. Shadows danced on the wall and cast part of his face in darkness, and I could not help but think that he appeared evil. Shelly tried to wriggle out of his grip, but he held on tight. It was not so much the broken glass crunching under my toes as it was the blind fury of this man invading my home and laying hands on my sister.

I did the only thing I could think of at the moment. Reaching for his arm, I tried to get between them. If he reached the door with her, there would be no stopping them. "Let her go! Get out of my house."

Nothing I did seemed to deter him. Frightened that he would get her out the door, I looked around the room desperately. The only weapon readily available lay at my feet in jagged pieces. I bent and picked up one of the broken shards from the table lamp and jumped forward. His forearm was exposed, so I lashed out and pulled it across the taut skin with enough force to leave a red trail behind my shaking fingers. I was rewarded with a howl from him as he jerked away and stared at his arm in disbelief.

In his distraction, he released my sister, but his arm swung out, striking me in an effort to get me away. Because of his unsteadiness, his full weight went with the blow from his elbow, and the impact knocked me down to the ground. I fell hard with a loud exhale, my head and cheek grazing the sharp edge of the coffee table. The cry that escaped my lips when I fell did little to stop the pain. Stars exploded in my head and my jaw felt as though it had been torn from my face. I could taste the bitter, salty taste of blood, and my tongue reached for the gash in my mouth. My teeth had sliced open the soft tissue of my cheek. It flamed and burned, and an instant swelling at the site made it even more painful. It hurt every bit as much as the throbbing in the back of my head.

I was aware of Shelly's voice, rising in a panic. "Cher! Cher? Are you okay?"

Blackness threatened to consume me. I believe the only thing that kept me conscious was the pain. The area where I had struck the table burned like an inferno, and I shook my head to try to clear it.

"Look what you did!" Stunned, Joe hesitated in order to stare down at the wound I had inflicted to his arm. "Goddamn!"

He stopped speaking and took a deep breath, but his fingers continued to clench and unclench as he struggled to control his temper. Starting over again, he tried to speak in a normal tone, but I could feel the rage emanating from him.

"Cher, this is a family problem that has extended too far tonight. All of this..." He pointed to the lamp on the floor and Shelly crouching beside me with a sweeping hand. "This is your fault."

I reached out to touch my cheek. My fingers were trembling, and I tasted blood when I spoke through stiff lips. "My fault? Are you nuts?"

His anger grew when I looked at him in disbelief. "This is not your concern. You need to stay out of this. She's my wife." He pointed at his chest as he spoke, and saliva spewed from his mouth as he fumed. "She needs to be with me!"

"You're in no condition right now," I sputtered, trying to sit up. It hurt so much that black spots teased the back of my eyes, causing me to fall back again and close my eyes. "You need to cool off," I finished weakly.

"Who are you to tell me what to do? You're just a pathetic kid, you know that?"

Coming to stand in front of me, he stared down but did nothing to help me up. His breath stank of whiskey and cigarettes, so pungent that I winced from the force of it.

Now I was beginning to understand. My cockiness was no match for his violence. "Back off," I said through narrow lips.

"Oh, so you think you're a big girl now? I remember you when you were still wearing training bras, kid." He stared down at my chest. "Not that you've grown out of them yet... You'll never be a real woman, Cher."

With one last glance at me, he shook his head in disgust. "You got what you deserved, little girl. If you hadn't gotten involved, you wouldn't be lying on the ground now."

He reached for Shelly again and began dragging her to the door by her arm. She did not fight this time. Instead she sent a worried glance at me where I continued to fight back the tears of pain from the blow to the back of my head. I knew he had won. There was nothing that I could do anymore to save my sister. I watched through blurred vision, fearing for Shelly's safety.

However, Joe never made it through the door. Over the rushing in my ears, I heard the forceful knock. Joe had not thought enough ahead to latch it behind him, and it swung open the second time. Once again, uniformed officers were standing in my doorway, and Joe hastily released Shelly and turned to run.

Though their voices were muffled from the continued ringing in my ears, I took in the sight with a deep sense of relief. The cavalry had arrived. Luckily, it was sweet little Jacob who came to the rescue. Awakened by my departure, he heard the voices and grabbed the phone off my nightstand to dial 911. Then my smart nephew climbed into my closet and hid behind the hanging sweater shelf while he waited for them to arrive.

"She's coming home with me," Joe snarled, reaching again for Shelly's wrist.

That was all the officers needed to act. While Shelly squealed and pulled away from him, they reached for his arms to restrain him. He continued to scream aloud his anger, and the rustling grew more heated as he began to struggle in earnest.

The room seemed to explode in activity, but I was unable to follow the fight. My mouth was filled with blood, and swallowing it only increased my nausea. I struggled not to be sick. There were voices all around me, but I could not understand their words. Then I felt a presence next to me, coming down on his haunches, and gentle hands lifted my head.

"One forty three, dispatch, I'm going to need EMS on site. Possibly two patients – both alert and oriented at this time."

A crackle of indistinguishable words responded, to which he calmly answered.

I opened my eyes then and read the name on the tag above his heart. Brandon Nicholson. The shining gold-plated badge marked him as a sergeant. Raising my gaze higher, I got my first good look at him. He seemed familiar, and I realized through my fogged brain that he had been there earlier. He was the third, authoritative officer who had spoken to Shelly. Now he was bending over me, breathing rapidly from his exertions, and a sheen of sweat glistened on his forehead and upper lip. I studied him while I struggled to regain my senses. Surprisingly, up close it was obvious that he was the youngest of the group. He was certainly a handsome man, with dirty blond hair in a closely-cropped fade, and large, deep-set blue-green eyes that reminded me of the Pacific Ocean.

Whether it was my hazy mind or the beginnings of love at first sight, his gaze immediately mesmerized me. Even though his face was emotionless and inscrutable at first, his eyes showed something entirely different. He was staring at me with an intensity that I found frightening and very powerful. Without a word, he gave me a once over, his eyes pausing on my legs, and it was then I remembered that my nightshirt was up. Reaching down quickly, I tugged it over my thighs.

His steady gaze returned to my face, and a frown appeared upon his sculpted, full lips when he saw the blood around my lips. The initial blank look was replaced with concern, and the tension in his primed muscles was quick to win me over. He was not acting. There was still a touch of formality in his tone, but the warmth in his eyes flowed right through me.

He really was worried about me.

"Are you all right, Miss Bridwell?"

"I've been better," I struggled to say. My lips felt stiff. "Where's Jacob?"

I could feel the warm stickiness of blood slowly drip from my mouth and grimaced. No wonder they felt stiff. His hands were gentle as he assisted me to sit up and straighten my shirt modestly, and at that point I saw a flash of exasperation and anger glimmer in the abyss of his eyes. "I know we asked earlier, but I have to ask again. Do you have any weapons in the house?"

I shook my head, unwilling to speak more.

With his bare hand, he gently tipped my face to examine the swelling of my cheek. His fingers were warm and tender as they tilted my head to the side. It hurt like the dickens, but I was so happy to see a friendly face that I willingly tolerated it. "What happened?"

"I cut him, and he knocked me down. I hit my head."

"We may need to take photos of your injuries..."

I nodded.

"You might need stitches, but your jaw seems okay. I've called for an ambulance." He turned to Joe, standing in the safe grip of two of the other officers with his head held low. "Is it not enough to beat on your wife? Now you have to get your kicks out of beating on her sister?"

Joe turned his angry gaze to me, his red-rimmed eyes spitting fury. "She got me first. Look at my arm. She gouged me. I want to press charges."

"I think self-defense is an excusable crime." The sergeant scowled fiercely. "We've already been here once tonight. You shouldn't have come back."

"This is my problem, not yours."

Seeing the sergeant stiffen, one of the other officers gave Joe a tug and shot his friend and fellow officer a warning look. "Nixs, no."

"She's my wife, for Christ's sakes. What right does *she* have to come between us?" Joe hissed angrily.

"Maybe if you'd stop slapping around your wife she wouldn't need to come to her sister's for help."

"This is none of your business, Sergeant Nicholson," he spat, drawing out the syllables of the sergeant's name with disgust.

"It is now. We were called here two times tonight. She asked you to leave her alone earlier. Now you can go to jail for domestic assault and trespassing."

"Oh, this is bull."

"You were out of line tonight, Joe."

The sergeant barely gave me another glance as he regained his feet. "I see you're not having any trouble breathing. Can you stand?" I shook my head and was rewarded with a curt nod. "Just stay put then until the medics come to take a look at you." He glanced over at Shelly, who was sobbing into a napkin in the corner. Her eyes continued to flick to her husband before returning to gaze in fear at the man in the uniform.

"Are you all right?" he asked. When she nodded he frowned. "Where's the boy?"

"Jacob?" Shelly asked, her voice quivering.

The sergeant's attention returned to me. "Is that his name?"

I nodded.

"Where is he, ma'am?"

"I imagine he's still asleep."

"Where was he sleeping?"

Though he appeared patient, I could sense his exasperation with my sister. Shelly had turned into an emotional wreck, so I inclined my head in the direction of my bedroom. The movement worsened the pain in my head, making me reach up and touch the spot where I landed. There was a large goose egg, and my fingers came away with some blood. Though technically an accident, I just could not believe what had happened.

The sergeant stepped around the tangle of legs and toes to make his way cautiously down the hall. I heard him calling for Jacob and then asking him to come out of the closet. One of the other officers left Joe in the custody of the tall, thin one and joined him, surrounding Jacob in order to shield him from the fiasco in the living room. I could hear them asking him questions about what had happened and bit back tears. How much had he seen or heard that made him dial 911 at the age of four?

Once again, lights flashed outside in the growing daylight, and moments later the officer standing in the doorway nodded in my direction. More uniforms entered, making me all the more self-conscious of my skimpy attire and bloody appearance. The paramedic team approached with arms weighted down with a heart monitor, oxygen and a jump kit. Humiliation and fear made the tears burn my eyes.

A female paramedic crouched down beside me with a polite smile. "Can you tell me what happened?"

As I gave them a summed up breakdown of the injuries, Shelly watched on with a worried look on her face. It only worsened when the two officers lifted Joe from the sofa and led him out of the way. When she stood to follow, they shook their heads sternly. She wrung her hands in helplessness and despair, knowing what I was just now beginning to comprehend.

It was not going to be good for her.

They half-led, half-dragged Joe from my apartment and began to guide him down the stairs. After only two steps, he stopped and retched over the wall. The officers shook their heads in disgust, though they stood patiently until Joe was finished. The tall, skinny one chuckled slightly as Joe wiped his face with the tail of his shirt, and Joe turned on him with blurred eyes. "Think that was funny? Maybe next time I'll puke on you."

His comment earned him a jerk from the shorter officer, and Joe scowled in the direction of Shelly. As they led him to a waiting patrol car, he shouted his anger at her, telling her that she would be punished for letting them take him away. I shivered. After what had happened, I believed him.

Chapter 3

No sooner had Joe been escorted back to one of the waiting cruisers than I was faced with a new problem. As the paramedics loaded me onto the stretcher, the nice female one advised me that it would take some time and I would need a ride home from the hospital. I glanced at Shelly, who had collapsed onto the sofa with Jacob in her arms. Tears left pale trails down her cheeks, contrasting sharply with the dark bruising around her eye, and I hope she would be able to pull herself together long enough to help me.

"Shelly, would you take my car and pick me up?"

She shook her head without hesitation. "I can't Cher; I'm going to have to go to the station to get Joe out. Can't you call your roommate?"

"I can't wake her up this early in the morning."

Shelly glanced around her as though trapped in a cage. "But Cher, I can't be two places at once, especially with Jacob."

Jacob had not lifted his head from his mother's shoulder. I grimaced. "He should not go near his father, especially when he's so scared."

"You're right... Maybe he should go to the hospital with you."

The two remaining officers exchanged glances after her comment, and I shook my head in disbelief. Betrayal and anger combined to make my slurred words sharp with disgust. "Oh, and that's better? Forget it Shelly, I'll just get a cab."

Even though I knew I was tired and ached everywhere, I could not help but feel irritated. Self-pity and exhaustion made me exaggerate her fear and worry for ingratitude. I did not understand how she could put her husband before me after what he had done.

"Just grab me my shorts and some shoes, please? I'll also need my wallet and mobile."

Shelly continued to sit and watch with a lost gleam in her eyes. My anger grew when Nicholson stepped forward, holding my purse on the tips of his fingers. "Where are your shoes?"

"In my closet."

He disappeared back into my room, only to emerge a few minutes later carrying my running sneakers and a pair of my jean shorts. "I hope these are yours. They're so small I thought they might be the boy's."

His face showed absolutely no sign of humor, but when the other officer chuckled, I realized that he was making a joke. I scowled the best I could. I had been insulted enough that night about my diminutive size. "I'm not a child."

He nodded sagely.

Turning my attention to Shelly, I gave her my best exasperated look. "Will you please get me?"

"I can't Cher... You just don't understand. He'll kill me."

After watching him in action that night, I truly did believe her. Even though every word was awkward and sent the taste of fresh blood into my mouth, I could not stop warning her. Someone had to get through to her. "That's all the more reason to stay away from him. Don't bother bailing him out. He's just going to hurt you again. What about Jacob? You have to think of him, too. How can you even consider going back when you know he'll just hurt you again?"

Shelly turned away from me then, blocking me out, and I felt the sting of tears burning against the back of my eyelids once more. Bravely, I held them in check. There was no way I was going to cry in front of all these men.

Seeing my frustration, Nicholson sank down on his haunches by the stretcher and stared at me, and I was captured by the intensity in his blue eyes. He saw the emotion on my face, and his lips tightened with unveiled irritation. "Miss Bridwell, I'm going to need to ask you some questions, and you'll have to make a statement. I'll swing by the hospital when I'm done with my paperwork and give you a lift home if you want."

I noticed the strange looks sent his way from the other officer and shook my head. "It's okay, really. St. Luke's isn't far. I can get a cab, and I'll swing by the station and answer your questions."

His head inclined slightly in response, his face impassive. As I stared at Shelly in despair, I was suddenly lifted on the stretcher and wheeled to the door. The EMS team carefully carried me out and into the bright lights of the ambulance. Shelly did not come out with me, and at that point, I did not expect her to.

In fact, I did not expect anything from her at all.

****

Three hours later, with four small dissolvable sutures and a prescription for Vicodin, I was dressed in the jean shorts and sneakers that Sergeant Nicholson had taken from my closet. It was a relief that the Emergency Room was having a slow morning because

I felt awkward being out in my nightshirt. Even though I suspected that others in the sparsely crowded emergency room had seen much worse than a braless twenty-something, I was still happy to have been in and out of there in record time.

My head continued to throb, and the pressure from the huge lump on the back of my head had only increased while I was there. The nurse, a sweet older woman with gentle brown eyes, was kind enough to send me along with my first dose of Vicodin, and it began working its magic quickly. As I waited to be discharged, the throbbing eased to the ever-present dull pain in the spot.

My mouth was still numb from the local, but my nurse had convinced me that I was not drooling and looked normal enough to get home. She also made me promise someone would be there to watch me for a while to ensure the bump on my head did not become more serious.

I promised, though I really did not expect Shelly to be there. I was certain that I had lost her the moment I left on the ambulance gurney. Shelly was too upset with the events of the night, and she would be doing whatever she could to get Joe out of trouble.

That was about all I was able to convince the nurse of. She insisted that I wait in my bed and rest until the cab showed up. Snuggled deep under warmed blankets, I lay back and nodded my acquiescence. When she pulled the curtain closed behind her, she promised me that the front desk would alert her when my ride came.

The nurse had shown more wisdom than I had the entire night, for no sooner had she pulled the curtain than I fell asleep. The noise of the people speaking and equipment working seemed to fade away, leaving me to fall into a deep but troubled slumber. However, it was short lived, for it seemed that no sooner had I closed my eyes than the curtain was pulled back again and footsteps approached my bed.

A warm hand landed on my forearm and gently shook me. "Miss Bridwell?"

Even though the deep voice was familiar, the sound and the touch startled me out of my dreams. Thinking Joe was back yet again, I shot up with a cry. My head screamed in pain, and when I saw the familiar face, I sank back onto the pillow with a groan. One shaky hand reached up to press against my throbbing temple. "You scared me, Sergeant Nicholson."

"I called your name first, but you didn't respond. I didn't think I could wake you unless I gave you a shake."

His face was still impassive, a look that I had always connected with officers of law enforcement. However, he was again staring at me strangely, making me very conscious of my appearance. It was disconcerting, and I began to feel as though I were in trouble.

"Is everything okay?" I asked.

"I've finished my shift. I figured if you were all set, I could bring you home."

My eyes widened, and I struggled to determine if he was this nice to everyone or if he somehow felt guilty for not being able to prevent the night's occurrences. Yeah, right, I thought, he probably saw situations like mine all the time. Nevertheless, I found myself studying him through blurred vision. As I expected, his face was inscrutable, completely unreadable, and almost as though he had no emotion whatsoever.

"Are you sure? I mean, the other officers looked at you a little funny when you offered before," I murmured.

He shrugged. "They're just not used to seeing me offer."

"Will you get in trouble?"

"No." His lips curved the slightest bit. "Do you want the ride or not?"

I sat up slowly, afraid of the possible aches I may find that I had not noticed before. Luckily, the painkiller my motherly nurse had given me was working. Though I had wanted to question him more, he reached for my arm and assisted me off the bed. My thigh brushed against his leg, revealing what I had already suspected and stealing my ability to speak. He was hard and lean, strong and well-defined under the pressed material of his uniform slacks. The man was definitely in good shape.

I had not realized just how tall he was until I was standing beside him. Granted, I was barely five foot three inches tall, but he stood over six feet easily, and his broad shoulders completely blocked my view of everything beyond him. In typical policeman fashion, he certainly did not lack in intimidation.

His hand maintained a loose grip, and his fingers were long and lean, easily able to encircle my upper arm. The effect his closeness left on me was a slight breathlessness that I tried to contribute to the medication, but it was no use. It was his presence that stole my breath away. Like a randy teenager, my palms grew moist and my heart pounded in my chest.

Leading me out into the hall, Sergeant Nicholson nodded in the direction of the nurse's desk, completely oblivious to the stares and coy smiles sent his way. I saw the covert glances and whispers behind their hands and inadvertently grimaced. Though I knew it should not have mattered to me that the nurses found him attractive, for some odd reason it did. I looked a wreck, had been involved in one of his nightly arrests, and here these nurses were, fresh and attractive. It was not fair.

He was *my* savior.

I wanted to pull away, fearing that I looked like a prisoner, but I found myself leaning into his touch instead. It was gentle but strong and gave me the support I so desperately needed at the moment. Things were fuzzy and a little out of focus, and the pain in the back of my head left me dizzy and lightheaded.

I felt awful. I hated Joe for placing me in this situation, especially when I was in the company of one of the most handsome men I had ever seen in my life, and I looked like something out of a horror movie. He paused once more at the admissions desk and asked another wide-eyed woman to cancel the cab while I stood next to him feeling like a transient.

Then we were on the move again, and his hand remained around my arm as we stepped out into the bright sunlight. My eyes burned painfully, increasing the volume of my severely protesting head, and I stumbled slightly while my eyes struggled to adjust. His fingers tightened immediately, and I threw him a thankful half smile. "Sorry about that."

He nodded shortly. "Not a problem."

Leading me to the police car parked illegally in the front of the emergency room, he opened the front passenger side door. I glanced at him again, my eyes shining with curiosity, but he merely assisted me in and shut the door behind me.

The radio crackled before me, and I was aware of the cage behind me. With glowing lights and beeps echoing in the small, tight area, I was struck with a feeling of claustrophobia. It was like sitting in the cockpit of an airplane, with switches, equipment and a computer screen filling the space around me. Never in my life had the front seat of a car felt so small and closed to me. When he bent his tall frame into the driver's side, I turned to him. "Am I allowed to ride up front with you?"

He closed the door and fastened his seatbelt without glancing at me, but when I opened my mouth to ask him again, he nodded in the direction of my hands. "Just don't touch anything, okay?"

I secured my seatbelt without responding, but it occurred to me that he was teasing me again when he put the car in gear and drove toward the exit. More relaxed than I had seen him before, he handled the car with utter ease. One arm rested on the windowsill and the other draped over the steering wheel. He spoke into his car radio and pulled slowly from the parking lot, leaving me to rest my head against the seat in silence. With my eyes closed, my other senses slowly took over. I could smell him, the leather on his belt and the slight tang of his aftershave. It bothered me that he could still look so good after being awake all night long.

"Do you have a prescription?"

My eyes opened slowly to find him staring at me, and I glanced around in surprise. We were stopped at a red light, the last in a long line of cars on Mill Avenue heading south. I knew there was a drugstore just another block down, and he could head back to my place a lot faster by taking Broadway than going through the university. When I returned my attention to him, I almost let it slip that I thought his eyes were beautiful. Catching myself just in time, I nodded slowly and focused on his question. "Yes, for Amoxicillin and Vicodin."

"Why don't you give it to me? I'll run into the pharmacy. Walgreens okay?"

I nodded drowsily. "I've had one filled there before. They have my information on file."

He pulled into the parking lot and held out his hand expectantly. Though my eyelids were growing heavier, I handed him the slip of paper, a twenty and my insurance card before I began to feel myself slip away. Although I wanted to tell him it was unnecessary, I could not find the words. I was so tired. Too tired to ask him – why me?

Falling asleep in Brandon Nicholson's police car was the last thing that I had wanted to do. However, the power of stress, lack of sleep, and medication took over all of my best intentions, and I became aware of my surroundings again when he gently shook my shoulder. With no memory of anything beyond the stop in Walgreens, it was startling to find the car door open again. The warm morning breeze rustled the tangles in my hair and promised another miserably hot day, and the ever-present dry heat sucked what little energy I had left right out of me.

When I opened my eyes, my gaze landed on the uniform-clad legs standing before me. Following them up to his face. I noticed he was smiling slightly. My heart responded by picking up in tempo, even as my cheeks flushed with embarrassment.

It was the small smile on his lips that held my attention. They appeared solid and firm. Through my sleep-fogged mind, I imagined what they would feel like, and my flush deepened as I hastily looked away. I must have been having a good dream in the car to be thinking in that way, and all I could do is hope he did not notice my infatuation.

"We're at your apartment. Are you okay to get in?"

I felt in my pocket for my keys, pulling them free with a triumphant grunt. "I'm not usually so dull," I said lamely. "But they gave me something at the hospital."

"I know," he said shortly, once more reaching for my arm.

Slowly and cautiously, he assisted me out of the car and helped support me as I slogged my way up the stairs. Strange thoughts continued to ramble through my head, things like kissing the man and then wondering if he had ever shot anyone before. I had never been that close to a police officer's gun before, and it was a little exciting as well as frightening.

When we reached the door, I turned to him and tried to smile. I wanted to thank him but could not think of any words to do so, and he merely stared at me with his impassive look. I could not see his eyes behind his dark glasses, but I could feel his appraising stare on my face. The scrutiny caused a faint blush to rise on my cheeks. The awareness that my shoulder-length hair was tangled beyond repair, my cheek was swollen, and my clothing was hanging off me only heightened my discomfort. I knew how terrible I looked.

Before I could speak, the door to my apartment was yanked open, saving me from my discomfort. Arianne stood on the other side, a fierce frown turning down her brightly glossed lips and her hands planted solidly on her round hips. "Cher Bridwell! What the hell happened here last night? There's glass everywhere, and there's blood. I thought you were dead!" She stopped and stared from me to my companion, her frown fading. "What happened to your face? And why are you with a cop?"

For a moment I was jealous of the appraising look my champion gave my roommate behind his glasses. Granted the view of his profile, I could see how his eyes swept her from head to toe, pausing momentarily on her plush hips and generous breasts. I could not help but bristle, considering how awful I looked and felt.

Of course, when one looked at Arianne, one would have to stare. Garbed in a skintight, red dress that ended at mid-thigh, Arianne posed a seductive picture. After a night clubbing in nearby Old Town, Scottsdale, she looked just disheveled enough to be sexy. Her long blond hair hung loose around her shoulders, and her wide blue eyes sparkled with anger and worry. Even though I felt the surprising urge to lean into Sergeant Nicholson and tell him that she was just about married, I stood silently.

After a moment, I sighed softly and glanced around the

apartment with a disappointed eye. The once immaculate gray rug had drops of blood on it. Mine, Shelly's, Joe's? Maybe from all of us, all mingled together in dark smears of color.

The lamp was still in shards on the floor, some small pieces ground in from the weight of the policemen's boots. The coffee table was askew, and Arianne's *Glamour*, *Cosmopolitan* and *People* magazines that once sat upon it were scattered from one end of the room to the other. It looked a lot worse than it had been, but I would have a lot of explaining to do.

"I'm fine, Ari. Everything's okay. Don't worry, I'll get this mess cleaned up."

Her voice was less frantic as she took my arm and stared into my face. "Cher, what happened here last night?"

"Well, remember I called to tell you that Joe and Shelly were fighting? The fight ended here."

She sighed heavily and turned away in disgust. Reaching down, she picked up the answering machine and set it back on the end table where it had once sat next to the lamp.

"Are they going to pay you for the lamp?"

I shook my head. "I'll take care of it next payday."

"Oh, like you ever have extra money," she snapped. "She brought this mess here, so why don't you ask her to take care of it?"

"She's not here?" I asked.

Arianne shook her head, still scowling. I was not sure that I was at all surprised, but I turned to Nicholson as if expecting him to have all the answers. He had stood silently during our exchange, but I noticed that his lips thinned to a narrow line. The shrug he sent my way held all of the frustration I felt at that moment. "Usually they go back to their husbands for fear of retribution. It's not unusual."

I shook my head. "She should know better. We weren't raised

like that."

"She's scared. Sometimes the abuse will get worse once he's been arrested." He shrugged again. "Other times it just sends the fact home that what he did was wrong and unacceptable. Who knows what Joe will do? If you were my sister, I'd be afraid to have him come back here and bang you up again."

When I did not answer, his hand came down to rest on my shoulder. He gave it a slight squeeze before stepping back outside. "The battle's just begun, Cherisse. I'd recommend you consider an Order of Protection."

"Me?"

I thought one of his long fingers might touch my cheek, but it hovered slightly above the swollen and discolored skin. "He took a swing at you last night. You said he's never done that before."

"Of course he hasn't. I never even knew he hit Shelly. Besides, he didn't really hit me. I went after him first, and he just knocked me aside. Maybe it was all because he was drunk – like Shelly said," I said hastily. Then I laughed which sounded hollow even to my ears. "Listen to me... Now I'm making excuses for him."

Again his lips curved slightly in a small smile, and I was aware of Arianne watching us closely. "Maybe so, but if she's come here for help, your place will be the first place he'll look next time. If he's comfortable enough to barge in and start banging her around while you're there, you might get hurt again." When he saw my eyes widen, he shrugged again. "Or not. It's not usual for batterers to bully family members other than their children. They choose to maintain control in their relationships by abusing the people they claim to love. I'm just telling you this so you're aware next time."

"But he was drunk. Maybe he just lost it. He's never..."

My voice trailed off, and I glanced down at my hands. There was blood under my fingernails. When I looked up again, I saw that his gaze had followed mine. There was the same tightening around his lips again, and I wondered how soft those lips would feel. Probably wonderful to his beautiful wife and two towheaded children at home – assuming he was married, after all.

Giving myself a mental shake, I swallowed hard. "What's going to happen to him now?"

"He'll have to go to court. They'll probably tell your sister to take out an Order of Protection and have him attend anger management classes."

"This is terrible." I sighed. "Why didn't she tell me sooner?"

Shrugging, he took another step away. "Call the station when you're able, and we can talk, okay?"

With a final nod at me and Arianne, he turned and descended the stairs. My gaze followed him until he disappeared from sight, and it was then I felt the exhausted tears fill my eyes. I needed a long, hot bath and a soft, clean bed. I needed to call in sick at work and just crash. I also knew that I needed to sit down and think about what happened and what to do about it. One thing was for sure, and that was that I was completely unprepared for Shelly's state of mind.

Chapter 4

Shelly returned to Joe as soon as he was released.

Unfortunately, he was considered a first-time offender and released on his own recognizance. Now that I knew it was not the first time Shelly had been hit, I was upset that he was let out so quickly. In my opinion, the man needed to be locked up for hurting the woman he was supposed to honor and cherish, and I strongly believed the system was flawed.

Without even an effort to find out how I was doing, Shelly returned to her small home in East Mesa with Jacob. Burning with a need to punish, I followed up myself. I did go to the station. It became an obsession for me, finding out all I could about domestic violence. Paying my own way through ASU with a scholarship and full-time work did not leave me with much extra time, but the small amount I had was spent surfing the Internet for more information. I read up on the laws that protected women and the laws that did not. It amazed me how many women went through what Shelly had, and her behavior was not so different from others. It had a name: Battered Woman's Syndrome.

I wanted to free Shelly from the prison called her marriage. I wanted give her and her son a chance at life, but she still was not ready. The phone calls and texts I sent out went unanswered, so I was forced to face the truth. Unfortunately, she was unwilling.

So many reasons screamed out at me as to why she would stay with the man who had hurt her so badly. Perhaps she was afraid he would kill her or try to take away Jacob. Or maybe it was because she depended on him to support her and was afraid to try it on her own. Maybe she thought he would change over time. Or the greatest tragedy of all: maybe she thought it was all her fault. Would I ever know?

Shelly finally called me two days later to say she was staying with her husband. Then she told me that Joe thought it would be best if they focused on their marriage for a while. That meant just the two of them and Jacob, without any outside influence – which meant me. He blamed my involvement for his violence and told her that things would be better if I stayed away. As sick as it was, she believed him and wanted to give him another chance. I did not remind her that I had only been involved in one altercation. How many had there been before?

Before we hung up, I let her hear my tears and my wobbly voice. "Shelly, are you really happy? Is this what you want?"

Her voice broke when she answered. "Things are good now, Cher. We'll be fine."

That was it. She hung up without saying another word, and I felt more helpless than ever. Remembering Sergeant Nicholson's kindness, I thought about asking him for help. It spurred me into returning to the station. Unfortunately, when I did go down, I did not see Sergeant Nicholson. Instead, I was led to a detective who asked me more questions about that night and compared it to the officers' reports. Everything matched up satisfactorily, and I was told he would be in touch for the hearing. They never called me. It was all handled without my presence, for one reason or another. When I called in, I was told rather briskly that he had shown up with a good lawyer, pled guilty, and had gotten off with probation.

A phone call to my parents did little to help. The way they spoke indulgently told me everything I needed to know. Shelly had spun her own story, and I knew how convincing she was after seeing her in action that night. They asked me to pass on my love to Jacob when I saw them next, and we hung up. I felt more helpless than ever.

There was nothing left for me to do except return to my studies now that the new semester had started. It seemed that with the yearly monsoon season came the beginning of classes at ASU, and despite the oppressive desert heat, the students returned with gusto. I did as well. Having no other choice than to move on with my life, I turned to my studies. Even so, deep down, I understood that I had changed. I was no longer an innocent and sheltered 23-year-old college student. I had a new awareness that the world was not a safe place and that terrible things do happen very close to home. With the knowledge that my sister was in trouble and that I could do nothing to stop it, I faced my days with a heavy weight upon my shoulders.

But my friends were persistent in dragging me from my internal reverie. A friend from one of my English classes, Paul, caught up to me on the steep road bridge over University Drive. Like the dozens of other students crowding around me, I was returning to my car after finishing up the day's classes when he shouted my name.

Stopping was hard to do. It was blazing hot and the sun beat down upon the top of my head brutally. With no shade around and crowds of people hurrying past, I was eager to escape to my car and its air conditioning. Wishing for nothing more than the safety of my home and a good cup of coffee, I hurried along. But Paul was insistent. He jogged up to me and grabbed my arm, his voice breathless after hurrying up the steep bridge, leaving me impressed with his stamina.

"Didn't you hear me calling you?"

I shrugged at the stocky, dark-haired football player whom I had dated on a couple of occasions. We had waited tables together during our sophomore year at a cantina in Tempe Marketplace and had hung out after work for a couple of months, but both of us knew that there was no spark. Luckily we had remained good friends, which was helpful since attending a college so large that making friends while commuting to classes was tricky for me. "I've got to get home, Paul. I have to work tonight and I have a ton of reading to do. I really don't have much time."

He studied me with his dark brown eyes. He really was a handsome young man, and the last I had heard, he had been on every sports recruiter's list to play pro. I wished him all the best. Paul was one of the few people aside from Arianne who I spent my sparse free time with, and it was as my friend that he persisted then. Falling into step beside me, he reached out and took my book bag. I almost protested, but figured in the end that it was just too hot to argue. He shouldered it and then turned his attention back to me. "So, how've you been?"

"I'm okay," I answered vaguely. "How about you?"

He sent me a sidelong glance. "What's the deal, Cher? You've been a little strange lately."

"Strange?"

He had the grace to look a little uncomfortable. "Well, yeah. You haven't been the same since you're uh...thing."

I smiled. "You mean Shelly?"

"I should take a ride out there and show Joe what it feels like. Want me to do that for you?"

Chuckling, I shook my head. "As much as I'd love to say yes, you're far more valuable than that. I don't want you to have any blemishes on your record due to me."

"What can I do then? You're not happy anymore."

"Things aren't so great right now. I've got a lot on my mind. That's all, really... I'll be back to my normal self soon. I promise." He looked so uncomfortable that I reached up on tiptoe and kissed his cheek. "That's all, Paul. Things will be fine soon."

"Well, I was going to ask you to come with a few of us to the movies tonight. It's Friday, you know. We're all going out."

"I can't. I have to work."

"What about after work? We can meet up in Old Town."

I sighed. It was too hot outside, and all the students returning to the dorms brushed past us like a school of fish. The feeling of being in a fishbowl was irritating me. "Can we do something next week? I'm not up for it tonight."

"You haven't been up to anything these last couple of weeks. Are you sure I can't do anything for you?"

"Look," I said a little sharply. "I'm fine."

He gripped both my shoulders with his hands and pressed his forehead against mine. His palms were moist against my skin and our foreheads were instantly hot. I wanted to pull away, but I continued to smile, despite the sweat forming between our two brows and my discomfort.

"You're a real pain, Cher. Are you sure you're going to be all right?"

To placate him, I smiled widely. "Call me tomorrow and we'll catch up. I have to work all day, but you can take me out to lunch or something, okay?"

He placed a kiss on my forehead before releasing me. "Will you call me if you need anything before then?"

"Of course. But you know that I can take care of myself."

"I do know." He smiled at me then and gave me a gentle shove. "Go home, Cher. I won't keep you any longer." With an exaggerated bow, he handed me back my book bag and turned to go, sending me a grin over his shoulders. "I'll call you."

"Thanks."

"You bet."

He strode a couple of feet then turned around one last time. "When do you want to hit the track again? We haven't done that in a long time."

"Not until it's below eighty in the morning," I returned.

"I'll keep checking the weather, and as soon as the temperature drops, I'll be at your door at six."

Laughing, I watched him jog off toward the Palo Verde Main dormitory. Most likely he was going off to meet up with guys on the team over at the Arena. I was planning on turning in the opposite direction, towards San Pablo Hall and Lot 59. Like all the other poor students, I could not afford to park anywhere else. With a final wistful glance toward Paul, I began to appreciate his concern. When he finally slipped out of sight in the crowds heading to and from their classes, I spun on my heel and slammed right into someone standing directly behind me.

My heavy book bag fell to the ground and several loose papers scattered everywhere while I let out a startled, "oof."

"Sorry," was the mumbled reply.

We both bent and reached for the books at the same time, bumping our heads in the process. Again I let out, "oof." This time, he echoed my gasp.

I had to laugh when we both reached for our heads and straightened, and I took my turn in mumbling an apology. In response, he handed me a handful of papers, which I took gratefully. While I awkwardly tried to get them organized, I did not immediately give the man my attention, but he continued to stand close, and his gaze bored into the top of my head.

"Hi, Cherisse. How have you been?"

It was the way he said my name that caught my attention and stirred my fogged memory. Not believing my ears, my head shot up, and I stared with narrowed eyes. He looked entirely different from the authoritative uniformed police officer that had kindly driven me home from the hospital several weeks ago.

"Sergeant Nicholson?"

"Brandon," he corrected with a short nod.

The first thing I thought of was Shelly. "What are you doing here? Has my sister gotten into trouble again?"

No sooner had I said it than I realized the implausibility of my thinking. Shelly was all in the way in East Mesa. It would be pretty unlikely that something happened to her in Tempe.

While I was rationalizing this, he glanced down at himself which drew my attention to his garb. He was not in uniform, and I was quick to notice that he was just as handsome without it. Though in street clothes, his bearing screamed military training. He held himself straight and alert, with his long jean clad legs spread wide, and I admired the way they hugged his narrow hips and clung to the long expanse of his legs. Leather and suede hiking boots covered his feet, and a battered Air Force T-shirt embraced his broad shoulders. I thought idly that no man had the right to be that handsome, especially in this scorching desert heat.

"No, not that I'm aware of." He shrugged. "I'm not on duty."

His eyes were impossible to read, hidden as they were behind his dark sunglasses. It was frustrating to have him stand so close, studying me, while I could not interpret his emotions. "Why are you here, then? Are you looking for me?"

His lips curved slightly upwards. "Why would I be looking for you? Have you done something illegal?"

Flustered, I shook my head. "No way."

When his lips began to twitch, I realized he was teasing me again. "I wasn't looking for you. I saw you with your boyfriend and thought I'd see how you were doing."

"He's not my boyfriend."

I was not sure why I corrected him so quickly, but his response was exactly what I could have hoped for. His brows rose inquisitively and the small curvature of his lips widened to a grin. There was warmth in his smile, and it sent shivers of pleasure down my spine. Reminding myself that he was probably married to a beautiful wife and had two gorgeous children, I mentally slapped myself to get back to reality and glanced away from his penetrating stare, aware that my palms were growing moist.

The silence stretched out for too long, so I looked up at him again. "Then what are you doing here?"

"I take classes here. Just finished one."

"You?" His brows rose again from behind his glasses. I grimaced in response. "Sorry. I didn't mean it that way."

He gave me another small smile. "Yes, I'm taking classes here. I'm working post-grad. Justice studies... Which is why I work nights."

I could feel my eyes widen in response to my surprise. "Wow, good for you."

"Thanks."

We stood awkwardly for a minute as I mentally calculated the distance to Wilson Hall. It was a long walk in this heat. "Why are you up here? Shouldn't you be at the other end of the campus?"

"I usually do," he responded easily. "I had lunch with a buddy, and he dropped me at Denny's on our way back from Phoenix."

It was well over a hundred degrees outside, and he was in jeans and hiking boots. How had he managed to get here and still look as though he was fresh from a shower?

"Long walk," I commented stupidly.

He nodded again then jerked his thumb over his shoulder. "Are you in a hurry? Going somewhere?"

I almost gave him the same reply I had used on Paul, but two things held me back. First, I knew he would not believe me. And second, I had so many questions to ask, and somehow I knew he would take the time then to answer them.

"No, I was just on my way home."

"Do you like coffee?"

I nodded. "Decaf."

"Would you like to go get a cup with me?"

"Will your wife mind?"

"I'm not married," he said with a surprised edge to his voice.

"Oh," I answered, my face coloring yet again.

Seeming not to notice my embarrassment, one brow rose above his dark glasses. "Join me?"

"Sure," I stammered, my heart pounding. "Where to?"

"There's a Starbucks over here, but I think we could both use some air conditioning. Do you feel up to walking down to the MU?" He cocked his head to the side, appraising me. "That way we don't have to drive."

I appreciated the thought. It certainly saved us both the effort of trying to find parking at one of the metered spots around the campus. The Memorial Union was a bustling center of student dining amongst other things, busy but not too far of a walk in the heat. With a nod, I shifted my bag and turned back to the road bridge with a sigh of resignation.

Falling into step beside him, I was quick to notice that keeping up to his long-legged pace would be difficult. By the time we reached the double doors, I was breathless, and my legs were straining. Naturally, he looked as cool as ever, and when he held the door open for me to pass, his nostrils flared slightly as I passed. I noticed and responded almost immediately with a nervous flutter in my chest. At this point in the afternoon, I was not sure there was any perfume left on me and feared all he could smell on me was sweat.

The Memorial Union was crowded but blessedly cooler than outside. The hum of people's voices echoed off the high ceilings, and throngs of people hustled by and between us, threatening to separate us into the crowd. Brandon stepped closer to prevent it, and his hand settled between my shoulder blades and remained there while we found our place in line. His fingers were splayed just enough to guide me, but I could feel the change in my breathing pattern. For the tenth time in as many minutes, I told myself to calm down even though I knew I was becoming even more hopelessly attracted to him.

Hiding my nervousness was more work than I imagined, and I noticed that my hands were shaking by the time we found a place to sit. It was difficult to conceal anything from his piercing gaze, so I did the best I could by adding the sugar and creamer and stirring my coffee for an unbelievably long time. He sat across from me with his back against the wall, watching the people pass by with his customary alert indifference. After a minute or so, and once he was satisfied with our surroundings, he turned his attention to me and watched my ministrations. I noticed that he added nothing to his coffee, and his fingers curled around his cup in a relaxed and easy grip.

Finally he sat back and raised the steaming liquid to his lips. "So, I see your face has healed."

My stirring stopped abruptly. Placing the stirrer on a napkin next to my cup, I reached up and touched my cheek. My fingers traced the spot that had landed against the coffee table all the way to the back of my head. The bruising had faded under my summer tan, but inside my mouth I could still feel the scar tissue with my tongue.

"Yes, the bruises have faded." I sighed. The bruises inside were a different story. Raising my gaze, I met his stare evenly. "I can't thank you enough for helping me out that day. I'm sorry I haven't had a chance to before now."

He shrugged his broad shoulders, his battered and worn shirt rising from around his narrow waist. "Not a problem. Just doing my job."

"I understand," I murmured.

He smiled. "You look a lot better without the chipmunk cheek. You're much prettier."

"Thank you," I said with a nervous smile.

"How's your sister – Shelly, right?"

I nodded in response. He had removed his glasses and the aquamarine of his eyes initially held me captivated, but the mention of Shelly brought me back to the present, and I reminded myself to get a grip. He was here, the very man I had wanted to talk to, and I was stuttering like a teenager. "She won't talk to me."

"He won't let her." It was more a statement than a question.

I nodded. "Yeah, Joe told her that she couldn't talk to me anymore, and now she won't answer my calls. I actually drove out there last week, but Shelly's car was gone and Joe's truck was there... I didn't stop." I inhaled slowly. "Two days ago I tried to call again, but he's changed the phone number."

"Isolation. It's not uncommon."

I nodded in agreement. "So how do you know so much?"

"I see it almost every day. The same people go back and forth over and over again."

"Why won't she just leave him? I mean, it's not like we were beaten as kids. My parents never hit us."

He nodded, almost as if expecting my answer. "Where are they now?"

"Who? My parents?"

"Yes."

"In Montana. I called to tell them what happened, but Shelly got to them first and said I overreacted. They won't come down here because they think Shelly's perfectly fine."

His lips thinned. "Sometimes it's better to let the players work on their own game."

"How can you say that? She's my sister. I need to help her."

"You can't help someone who doesn't want to be helped, Cherisse."

"I won't accept that," I said in a hushed tone. "Why can't you go arrest him?"

"Believe me, Cherisse, I would if I could," he replied with a hint of emotion, "but there are laws to follow, and he's got to break them first."

"How? By killing her? I've done some research; I've seen how badly the system works."

I saw the anger flash in his eyes and thought I might have offended him. Yet when he leaned forward, his eyes were urgent. "You have no idea how hard it is to watch the same couples go at it time and again. Do you know how frustrating it is to see a child after he's watched his father beat his mother? They stare at you with a mixture of relief and disgust. They love the cops to help them but hate them for doing their job and taking their parent away. And then, after I arrest the father, that same child has to call me back two nights later for the same thing. After he's been to court... all because she's too scared of him to leave."

"Yes," I hissed. "Just a few weeks ago I had my first experience with that. You and I both know he's going to hurt her again. What about Jacob? What's all this going to do to him?"

"He should be in counseling. And if he doesn't get it, he could end up just like his father."

"I should go and kill him myself."

"And end up in jail." He chuckled. "Remember who you're talking to here."

When I looked away, he leaned forward to capture one of my hands in his wide palm. I was again aware of the fluttering in my belly and considered pulling free before I blushed again, but his soft voice stilled me. "You're a dangerous young woman, Cherisse, and he sees you as a direct threat. He's used to Shelly doing everything he wants her to, and then you come along and have him arrested. Abusers want control. They don't usually hit people other than their wives."

"I went after him to get him off my sister."

"And he completely lost it and hurt you. You're way too feisty to get involved. You'll be the one to end up hurt."

"But that's my problem."

His eyes smoldered as his lips narrowed to a thin line.

"The very last thing I would ever want to do is find your body one night after another 911 call from your nephew, Cherisse."

"I don't want you to either," I answered softly.

Sighing deeply, Brandon released my hand and sat back in his chair. Pushing it back on two legs, he studied me for a moment. His frustration wavered slightly under my wide-eyed scrutiny, but I continued to wonder what he was truly thinking. It was too easy to develop a crush on one so enigmatic.

"Enough said," he said abruptly, dropping his chair back on all four legs. "We're arguing like an old married couple and we've only been here for thirty minutes." He gestured with his hand to the pile of my books beside me. "What's your major?"

"Education."

"You want to teach?"

I nodded with a shy smile. "High school."

"What year are you?"

"Junior."

"So you're how old?"

"Not a child," I quipped.

He smiled a heart shattering, breathtaking smile that I felt down to my toes. It bothered me that he could have such straight, even teeth. Of course he was a policeman, he would be perfect. Or at least pretty close to it. "How old are you, Cherisse?"

"Twenty-three last April."

"So you didn't come here right away after finishing high school?"

I shook my head. His questions were starting to get more personal, and I was not sure if that was a good thing or not. I told myself that he was inquisitive because of his job, but he seemed so earnest that I was unable to hold back. "No. I worked for two years to raise enough money. I still work now."

"Do your parents help you at all?"

"No," I muttered. "They're retired up in Montana. They spend all their time either hunting or fishing. They don't really care what Shelly and I do now that we're adults. But I have a scholarship that helps a lot. Tuition increases are killing me."

"So, I guess they don't approve of your chosen major either?"

I laughed. He had them pinned. "How'd you guess?"

"It's my job," he answered with a shrug.

I counted off on my fingers. "They say I won't make any money. They say that I'll be burnt out in a year or two. They say it's an undervalued and underpaid job that politics tries to maintain too much control over. They say I'm wasting my time and my mind. And, of course, they say I won't even be able to find a job after student teaching."

"You know what I think?" He paused and downed the rest of his coffee.

"What?"

The room seemed to grow quiet as I waited expectantly for him to answer. Despite the people that mingled and chatted around us, despite those who paused next to our table to share a few words, I was aware only of him. He took his time, his eyes twinkling.

"Life is what you make of it. You can choose to succeed and pursue your goals, or you can sit back and let life pass you by. Hopefully, you'll always have that ability to taste your hope."

"Taste hope?" I asked. "What's that exactly?"

He pursed his lips together as though considering my question carefully. I liked the intent look on his face. "When you know what you want and go after it. Hope is tangible. Hope is ever-present. When someone has the ability to taste hope, they catch it, they hold it in their hands, and feel it in their hearts. I think you're a tough young woman who can achieve whatever goals you set for yourself. You should do whatever you want, especially if it makes you happy. Besides, teaching is an honorable job, no matter what anyone else thinks. You'd be shaping the kids of our future."

"Wow, thank you," I said, following his example of drinking the rest of my coffee. I grimaced immediately. The coffee had turned cold, and I was surprised to notice how much time had passed. The sun had moved from its position just over our heads to glare through the glass windows. "Gosh, look at the time."

"Can I walk you back to your car?"

I nodded and came to my feet, gathering up my books as I did so. Side by side, we exited the building, both inhaling sharply as the heat outside blasted our faces. I fell into step beside him again, matching his long strides equally this time. He was so close I could hear the slight sounds of his breathing. I liked it, probably more than I should have.

A long walk through the crowds mingling on Palm Walk in the burning heat of late-August kept me somewhat grounded. I was able to answer his casual questions as we again hiked up the steep bridge across University Drive and pass through the dormitory area over to Lot 59. My car was approaching, and I resigned myself to ending our pleasant meeting.

Disappointment slowed my steps, causing him to glance down questioningly. "That's it over there, right?"

He pointed to my small blue Kia Rio just a mere ten paces away, and I nodded. At this point I knew better than to ask him how he knew. More than likely he had seen it in its assigned space that night he was at my apartment or perhaps when he ran my license. "It's not much, but it's paid for."

"And it runs," he finished with another heartbreaking grin.

"Most of the time," I said lamely, pulling out my keys.

He took them from me and deftly opened the door, holding it wide for me to get behind the wheel.

"Thanks for letting me vent," I said before I climbed in.

He smiled again and nodded his head. "It was good to see you. I'm glad you're doing well... Maybe I'll see you around campus sometime."

Ducking into the car, I paused to search for something that was not forthcoming on his face. "Yeah, I'll look for you."

Once I had placed my purse and books on the seat beside me, he closed the door and handed me the keys through the open window. It was hot inside the car, and the smell of my air freshener combined with the wave of hot air out the window to wrinkle Brandon's nose. "Berries? A new one, eh?"

"I guess I do whatever it takes."

"Yeah, that's what scares me."

Before I could question him, he reached across me into the car, his forearm brushing my chest. I leaned back in surprise, but he merely picked up my notebook and took out his pen. As I watched he scribbled something on the last page, and then folded the notebook over and handed it back to me. Three phone numbers glared back at me, written in neat, block-style handwriting.

"The top one is my mobile, the middle one my home phone, and the last one the number to the station. If you ever need me, Cherisse, you call me. I'll do what I can to help you out, okay?"

It was not an invitation for a date, and it certainly was not a promise of one, but as I stared down at those phone numbers I felt my heart tug. It was not a huge lurch, but it was something. I knew then that he cared at least a little.

When I did not immediately speak, Brandon tapped the top of my head with his pen. I glanced up, smiling, to meet my reflection in his glasses. "Thank you, Sergeant Nicholson," I murmured, hugging the notebook to my chest. "I promise I won't abuse your generosity."

He smiled again. "I trust you, Sunshine. And call me Brandon."

No sooner had the words left my mouth than I was feeling like an idiot. What was I thinking? Why had I said something so childish, so foolish? I could feel the blush burn my cheeks, growing hotter when he raised his hand to wave back. I did not wait to see him climb into his own vehicle. I sped away home as fast as I could so I could hide my burning cheeks under the covers of my bed.

Chapter 5

"I promise I won't abuse your generosity? You said that Cher? What's wrong with you? Haven't I taught you anything about flirting in all this time?"

I wanted to reach out and kick Arianne's foot out from under her. Two weeks ago I had developed a teenage-like crush on Brandon Nicholson. Just that day, I finally revealed my embarrassing secret to my roommate while we jogged around the track at the campus. Her response was a loud, enthusiastic laugh which made me scowl.

It was another hot morning, despite the recent departure of the monsoon season. Labor Day usually indicated the end of the summer season for the folks in the colder climates, but not here. Labor Day had come and gone, and we still had temperatures over one hundred degrees. Our heat showed no sign of waning any time before rapidly approaching October.

As I had reminded Paul, I refused to run before the morning low dropped below eighty degrees, and this morning was the first that we had been able to hit the track. Unfortunately, Paul had not made it. Though we were jogging early, I could already feel the stickiness of my sweat trickle down my back, and we were only halfway through our three-mile run.

"He really called you 'Sunshine?'"

"Yes," I grunted.

"I don't know, Cher. He did look a bit worried about you that day he dropped you off."

"Nice try, Ari. You saw how he's made hiding his emotions an art form."

"And I just thought it was his body that was the art form."

I gave her a quick shove, sending her jogging on the green grass next to the track.

"Hey!"

"You're not helping."

"Well, he is handsome as sin."

"And I'm just wasting my time." I took a deep breath and let it out. "Besides, he was staring at you."

Arianne glanced at me, sizing me up. "Cher, don't sell yourself short. You are a beautiful girl, you know, and I would kill to have a figure like yours. Unlike me, you don't need to be out here running every day. You eat whatever you want and don't put on a pound while I have to struggle to keep in my clothes."

"You have breasts, Ari, and I have molehills. And he *stared* at you when he saw you."

"It's not the size, babe," she purred. "Besides, those *are not* molehills."

"I look like a boy."

She laughed. "I can't think of a single guy out there that would agree with you." I didn't tell her of Sergeant Nicholson's comment that night over a month ago. "And you have a gorgeous head of hair and huge blue eyes. Like that's not stunning?"

"I'm plain."

61

"Your modesty is growing thin." She waved her hand, throwing aside her voluptuousness. "You're not plain at all, Cher. I think it's just that we're never happy with what we have. It's unfortunate but something we have to live with. But I'll tell you, if your cop's butt was within my reach I would grab it. Like this guy here – I've never seen him here before... Look, it's a new guy."

She gestured to a jogger who had just arrived on the track. He moved slowly to warm up, and we were catching up quickly. His feet were clad in worn running shoes, and baggy sweats covered his body, hiding his form, all except for his derriere. It was taut and muscular, and it clung to his gray sweats enticingly. A worn baseball cap covered his head, but at that moment we two were not staring at anything but his behind.

Much to my dismay, as we came up behind the jogger, Arianne reached out and pinched his buttock on the side I jogged on, leaving me to get the surprised, "Hey," shouted our way.

"Arianne," I gasped. "Why did you do that?"

"Don't worry about it, Cher. He loved it. You know guys love it when a girl takes the initiative."

"But I don't know him. What if he catches up to us? What if he thinks I was hitting on him?"

"Who cares? You'll probably never see him again. But boy, did he have a nice butt."

"I'm out of here."

Forgoing my stretches, I ran right to the locker-room. I didn't care if Arianne followed. Naturally she did, and she was merciless when she teased me about finally falling for a guy. "It's about time, Cher. I was beginning to wonder about you."

"Wonder what? I'm just too busy for a relationship."

"But he's too good looking to let slide. Any fish is good if you've got him on a hook, Cher. I say go after him."

"I'm done listening to you, Ari." I scowled at her. "Let's just go."

Reluctantly giving up, Arianne finished dressing and tossed my bag to me. I slipped my flip-flops on and gathered my stuff, hurrying out behind her, only to see the jogger standing outside waiting for us. He was leaning against the wall, his arms crossed over his chest, and I immediately realized that there was no way he could have missed our conversation.

Then it occurred to me that there was something familiar about him, about his form and the way his T-shirt was clinging to his damp skin, outlining the firm muscles of his chest. It was a broad chest, smooth and sleek. Though his hat hid his face in the shadows of the early morning sunlight, I was certain I had seen him around before. That only made me even more ashamed. Arianne elbowed me as I caught sight of him, stopping me from breaking into a run.

My mouth dropped open in a surprised gasp instead, and I began to stutter almost incoherently. "I'm really sorry about that. It was just a misunderstanding."

The jogger pushed himself away from the wall and shoved his cap back on his head. It felt as though the ground gave way beneath me as the realization of who it was hit home.

"Jesus, Sergeant Nicholson. I had no idea it was you."

Arianne's eyes widened too, and for once she was speechless. The irony was not lost on her, either. She stared down at her hands, a blush rising up her cheeks. I knew that it would be up to me to explain this one, and that Arianne would be cooking me dinner for at least the next two weeks. I shot an angry glance her way.

"Obviously... Do you know that sexual harassment can go both ways, ladies? I could arrest you."

I gasped and sent another look at Arianne, this one frantic. Her blue eyes were wide with surprise and a little fear. I peered up at Brandon, trying desperately to read his emotions, but his face was a blank mask – as usual.

"I'm really sorry, I didn't mean to..."

"Why are you apologizing, Cherisse?"

"Well." My voice trailed off. "Aren't you mad?"

"I want to hear your roommate – what's your name?"

"Arianne, Sergeant." She used her most enticing voice and nearly batted her eyes at him, and a spark of jealousy ignited within me, growing to a flame when he smiled down at her. I was reminded how long it took him to smile at me and felt a surge of envy. It had never bothered me before, her easy way with men. This time, however, it bothered me a lot. Brandon had been my find, my friend. Ari would eat him alive, and probably he her. That thought bothered me very much.

However, when he spoke I realized that I was completely wrong.

"Arianne. I want you to apologize."

"How did you know?" I blurted.

He chuckled. "Your fingernails are cut pretty close, Cherisse. I'll have a bruise from the daggers on her hands."

I glanced at my hands in surprise. When had he noticed my hands? Then I remembered the morning he brought me home. We had both seen the blood under my nails.

Ari flashed him her white teeth and bowed, giving him a view of the tops of her breasts beneath her square neck tank top. "Sergeant Nicholson, I'm very sorry. I meant you no harm, believe me. We were just talking about a guy with a nice butt. and you were there. You know how it is."

I was aware of Brandon's curious stare and glanced away. I refused to meet Ari's eyes as well.

"Not a problem, Arianne, just don't do it again. Any other guy could've gotten the wrong idea."

She bowed again and reached for my arm, intent on leading me away, but Brandon shook his head and reached for me first. "Wait a minute, Cherisse. Got a minute?"

Arianne stepped away, smiling at me with a knowing look. With eyebrows raised over dancing blue eyes, she nodded in my direction. "I'll meet you at the car, Cher." She waved. "Ta ta."

He remained silent for a time, re-crossing his arms across his chest and spreading his legs in an authoritative stance. I hated the way I could not see even the slightest glimpse of any emotion on his face, and the way he continued to stare at me had me shifting uncomfortably. My discomfort grew until I could not stand it anymore. "You wouldn't have arrested us," I accused.

"I know." He looked surprised at my sharp words, and his voice grew warm when he spoke again. "How are you, Cherisse?"

"You know we didn't know it was you."

He laughed aloud, a wide smile upon his angular face. "I knew that, too. I was just giving you a hard time. The only reason I came over here was because of you." He pointed at me in a sweeping gesture. "I recognized you."

"Oh."

"You haven't called. I was worried."

I was caught off guard. Now that was the last thing I had expected him to say. He had wanted me to call him? It was almost too good to be true. Struggling to hold back my goofy grin, I stared at him in confusion, wishing I could read him as easily as he could read me.

A breeze stirred my hair, and I took a moment to tuck it behind my ear while I regained my composure. "Umm, well I'm okay. I thought you told me to call you if I ever needed you. I haven't had any murderous thoughts lately, and I haven't gotten into trouble."

With a soft chuckle, he shook his head. "I didn't mean to save you from a speeding ticket, Cherisse."

"What did you mean, then?"

"If you need a friend or a companion, I'll be here for you."

My mouth dropped open stupidly. "Are you sure you're not married?"

He shook his head, smiling down at me. "No."

"Involved?"

"If I was, I wouldn't be here, would I?"

"How would I know? I don't know you at all, really. I mean, you know all there is to know about me, and I know nothing about you except for your name."

"Let's fix that," he said softly. "I just had a schedule change to accommodate my classes, so I come here some mornings before I head in to campus. I know you're busy too, so how often do you come?"

"Just about every morning now that it's cooler."

"Do you want to meet Tuesdays and Sundays? Say around seven o'clock?"

I could barely find my voice. Apparently he did not think I was a dork after what I had said the last time we parted ways. I was so excited that I wanted to throw my arms around his neck and hug him. Instead I nodded my head, my eyes shining with excitement.

He smiled back then, and my heart stopped. It was an angelic smile, one that reached all the way down to my toes. For the first time since Shelly had called me in tears, I felt happy – truly happy. He wanted to see me twice a week, which was more than I had ever dreamed of. "That would be great," I mumbled.

"Great. Until then. " He walked backward for a few steps. "Look, I've got to run. I'll see you later."

He jogged toward the men's locker room, his sneaker-clad feet slapping the pavement, and I watched him go, unable to drag my eyes away. They remained on the spot I last saw him for several minutes before I shook my head to clear it and went off to find Arianne. She had to know, and I could not wait to tell her.

****

Despite Arianne's initial disappointment at my refusal to jog with her two days a week, she ended up coping rather well and encouraged me to keep at it. During this time, Brandon treated me like a friend, perhaps even one of his buddies. Despite my hectic schedule and my comment to Arianne about how I had no time for dating, I found myself growing even more attached to him and his increasing role in my life. We talked. We shared our dreams and goals, and I loved speaking with him. It was so easy. I could be myself, say anything, do anything, and he accepted me and my antics with a good natured chuckle.

He opened up to me as well, telling me that not only was he a Sergeant on the police force, but he also was a member of their Tactical Unit, which required extra training every month. In the beginning of each year he would take part in a training course which lasted a week. It was a full week, but he enjoyed the challenge.

His enjoyment of challenges extended from his time at Luke Air Force Base in the West Valley. As I had suspected, he was ex-military and very proud to have served his country. Straight out of the military, he joined the police department and finished his college degree. With a graduate degree his next challenge, I learned that

Brandon was not one to sit idle.

Because of all of this, I was finding it hard to believe he had not made any attempt to make a pass at me. I wondered sometimes if he wanted to go further, but even if he had, I could never tell. The man was a master at maintaining an expressionless mask, even when he was courteous. For my part, my secret crush turned into hero worship, and it was a struggle to hide my impatience from his observant stare. The discouragement that I felt was growing to the point where I was preparing to come right out and ask him, but he finally beat me to the punch on a Sunday in mid-October.

That day was a beautifully sunny one, and the weather had finally cooled enough to make jogging more pleasant. To accommodate both our schedules, we had changed our Sunday jog to eight that morning. The sun was warm as it beat down on us from the deep blue sky, though there was a pleasant breeze to keep us cool.

We jogged side by side, with Brandon doing his best to accommodate my shorter legs. In the month since we had begun running together, I noticed that I was stronger due to the difference in our styles. The irony was not lost on me that it was mostly due to my struggle to keep up with him.

Since it was a cooler morning than usual, I had thrown a sweatshirt and pants over my normal jogging tank and shorts when I left my apartment. Now I was regretting my decision. The day was growing warm, and I was already overtired. I had worked an extra shift the night before, and I just did not have the energy to go all out that day. By the time we passed our halfway point, I was slightly breathless and feeling worn out, and after another lap, Brandon astutely noticed my weariness. Giving me a slight nudge, he nodded in the direction of the bleachers. They were empty, and I fell onto the bench with a heavy sigh.

"Wow, I'm pooped," I muttered.

"You look a little red," he said, smiling.

"Thanks," I said wryly. "I had a late night."

"Yeah I can tell. You looked tired when you got out of the car this morning," he remarked.

"I've been working all week. One of the girls is really sick."

"After classes? That's a long day."

"But it's good money. Remember, I have to save up to make it through student teaching. I'll have no income then..." I heaved another deep breath and waved my hand dismissively. "I'll just crash later."

He sat beside me and stretched out his long legs, and my lips twisted when I watched them extend way past mine. "Do you watch what you eat?" I asked suddenly, remembering my conversation with Arianne.

"Like dieting?" He glanced at me in surprise when I nodded. "No. Do you?"

"No."

He chuckled. "Why do you sound so disappointed?"

"What I meant is..." I said awkwardly. "Do you work out just because of your job or because you have to?"

"Mostly because of my job. You'd be surprised how many rabbits there are around here. It's amazing how fast people can run when they're afraid."

I laughed. "So why do you do it?"

He was quiet for a moment, as though pondering my question. I glanced at him and saw the color that had risen on his cheeks.

"Well?"

"I guess I thought I could help," he admitted.

"You don't think that anymore?"

"Oh, I'm sure I've helped some people, but not in the way I thought. There are a lot of ungrateful people out there. I mean, people hate cops. They don't trust us any more than we trust them. It's tiring sometimes." He shrugged and glanced at me. "Why did you ask anyway?"

Sensing his discomfort with the turn of our conversation, I raised my eyebrows at him. "It's not right that a person can look as good as you do and not have to work hard at it."

"I could say the same thing about you, couldn't I?"

I snorted in surprise. "Me? Why me? I'm not handsome."

He smiled at me as he shoved me lightly with his shoulder. "Not handsome but very pretty."

"You think so?"

He nodded slowly, his head dipping ever so slightly. "I do, yes."

"Oh."

Before I could stop myself, I reached up and cupped his cheek in my palm. It was moist, and I could feel the stubble there. My thumb stroked his strong cheekbone along the underside of his eye. He was so real, so utterly male, and just so handsome, and he was staring at me with a look on his face that I had not seen before.

Suddenly I knew. He was finally going to kiss me. There was a glow in his eyes that I had never seen before. It shone like fire within the oceans of his gaze. Excitement coursed through my veins as I prepared for my first touch of his soft, full lips, and I wondered how many times I imagined this moment.

His determined stare captured my attention, and his face descended ever so slowly. I was powerless to look away. The heat from his body enveloped mine. That, coupled with the desire showing plainly in his eyes, promised me that this was not going to be an ordinary kiss. My heart pounded furiously in anticipation, and

I felt my lips part. When his fingers reached up to tip up my chin I thought I would die of excitement.

It was finally happening.

The texture of his lips was everything as I had expected. They touched mine gently, brushing ever so slightly, before drawing away. While I wanted to wrap my arms around him and pull him close, he continued to exercise his magnificent control. When he pulled away, I sighed softly in protest. The corner of his mouth deepened in a tiny smile before he dipped his head again. The whole time his gaze held mine, intent and solemn.

"I'm going to kiss you," he murmured.

"Oh...yes."

As his moist lips settled upon mine again, I felt my eyes slip closed. Taking his time to explore my mouth thoroughly, Brandon held himself in check while I relaxed and let him take control. His free arm slipped around my shoulders, pulling me closer to him, and I settled into him happily. He was strong, and his arm was demanding where his lips were not.

For many hours I had speculated and dreamed what his close cropped hair would feel like, and suddenly given the chance I eagerly reached for the short pieces. My fingers stole up his powerful neck to wind in the short, silky strands. Much softer than I had imagined; it was so much more luxurious. I was in heaven until he slowly pulled away from me, pressing two small kisses to the corners of my mouth before he lifted his head. I made a protesting sound in the back of my throat, but he continued to move away. The snickers not a hundred feet away brought me back to earth with a solid thump.

"Someone's coming," he murmured in explanation.

Disappointed with the intrusion, I was surprised to realize that I did not care if someone saw us. Brandon released his hold on me and straightened, holding out his hand to help me up. "Come on. I don't need an audience."

I wanted to protest, but he pulled me to my feet and wrapped his arm around my shoulders as we walked back towards the locker rooms. Coming towards us from the parking lot was another couple, and they sent catcalls our way. I tensed up, ready to tell them to butt out, but Brandon's grip on me tightened. A moment later, I realized why. I recognized the approaching blond head and curvaceous body.

"Couldn't wait until you got home, eh?"

"Ari! Really!"

She wagged her eyebrows at me and elbowed her boyfriend, Mike. "Aren't they so cute, Mike? So perfect together."

Mike smiled at us as he shook his head in understanding. It was so typical of Arianne to be suggestive, and it was one of the many reasons Mike loved her. He held out his hand to Brandon, who shook it quickly.

"You have bad timing," Brandon said.

"I noticed," she said, laughing. "But I think we came just in time. If we hadn't you may have been naked within minutes."

Mike grinned. "Good thing the locker rooms are locked, eh?"

"Knock it off! Just go... go away, Arianne," I snapped.

"We just got here. Why don't you go home and do it in private? Aren't you the first one to complain about PDA? So hypocritical."

The color rose on my cheeks and everyone noticed. While Arianne giggled, Brandon gave my sweatshirt a tug. "Let's go." As soon as we were out of earshot, he turned to me. "Have I told you how obnoxious I think your roommate is?"

My eyes went wide. Usually men adored her, especially her flamboyant ways. "You think she's obnoxious?"

"Yeah." He gave me a sidelong glance. "Why do you sound so

surprised?"

"She's very sexy."

"So?"

I was honestly surprised. Most guys I knew would love a shot at Arianne, given the chance. "I just assumed that you'd like to..."

For the first time, I heard his full-blown laughter. Though I wanted to be irritated, the sound was so infectious that I smiled. too. "You're too much. No, I don't want anything to do with your roommate. She's definitely not my type," he said.

I was granted his most angelic smile, and I felt it down to my very toes again. "I'm glad to hear that," I managed to say.

His arm tightened around my shoulders, and I leaned into him. It was nice to be held like that. I felt so protected.

"Cherisse, we've been meeting up for a while now, and I really like hanging with you..."

"But..."

He was silent for a moment, and his hand slipped away from me. For a moment, I felt loss and looked up at him nervously.

"I want more."

"More?"

"Yes, more. I like running with you. We talk all the time, and I enjoy texting you. But you've said you don't have time for a relationship. I want to work on that. I think we could make it work, even though your schedule's full." He sighed and glanced away. "I'm in a wedding next Saturday, the best man."

My heart was racing so fast that I could barely get the words out. "Saturday? Okay."

He nodded. "Are you working?"

"Yes."

Seeing the flash of disappointment in his aquamarine eyes, I smiled apologetically. "Why, what's going on?"

"I want to bring you with me. I want it to be a date," he said in a rush.

It was finally happening. He wanted more! He wanted to make it work. I was floating on air, so excited and joyful that most of my problems seemed insignificant. Schedules be damned. We could do this. I thought of the fool I would be if I let this opportunity pass. With all the extra shifts and covering I had done recently, I just knew that someone would repay the favor, and I was grinning so wide that I thought my face would crack. "I'll see if I can switch with someone and make it up some nights this week, okay? What time is the wedding?"

"Ten."

I was surprised. "But don't you work the late shift?"

"Just until midnight. All the more reason for you to come."

"Why's that?"

"So you can drive me home when I pass out."

I laughed, and Brandon kissed me again. The second kiss was different from his first one. Gone was the exploratory hesitance. In its place was what I believed all those heroines in romance novels experienced, when the hero pulled her close and held her tight against his body. There was so much honesty in the hungry pressure of his mouth that I felt devoured. It was magical.

When he finally lifted his head I was swaying on my feet. Seeing this, a look of satisfaction replaced his hesitancy. "Will you try to come with me? I'd really like your company."

"Definitely."

"Great. Can I call you later?"

"Yes. I'll ask to cash in a favor and let you know."

"I'm working tonight, so I don't know when I'll be able to break away. I'll make sure I call before eleven, so you can get some sleep tonight. Okay, Sunshine?"

I wanted to shout that I would wait up all night, but instead I merely nodded. He took my keys in what was fast becoming a habit and opened my door for me. Once I climbed in and began to secure my seatbelt, he shut it. "I'll talk to you later."

I nodded as he turned and walked away with his customary wave. I watched him go until he reached his truck and opened the door. All too soon for my hungry eyes, he had disappeared into the dark tinted confines. At that point, I allowed myself to squeal in delight.

Two kisses! Two kisses in one day. What had I done to deserve it?

Chapter 6

I returned home, showered, and then waited anxiously for Arianne to get in. While I passed the time, I set about vacuuming and dusting, two chores neither one of us enjoyed doing. Luckily, we were not home all that often and never managed to get the place too dirty. Since I knew that she and Mike would return at least long enough to shower before setting out for the day, I hurried to complete the light chores to help boost my case. It was just a matter of patience.

When she finally walked in the door, I greeted her with a wide smile and a pleading look in my eye. "Do me a huge favor?"

Suspicion narrowed her eyes, and Mike chuckled as he entered behind her. "Payback, my darling."

"You're right," I said.

With an exaggerated sigh, Arianne threw herself down on the couch and kicked off her sneakers. "Fine. What's up?"

"Will you work for me Saturday?"

A pained look appeared on her face. "You mean all day?"

"I promise I'll make it up for you during the week. Please, Arianne, please!"

"Why do you have to pull full-time hours in three shifts, Cher? I don't want to be there all day."

"It's only open to close one day. You'll be home in time to go out."

"But I'll be so tired I'll just want to go to bed."

I knew how she felt. I worked three shifts, twelve hours each, at a popular American-style restaurant on Mill Avenue. Food service was exhausting, and by the time I got home on my days without classes all I wanted to do was lay down and put my feet up. Arianne worked nights at the same restaurant, but she only did part-time hours. I considered her to be one of the truly lucky ones. Her family helped her pay her way through school, handling her rent and most of her expenses. Although I used to be jealous of her generous relations, when I finally saw my parents settle themselves up north I learned that it was better to be self-sufficient. All that mattered to me was my goals in life. No matter what it took, I knew I would succeed. I would have done it all on my own, too.

"Please, Ari?"

Mike squeezed Arianne's thigh, nodding in my direction. After my pleading look sent in his direction, he spoke up on my behalf. "I'm sure it's an important reason that she's asking you, Ari. Why don't you do it?"

She scowled. "What's going on, anyway?"

I could not hold in my smile. It spread across my face like a blossoming flower. "Brandon has asked me to go with him to a wedding."

Arianne sat up suddenly, her eyes wide with surprise. "You mean, he's actually asked you out?"

I nodded.

"To a wedding?"

My head bobbed again, sending loose strands of my auburn hair flying.

She laughed. "It's about time. I didn't think that piece of wood would ever make the move on you. I guess your kiss really hit a nerve."

"Ari, please."

Mike laughed. "I think that's great, Cher. He seems like a good guy."

"Who are you kidding, Mike? The man's gorgeous," Arianne said with a shake of her head.

"Looks aren't everything," I said softly.

Mike agreed, though Arianne waved her hand in dismissal. "It may not matter, but, boy, does it help."

"So you'll do it?"

"The romantic in me has agreed," she said with a dramatic tone. "But Cher, you need to get him into bed and decide if he's worth all this time you're giving him, okay?"

I felt the blush rise on my face again, but in an effort to placate my sensual roommate, I agreed. I would give her a good show, and who knew? Maybe Brandon would get drunk and save me the trouble.

****

I knew I needed to find something suitable to wear, so I took off later that day to go to the bank and head to the mall. Although I was alone, I felt good about shopping for myself. It could not be that hard to find a dress to wear to a wedding. Unfortunately, I was more wrong than I had imagined. It took a quick dinner at the mall, three department stores, and several hours of window shopping at the smaller stores before I found some things in my size that would look good enough with my flaming, auburn hair.

When I finally got home with a couple of dresses to model for Ari, I found two messages on the home machine. Since both Ari and I were on our mobile phones all the time, it was very rare that anyone would call the home phone. Sales calls, I thought to myself, ugh.

But they were not sales calls.

"Hi, Cher, this is Shelly. I just wanted to let you know that we're gone. I've left Joe and am going into hiding for a while... Um, jeez, I hate these machines... He hit Jake today, Cher. My baby got hit and not just on the bottom. I can't let him hurt my son, Cher. I hope you understand." I heard her laugh sarcastically. "I'm so sorry, Cher. I should've listened to you. I should've left him a long time ago, before it got this bad. I'm afraid he's going to call you. I hope he doesn't, please believe that, but if he does, just tell him I'm in hiding, okay? Thanks, Cher. I'll call you."

The message ended and the machine beeped. Rather than listen to the other message right away, I picked up the phone and dialed my parents. To no surprise, I got their answering machine. As I listened to my mother's senseless chatter, I debated hanging up, but the machine beeped before I could, and I felt compelled to speak.

When I finished, I decided to listen to the other message. What I heard chilled my bones.

"Cher, I was just there looking for my wife," came the angry voice. "She's not here, Cher. I don't know what lies you've been filling her head with, but if you know what's good for you you'll stop... Stop. Interfering. Now. I think you should hear both sides of the story before you go butting your nose in places it doesn't belong. You owe me an apology."

Suddenly the voice changed. It became sad, depressive, and weepy. "When you two get in, I want you to send her home – right now. Tell her it'll be okay if she gets home soon. She just needs to come back. I need her here."

When I stepped away from the machine, I noticed my hands were shaking. Cold fear filled my belly and left me uneasy. The memory of the angry face that had burst into my home, turning a man I had grown up knowing and trusting into a monster within the space of a few minutes, scared me. He had come to my apartment looking for Shelly, and that reminded me of what Brandon had said. I would be blamed.

I was alone tonight. Arianne was spending the night at Mike's place.

For a few moments, I considered calling Paul, but the fear of Brandon misunderstanding held me back. I knew Paul would come and stay however long I needed him to, but I did not want to do anything that might ruin the finally deepening relationship that Brandon wanted. So I sat and waited. Growing nervous with the coming darkness, I hurried around the apartment and secured the locks on every door and window then cursed aloud for being so frightened. After checking that the house was secure, I turned off all the lights and sat on the sofa, staring at the door and allowing my imagination full rein of what could possibly happen if he did show up.

Tense hours passed. I finally fell asleep on the sofa, too tired to keep my eyes open any longer. Unfortunately, it was not long before the ring of the home phone shook me awake.

The machine answered after the fourth ring. I heard Ari's cheery voice asking the caller to leave a message and closed my eyes in dread. I felt cold from the fear, and tucked my legs beneath me. I was growing smaller, shrinking away in fright, and the blinking light prepared me for the worst.

"This is Joe. You troublemaking little brat, where the hell is Shelly? I'm coming to get her if she doesn't get home within an hour, and you're both gonna regret it. Do you understand? Pass on the message."

His words were slurred with the effects of alcohol. He had been drinking again. I realized he would know that I had checked my message, since it had not beeped two times before he was able to speak. Cold dread filled me. Was he outside, waiting? More than anything, I was terrified of another violent scene at my apartment.

Reaching for the phone, I hastily looked up the Caller ID. It was their home phone number that he was calling on, but I knew he could hop on the highway and be at my apartment in just 30 minutes. For a few seconds, I considered leaving and finding a place to hang out. Still, everything closed at some point, so I would have to come home to the dark, empty apartment. In the wee early hours of the morning, who knew what could be lurking in the shadows by the stairs. Even more frightening was the idea that I could try to leave the apartment, only to come face to face with Joe in the parking lot. I felt trapped.

Over the course of the next forty minutes, the house phone rang six times, and each time the caller hung up after a long pause. The Caller ID told me it was him. Fifteen minutes later, he switched to my mobile. The vibration shook the sofa cushion several times while I considered shutting it off for the night. His persistence bothered me. Who knew what he would be capable of if he continued drinking?

My nerves grew increasingly frazzled while I waited. I sat and waited for I don't know what. It was nearing midnight, but I was too frightened to go to bed. After another twenty minutes, my mobile vibrated again. It so startled me that I cried out in alarm.

Angry with myself for being so frightened and angry at him for calling me over and over again, this time I answered. My voice shook with fury, but I felt I was putting on a good show in any case.

"You'd better stop calling me, Joe. Stop it right now. Shelly's not here, and I don't know where she is."

"Cherisse?"

I jumped at the sound of the warm voice at the other end, a voice now filled with concern. "Brandon, I'm sorry," I stammered. "I didn't know it was you."

"What's going on, Cherisse?"

Hearing the hard edge in his voice, I struggled to laugh. Tears filled my eyes from rage or fear, I could not tell. As I struggled to form the words in my mind, I heard Brandon again.

"Cherisse, are you okay?"

A hiccup sob sort of escaped my lips before I was able to take a deep breath to steady my words. Hoping he would think I was laughing, I schooled my voice to sound as flippant as possible. "I'm fine. I thought you were a prank caller."

Naturally, he did not buy it. "A prank caller? Named Joe? Come on, Sunshine, what's going on?"

I sobbed again, this time the tears spilled from my eyes like hot drops of acid. "Brandon, I think I need you."

"I've got some paperwork to finish, but I can be done in about a half hour. Can you wait that long, or should I send someone over now?"

I sniffled. "No, no, come when you can. I'm sorry."

"Don't be sorry. I'll head over straight away."

"Thank you," I said, almost inaudibly.

"It's not a problem," he answered, his voice sounding like warm honey. "You have my number? Call me back if you need me."

"I will."

The minutes ticked away like hours. With an angry huff, I stalked from one end to the next in my small bedroom, stepping over the basket with clean laundry needing to be folded. I was far too anxious to fold them now. Even though they would be wrinkled by morning, I ignored them completely. Tossing down the phone on my dresser, I cursed softly as it knocked over my small collection of unicorns.

Telling myself to calm down, I went to the window that overlooked the parking lot and waited. Once more I huddled, sitting with my knees to my chest as I waited for something to happen.

The lights in the parking lot shed an orange glow on the cars below. It was a well-lit, but loaded with dark shadows. Three cars passed through that late at night. With every glimpse of the white headlights, my breath caught in my chest. I watched them approach slowly, my heart thudding within my chest, as they continued by. Only one could have been Joe, but it too passed by when confronted with the black interior.

Some part of me doubted that Joe would really come back here, but at the same time I knew he was not acting rationally and that could mean he would do just about anything to regain control over his wife. I also knew that he now blamed me for her defection. Brandon's words once more rang in my ears. He had warned me that Joe had something against me. Evidently he did.

Almost a full hour passed before I saw another pair of white lights. They entered the parking lot at a fast clip, faster than most vehicles would. Up and over the speed bumps it went, and I peered at it as I considered my two options. It was either Joe, in a hurry to collect his wife, or it was Brandon, hurrying because he was later than he had promised.

With a happy squeak, I observed the white Frontier pull into an open visitor's spot. Peering out into the darkness, I watched as the headlights went out and the door opened.

The interior light cast a glow through the tinted glass. It was enough that I was able to witness him emerge from the car like a beacon on a foggy day. My knight in shining armor had arrived.

He had removed his uniform shirt, and was dressed only in a white T-shirt tucked loosely into his slacks. His black boots gleamed in the night, and my heart hammered. He was so tall and handsome, so cool and deliberate. I knew at that moment that everything would be okay.

I watched him until he was out of sight, and then I hurried into the living room where I waited for him to reappear. He mounted the steps at a jog and took them two at a time in his haste to rescue me. Without a thought, I threw back the deadbolt and opened the door.

With an embarrassed flush and a relieved smile, I greeted him in the doorway. Then I promptly threw myself at him, hugging him tightly and never wanting to let him go. After a surprised grunt, his hands went around my waist, and he gently backed me into the apartment.

I stepped back with an embarrassed laugh. "I'm so sorry for making you rush over here. But thanks for coming."

I stepped aside so he could pass and close the door behind him. Once I had set the locks, I turned to face him, my hands clasped together in front of me. I waited breathlessly. For what, I was not sure. Maybe I waited for his embrace or even just a smile. My nerves were jittery, but it was no longer fear. I was thrilled he had come.

He glanced around, his senses heightened by the darkness. "Why are all the lights off?"

My flush deepened. "I was afraid he was coming."

"Who? You mean Joe?"

When I nodded, he scowled. I hurried past him and switched on the light, casting a dim yellowish glow upon the living room. That was when I noticed how agitated he was. The mixture of anger and relief on his face burned like a raging fire. "What happened?"

Instead of speaking, I pressed the play button on the answering machine and let him hear all the messages, starting with the one from Shelly. He listened, his face impassive, as Joe's voice filled the apartment, angry and forceful. Now that Brandon was here and I had company, I could feel my anger rise. How could I have been so scared of that man?

The answer was simple. He had acted so out of the ordinary in August that I did not know what to expect from him.

When all the messages played back and he saw the number of calls on my Caller ID, Brandon shook his head, his lips a narrow line. I stared up at him, noticing for the first time the small lines around his eyes. Laughter lines. A strange occurrence, since he laughed so rarely. "Has he called you before?"

I shook my head.

"Have you seen his truck around here?"

"No."

"You should save those messages for evidence. If things progress, it can help you and Shelly fight him in court."

When I sighed, he frowned down at me and placed his hands on his hips. "Where's your roommate?"

"She's been staying at Mike's. She comes home Monday's after class."

"She won't be back tonight?"

When I shook my head, he sat on the couch with a heavy sigh.

"Can you call her?"

"I can't call Ari over this. I mean, what if he comes here, and she gets caught up in this?"

"You're right." He leaned forward and tugged on the side zipper of his duty boots. They fell to the floor with a solid thump. An exasperated sigh escaped his tightly compressed lips. "I don't think you should be here alone, especially when Shelly doesn't go back at all tonight."

Waiting for an offer that did not come was not heartening. Feeling rejected, I stared at him for what seemed an eternity, but he merely met my eyes with his somber gaze. My heart sank. He did not want me to be here alone, and he wasn't offering to stay.

Swallowing every last shred of pride I had, I glanced down at my hands. "Would you stay?" I asked hesitantly. "I can cook you some dinner if you haven't eaten yet. Ari's always dieting, but I have some stuff in the fridge."

"Of course I'll stay."

He continued to stare at me, his face still impassive.

"Are you hungry?"

"I ate this afternoon," he said with a small smile. "Come here."

He patted a spot beside him on the couch, and I only hesitated a minute before I climbed over the long expanse of his legs and sat down, my hands wound tightly in my lap. Though he did not seem too thrilled with the idea of staying, I could not deny that I was relieved he was there.

Reaching over my head to shut off the light, Brandon cast the room into darkness once more. Then he picked up the TV remote and turned the set on, immediately finding the all-night news channel. Fiddling with the remote for a moment, he set about finding a setting he approved of and then set it down.

When he was satisfied with the low volume, he reached over and pulled me into his arms, wrapping them tightly around me and pulling me close. His hands locked together around my waist, leaving me cloaked in security.

"This is not a good way to finish a good day," he murmured as I leaned into him.

I landed upon his chest, my palm coming to rest upon the steady beating of his heart. He was warm and smelled again of the lingering remains of after-shave. I inhaled deeply. For the second time that day, I felt what romance novelists wrote about. Raw, throbbing desire was a real thing. I knew now because I was experiencing it, even if Brandon did not. Considering the hours I had sat alone in my apartment, I assumed that my tension was the reason I was so hyper-aware. Whatever the case, it was new to me.

"We'll just watch some TV for a while, Sunshine. That way you can calm down a little." His voice rumbled from deep in his chest, and his breath tickled my ear and stirred the loose strands of my hair. I felt like a child, curled in his lap. When I nodded, he placed his chin on the top of my head, bending just once to press a kiss in my hair. "You scared the daylights out of me, you know," he whispered.

"I'm sorry," I whispered. "I didn't want to be alone."

"I'm here now. I'll take care of you." He chuckled. "Besides, I think he'd be nuts to try and tangle with you again. You did a number on his arm."

I giggled, remembering the glass on the floor and the gouge in his arm. Then I remembered the hard blow to my face, and it immediately sobered me. "He got me pretty good, too."

"I won't let him touch you again, Cherisse. You have my word on that."

"My hero," I whispered, meaning it wholeheartedly.

"It's my job," he said.

Though his words were matter-of-fact, he gave my waist a slight squeeze of approval. My heart swelled so much at that moment that I could feel fresh tears sting my eyes again. My voice shook with emotion when I lifted my head to smile bravely at him. "Thank you Brandon. Thank you for everything."

He smiled then, flashing his white teeth at me with heart-stopping effects. "Just relax."

It could not have been fifteen minutes before I was fast asleep, and I remained asleep until the buzzing of my alarm shook me awake in the morning. Reluctantly, I opened my eyes. At some time in the night, Brandon had carried me to bed. He had tucked me under the covers and pulled me close, with a strong arm wrapped snugly around my shoulders and a hand resting on my waist. As I slowly regained my senses, I realized that my right hand was resting upon a flat midsection, a strong one at that. My other hand was tucked under his shoulder, trapped between our bodies. Not only that, but my leg was thrown over a pair of muscular thighs. I had slept the whole night with my cheek pressed against his chest, soothed by the steady sound of his heartbeat and my head tucked safely in his shoulder.

I had spent the night with Brandon.

Considering the amount of times I had romanticized that very moment, nothing had come even close to the reality of the chaste night we spent together. It was nothing like I imagined.

I slowly lifted my head, careful not to disturb my sleeping companion. Luckily, he did not flinch at all as I eased my way out of his embrace to reach for the buzzing clock. I glanced at the time with a groan. It was 7:00 am. I had my first class in two hours.

With a sigh of regret, I eased back the covers and slipped from the bed as quietly as I could. Finding it impossible not to stare, I glanced down at Brandon in the gray morning light. His face was completely relaxed, and surprisingly undisturbed by my movements. He looked like an angel – my guardian angel. His short hair stood up in spots, lending him an untidy look, but a very endearing one at that. I could see the brownish stubble on his cheeks and curled my fingers into my palm to keep from reaching out to feel it. After his selflessness the night before, I knew for sure that I had found a good man. I only hoped I could hold on to him for a while. As I quietly made my way down the hall to take a shower, I could not help but smile.

It was nice to sleep next to a man, curl against him, and relish in his warmth and even breathing. We were alone in the apartment, and as I showered I fantasized about opening my eyes and finding him standing gloriously nude before me. However, he was still sleeping soundly when I emerged, his even breathing carrying through the bathroom door. Poor guy. He must have been exhausted.

With nothing to dress in, I reached for Arianne's red silk robe, a mid-thigh cover-up that clung to my damp body. In total Arianne style, it was low cut and sexy. Unfortunately for me, it was two sizes too big for me and dipped quite low in the neckline, revealing the curve of my breasts through the gap. It was difficult to keep it closed, and as I wandered about in the kitchen preparing breakfast, I kept one hand at my neckline.

I had just finished pouring our coffee when I heard Brandon emerge from my bedroom. After a brief sojourn to the bathroom, he came up behind me, wrapping one hand around my waist and reaching for his coffee with the other. "Mm, coffee. You're a saint."

I felt a mixture of excitement and nervousness. He was close behind me, with my buttocks pressing against his upper thighs. I could feel every line of his body against my back, and it felt good. I leaned back against his chest, the top of my head just barely touching his chin. He lowered his face to rest it on my crown, inhaling deeply the scent of my freshly washed hair. "You smell good."

"There's a towel on the sink if you want to shower, and I have a new toothbrush next to it if you want to brush."

"Wow, my own toothbrush? After only one night?"

I chuckled. "I wasn't sure how grouchy you'd be in the morning."

"I'm never grouchy."

I laughed again, and he responded by giving me a slight squeeze.

"I'll just have my coffee first, if that works?"

"I don't know how you like it."

"Black is fine," he murmured. A short moment later, he laughed. "You don't know how I like it yet? After all those cups we've shared."

"All? I remember only two."

"Okay, two. Still..."

With a small laugh, I placed down my spoon and turned around to face him. He pulled me closer, wrapping both hands around my waist. Hugging him was so easy, and I pressed my cheek to the spot where I could hear his steady heartbeat the best. Closing my eyes, I inhaled deeply and listened. So smooth and even, his heart thudded gently under my cheek and soothed my nerves.

"Thank you, Brandon. Thank you for dropping everything and coming here. I feel silly now. He probably never would've come over last night."

Even though I could not see it, I heard the smile in his voice. "It's fine, so stop thanking me... While it wasn't quite the way I imagined our first night to be, I'm glad I could help you relax."

"That you did."

"Just remember that if he had been drinking as much as it sounded like he had, he'd probably have passed out before he got the car started anyway, or DPS would've picked him up for a DUI. Either way, I doubt he would've made it here last night. Not that I minded coming to your rescue last night. I kind of like taking care of you."

I raised my eyes, expecting to see humor, a gentle teasing, perhaps, on his face. Instead he appeared once more to be deadly serious. "You do?"

He responded first by lowering his hands from my waist to the curve of my buttocks, resting in the small dip with moderate pressure. I felt him against my belly, firm and eager and very much alive, and I grew warm all over. "Yes, I do. But I'd like it even more if you would wear that robe every time I see you. It's driving me nuts right now."

"It's not mine, it's Ari's. I didn't want to wake you up, so I just put it on."

He chuckled. "I can tell. It doesn't fit you very well." One of his hands left the small of my back to toy with the lapel of the robe. His long fingers lightly stroked the silk and my skin underneath, gradually going lower until he was within inches of my breast. "You could've dressed. I certainly wouldn't have minded if you woke me up fresh from a shower."

"You looked so tired that I doubt you would've noticed me walking around in there," I said, my heart pounding wildly. "I still feel really bad about asking you to come over here. Were you able to sleep?"

"I slept very well," he replied huskily. "You're pretty cute when you're relaxed."

"I was being serious," I reprimanded softly.

Brandon's hand fell away from the robe, and he released me. Still leaning against the counter, I watched while he strode to the small dining room table and pulled out a chair to sit. He pushed aside my purse and placed down his coffee with a soft clang on the freshly wiped glass surface, his gaze never leaving mine. "I'm glad you asked me to come over, Cherisse," he said. "The only thing that bothers me is your fear of Joe."

"I'm not afraid of him," I protested.

Before the lie left my tongue, I knew we both knew it was a pathetic attempt at bravado. He smiled grimly. "You are, and that's okay. I didn't think he'd try to break into your apartment last night, Cherisse. But I do think..."

"What?"

He glanced at his coffee, slowly swirling the black liquid around in the cup. I glanced at the mug. It was a photo of me and Shelly when we were children. I fought the urge to laugh bitterly. "How often are you alone here at night?"

"Just weekends."

"Does he know that?"

"I can't see how. I don't even think Shelly knows."

"And now Shelly has taken Jacob and left. If she doesn't come home, he's going to start looking for her."

"Do you think they'll be okay?"

"They will as long as she doesn't cave in to Joe. He's not going to be happy to have lost her."

"So you think that he'll come here and give me trouble?"

"Better to be safe than sorry, Sunshine. That's all I'm saying. You did the right thing by calling me." Another charming smile appeared. "I'd like to think you asked me over because you missed me."

I took a deep breath and nodded, knowing instinctively that this was some sort of test. "I was glad when you said you'd come over. Really."

"Not just because of Joe?"

"No. I like being with you, Brandon."

He smiled again. "So can I have a drawer now?"

"You can have two."

Appearing busy by preparing two plates with bagels and cream cheese, I handed him a plate and took the chair opposite him. Over the rim of my coffee mug I watched as he lathered a liberal amount of cream cheese over his bagel before sitting back and taking a bite. He caught my stare as he chewed, and I looked at my plain bagel with a guilty flush. I still had no appetite.

After several bites, he glanced up and again caught me staring. His gaze dropped to the gaping neckline of the robe, and when I followed his stare I noted that it had fallen open to reveal a lot of skin. "What time is your first class?"

His voice had grown husky again, and my heart immediately responded. I glanced at the clock a little nervously, my hand returning to the neckline of my robe. "I have a half hour. You're welcome to stay here for a while. I don't know how far away you live."

He shrugged, though his eyes danced with mirth. "It's not that. I was thinking something else."

"Oh," I said, understanding his insinuation. I stared down at my plate again, completely at a loss for words.

"Cherisse, I meant what I said before."

"That you want more?" I asked.

His mouth opened with words that would not come out. Finally he nodded his head. "Yes, I do." He sighed. "I do want more,

Cherisse. I want to take you out. I want quiet dinners and private mornings like this. I want to hold you at night and cook for you. I want to show you my house."

"I don't even know where you live," I commented.

"I want to remedy that."

I smiled. "Let's start with the wedding then, okay? I got Ari to fill in for me. I have the whole day off and don't work Sunday."

"Good." He came to his feet and reached for me, pulling me from my chair to the firm warmth of his chest. I went willingly, happily. "I am a bit older than you," he said, his thumbs stroking my back. "Does that bother you?"

"How old are you?"

"Twenty-nine."

"That's not that much older," I said with a laugh.

"I guess you're right." He released me with a sigh. "I should probably let you go get ready for class. Are we still on for tomorrow?"

I nodded. "Of course."

"Great. Now get going before I can't stop myself." He winked at me, and I felt dizzy with excitement. "We'll talk more about the wedding when I see you then."

I backed out of the room, reluctantly leaving the man who made my toes curl.

Chapter 7

Tuesday came, and still no word from my sister. With my growing relationship with Brandon and my own hectic life, time had passed quickly, and I hardly thought of her. However, all of that had changed when Shelly left a message on Ari's answering machine. Suddenly I was again worried and concerned about her and Jacob. The not knowing where she was hiding bothered me, so much so that it was always in the back of my mind, hoping they were both safe.

During our Tuesday jog, Brandon gave me the number of a friend of his. I had stared at the name Mary and felt a twinge of jealousy, but then Brandon explained to me who she was. A counselor at one of Mesa's crisis shelters, she and Brandon had been friendly when she worked for the City. She had left to open a center of her own, and Brandon had kept in touch.

All week I held that slip of paper with her phone number on it, debating whether to call and wondering if it would be necessary. It slipped away in my book bag, forgotten, as the week flew by. Before I knew it, Saturday arrived, and I was to have my first date with Brandon. I spent most of the morning trying to make myself beautiful. Of course, in my opinion, it was a daunting task. Yet, by the time I had applied my pink lip gloss, I thought I had achieved pretty good results.

As I waited for Brandon to pick me up, I paced the living room from one end to the other, pausing only long enough to once more check my reflection in the glass. While I did so, Ari, who had risen early to do my hair, lounged on the sofa and watched. Though she was due to be in work, she refused to leave until she had seen Brandon's face. She smiled like a cat who had stolen the canary, her eyes triumphant with my appearance.

I worried that the royal blue, form-clinging dress with the black trim was too sexy to wear to a wedding. The sharp V neckline tapered, showing a healthy portion of cleavage, and, at Ari's insistence, I wore a push-up bra, which enhanced what I had so little of. The skirt ended mid-thigh, showing off a good portion of my well-toned legs.

Coming to her feet with a sigh, Ari stood in front of me, eyeing me from head to toe. "Stop fidgeting, Cher, you look fabulous."

"By your standards," I said dryly.

Ari smirked at me as she pushed some of my hair behind my ear. "You look so good, Cher, he's going to want to rip your clothes off."

"Oh, that's useful when we're going to a wedding."

"It's just as well. He'll have to suffer all day. By the end of the night, there'll be no stopping him. It's past time you dangled the carrot in front of that horse's face."

I shivered at the thought. There was no doubt in my mind that I was ready, especially after he had taken such good care of me without the pressure of payment. However, there was still a slight fear within me. Something I had not shared even with Arianne. I had only been intimate with a man once before, on prom night in high school, and it turned out to be a total fiasco. Talk about performance anxiety.

"Don't worry so much. I've seen him watch you when he thinks no one is looking. The guy's crazy about you. He just has a... weird way of showing it."

"That's an understatement."

Almost as if he knew we were speaking about him, Brandon chose that moment to pull into a spare spot in the complex. Turning to Arianne, I ran my fingers down the bodice and pinned her with a steady stare. "He's here. Are you sure I look good enough for a wedding?"

"You look great. Just remember, these are people you don't know, and who knows if you'll ever see them again. It's his attention that you're trying to keep."

His knock stopped any further conversation, and I reached for the door with a shaking hand. His dark glasses hid the emotion in his eyes, but the slow smile that spread across his face proved Arianne right. He stared at me, his smile widening with pleasure. "You look fantastic," he said softly. "I knew you'd dress up nice."

His gaze wandered down, and I felt it like a heated brand. Glancing behind me quickly, I caught Arianne's gaze. She flashed me another triumphant smile.

"Wow, Cherisse."

His words brought me back home, and I managed a nervous laugh. "I could say the same for you."

He wore a dark gray tux with tails. It made him appear taller and more handsome than ever, and I heard Ari whistle behind me. I did not dare turn for fear of seeing her leer at him, but Brandon smiled at her and gave her a mock bow before his gaze returned to me almost immediately. I could feel my heart swell.

He was clean-shaven and smelled fresh from the shower. I

noticed his hair was still damp, and he had cut himself shaving. "Were you in a rush this morning?" I asked, reaching up to gently touch his jaw.

He gave me a sheepish grin. "Yeah, I overslept a little. I ran into trouble early this morning, a bit of a scuffle. I had to get checked before I left."

"Checked?"

"It's nothing. I'll tell you about it later. Let's go."

"Well, I certainly won't be waiting up for you tonight," Ari said dramatically. "I'll probably go right to bed once I get home from work."

"With Mike, right?" I asked, laughing.

"Hopefully. Ta-ta, kids... behave tonight."

Brandon waved and reached for my arm, holding it loosely as we descended the stairs and walked to the car. As usual, it was a beautiful day, with bright blue skies and not a cloud in sight. Birds sang their happy songs of the morning, and the slight breeze promised glorious temperatures by mid-afternoon. The bride and groom chose a great time of year for a wedding.

"The bride is lucky. No rain," I commented as he opened the car door for me.

"Yeah. She's excited." He helped me into the Frontier and shut the door, walking around the front to hop in beside me. I took a moment to glance around at the interior, taking note of how neat it was despite its older-model year. Considering he usually took little notice of his garb, I found it surprising that he would think of his car.

When he closed the door and started the engine, I turned to him. "Did you just have this cleaned?"

He smiled sheepishly. "How'd you guess?"

"It was obvious."

"Yesterday."

I grinned. "All that for me?"

"I wanted to make a good impression."

"It's neater than mine."

"I've seen."

"Thanks a lot."

He chuckled, and I fell silent as he pulled away out of the spot and wove his way out of the complex. We did not speak until he pulled onto the highway, heading up to North Phoenix. I was growing more nervous with every mile that passed, fearing that his friends would not like me. I began to think that maybe I should not have agreed to go to a wedding as a first date. Such a huge first step.

He turned to me after several miles and smiled. "Chuck Evans is meeting us at the church. His wife is home with a new baby and couldn't come, so he's going solo. This way you don't have to sit alone during the ceremony."

"Chuck?" I asked, frowning.

"Yeah, you met him the night Joe was arrested."

"Oh, great," I muttered. "He ought to love me. Just another one of the girls you've met on the job."

He reached for my knee and gave it a slight squeeze. His eyes were dancing. "Not at all. He thought you were pretty brave. You had quite the reputation at the station after that night. The guys told the story about the 'little spitfire' for about a week or two after."

"That doesn't make me feel any better," I whined.

"You look beautiful, Sunshine. I'm afraid you will be the center of attention today instead of the bride."

"Yeah, right."

"Will you trust me, Cherisse?" He knew what he was asking, and I knew how I would answer. This would be the deciding moment, and I had no intentions of blowing it.

I smiled at him. "I already do."

****

Meeting Brandon's friends proved even more difficult than I had feared. I was jealous of the camaraderie between Brandon and the bride, Kerri Vasquez. The fellow police officer who looked lovely in her white sheath dress and obviously was held in high esteem by Brandon elicited an uncharacteristic possessiveness that made me want to hate her. Perhaps I was a catty female after all.

The way his eyes had shone during the ceremony, almost as though he was the proud father giving away the bride, that concerned me. All throughout the service he stood proud and tall with the other groomsmen, looking more handsome and debonair than the lot of them. He exuded happiness.

He also oozed charm. I could see the dreamy look on the maid of honor's face as he escorted her out of the church. It was a look I was sure I had given him a time or two, and I clenched my teeth with irritation.

"He's going to meet us outside by his truck," Chuck said as they passed. "They're doing a receiving line at the reception rather than have everyone stand outside and sweat."

"Good thinking," I murmured.

Brandon had glanced over and bowed his head in greeting as he passed, slowing long enough to send me another of his angelic smiles. From the corner of my eye, I could see my new friend, Chuck, watching the exchange with interest. No sooner had they passed than he reached out and took my hand. "Come on, Cher, let's catch up to them."

Chuck had proven to be just as nice as Brandon promised. The same officer who had questioned me the first time, I remembered how polite and courteous he had been then. He had a cheerful smile in a large, round face and happy, dancing eyes. Gone was the stern policeman. In his stead was a man who appeared to enjoy everything about life. I assumed Brandon had paired me up with him because he was in his forties and safely in love with his wife. They had just had a baby to boot, their third, so he was a safe escort. That much Chuck had told me himself.

And here I was, watching Brandon escort a pretty blond wearing a deep green bridesmaid gown.

"How does he know the bride so well?" I asked as casually as possible.

"Oh they dated for four years back in college. They've known each other for years."

"Oh." I felt sick to my stomach, but I managed to keep my face as neutral as possible. While part of me wanted to know about Brandon's past loves, the other part was distinctly uncomfortable with the knowledge. How would I rank?

Chuck chuckled. "I wouldn't worry about them, Cher. They've been the best of friends for about three years now. She's so in love with Lieutenant Moore that Nixs means nothing to her. I'd tell you if I thought otherwise."

"That's good to know."

The bright sun outside greeted us with its bright warm rays. I shielded my eyes from the glare and scanned the parking lot for any sign of Brandon. There were plenty of people around. Some stood in small groups, while others made their way in pairs to their parked cars. It took me a few moments, but finally I was able to find the Frontier. Brandon stood beside it and waited while we approached.

A gentle breeze blew the tails of his tux around his legs and threatened to undo the elaborate curls that Ari had labored on, but neither of us noticed at the time. Our gazes locked, and he grinned as we neared, pushing himself away from the front of the car to meet us halfway.

Smiling down at me, he wrapped an arm around my waist. "See? That was painless."

"She's a beautiful bride. They make a lovely couple."

"Yeah, she's very happy." He squeezed me gently. "I hope it works out for them. They're good people, considering he's one of *them*."

"Them?"

"Management," Chuck said in explanation.

"But aren't you?" I asked, confusion drawing down my lips in a frown.

"I'm different," Brandon claimed, smiling. "I'm still one of the guys."

I found myself staring at him, watching his every move as he spoke. I could not see any regrets in his eyes. Instead I could only see a man happy with the way things had turned out for his friend. I began to feel better.

He turned to Chuck and held out his hand. "Thanks for taking care of Cherisse. Are you going to ride with us?"

"No, no," Chuck said with a small shake of his head. He gripped Brandon's hand with a wide smile. "I'll catch you two there. Cherisse is sitting with me, right?"

"Just until the dancing begins," Brandon warned. The sidelong glance that he sent my way promised his continued presence.

Chuck made a tsk-ing sound. "Sorry, Cher's already said she's saving them all for me. She said you'd be too busy with that cute maid of honor from the Assistant DA's office to bother with her."

I could feel my color heighten, for even though I had not said it, I had still felt it, and obviously Chuck noticed.

Barely giving me a glance, Brandon cocked his head to the side and smiled threateningly. "What's your home phone again, Chuck? I think I'll give your wife a call and tell her how you're flirting with a much younger, very beautiful woman."

Chuck bellowed his laughter. "Touché."

"I don't share very well," Brandon explained.

He wrapped his other hand around my waist, and though I was pleased, I pushed away playfully and acted indignant. "If I decide I'm going to dance the night away with Chuck, that's my choice, not yours."

Brandon raised his eyebrows and glanced at Chuck. "You see what I put up with?"

"You've definitely got your hands full there."

We all laughed then, and Chuck turned to go. "Look, kids, everyone's leaving. You'd better get straight there, or they'll take pictures without you."

As soon as Chuck was out of sight of the car, Brandon opened my door and went around the other side. This time, instead of starting up the car right away, he closed his door and leaned across the seat. "I'm glad you came. It was nice to look out and see your face in the crowd, Sunshine."

Before I could answer, his head bent and his lips met mine. When he finally lifted his head, I stared up at him, smiling happily. He reached over and cupped my cheek in his large hand, lightly stroking my cheekbone while I reached up and wiped at the lip gloss smeared across his lips. The smile he returned just before he grasped my hand and brought my thumb to his lips, kissing it first and then nipping it slightly.

"Hey," I complained, pulling away.

His eyes churned like a stormy ocean. "Are you sure you don't want to just go to my place for the afternoon?"

Even though I laughed at his absurd comment, in my heart I realized that I really did want to disappear with him for the afternoon. "Don't tempt me."

"Ah, would that I could," he said. Smiling boyishly, he started up the truck and pulled out of the parking lot, his face once more smooth and relaxed.

"Just a few more hours," I offered.

"True."

Once we had pulled out into traffic, I turned to him. "So tell me about the bride, Kerri."

"What do you want to know?"

"You used to date?"

"Yep, for four years," he said without hesitation. "Back in college we were an item, but we were too good of friends to make good lovers. You know what I mean?"

"Yes. Me and Paul."

He nodded. "You dated him?"

"Not for four years. We knew straight away that nothing would come of it. He just hangs around as a friend."

"Hangs around is an understatement," he muttered.

"What do you mean?"

"I saw him with you on campus – twice now. He follows you around like a puppy."

"He does not," I protested.

Brandon's lips twisted. "What would you call it?"

"We have a few classes together and walk together, and he

sometimes walks me to my car... You do as well." I crossed my arms over my chest. "You sound like you're jealous."

His mouth closed abruptly. In another moment, he snorted and then laughed. "You know, you're right. I guess I'm no better. You see what effect you have on men?"

"Not really."

"What would you call it?"

"Kindness."

"And I'm jealous?"

"I'd like to think so."

He chuckled again. "What about you? You started it."

"I don't know much about you, that's all. It came as quite a shock to see you as the best man in an ex-girlfriend's wedding."

"I'm trying to remedy that, Cherisse, honestly. Give me some time."

"I am... I am."

He reached again for my knee, his long fingers spreading out over it. "You're right," he whispered. "I was jealous." When my mouth opened in surprise, he smiled sheepishly at me. "Each time I've seen you with him, I've wanted to interrupt."

That was a surprise. The first time he had seen me with Paul was when we had coffee. How on earth could he have been jealous then? "Why didn't you?"

He shrugged. "I didn't want to overstep my bounds."

"That's okay within reason." Even as I spoke the words, I realized how close I had been the week before in causing a problem with this budding relationship. I knew then that I was of the same mind as Brandon. I wanted to make this work, and that meant not doing anything to jeopardize things with him.

"Fair enough. So who else have you been seeing lately?"

"No one you know," I answered.

"I could find out," he threatened.

The fact that I did not doubt it should have made me worried, but I grinned instead. "No one in a long time, Brandon. Just a few dates here and there since I've been in school. My classes have meant more to me than the dating scene."

With a nod of understanding, Brandon fell silent again. I wondered briefly if he would ask about now and whether I would tell him what had just occurred to me: everything had changed since I met him. It was frightening and exhilarating at the same time.

But he never asked. Instead there was silence in the vehicle until we reached the reception site. It was a beautiful place, with a Spanish-style courtyard containing a large stone fountain in the center. The whitewashed walls appeared stark against the bright blue sky, and the rustic wood ceiling lent the setting an intimate charm. I was impressed.

Once again, I was placed in Chuck's capable hands while Brandon joined the others for photos and the receiving line. Chuck escorted me down the receiving line, and I waited with bated breath to meet the new bride and her husband, Jeff. Everyone seemed to know about me and smiled their greeting with appraising looks. It was slightly disconcerting until I met Kerri.

The bride was just as pretty up close, and I noticed that beneath her sheath dress she was fit and trim. She was tall with shiny black hair and wide brown eyes. Her caramel skin contrasted sharply with the ivory of her gown, giving her a glow that went above and beyond her obvious happiness. When she saw us approach, she pushed Chuck away and reached for both my hands.

"Cher! Thank you so much for coming. Nixs has told me so much about you, I feel as though I know you already."

"Thank you," I said with a smile. "And congratulations! I'm honored to be here."

"Are you kidding?" she said with a laugh. "I was dying to see you. Nixs keeps saying all these nice things about you, I thought you were an angel and wondered if you were for real."

Surprised, I glanced over at Brandon, but he was talking to another man further down the line.

Kerri grinned again and squeezed my hands. "He's a real good guy, Cher. I hope things work out for you."

I smiled, sure that my own hopefulness glimmered in my eyes. "I hope so too... And I should say the same for you two."

Her husband, Jeff, grinned. "I'm not so worried about that."

"Don't speak too soon," Kerri admonished gently. "You never know."

I laughed at Jeff's wounded look, and Chuck reached out to grasp my arm. "Come on Cher, we're holding up the line."

"Hook up with me later," Kerri pleaded. "I'd love to sit down and chat with you for a little bit."

I smiled again. "I'd like that."

"If not today, maybe sometime soon?"

I nodded my head as Chuck pulled me away. After stopping at the table to find our names printed in fine calligraphy, he tucked my arm under his and proudly led me through the groups of mingling guests who all watched us closely. Finding our table number, he led me inside the spacious ballroom. The high ceilings echoed with laughter, and the arched windows sent light streaming down upon the candlelit tables.

The reception was even more beautiful than the ceremony, with colorful floral centerpieces set in crystal vases on every table. The fine china sat atop a dark green tablecloth, and green candles surrounded the table. They cast a soft glow around the guests.

I took my seat to the left of the head table, within view of Brandon. Once the wedding party was comfortably seated, I could feel the weight of his stare on me every few minutes, and when I turned my attention to him, he would send a smile my way. In this new element, I noticed that it was the most relaxed I had seen him to date, and I admired the new Brandon as much as the old.

As the room filled with guests, I was quick to learn more about him through his friends. Many of them stopped by the table to introduce themselves and to tell me short tales of Brandon's bravery and reliability on the job as well as his continued hunger for an education. He was dependable and honest, and everyone agreed that he was destined to go far without the usual mistrust that inevitably happened when one went into management.

While shocked at how curious people were about me, I enjoyed hearing about this side of Brandon that I was previously unaware of. My wonder at this different man increased tenfold when he stood to toast the bride and groom. The giggling pair ducked their heads and winced, obviously fearing his words, but he stood proud and tall, loosely holding the champagne flute between his fingers. I was sure I saw the mischief in his eyes, and it glowed when he once more glanced over and smiled at me.

"Ladies and Gentlemen, we're here today to celebrate the union of Kerri and Jeff." I closed my eyes and listened, allowing his deep, confident voice roll over me. It was not until I heard his joke did I open my eyes again. "...And most of you know that Kerri and I dated many years ago. We've maintained a close friendship, and she even considers me her closest confidante. What most of you don't know... is that Jeff has no clue to what he's in for. He still doesn't realize that Kerri will have more power over him than the Chief and plans to use it well. After all, what other use is there in fraternizing with management?"

Amid the strangled gasps came the loud guffaws, and Jeff reached over to playfully punch Brandon before he finished. They embraced quickly; then Brandon bent and kissed Kerri on the forehead. She laughed as she reached up to hug him. I smiled too, enjoying his scandalous toast as well as his playful manner.

He straightened and winked at the crowd. "Actually that's not true. But one can hope." Raising his champagne flute, he gestured to the bride and groom. "To their happiness, ladies and gentlemen."

"Here, here," came the chorus.

The discussion at our table was lively and entertaining, and I soon felt comfortable enough to enter the conversations around me. I barely spared another glance at ever-watchful Brandon until the head table rose to dance. That was when my jealous side rose again. Watching him sweep the fawning maid of honor into his arms and skillfully maneuver her around the dance floor had my nerves on edge. He knew how to dance well, and he easily guided the young woman around the floor. Even though his hands were modestly placed and he kept her at a chaste distance, I could not help but seethe. She batted her eyes at him and chatted away gaily, and though Brandon's face remained dazzlingly unexpressive, it was not until they switched off that I breathed a sigh of relief.

Although I knew Kerri and Brandon were old news, I watched them as they danced, too. It was a touching scene. They spoke amiably during the rest of the dance, laughing at shared jokes and memories. That was when the other guests were invited to join the wedding party, and Chuck good-naturedly pulled me to my feet and swept me out onto the floor. I went somewhat unwillingly because I feared my horrible two right feet.

"I can't dance," I muttered.

"I can't either," Chuck said lightly.

"Oh, great, so instead of stepping on each other, we'll just step on the other people out here."

Laughing aloud, Chuck gave my waist a squeeze. "That's the plan, Cher."

"Nice."

"Just close your eyes, darlin'. Let your feet move, and we'll find a rhythm. All you have to do is what your body feels is natural."

It was my turn to laugh. "Great. Next thing you know, we'll be doing the funky chicken."

He glanced down at his rotund belly. "Not fair. I'm a good dancer actually, as long as I have a good partner."

"Hey, be nice," I snapped playfully.

He winked, and a few seconds later I was spinning around the dance floor and holding on to Chuck for dear life. Other couples either stepped or ran out of our way, leaving me to squeeze my eyes shut in fear.

"You see, we're the talk of the wedding," Chuck gasped.

I inhaled deeply and held my breath. "That's because we're going to crash."

"No, but now we're going to stop."

Even as he said it, he came completely still, and I opened my eyes to find Brandon frowning down at me. "You two are having way too much fun," he grumbled.

"Not at all, I was just delivering her to you."

"Thanks, now you can go."

As Brandon waved Chuck away, I grinned. "Thank you for scaring the wits out of me."

"Not at all. Anytime," he said. "But if you decide you want more of my fancy footwork, you might have to get in line."

Sure enough, when I glanced behind him, the ladies were lining up to get a twirl around the floor. Good luck to them, I thought.

"Are you having fun, or are you bored out of your mind?" Brandon asked, wrapping an arm around my waist and pulling me up against his hips. I breathed a sigh of relief when I heard the band strike up a slow number. Now that was a dance I could handle. I pulled away slightly in order to avoid stepping on his feet, but his arm tightened.

"I'm having a wonderful time."

"Of course, dancing with Chuck is always a treat," he said sarcastically.

I laughed. "I had no idea."

"Now you do. I've seen him before, and he's quite a sight." He smiled down at me, and for a moment time seemed suspended. I was trapped in the heaven of his stare, held captive by the power in his hands, and I was enjoying every minute of it. When he spoke, small shivers coursed up and down my spine. "Have I told you how beautiful you look, Sunshine?"

"Yes," I said softly. "But you can tell me again if you want."

His head dipped slightly, closing the large gap between us. "I think you look stunning, Cherisse, even more beautiful than the bride."

"Wow, a high compliment considering you used to date her."

"I mean every word of it."

"You look splendid, too." I laughed. "And here I didn't think you could get any more handsome."

"Thank you."

The hand around my waist tightened, and I moved closer to press my cheek against the warm smoothness of his tux. He felt so solid under my face, and for the first time ever I felt sexy in his arms. Closing my eyes, I imagined myself as the bride and he the groom and felt my heart swell with pride. "Are you tired?"

I lifted my head and smiled. "No, not at all."

"Mm, snuggling?"

"I guess you could say that."

He bent his head and pressed his lips against my forehead. "There's been talk of going to a nearby club after the reception. Do you want to go or head out from here?"

"I'll do what you want to do."

His lips twisted. "Oh no, it's your date. Besides, these are my friends, Cherisse. I feel bad dragging you right into the midst of them."

"I've had a good time, and everyone's been nice." I grinned. "And I feel incredibly safe considering everyone here knows how to use a gun."

He made a show of looking around, nodding and shaking his head as needed. "No, not everyone. Probably eighty percent or so."

"If you want to go for a little while, I'm game. I mean, I have the whole night off, so I'd hate to waste it going home." I did not add that I did not want to let him go either. I wanted to stay with him as long as I could, even if it meant going to a bar.

He beamed, his aquamarine eyes glowing with delight. "Fine. Just for a little while."

The music stopped, and I stepped out of his arms. "Chuck kept buying me drinks."

"Nature's calling?"

"The polite way of putting it."

He seemed reluctant to release his hold, but eventually he did with a smile. Realizing that the pressure on my bladder was increasing with every step, I hurried to the restroom. The smooth door opened with a soft whoosh, revealing a surprisingly empty, spacious restroom lit by bright fluorescent lights. There was a basket of flowers on the recently wiped sink, and a small cabinet holding mouth wash, hand soap and lotion. On the other side rested a basket with every possible feminine necessity, from breath mints to tampons.

Whistling under my breath at the luxury of it all, I made my way to a large stall. No graffiti marred this beautiful hall, not that I expected it to, and the floors were immaculate.

I was rearranging my dress over my hips when I heard the door open again. My solitude destroyed, I was reaching for the door handle when I heard the voices. They stayed my hand.

"Nixs was funny."

"Yeah, he's such a peach, isn't he?"

I grimaced. It was Kerri and the fawning maid of honor, Connie. Deciding to wait until they had left, my hand dropped to my side.

"Well, he hasn't been exactly nice today."

"What do you mean?"

I heard the faucet and rushing water, a sound that almost drowned out their voices. "Well, he's been so distant. I tried to talk to him during the one dance we shared, but he just nodded and shook his head. It was very frustrating."

I heard Kerri laugh. "He's been watching his new girlfriend the entire night. He's had eyes for no one else."

"Who's the girl?"

"The pretty redhead with the blue dress. She's been sitting with Chuck Evans all night. Sweet girl, from what I could tell. I've only spoken to her for a minute so far, but Brandon's spoken of nothing else since he met her."

"Good for him," I heard Connie say though her voice lacked true conviction. I sensed she was missing his good looks already.

"Yes, I hope so. He's been alone for so long even though I know he wants to settle down. I'm pretty sure he believes this is the one he's been looking for all his life."

"How can you be so sure? Jeez, you sound like a bride!"

"I am, silly."

Kerri dropped her lip gloss, and it rolled perilously close to my stall. Terrified of being found out, I was tempted to climb up on the seat, but Connie passed by on the search.

"Thanks," Kerri said when Connie handed it back to her. "Anyway, if you look at them together you can see something. It's weird, I dunno. I just saw something there." She sighed. "You'll just have to look for yourself. They're probably still slow dancing and staring at each other like there's no one else in the room."

Connie chuckled, and I pressed two fingers against my lips to hide my laugh. Is that what we looked like? Though embarrassed, I was also filled with hope and glowing with the idea that Brandon was so proud of me. While I thought it was a heavy expectation to fill, I wanted nothing more than to live up to his high praise.

"Come on, Kerri, your groom is probably looking all over for you. Talk about a pair who only has eyes for each other."

Kerri laughed again, her voice happy and breathless. "I'm allowed. It's my wedding."

"Too true," Connie answered.

With a rustle of silk, the pair departed, leaving me leaning against the bathroom wall. In the back of my mind, a lingering fear of commitment hovered, but the foremost part of me, my very essence, was all for it.

I was head over heels myself.

Chapter 8

Once the hall outside the bathroom grew quiet, I slipped out and made my way back to Brandon. I never had a chance to sit down and talk to Kerri. When she made her round to our table I was dancing with Brandon, and then she was suddenly cutting the cake. The day was progressing much too fast, and I was helpless to stop it. All too soon, she was tossing her beautiful orange and red rose bouquet with the white calla lilies. Her gaze captured mine, and she gave me a wide grin and a wink just before she turned around and threw her bouquet. Much to my dismay, I realized that she deliberately aimed for me when I caught the exquisite and colorful bunch.

My suspicion only deepened when Jeff tossed the green lace garter in the direction of Brandon. With a broad smile, he caught it in one hand and held it up with a shout of triumph. Yes, I concluded, it was definitely rigged.

Loud cheers and encouraging whistles resounded in the room as I was guided to the chair Kerri had so recently sat in. Brandon stood nearby, his hand around my arm and a smile on his lips.

"Now don't be too X-rated, Nixs," Jeff called, wrapping his arm around Kerri's shoulders.

Brandon grinned at him over his shoulder before sending me a brow- wiggling smile. "Are you ready?"

I took a deep breath and settled firmly down on the chair, sending another word of thanks that I had hit up the shoe store and picked up some pretty blue satin sandals that matched my dress so well. Never had I expected to be on such display at a wedding where I knew only two people, one of which was now on one knee in front of me.

Our gazes locked.

"Be nice," I whispered.

I could feel a blush climb slowly up my face, but Brandon was no longer looking at me. His heated gaze burned the skin of my ankle as one hand slipped my sandal off while the other carefully spread the garter to slip it over my now bare foot. Too afraid to watch the excited sea of faces, I stared down at the top of his head with my own smile wavering nervously.

Catcalls and raunchy music invaded our privacy, and I lowered my head even more, peering down at Brandon's long fingers. A tremor shook them. It was not an overly obvious shake, but I felt the same nervousness in the pit of my stomach.

"Come on, Nixs, stop procrastinating."

"He just doesn't want to show off Cher's legs," Kerri said with a giggle.

"She's got great legs, Nixs, come on!"

Brandon lifted his head and smiled at me. Pride glimmered in his eyes. "It's all that running."

"Keeping up with you, you mean?" I whispered back.

His hands squeezed my calf slightly, the pressure increasing as he raised the garter up and over my knee to my thigh. With a smile for the crowd, he withdrew it slightly to more cheers from the onlookers. Then he slipped it up higher, his fingers sliding against my bare skin. My breath caught, and I wondered just how far he was going to go. The whistles grew increasingly loud and loud clapping echoed off the ceiling and reverberated through my ears. His hand slipped under my skirt, dragging the pliable material up with it. Gasping, I began to reach for his hands, but he stopped me with a look and a quick shake of his head.

"Brandon," I hissed.

"You're fine," he answered. "Trust me."

His performance was a deliberate show for the crowd and a more private show for me. His fingers stroked my upper thigh, mere inches away from my black lace panties. The impression of his fingers stayed long after he gave my thigh a final squeeze and withdrew his hand.

As he guided me to my feet, I was appreciative of the arm that landed heavily around my shoulders. He smiled again and bent to kiss my cheek very enthusiastically, but I could see that he was not as unaffected as he seemed. The tension was indeed growing.

"Are you angry at me?"

I grinned. "Should I be?"

"No, I enjoyed myself very much."

"At my expense?"

"Didn't you?"

My lips twisted wryly. There was no doubt in my mind that he had seen my heightened color. "It would've been much nicer if we were alone."

He gave me a slight squeeze, and his eyes held much promise. "You really have great legs."

"So I've heard."

He chuckled. "But not from me."

"That's true."

Chuck arrived then, bearing a glass of wine for me and beers for himself and Brandon. Once he had handed over our drinks, he clapped his hands and winked at me. "Great job, Cher. You did good."

Brandon's brow rose in mock protest. "What about me?"

Chuck grinned. "Sorry, Nixs, I wasn't even looking at you."

Brandon laughed again. "I suspect no one was looking at me."

"At least not the male half."

"Oh gosh," I muttered.

Brandon shook his finger at Chuck, his eyes dancing. "Stop it, Chuck, you're embarrassing my date."

"Don't be silly, Cher, you were great. I'm sure half the ladies here are pea green with envy. You're a looker, sweetie; flaunt it, as my wife would say."

"I'd like to meet your wife," I said half-joking.

"Yeah, I'm sure she'd love to meet you, too. Maybe we could all hook up for dinner soon."

I looked up at Brandon, who grinned as he nodded. "Definitely soon. When she's not working."

"I'll talk to you about it during the week, Brandon. I've got to run now. My mobile's been vibrating for the last fifteen minutes, and I've had three texts in that time. Diaper emergency, you know?"

I did not know, but I nodded in understanding anyway. "Thank you very much for escorting me today, Chuck. I had a nice date."

Brandon sent a frown in my direction, but Chuck beamed with pleasure. "Yeah, I know what you mean. You've spent more time with me than with your boyfriend."

"I'm remedying that later," Brandon grumbled.

"Oh ho, I bet!"

I cocked my head to stare up at Brandon, a secretive smile on my face. "Really?"

"Well, he's leaving now, so you're stuck with me for the rest of the evening."

I leaned towards Chuck conspiratorially. "And that sounds so appealing?"

"Honey, if you get bored with him, you just call me. I've got loads of diapers to change, spit-up to clean and bottles to prepare."

"As romantic as that sounds, I'll have to respectfully decline," I said.

"She'll be too busy for that anyway," Brandon claimed.

"Okay, I got you," Chuck said. "I've got to run. See you Monday night, Nixs. Have a nice evening."

He winked in my direction and then sauntered off, stopping several times to speak to the other pretty ladies. I grinned as I watched him go. Chuck Evans was quite a character, so different from the man in my living room those months ago. For a moment, I felt guilty that I was having that much fun with these people. The memory of my first interaction with Chuck reminded me of my sister. Worry for Shelly gave me pause, and I hoped that she and Jacob were doing okay. Then Brandon's arm was leading me back to the party, and once again Shelly was tucked into the recesses of my mind.

With the reception slowing down, he escorted me to his other friends, the fellow officers on the Tactical Unit. A tight-knit bunch of strong, hearty men, they greeted me as warmly as everyone else had. As Brandon made his introductions, he kept his arm comfortably around my shoulder and tucked me into his side. My head was left spinning, and I quickly gave up trying to remember names. Sympathetic smiles were sent my way, as if they understood how overwhelmed I felt.

Even this visit remained short, and with tremendous relief I found myself following Brandon as he weaved his way through the remaining guests making our farewells. All I could think of was that Brandon was deadly serious when he said he wanted to change the fact that I knew so little about him. Now it seemed as though I had an overload of personal information about him. At least he was just as appealing to me then as he was before.

Head still spinning, I let Brandon usher me out to the relative calm of his Frontier, where we were once again on the highway heading off to Desert Ridge. I was filled with excitement, feeling as though the worst was over and the evening just begun. All throughout the afternoon I had pondered, and by the end of the reception I made up my mind. Tonight was the night. I was going to seduce him, whether he was ready or not. After the episode with the garter, much less his hints Monday morning at my apartment, I highly doubted he was not.

Despite the size and amount of choices to hang out, Desert Ridge was busy every Saturday evening, and The Sandbar was a popular spot to hang out. Familiar faces surrounded us there, and a few early goers had managed to sequester a table outside, warmed by the running heaters. Though not too keen to wander in the sand with sandals, I bore the discomfort and followed Brandon cheerfully. I noticed that though more beer was ordered, Brandon nursed a Coke for the rest of the evening. He seemed content to watch me lighten up as the alcohol went straight to my head. I was both surprised and thrilled with his dependability, for in my mind it spoke volumes about his convictions.

Sitting back to watch his interchange with his friends was enough for me at that point. I admired how they all spoke and ribbed one another like family. A close knit, almost cliquey, environment surrounded me, and I could see that trust was very important to them. It was obvious that Brandon had long ago earned theirs, and I liked watching his interplay with the people he knew so well.

Though I was comfortable enough with the group date, Brandon jumped at the chance to leave the party and claim a table away from the others. As soon as one opened off to the side, he tugged on my hand and stared at me with his brows raised in question. I nodded and followed him away from the crowd. The loud hum of the voices was punctuated by a loud cry intermittently, and we retired to the table for two and shared some small talk as we watched the others continue partying. The loud music and conversations seemed to thin out where we settled. I preferred it that way, and I was silently thankful that Brandon had taken me away from his half-drunk friends.

We were not there long before one of his fellow officers, Ethan Schor, came up and leaned over our table. The younger officer had already had a few too many, and his words were slurred as he grinned at Brandon. "I heard about last night. Arrested a guy for assault with a deadly weapon, eh?"

"What?" I asked.

"You didn't tell her about it?"

Brandon shot a quick look my way before he casually shrugged his shoulders. "It was nothing... Just a drunk who had decided to run."

"Run?" Ethan said with a laugh. "With his car? I heard he ran you right off the road. Literally. Did you have to do a flying leap?"

"Nah. Well, his intent was to run me over. Problem was that he was so drunk he would have run right into my cruiser."

Ethan laughed again. "Too many weirdoes around nowadays...

They all seem to have one too many."

"And you're any better?" Brandon asked wryly.

"Ah, but I'm not driving." He pointed to his wife with his beer bottle, a friendly woman I had met at the wedding. She smiled and waved back. I noticed that she too was drinking soda and grinned in her direction.

"Well, good job anyway," Ethan said, pushing away from the table. "Glad you're okay."

"Thanks."

Without another word, Brandon went back to his drink, taking a deep swig without even glancing my way. I suspected there was more to the story than what they had just shared, but his closed features prevented me from speaking of my concerns aloud.

It was a fact that every day Brandon put his life in jeopardy. I had watched *COPS*, and I saw the news. Shootings and stabbings, car chases and people resisting arrest. Not to mention the stand-offs and hostage situations he faced on the Unit. It was a dangerous job. While I had never considered it before, Ethan's comments brought the reality to the forefront. The question was whether I was ready to deal with it. Perhaps at that time, after watching him interact with his friends, laugh and joke, I did not see beyond the immediate. In addition, everything was so new and exciting that I thought at that moment my feelings for him outweighed my concerns. I assumed I could do it.

"Do you want to leave soon?"

I jumped at the sound of his voice, so close to my ear. So lost in my reverie, I had not noticed him slipping from his stool. It was loud, not quite the place to share a decent conversation, and I was growing happier and looser with my second beer since we had arrived. I knew what I had planned to do, and three glasses of wine, a champagne toast, and now two beers was helping me do it. That was the most alcohol I had drank since I turned legal age.

"Yes," I said, nodding my head.

He smiled at me, a wide smile.

"I'd like to hear more about your evening, too."

As if not at all surprised, Brandon nodded and gave my arm a gentle squeeze. I knew it was his way of accepting my fears, my concerns. Instinctively, I became aware that it mattered to him and that he did not want to frighten me. "Let's talk about it later, okay?"

"Let me just make a quick stop."

He glanced towards the ladies room and nodded. "I'll walk you over."

"That's okay," I said flippantly. "I think I can find it."

His hand dropped away, and he shrugged. "I'll be over there then."

He pointed in the direction of the bar, and I waited for just a moment to watch where he ended up. Confident I would be able to find him again, I twisted and turned through the crowds, getting bumped and jostled along the way. It was times like those that I hated being so short. People could not see me, and a rare few took me seriously.

As usual, the public restroom was just as crowded as the club itself, with girls lining up almost out the door to use the facilities. I sighed and went for the mirror, checking my makeup and pile of curls that had held up nicely thanks to Arianne. With every passing moment, the line grew longer, so I decided to wait. More than anything, I wanted to get out of there, away from the hot press of the overly perfumed bodies.

I was barely out the door when a sudden lurch in the crowd threw me several steps forward, right into the back of a man by the door. He cursed and spun around, his face furrowed in a deep frown as he stared at the beer that had spilled down the front of his shirt.

Smiling apologetically, I reached out to try and brush it off. "I'm sorry, I was pushed."

He swayed on his feet for a moment, and I watched him try to focus on me without much success. Suddenly his hand was on my shoulder, and he was gripping me tightly.

"Uh, let go," I said as loudly as I could.

He grinned down at me and then smiled at his buddies. "You're hot. Let's dance."

"No, thanks. I'm with someone." I tried to twist out of his reach, but his grip was too strong. His fingers bit into my shoulder blades with bruising pressure, and his buddies laughed at him.

"Lemme see your hand."

Swaying violently, he leaned over me, earning a bunch of ribald comments from his friends, and examined my left hand. I began to struggle again, hoping I could catch him off balance, but he was too strong. Seeing no ring, his smile widened. "You're not married."

Spoken more as a comment than a question, the young man pulled me a little closer. I went rigid, and irritation made my eyebrows draw together. Ready to give him a piece of my mind, I scowled as fiercely as I could. "Let me go. I'm with someone."

"But you can at least dance with me."

"Sorry, I'm not interested."

No sooner had the guy loosened his grip than another hand came down on my shoulder on top of the man's. "Sorry, buddy, but you better look elsewhere tonight."

I felt myself relax slightly when I heard Brandon's voice directly behind me. He sounded almost pleasant, but when I turned I could see the anger flaring in his eyes.

"Let me go," the young man growled.

"Let her go," he advised evenly.

"She with you?"

Brandon nodded once, curtly, his lips thinning with restrained impatience.

"She's not your wife. I want one dance. C'mon... You can let her dance once."

"I don't think she wants to dance with you."

I shook my head and again tried to twist away from him. The guy lurched forward, causing Brandon to make a quick move. A fleeting look of surprise crossed over the man's face as Brandon swiftly swung the man around and pinned his arm behind his back with one hand. I blinked and it was over, with only the sound of the man's angry complaint ringing in my ear. Seeing Brandon's threatening frown, the man nodded his head and Brandon let go.

Taking a hold of my arm, Brandon gave me a half smile. I wanted to get away right then, to slip from the drunk's line of sight before he changed his mind. Even though I was sure Brandon would react if the man did, that was the last thing I wanted. The thought of causing a bar brawl because of one blue dress was too horrible to consider. Fortunately, one of the young man's friends magically appeared and took a hold of him. "Back off, bud, he's a cop."

Some glimmer of recognition entered the man's fogged mind, and he did take a step back. He lowered his beer and grinned sheepishly. "Sorry, lady."

Nodding my acceptance, I quickly moved away with Brandon close behind me, his hand once more pressed into my back. His face was cool and collected, and his clothes were completely unruffled.

"Let me just say goodbye to a few people, okay? Come with me?"

"Of course."

Interlocking our fingers, Brandon and I said our farewells to his friends together. It was a nice feeling, this togetherness. For too long I had been all about work and school, handling my day to day activities and going straight home after. That meant forgoing the company of friends and a good night out. I was suddenly even happier that my first date with Brandon included a large group of people. I liked these friendly strangers, even though they were not happy that we were leaving the scene so early. Some complained a little about missing last call, but others were drunk enough to make naughty comments.

Naturally Brandon shrugged it all off, and his happy smile had returned by the time we made our way out to the parking lot. When he spoke outside, his voice seemed loud after the raised voices in the bar. "You all right? You haven't said a word."

"I'm fine," I said softly, suddenly unsure of what to do next. "You were pretty impressive. Thanks for coming when you did. He was really drunk."

"Yeah. Remind me never to take you to a bar again."

"I guess I could say the same about you," I answered softly. "Going out with you is quite interesting."

Both of his hands came down on my shoulders, and he pressed me up against the side of the truck. His hands rounded the curve of my shoulders to stroke my upper arms, up and down, slowly and carefully. He was so close I had to tip my head back to see his face, but with it hidden in the shadows, it was completely unreadable.

"Are you mad at me?" I asked.

"Mad at you? No, of course I'm not mad at you."

As I watched, his head dipped. Suddenly I was caught between him and the truck. My lips parted just in time for yet another surprise kiss from him. Despite the chill in the cool autumn air, I felt

127

warm inside. His body was hard under my hands, and his heart was beating as quickly as mine. I stroked his chest, my hands balling into the material of his crisp, white shirt. It was over too quickly, for Brandon lifted his head and stared down at me. "Did he hurt you?"

"Nah. He was just drunk."

His lips thinned. "I told you I'd go with you."

"I didn't think I'd need an escort to the ladies room."

"Obviously you did."

I frowned. "Are you sure you're not angry?"

"At you?"

When I nodded, he shook his head.

"Not at all. I'm angry at him. He had no right to grab you like that, and he should be cut off, if not kicked out for the night."

"I know. I guess that's why I don't go out that often."

In the darkness, through the cool breeze, I thought I glimpsed a slight smile. He was like a furnace, emanating heat and anger all at once. Beginning to feel the chill, I burrowed against his chest in an effort to stay warm. As soon as the sun had set, the desert had grown cold, and neither of us was dressed appropriately for the weather. The chilly breeze made me shiver from the cold.

Sighing reluctantly, Brandon stepped back a step and reached into his pocket for his keys. One hand remained around my waist as he opened the door and stared expectantly down at me. "You're freezing. Ready to go?"

Clearing my throat, I smiled hesitantly. "Brandon?"

"Yeah?"

I swallowed hard, thankful for the darkness that now shadowed my face. "I want to go home with you. I want you to bring me to your house."

My words came out in a rush, so fast he looked confused for a moment. Then he chuckled. "I was hoping you'd say that."

"You were?"

He laughed. "You have no idea."

He helped me into the Frontier and shut the door behind me. As I fastened my seatbelt, I took several deep, calming breaths. I had done it. I had offered myself to him, given him my complete trust.

What surprised me most was that I was not regretting it at all.

Chapter 9

Truth be told, I did not know what I was expecting when Brandon pulled into the quiet neighborhood in South Tempe. It certainly was not the well-lit single-and-two-story homes with earth-colored stucco fronts, surrounded by towering queen palms and green grass. The front yards were well-maintained, with manicured sage bushes, birds of paradise, and multi-colored lantanas planted in leaf-free gravel.

I watched in open-mouthed awe as he pressed the garage door opener in front of a towering two-story at the end of a cul-de-sac. The wide double door opened to reveal a neat garage, with hand and yard tools all neatly stacked on or near the organizer. Nothing appeared to be out of place, and my awe grew.

"I thought men were supposed to be slobs," I commented as he shut off the engine.

"Five years of active duty did that to me." He glanced over and grinned sheepishly at me. "Actually, I was hoping to have company tonight. I spent yesterday afternoon picking up. Good first impression, you know?"

I nodded my approval and smiled back. "I don't think I could be any more impressed. No one's ever gone to that much trouble for me before."

"Then I did well."

He hopped out and went around to my side to help me down. I was suddenly nervous and noticed with chagrin that my palms were moist. Curling my fingers into them, I felt my nails bite into my flesh and grimaced. I had never done this before. Would I know how to act and what to say?

Brandon was smiling when he reached for me. He seemed totally relaxed and unconcerned with my presence, as though he did it every day. I began to wonder just how many he had entertained, and just as quickly decided I did not want to know.

"Come on in," he said, his voice warm and encouraging.

The interior of the house was dark when we first entered, and Brandon left me by the door removing my sandals as he went around and turned on some of the lights. I was impressed with what I saw. The hallway and kitchen were tiled, yet the other areas sported a plush tan carpet that felt heavenly under my tired feet.

Though I was still surprised at this very domestic side of Brandon, I was eager to view his home now more than ever. From what I could see, it was a large house, with several bedrooms upstairs and a guestroom with a private bath downstairs off the living room. I wandered around, following the trail of lights behind Brandon.

The few pieces of furniture he had were simple yet elegant. Obviously, he had not yet finished furnishing the house. No stools lined the breakfast bar, and no china resided in the built in hutch. There was so much space in the house that it did not surprise me in the least. It would take me years to fully furnish it on my salary.

He paused at the foot of the stairs to drop his vest and jacket over the railing then glanced back at me. For a minute, I panicked, assuming that he was ready to tumble in his bed, and I hesitated with my hand on the railing. Though he had not noticed my hesitation, he quickly put my fears to rest. "Take a look around upstairs and then we can come down and have a beer or something."

"Sounds great. Thank you."

"I'm just going to change out of this monkey suit. Do you mind?"

"No, not at all."

As he climbed the stairs ahead of me to the dark cavity above, I followed slowly and stared around me in wonder. He disappeared into the master bedroom, and I saw the lights go on behind him.

The four bedrooms upstairs were almost as empty as the rooms below. The most hidden bedroom was used as an office. Wall to ceiling bookshelves sported all kinds of hard and soft cover text books and a few paperbacks, though it was not nearly filled completely. I could not read most of the titles, but it was obvious that he held the books in high esteem. They were well-dusted and neatly organized.

Upon the walls were framed certificates, and, as I perused them, I noticed he had been commended for valor on at least two occasions. I was not at all surprised. After all, I had seen him in action and knew he took his job seriously.

He also had a computer desk in that room, and papers were scattered across it. A small grin appeared. So far it was the only messy spot in the entire house.

Only one spare queen bed lay in the room closest to the master, and the room at the front of the house had a workout bench. I examined the weight set, and, while nodding my approval, went in search of my elusive host.

"Do you like it?"

Brandon stood in the doorway to the master, dressed in jeans and another battered T-shirt, his feet bare. His arms were crossed over his broad chest and his feet at the ankles as he leaned against the door jame. I took in his appearance with a steady eye, even though I was so nervous my hands shook.

"It's huge." I waved my hand around. "Why did you buy a house so big? I mean, it's just you."

He shrugged. "Not always. I mean, I do plan to marry and have kids. This saves me time and money. I bought this after the housing crash a few years back. It was an investment property that some people from California couldn't keep. It was a foreclosure."

"What if your wife decides she doesn't like it?"

"Then I'll have to find another wife," he said with a wink.

At my surprised look he grinned, his smile lines deepening. After hearing him at the wedding, I realized that he really had a well-rounded sense of humor. It was becoming more obvious to me that the true Brandon was pretty well hidden from those he did not know well. That he was showing me his other side was flattering.

"Easier said than done."

He straightened from the doorway with a chuckle. "Then she'll have to settle for this." His arms made a sweeping gesture, and my eyes followed it to the high, vaulted ceilings. "Do you like it?"

"Yes, I do. It's a beautiful house."

"Thank you."

"How do you afford it?"

Even as I asked, I could feel a blush creep up my cheeks, but Brandon did not hesitate to answer. "I did a lot of overtime before I met you. And I saved for a long time. This house came pretty cheap too, so the mortgage is probably less than your rent."

"Oh."

"After I got out of the Air Force, I went straight to college, and, like you, I worked while I studied. As soon as I was able to get on the force, I did, and I've stayed there. Schedules are four days a week, freeing up time for school and overtime." He headed for the stairs, reaching for my hand as he passed. I felt his fingers wrap around mine and smiled again. "It's still early. Let's go downstairs. You look a little tense."

He gave my hand a little tug. I followed him back into his den. As we went, Brandon shut off some of the lights, casting a warm glow on the remainder of the house. It softened the mood, made it more romantic, and the fluttering began in my belly again.

The den was a little less Spartan than the remainder of the house. I could tell that this was the area he enjoyed most. A 55" wall-mounted television sat high upon the wall above the remainder of the entertainment system, and multiple surround-sound speakers engulfed the room with noise as he flicked the system on with one push of the button. Settling me on the soft leather sofa, he handed me the remote and returned to the kitchen. I heard him ruffling in the fridge and took the opportunity to stretch my tired feet. As I wiggled my toes and flexed my ankles, I rested my head against the plush sofa backing. My eyes drifted closed as I relaxed, even though I could hear Brandon in the next room opening a beer.

"Here you go." He handed me the beer and sat down next to me, reaching forward to pick up the remote.

I greeted him with a welcoming smile. "Thank you."

"What do you want to watch?"

"Jeez, I don't know," I answered with a shrug, looking everywhere but at him. "I never watch TV. I have no idea what's on."

He glanced over and searched my face for what seemed an eternity. His head cocked to the side as he continued to stare, and I grew increasingly uncomfortable with his scrutiny.

"What's wrong?"

"I was wondering the same thing." He sighed. "Are you okay with this?"

Even though I knew what he was referring to, I frowned with feigned ignorance. "With what?"

His lips curved in a half smile, a knowing one at that. "Cherisse, you've been jumpy since we got in the car. Are you sure you want to be here?" I opened my mouth to answer, but he glanced down at his beer. "I don't want you to do something you're not ready for... I can take you home."

"No." I flushed guiltily. "No, it's not that... I'm just not used to this sort of thing."

Staring down at my hands, I noticed they were tightly entwined around the cold beer bottle. In an effort to give me more time, he crossed to the entertainment center against the wall and turned on the radio. He spun the dial until he reached a country station. After a short bout of talk, the soft croon of Lonestar's "Amazed" began, and Brandon came to stand in front of me, holding out his hand. "Come here. Let's dance."

I smiled. "Haven't we danced all night?"

"Not like this, not in private."

Giving my hand a tug, he pulled me to my feet and into his arms. One hand held mine in a loose hold while the other went around my waist snugly. I closed my eyes and listened to the words, feeling my heart tug at the appropriateness of the older song. He sighed, almost as though he was feeling the same, and his breath stirred my hair.

"I've wanted to have you here like this for so long," he said softly into the top of my head.

"You have?" I glanced up at him in surprise. "But you've never said anything."

Our gazes locked as we moved slowly against each other. His hands tightened. "Yep, I wanted to make sure I did it right. I wanted everything to be perfect."

"I had no idea."

He chuckled. The sound came from deep in his chest, and I pressed my ear against the firm plane. His heart beat steadily, unlike my own pounding in my chest. "I didn't want to scare you off. You're pretty independent."

Lifting my head, I leaned back so I could meet his gaze again. "Scare me off? You almost did by not making any moves. You're the first guy I've ever had to pursue." I blushed. "I mean... it's not like I do this every day. It's just that I've never asked a guy to take me home before."

He smiled down at me, the look in his eyes soft and warm. His hand tightened around my waist, pulling me up against his hips. "I'm honored that I'm the first man you've pursued, and if you're still willing, I'd like very much to prove that to you."

This was the moment of truth. From that moment on, our relationship would be changed forever. If things did not work out, that would be the end. But somewhere in the back of my mind, somehow, I knew that it would. I knew that being with him would be incomparable to anything else I had ever known, or would ever in the future.

"Brandon, I'm very willing," I whispered.

His eyes seemed to darken before me, and he bent his head without another word. The kiss was brief, yet there was no doubting his growing desire. As soon as he lifted his head, he swept me into his arms and carried me all the way up the stairs to the master bedroom. I knew then that I had made the right choice, and I was certain I would never regret it. Breathless with excitement and a touch of nervousness, I squeezed my eyes shut until he gently set me down. The next thing I knew I was staring at a totally different part of the house.

The simple elegance of the lower floor and the sparse emptiness of the other bedrooms was gone, replaced by another world altogether. A fierce looking gargoyle face was mounted above the headboard of the king-sized, four-posted bed. Across the room on the other wall was an assortment of masks, African, South American, Asian, all set in a tastefully done pattern of the world. Some were fierce looking while others were beautifully done.

Beside the bay window on a solid oak table rested a chess board with a game in progress. I stepped closer and noticed that the marble pieces were the gods of Greek mythology. The pieces were magnificently carved, and it did not have even the slightest trace of dust on it.

In his room also was a large, highly polished samurai sword mounted on the wall with dragon talon hooks. I shivered and turned around to face him, my head cocked to the side. I could tell that Brandon appreciated his odd treasures. He seemed to hold them in the highest esteem by housing them in his most private sanctuary. It was yet another side to the quiet man I was hung up on.

He stood in the doorway, watching my face closely. I knew he was waiting for my reaction to his odd collection, and I was positive he wanted my approval.

I smiled widely. "You have some weird stuff. Where did you get it all?"

"I picked some of it up when I was in the service. Other things just here and there."

He approached me, his feet silent on the plush carpet. I waited for him with my hands lying limply by my side and my heart fluttering wildly.

"Cherisse."

His voice was soft. I could feel the hint of a smile spread my lips and slowly raised my head. There was something so raw and primal in the look he gave me before his hands reached up to undo the mass of curls painstakingly pinned on the top of my head. I shivered as it tumbled down over my shoulders.

Brandon watched too, mesmerized as the strands fell free. Then his hands reached for the sides of my face, and he buried them deep within the mass before pulling my face up to meet his. "Your hair is beautiful. I've wanted to do that all day."

His lips were soft as they covered mine. I felt my eyes slip closed and relaxed into him, closing the short distance to press myself against his body. He tasted of beer and smelled of his sweet cologne.

"You always smell so good," I whispered.

Inhaling deeply the fragrance of him, I slowly lifted my hands. They first came into contact with the hard flatness of his belly. It contracted under my searching fingers, quivering as I languidly lifted them higher. Up and over the mounds of his pectorals my hands went, all the way to the strong muscles of his shoulders.

I felt the brisk air on my back before I realized that he had found the zipper of my dress. He continued kissing me, and suddenly I was no longer nervous. Instead, I wanted to be filled to the brim with the tension that was increasing with every second I was in his arms.

His fingers escorted the zipper down, lower and lower still to the curve of my buttocks. His hands were pulling the dress over my arms and around my waist. It fell to the floor in a soft mass of blue, giving his wandering hands the freedom to touch my skin.

I was quick to return the favor. I reached around his waist and lifted his shirt slowly over his waist, and he stepped away from me long enough for me to pull it over his head. It dropped to the floor next to my dress, unforgotten and unwanted, allowing my hands to explore in the same manner as his.

My hands crept up and over his shoulders and down his arms. It was then that I felt the raw and ragged skin that extended from forearm to elbow. With a startled gasp, I dropped my hands and stared up at him questioningly. "What's this?"

His eyes were glazed and unfocused as he stared down at me uncomprehendingly. After a moment my words must have sunk in his desire-ridden brain, for he shook his head and twisted his arm to peer at the long abrasion. "It's nothing," he said with a shrug. "Just a scrape."

He reached for me again, his features softening. His hands circled my waist, but I held firm. "It happened last night," I said aloud.

"I'm fine, really."

"He hit you with his car?"

"I jumped out of the way."

When my scowl deepened, he grimaced. "Cherisse, it's nothing. Come here." He pulled me harder, his long fingers tightening around me. "My God, you're so damned beautiful," he said, almost inaudibly.

My hands slipped away from the waistband of his jeans, and I gazed up at him with wide eyes. When I spoke, my voice reflected my awe. "You're shaking."

He released the hook on my bra and glanced at his hands in wonder. "Now you know how badly I want you." He smiled. "I've waited so long to have you here, and now I can hardly believe it's really happening."

"Wow." I sighed heavily, my eyes drifting closed again.

"I've waited too long trying to make it perfect."

"I don't think there's anything about you that's not perfect, Brandon," I whispered.

In the silence of the room, our soft moans and mingled breathing echoed. Through the pounding of my blood in my ears, I discovered just what Brandon liked. How he squirmed under my probing hands and sighed when I kissed the base of his neck. From head to toe, he kissed every part of my body and smoothed away the day's tension with his hands.

Although I could sense his urgency, he was a gentle lover and very much an experienced man. As he raised himself above me, our eyes once more met and locked. The look in his eyes, the longing and respect, was breathtaking. I understood how he felt, how he cherished me at that moment.

"Please," I whispered.

That was exactly what he did, and because we fit so well, he was slow to roll away. When he did, I sighed once more and closed my eyes, my heart slowly returning to normal. Brandon bent and placed a kiss on my chin. Then his lips worked down the side of my neck, and I could feel a smile tug on the corners of my mouth.

"Mm," I murmured, arching my neck for better access. "That's very nice."

"You're very nice," he said, lifting his head long enough to smile down at me.

"That was good then?"

His smile broadened to a wide grin. "That was amazing, Sunshine."

"Mm, I thought so too."

I heard him sigh. It was a peaceful sound, like that of a man satisfied. "Cherisse, I want you to stay here with me more often. Maybe on our nights off we could get together. Something more than just two days a week."

"I'd like that very much."

His nostrils flared as he smiled down at me knowingly. Once again his hand began exploring, and his voice was husky when he leaned over me. "Me too, Sunshine."

Talk done, things settled, I closed my eyes and relaxed in his arms. With his heat, my body began warming with a new need. The need to be loved by Brandon.

Chapter 10

The newness of sleeping with another person was eclipsed by the newness of sleeping in the nude. During the night, I was very much aware of our bodies. With limbs entwined, warm skin against warm skin, I awoke in the middle of the night and found myself watching Brandon sleep. He was lying on his back, one hand wrapped around me and the other sprawled over his head. His face was totally relaxed in the semi-darkness, and his long lashes rested against his high cheekbones.

I eased back a little and propped myself up on my elbow to watch him. His lips parted slightly with my movement, and his arm tightened momentarily. Seconds later, he was sleeping heavily once more, and I could not help but smile.

The young men I had dated had never made me feel the way Brandon did. I had no idea just what I was missing all this time. No wonder Arianne was always so vocal. I, too, wanted to scream aloud just how wonderful a lover Brandon was and how amazing I felt inside.

Unable to stop myself, my fingers reached up to trace the outline of his face, from his full lips to his strong brow. His skin was smooth there too, not furrowed in his sleep. I liked the scratchy feel of his cheeks and square jaw. I loved the way his straight nose flared at the end, and how his wide his blue-green eyes were.

My fingers continued to stroke his face until his eyes fluttered and opened. When he focused on me, he smiled. "It's not morning yet," he said, his voice a little groggy.

I grinned. "I know."

"You're astonishing," he complained gently.

"I know."

****

By the time I woke, I could not remember just how many times we made love during the night. I opened my eyes slowly, feeling satiated and complete for the first time in my life. A slow smile parted my lips, and it widened when I found Brandon sitting next to me with a charming half-smile on his face. His hair glittered with drops of water from his recent shower and stubble roughened his cheeks. In his hand he sported a sapphire blue silk robe, cut to mid-thigh, and more my size judging by the look as it rested on a padded hangar.

Reaching up to wipe at my eyes, I slowly sat up and stared at the robe. "What's that?" I asked, stretching lazily.

"It's for you."

I smiled. "I would hope so."

"Do you remember the other morning? I said I'd like you to wear that robe every morning."

I laughed, and my heart sailed with joy. "You went out and bought me a robe?"

"Well, yeah, that very day, as a matter of fact. I've had it here all week. I just couldn't resist."

I reached out and grasped one corner. It was fine, soft silk. "You want me to wear this all day?"

He took the robe off the hangar and held it open for me to slip in. I was hesitant as I dropped the sheet, but his warm smile never wavered as I slipped my arms inside. With glowing eyes, his hands fell away as I secured the thin tie around my waist, yet he continued to peruse me with his head cocked to the side.

"Absolutely. Actually, I think you should wear that every time you're here, Cherisse."

He reached for me and pressed his lips against my neck. Though laughing, I arched my neck, giving him unlimited access. I was giggling by the time he raised his head.

"Do you want some lunch?"

"Lunch?" I squeaked.

His eyes crinkled with mirth. "It's almost one o'clock, Sunshine. You've slept the whole morning away."

"Oh my gosh! It's a good thing I got coverage for today. I've never slept this late before. This is awful."

"I'll take that as a compliment," he said warmly. "But today is a new day. Come on, lazy bones, I'm hungry."

"Do you have shampoo?" I asked, my hands going to my tangled hair.

"I don't know, I kind of like you all messed-up like that," he teased.

"Seriously..."

"Right in the bath, Sunshine. There's a towel out for you."

I hurried into the bathroom and stared at the large whirlpool tub next to the shower. Thoughts of Brandon and I in the tub full of bubbles with a bottle of champagne teased me. Granted, the tub was barely large enough for one person, but I was able to think of interesting ways to make it work. However, my body ached in strange places from the night before, and I realized it was a fantasy for another night. Even so, when Brandon appeared behind me and found me staring at the tub longingly, he was quick to act. Without a word, he reached forward and turned on the faucet, running it hot and deep.

While we waited, his arms went around my waist from behind, and his fingers deftly untied the sash of the robe. His fingers were gentle as he slipped the robe from my shoulders. It fell down my body in a teasing caress, falling to a heap on the floor. "Go ahead and relax. I'll wash your hair."

I shivered. His breath, warm and moist, teased my neck, and his husky voice sent more shivers of delight down my spine. The jets began to flow, making the steaming water bubble violently. It looked inviting.

Moving away from him, I stepped into the tub and sank into the water with a hearty sigh. Brandon's hands disappeared into the water, resurfacing moments later filled with water. He spilled it over my head, the warm rivulets careening down my shoulder length hair and down my back. "Mm, that's nice."

My eyes again drifted closed as his long fingers gently massaged the shampoo in. I was in pure, unadulterated heaven. Thousands of bubbles caressed my skin beneath the water, and Brandon's hands worked magic on my head. I almost fell asleep under his tender ministrations. He washed my hair and soaped my shoulders while the jets massaged the rest of my aching muscles. I was slow to finish soaping, unwilling to end the decadence. When I finally emerged, I felt both rejuvenated and exhausted.

"Is there anything you're not good at?" I asked in amazement.

Brandon held the towel open for me, and hugged me tight when I stepped into it. He did not seem to care that I soaked his shirt with my dripping hair. And all I cared about was being close to him, smelling his clean scent, being with him.

"You're mine now," he murmured into my hair.

"Maybe so, but you're mine too."

"You're right." He bent and kissed me lightly, sealing our words on our lips. I suddenly remembered Kerri's words in the bathroom. There was no doubt in my mind that this was the man that I would marry. I was sure of that more than anything else in my life. My only problem would be convincing him. It might take some time, but I was sure I could do it.

****

"How many girls have you dated while working?"

"What?"

I knew I had caught him totally by surprise, but after the incredible night we had shared, as well as the lazy afternoon, I felt as though I needed to know more about his past. "Have you dated other girls you've met on calls?"

"No, never," he said, shaking his head.

"Come on? With all those girls offering?"

He slowed the car, pulling up to a red light. As soon as we stopped, he turned to me and stared. "Where's this coming from?"

I shrugged. "I was just curious."

"Sunshine, most of the people I meet while I'm working aren't usually the dating kind. Sure, there are those who'll come on to you just because you're in uniform, but they're not exactly someone I'd want to bring home. I don't bother wasting my time."

"Why me then?"

It was his turn to shrug. He was still staring at me, his face unreadable, his eyes masked by the sunglasses that protected his eyes from the late afternoon sun. "I don't know. It just happened."

"What, exactly?"

Several silent moments followed. His discomfort grew under my steady gaze. I could see it in the tightening around his lips. "I don't know. I just looked at you and something clicked. You were so angry and... defiant. I was impressed. I could tell that you weren't some kind of floozy but a hard working girl who was in trouble."

A horn sounded behind us, and Brandon returned his attention to the road. I watched him drive, easing his way expertly through the traffic. Two more lights and we would be at my apartment complex. The glorious day was about to end.

When he pulled into a free space, I unbuckled my seatbelt and slipped it off my shoulder. I felt awkward still dressed in the blue dress from the day before, but Brandon did not seem to mind. He shut off the engine, unbuckled his seatbelt, and reached over to pull me close. "I don't know why I did what I did. I've never done it before and probably won't again. It's generally not a good idea to get involved with someone you're trying to serve and protect, you know?"

I nodded.

"I have no idea why I feel like I do when I'm with you. All I know is that I like what's happening to me, and I don't regret a minute of it." He kissed my cheek, the corner of my mouth and then my lips. "Do you?"

"No... Not one bit."

"Then why do you ask?"

"I just wanted to know if I was just a fling."

"A fling?" He chuckled between spreading more kisses along my chin and neck. "Damn, Cherisse, you're definitely not a fling."

There was a tone of wonder in his voice, almost accusing, and I knew he was referring to the previous night. I felt the same as he did. Nothing could compare to it, and I suspected nothing ever would. "I'm glad you say that."

"Come on, I'll walk you up."

He released me and hopped down, coming around to my side with a quick step. His arm came to rest around my shoulders as we crossed the parking lot and climbed the stairs.

"Do you want to come in?" I asked as I fished for my keys.

"If I stay I may not leave."

"I'd like that."

He smelled clean, like soap and the slight traces of blueberry muffins and oranges that we had shared for lunch hours earlier. I inhaled deeply, committing those scents to my memory, as well as the feel of his arms around me. He hugged me close, a chuckle resounding in the cavity of his chest. "As much as I'd like to, we both have things to do tomorrow. Besides, your bed is way too small. What time is your class?"

"Eight."

"Maybe I'll see you later? I'll call you."

"Promise me?"

He looked surprised. "Of course."

"Fine, then. I'll talk to you tomorrow."

He kissed me then, the same powerful kiss he had used the night before to make my toes curl. When he raised his head, he was again smiling a secretive, knowing smile. "I *will* call you."

My arms went around my waist when he released me, feeling the loss of his warmth immediately. My heart felt it too. I wanted to call him back as I watched him leave, but my tongue remained silent. Sighing softly, I unlocked the door and entered my silent, dark apartment, feeling lonely and alone.

The phone rang as soon as the door was locked behind me, causing me to jump. But the caller ID did not identify the number, so I answered it. Boy, was I glad I did.

"Hello, Cher?"

I sat down hard on the sofa, my heart soaring. "Jeez, Shelly! How are you? Actually – where are you?"

I had not spoken to Shelly in too long and had not heard from her since she had left that message on my machine. Here I was so wrapped up in my new relationship with Brandon that I had barely given my sister a thought. Guilt briefly glimmered in the back of my mind, but I tucked it away as Shelly began to speak once more.

"I don't really want to say," Shelly's voice trailed away for a moment, "just in case he comes looking."

"Are you still separated from Joe?"

"Yes. I went back today while he was out with a civic stand-by to pick up some things, like Jacob's birth certificate and my passport. He had tried to hide them, but I knew where to look."

"Good for you, Shelly. Do you need anything? Is there anything I can do? Do you need any money?"

"No, no, we're okay. I'm calling you because I'm afraid he's going to call you again."

"How did you know he called?"

"I spoke to him that first night and told him we were through. He told me he was on his way back to your place. He's upset about Jacob, I think, more than me. He's threatened to kill me if he catches us. I just got the permanent restraining order, but we're going into hiding for a while. I need to get some job training and start all over again."

"Why don't you go home to Mom and Dad?"

"Are you kidding? That's the first place he'd look after you, and they'd defend him until the cows came home. That's why I want to stay away from you for now also."

I grimaced. Of course she was right. "I'm sorry. Well, what else can I do for you? When can I see you and Jacob?"

"Nothing, hon. I just wanted to let you know that Jacob and I are all right. I've finally got my head on straight and wanted to say thank you for trying to help me. The place we're at is great. We're going to move on, but I'll keep in touch when I can. I'll let you know when it's safe to see you, okay?" She paused, and I heard a strangled sound, almost like a sob, through the receiver. "I wanted to update you just in case he tries to question you. I hope he doesn't bother you anymore, but just in case. At least you know we're safe."

"I understand."

I could feel tears of my own rise in my eyes, but I blinked them away. "Shelly, I'm so glad you're doing this. If you need anything, any help, let me know. I've become friendly with one of the officers who came here that night. I'm sure we could help you if you need it."

"Oh, honey, that's great. Thank you so much. But I think it's better if we go farther away. I don't want to risk his finding us so close by, and I don't want to involve you in my mess anymore. This is for me to straighten."

I sighed. "Will you give Jacob my love? Give him a big hug and kiss for me."

"Oh, I will. He's asked about you a lot lately. I'm sure he's going to miss you."

I felt emotion rise in the back of my throat, but my voice was steady when I spoke. "Please take care of yourself, Shelly. Keep in touch, and let me know how you're doing."

"I will. And give that big, blond hunk a hug for me. Thank him for trying to help us."

"How did you know?"

"Who else would it be?" She laughed. "I knew it wasn't the older man, and the others that showed up the second time didn't stare at you like he did. Of course it was him."

I swallowed my sob in a chuckle. "Well, you're right, and I will hug him for you."

"Okay, Cher. I'm going to run now. Take care of yourself. I love you."

"I love you, too," I whispered, tears spilling over my lashes. "Tell Jacob I love him."

"I will." She inhaled a ragged breath, and I could sense the tears in her eyes as well. Eyes so like my own. "Bye, bye Cher."

"Bye, Shelly. Good luck."

The phone went dead with a click, leaving me alone again. As I stared at the silent handset, horrible thoughts went through my head. Would this be the last time I ever heard from her? Would I ever see her or Jacob again?

Chapter 11

Thanksgiving Day began with Arianne testing out her culinary skills by putting the turkey in the oven. She had left it up to me to remove the innards and the neck, and I was the one who put the orange inside the belly, a trick my mom had given me to keep the meat moist. I was also in charge of the green bean casserole, the dinner rolls, the cranberry sauce, and the stuffing, while she handled the gravy and potatoes. The inequality was fine with me, since Arianne was constantly on some sort of diet, and I feared what she would cook otherwise.

I was slow to get up that morning. It was a brisk outside, and the chill in the air made me feel lazy and want to spend the whole day under the covers. I had wanted to do just that, but the knowledge that Mike was coming over shortly and Brandon as soon as he was done working spurred me to get started.

After taking a quick shower, I opened the window in my bedroom and inhaled the brisk air. The skies were bright blue, not a cloud to be found, and the weatherman behind me was promising a day in the low-seventies. Gone was the heat of summer, and in its place was Snowbird season and calmer temperatures. The semester was winding down to finals week, and I would be student teaching next fall. It was one of the happiest moments of my life. In fact, I did not think I could be any happier.

Therefore, it was with a light heart that I went to the kitchen and poured myself a cup of steaming coffee.

"Starting early?" I asked Arianne as she turned on the oven light.

"Mike wanted to eat early. He wants to go to a movie later on this afternoon after we eat."

"That sounds nice," I said, reaching past her for a muffin I had baked the day before.

"You've been baking. What a surprise."

I grinned. "I'm showing off my skills, too."

"Cher, you've too many to count. Don't bother showing them off," Arianne muttered, her lips twisted with dry sarcasm.

"Why, thanks. What a nice compliment."

"Do you and Brandon want to come with us to the movie?"

With a neutral shrug, I lathered some butter on my muffin. "I don't know. I'll ask him."

"In other words, no, right?"

"I didn't say that."

"But I can tell you're still not ready to share him yet."

That Arianne knew me so well was touching as well as unsettling. I watched as she strutted into the living room and plugged in her iPod. Of all of my friends, Arianne had by far the most eclectic music collection I could imagine, and today she was opting for New Age. The soft sounds of the music strained to reach me in the kitchen, but I could hear Arianne singing. When she came back in I managed to smile.

"I do understand, Cher," she said, understanding my smile. "Really, I do. I wish I had found him first, but hey, you can't win them all."

"Really, Ari, don't get me jealous again," I said.

"One look at you had that man lost to other women." She laughed. "Trust me, Cher; he is the man you're going to marry. At least you haven't completely written us off yet."

"I could never do that," I objected. "And marriage is still a long way off for me."

"I bet he could change your mind if he set out to do it."

"It's not that easy."

Arianne was about to answer when a knock sounded on the door. She glanced at me with her eyebrows lifted. "That's probably Mike. Will you get it? I haven't showered yet."

As Arianne hurried into the bathroom, I headed to the front door. I heard the bathroom door close solidly behind her as I pulled back the locks. A blast of cool air hit me in the face, and the bright early morning sunlight caught me off guard. All my excitement and happiness fled when I saw who was there.

It was not Mike.

I quickly pushed the door back as hard as I could, but he was faster. His booted foot blocked the latch, and with a heavy thrust he shoved at the door, throwing both me and the door aside.

"Cher, how are you?" Joe asked, stepping into the living room.

"Get out," I demanded.

He smirked in my direction before wandering further into the apartment, his eyes taking in everything from the muffins on the counter to the turkey in the oven. Down the hall he went, looking in my small bedroom for anything resembling Shelly's. Arianne and I had spent almost the entire evening cleaning everything we could. The apartment was spotless, freshly vacuumed, and smelling of the vanilla candles Arianne had just lit. There was no way he would find any hint of Shelly or Jacob. Anything they might have left behind would certainly have been put away by now. Let him look all he wants, I thought to myself, and then he can leave.

I shut the door, careful not to lock it, and stood with my back to it. My hands crossed over my chest when he came back to the living room. "What are you doing here? You're no longer welcome here."

"That's no way to talk to your brother-in-law." When I snorted, his lips twisted angrily. "I want to know where my son and my wife are."

"Even if I knew where they were, Joe, you'd be the last person I'd tell."

"That's exactly why I'm here. I know that. This is your fault. Not only have you ruined Shelly's state of mind, but you've even gotten to Jacob."

"At least there's finally some sanity in his life," I snapped.

For a moment I was scared, frightened that Arianne, who was now running the shower, would enter the mess and maybe get hurt. Or even more likely – that he would come after me again.

"I knew you'd say that, Cher, which is why I've been watching you. I know Shelly hasn't been here, but I also know that she might call you on this holiday."

"You're not staying here, Joe," I said, furious that he would have the gall to assume I would meekly stand by. "You're not welcome, and I have company coming."

"Wouldn't be that guy you've been sleeping with?"

I could feel the color rise on my cheeks, though I refused to show him what I was really feeling. There was no way I would let him see how frightened I really was, how wildly my heart was beating in my chest. "That's none of your business. You'd be best to stay out of my life, Joe. You hit your wife, and she's had enough. She wants to start over again. You need to focus on getting help of your own. Maybe then you'd have another chance with her."

The color in his face faded away before flooding it until it was bright red. Though I spoke softly and reasonably, I feared I had pushed him too hard and mentally prepared myself for his blow. With my head held high, I watched him take two steps towards me. This close, I could smell the alcohol on his breath, on his clothes, and stinking up the air around us. I wrinkled my nose in distaste. He had gone downhill so quickly, and it was so hard to remember the nice man my sister had married just years before.

"Joe – go home," I whispered, feeling my voice quiver just slightly.

He noticed and took another step closer, his fingers tracing the line of my jaw. I shuddered in distaste and turned away, but he followed me. I was pressed against the door, the knob pressing painfully into the small of my back.

"You got stitches I heard," he said softly, his voice cold and controlled. He smiled, but it appeared more of his lips spreading over his teeth in a snarl. Meanwhile, his hand cupped my chin and squeezed slightly. "You know, I should've gotten some, too. Do you want to see the scar you gave me?"

"Back off!" I shrieked, slapping his hands away.

His hand returned to my face, lightly stroking my cheek before it slipped around my neck. He did not tighten his grip but held me loosely. I could not move, and fear made my palms moist.

"Joe, if you don't let go, I'm going to scream as loud as I can."

"How long could you scream before I cut off your air supply?" He asked softly, his fingers tightening just a little. "Where are they?"

As much as I wanted to turn away, I did not. I struggled to keep my face emotionless, to hide the fear that pounded in my breast. Our eyes locked, and he moved closer still to speak but stopped when the bathroom door opened.

Like a breath of fresh air, Arianne appeared with a towel around her hair and her slinky red robe tied loosely around her waist. "What's going on here?"

When she saw Joe, her hands immediately went to the neckline of her robe, tightening it against Joe's curious gaze.

"Call the police, Ari," I muttered softly, hoping she would have enough sense to do just that. "He has a stay-away order for this address." I returned my attention to him. "How would you like to spend the holiday in jail, Joe?"

His fingers tightened again slightly, but then a slow smile spread his lips. "Court's done, baby. I got probation. Your stay-away order isn't in effect anymore."

My eyes widened just enough for Arianne to jump to action. Her voice rang out in the small room, catching both of us off guard. "Get your hands off her!"

Joe released me quickly and took two steps back, a charming smile on his face and his hands held up in surrender. "Relax now, ladies."

Arianne reached for her phone as she glared at Joe. "Get out of here, buddy. You're invading my apartment. Go now, or I'm calling the cops."

"Put the phone down," Joe warned in an even voice.

"Not until you're out of my place," Arianne snarled.

"Put the phone down, Arianne," he said more forcefully, taking a step toward her.

I shook my head at Arianne, warning her that he meant business. With her eyes glued to me, Ari began dialing. Before she could hit the final number, Joe advanced quickly and ripped the phone from her hand and threw it against the wall. Allowing her hand to fall back to her side, Arianne glared at Joe. "What do you want anyway, Joe?"

His face became mottled with rage. "I want my son!"

My eyes closed as I flinched. That sound brought back horrible memories, those of pain, anger and suffering. I was scared now, filling with panic. It glimmered in Ari's eyes as well, and both of her hands went to her neckline.

"She hasn't involved me in any of her plans. You'll have to wait and hear from the courts," I said forcefully. "And you will get nowhere but to jail unless you leave now."

I reached for the doorknob behind me, but as I did so, it spun easily. Mike, I thought with a glimmer of relief. As we did battle with the doorknob, I hoped Joe would not notice that we had company. My eyes clashed with his, and I prayed my increasing fear would appear as defiance in my gaze.

I stepped away from the door, opening it behind me. Mike stood on the step, his face showing his surprise. Yet it quickly turned to anger when he saw Joe standing in the doorway to the kitchen. "What are you doing here?"

"I was just leaving," he said sourly.

I shuddered again as he passed, knowing without a doubt that he would not just give up. He would be back again, and I would constantly have to be on my guard now.

I was being watched.

In the doorway, the two men glared at each other. Joe shrugged after a moment and went down the stairs. When he reached the bottom, he glanced up at me one last time. "I'll see you soon, Cher. And when you hear from Shelly, you tell her that."

I shook my head, refusing to believe it. Shelly was not going to call me. She knew better now.

Yet how did I know? And what would happen to her if he found her? She was in deep trouble in his eyes, and I was afraid I was just drawn into the middle.

****

Brandon had once told me that he was never grumpy. True to form, I had never seen Brandon actually furious before, but once I did, I decided at that moment that I never wanted to again. Not only did he look fierce, but he also sounded ferocious when he wanted to. It was intimidating.

He stood before me with his eyes narrowed dangerously and his lips compressed in a thin line. I saw a muscle work in his jaw, and his teeth were clenched tightly together. After glaring at me until I looked away again, he resumed pacing in front of me.

"Why didn't you call?"

"Why should I have? He left."

I was aware that my voice shook ever so slightly and bit my lower lip in dismay. He stopped again and frowned at me, his face once more impassive, and I was immediately reminded of the police officer in Brandon, the man who heard all kinds of lies while he was working. Oh yes, there were the lies and outrageous stories in addition to tales of woe and joy. He knew what I would say before I could say it.

"You said he stunk like booze. He could've been picked up for a DUI at the very least. What if he got into an accident, Cherisse? What if he killed someone on his way home?"

I had never considered that, and my hand flew to my chest as the idea filled me with fear. "Oh, gosh!"

"And now you tell me that he put his hands on you again?" His voice was incredulous.

I shot Arianne a fierce scowl, but my roommate shrugged as she came to her feet.

We all had sat comfortably in the living room after finishing our turkey dinner. All had gone smoothly, including Arianne's preparations, until my roommate commented on how thankful she was that Joe had left peacefully. Brandon's eyes had immediately narrowed in anger, and since then he had been glaring at all of us.

"I'm glad he's angry at you," Arianne said softly. "Maybe he can talk some sense into you... We're leaving."

Mike held out his hand to Brandon as an offering of peace. "Happy Thanksgiving, man."

Brandon shook absentmindedly, his eyes still threatening me. Still, he remained his polite self. "Yeah, you, too. Thanks for dinner, Arianne. It was delicious."

She smiled at him, her eyes no longer dancing with unleashed flirtation. I could tell that they were both anxious to get out of the way. They felt as I did at that moment, that we made a mistake and never should have tried to hide it from him.

They slipped away, reaching for their coats hurriedly as they hurried out the door. I heard it close behind them and felt a glimmer of panic. I was alone with Brandon, and he was furious.

He waited until he heard them lock the door behind them. As soon as their footsteps retreated to silence outside, he approached the sofa and stared down at me with his hands on his hips. "You need to take out an Order of Protection."

"I don't think he's coming back. He knows about you."

"He's been watching you. That's called stalking. You need to get some protection."

"From who? You cops take fifteen minutes to get here. He could kill me in that time."

Brandon's face went white with surprise before all the color returned in a deep flush. "Damn, Cher."

I glanced down at my hands, guilt causing me to avoid his eyes. "I'm sorry, that was uncalled for, and I certainly didn't mean it the way you're thinking."

"But you said it," he whispered. His statement hung in the air between us like an executioner's ax for long, tense moments. Finally Brandon sighed in frustration. "What you don't realize is that with an order you could put a stop to it right away. All he has to do is violate it once, and he goes to jail."

I watched as he fell to his knees in front of me. Both hands came forward, a move that made me flinch involuntarily and made him curse. Without coming any closer, he allowed his hands to fall limply back to his side, but I saw a glimmer of betrayal in his eyes.

"I can't believe you still don't trust me," he said softly.

His words brought my face swiveling back to face him. My eyes filled with tears, and no matter how I longed to hide them from him, to keep them leashed, they spilled over my lashes. "It's not that, Brandon, really it isn't. You know I trust you."

He shook his head. "Well, what do you expect me to think?"

He stared at a single tear as it careened down my cheek. For a moment I thought he might reach over and wipe it away, but as I watched his hand curled into a fist, and he scowled once more at me. "Why would you try to hide something like this from me? I'm a cop, Cherisse, how did you plan to hide it? All of you – all afternoon – have been sitting silently, barely eating. Obviously, you were hiding something. Did you really think you'd get away with it?"

"I wasn't trying to hide anything –"

"That's not true," he snapped.

"It is. I just didn't want to involve you – that's all," I finished lamely.

"Involve me? Who better to involve? I could protect you better than Arianne or even Mike." He cursed again. "That's what I mean about trust, Cherisse. You don't trust me."

He turned to stare at me again, his face burning with disappointment, and the look cut me to the bone. Those same eyes had been dancing with humor before dinner, glittering with a promise of what was to come later. Unable to bear the condemnation there, I once more lowered my head, turning away from him. He was right. My fear to show him my feelings was a question of trust – the only thing he had ever asked me for.

All this time I had thought I did, but he was right. I still held a piece of myself from him, and now he wanted and expected more.

"I'm leaving, Cherisse."

My head snapped back. "Where are you going?"

He turned away from me, leaving me to stare at the broad shoulders encased in a pale blue dress shirt. It was the nicest I had seen him dress since the wedding. He was just so handsome, downright beautiful even, and I was flattered that he had dressed up so nice for our cozy meal.

He did not turn around. His shoulders remained stiff and unyielding, as formal as the tone of his voice. "I don't know, home maybe." He laughed, and I winced at the sound. "I think you have a lot to think about, and I, apparently, can't help you."

He reached for his coat, the heavy leather jacket strewn over the chair. He slung it over his shoulder and strode to the door, his steps purposeful.

"Will you call me?" I watched for a moment, thinking he would turn around and say something, anything. But he did not. I never got an answer.

He pulled the door open, not hesitating at all. As it swung open into the dimming afternoon light, I watched him take two steps. My eyes burned with unshed tears. My mouth felt dry. I could not allow the one man who had captured my heart leave my life.

He was about to close the door behind him when I jumped up from my seat on the sofa and ran after him. I caught the door with my fingers, jamming them soundly, and I pulled back with a sharp cry. I shook them out while my other hand pulled it open.

"Wait," I cried out, reaching for his arm.

He was stiff beneath my fingers, his muscles rigid with restrained anger. I pressed my throbbing fingers to my lips and grasped him by the shirt with my other hand.

"Is that it, then? You're just going to walk away?"

His lips thinned, and I saw a muscle work furiously in his jaw. Oh yes, he was angry. In fact, he was furious. But too, I knew he was scared. He was just as frightened of losing me as I was of losing him.

Swallowing my pride, I tightened my fingers around his shirt. "Don't go, Brandon."

He did not move an inch, but neither did he walk any further. Pressing myself against his back, my arms surrounded his shoulders. I buried my face between his shoulder blades and squeezed him tightly. The smell of his leather jacket permeated my nostrils, and I could smell his subtle cologne as well, both scents I would love forever.

"Don't leave angry," I said, my voice muffled by his shirt. "Please, come back inside."

I felt rather than heard the negative answer. It cut me to the quick. "I don't think so."

"I'm not perfect, Brandon, believe me, I know that. I'm sorry I didn't tell you. I was embarrassed and afraid of your reaction."

"Could it have been any worse than this?" The sarcasm nearly dripped from his voice.

"Please come back inside and discuss this with me," I whispered.

He sighed heavily, so forcefully that my hands fell away from his shoulders. I kept them at my side. "Fine," he muttered.

I knew I had much to explain in order to ease the anger from his formal tone, so I reached for his arm and tugged him back inside. As soon as the door shut behind him, I threw my arms around him again and opted for honesty. "I didn't want you to know because I was embarrassed."

"What for?"

"I didn't want to remind you that my family has problems, or that you met me on one of your calls."

"That's ridiculous," he said tightly. "When have I ever given you the impression that I disapprove of you or your family?"

I put my face in his chest again, hoping he would soften toward me or give in just a little. He did not. He remained as rigid as before, his heart beating steadily under my ear.

"I know you haven't," I said with a small laugh. "But I've told you I wasn't perfect, and it's true. I'm not."

"Nobody's perfect," he commented dryly. "Believe me, I see it every day."

"That's why I wanted to be different."

"You're going about it the wrong way."

"I'm scared," I blurted. "I was terrified of him, and it embarrassed me. I didn't want you to know how weak I was, especially since you're always so controlled and know exactly what to do."

I heard the leap in his heart and raised my head. I had gotten through a little, and that was a start. He was staring at me expectantly, waiting for me to continue. Letting down my guard was new to me, but I really did want to prove to him that I did trust him. "I've never felt this way about another person in my life, Brandon. I didn't want to scare you away."

Having said it, I felt a tremendous burden lift from my shoulders. At last the full truth was out. He could accept me or reject me, but at least he knew the truth.

Another heavy sigh escaped his tight lips, and I felt his breath stir my hair and warm my face. To my delight, one of his hands came up to rest around my waist. His other hand reached for my hair, and he tucked a lock around my ear gently.

"You almost did," he said softly.

"I know, and I was so terrified," I said on a sob.

"Why are you so afraid to trust me? Have I ever hurt you?"

I shook my head. "No... but I care for you so much it scares me."

His eyelids lowered for just a second, but I knew I had done the right thing. When they opened again, I was captured by the intensity of his blue-green eyes. "I've been waiting to hear that for so long, Cherisse. I'm glad you finally said it."

Before I could ask him if he felt the same, his mouth came down on mine. It was a hard, punishing kiss, but there was desperation in it as well. I reached for him and held on tight, too afraid to let him go, even after he slowly raised his head.

"Our first fight," he murmured.

I nodded in return and squeezed him tighter. With a growl of triumph, he bent and swept me into his arms.

"I think we need to kiss and make up now," he said softly.

I blinked up at him. "You're not angry anymore?"

The look he gave me was stern, a total cop face. "We'll talk about that later, Sunshine, but one thing's for certain. I've learned a lot about you in the time we've been together. You are a strong woman, but you shouldn't be foolish. It's time to be more proactive. Terrible things happen to even the nicest people, especially the ones who say, 'it could never happen to me.' It's time to do something to stop Joe from bothering you."

Feeling chastised, I nodded my head in agreement. With a half-smile, he reached for me. "I promise that we'll discuss that much later."

Burying my face in his neck, I relaxed in his arms, even though I knew he meant it.

Chapter 12

A pattern formed during the holiday break. Since Arianne spent her weekends at Mike's, Brandon extended the same invitation to me. Our schedules still conflicted, with him on nights and me working all day, but we managed to have some Sundays together. During the short break between classes, I picked up a temporary job in retail. The second job would help to get me through the following semester without having to stress about money, and I was able to pay my entire year's car insurance with the check.

Since I was not around as much, Brandon took some overtime as well. We did not see much of each other, but we developed a little routine to make us both content.

After Thanksgiving and our first fight, our relationship ascended to a new level. The feelings I had for him had deepened to love without my knowledge, and having him in my life took on a whole new meaning. Because of this, when he expressed his displeasure at my refusal to prosecute Joe for his assault, I promised to call his friend, Mary, in order to ease his worry somewhat. The woman's name remained on a slip of paper in my book bag. I would see it occasionally while sorting out papers and writing utensils, but I had never taken the time to call. In order to placate him, I promised to call her as soon as I got through the holidays.

In all that time, I did not hear from Shelly, so the presents I had bought them remained wrapped in my closet high on a shelf as a daily reminder of the trials they were going through. I spoke to my parents over Christmas weekend, and they revealed that they had not heard from Shelly, either. Promising to visit in March, I was comfortable with making everything seem more pleasant than it was. Besides, things were still new with Brandon, and I much preferred spending what little free time I had with him instead of entertaining my parents.

Brandon's parents now lived in Payson, which was two hours north. Like my parents, they too had decided to retire in the mountains, although they still took the time to check in on Brandon on Sunday mornings. I had taken up the habit of sitting in the den while he spoke to them, watching the easy camaraderie they shared. It was with a touch of envy that I peered on, for I wished that my parents were as open as his. Where Brandon told his parents everything he knew about me, I still had not even told my parents that I was seeing someone – let alone seriously.

For Christmas, Brandon bought me a full spa package, and I came up with a shotgun ride in a NASCAR stock car over at Phoenix International Raceway. It must have been an ideal gift for him, though, because his eyes danced with excitement when he opened the box and read the description. Since I was all alone for Christmas, Brandon insisted that I join him and his parents for dinner. They made the ride down to share it with us, so Brandon and I set about preparing a respectable Christmas meal. Although I was nervous at first, his parents set me at ease rather quickly.

Kenneth Nicholson was tall and broad like his son, and they also shared the same calm self-assurance that I loved so much, which made it so easy to feel at ease around him. Meanwhile, Brigid Nicholson was a tall, beautiful woman, who at sixty-eight carried herself with the pride and self-confidence of a forty-year-old. She eyed me carefully when they first arrived at Brandon's house, but by the end of the evening she was filling my head with Brandon's childhood antics. I enjoyed these stories, for it gave me that much more insight as to who he really was.

The meal that we shared taught me more about Brandon's family. I learned he had a brother, Adam, and two sisters, Gina and Lori. Lori was the youngest and his closest sibling, with him being only eighteen months older than her. The two eldest children were older by six and ten years respectively, and they both had children as well. Brandon had a niece and two nephews, and all had moved away to different parts of the country, coming back once a year in the summer.

During the time we had together, Brandon kept us busy. Instead of telling me something that he enjoyed, he would show it to me and watch my reaction. Fortunately our similarities proved deep, from hiking in the mountains east of Phoenix to climbing in the car and driving out to Sky Harbor Airport to watch the airplanes take off and land. He taught me how to shoot a gun in self-defense and then moved on to teach me some martial arts moves. He had been training since he was a child and knew far more than I ever expected, and more often than not I ended up making him laugh at my clumsiness.

The New Year found us celebrating at Chuck's house with many of the officers and their spouses that I had met at Kerri's wedding. We celebrated the New Year with a long kiss in the darkness of Chuck's side yard, listening to everyone else sing "Auld Lang Syne" in off-key drunkenness.

And shortly after the New Year, I finally heard from Shelly again. Phoenix was in the midst of a winter storm, and I had arrived at Brandon right when the downpour started. It was just my luck, as not three miles away there was not a drop to be found. Brandon had promised to give me a garage door opener, but since he had removed the old batteries from them, I was still out on the driveway. The new ones were currently in the bags of groceries I was struggling to get in the house, and I was cursing the irony of it when the phone began the "William Tell Overture." Fumbling blindly, I reached for the phone without checking who was calling.

"Hey Cher!"

It took me a minute to realize who it was, and when I did, I tossed the groceries on the floor of the garage, completely forgotten. "Shelly? Is that you? It's raining like mad, and I can barely hear you."

"Yeah, I'm having rough weather like you."

"Where are you?"

I had so many questions that I wanted to ask, but I was afraid she would not be able to answer any of them. Follow her lead, I thought. Let her tell you what she wants you to know.

"Jacob and I are in Tempe."

That she was so close made my heart sing. "Can you come and see me? I'm in Tempe, too."

"But you're not at your apartment. I was there earlier. That's when I remembered you gave me this phone number."

"You were there? You're out of hiding!" I hastily scanned the house with a critical eye, looking around for anything that out of place. It was neat as a pin, as usual. "I'm never at the apartment when I can help it. I'm at Brandon's. Can you come over? I'll give you the address..."

She arrived ten minutes later, driving an unfamiliar used sedan that had seen its better days. It sputtered when she turned off the engine in the driveway, emitting one last cough as she opened the driver's side door. With a happy wave, she reached for the passenger door behind her, and a taller and chubbier Jacob scrambled out and ran to me as I waited on the front patio. He scrambled into my arms and wrapped his little legs around mine tightly. I was surprised to feel the tears that filled my eyes. It was a strange feeling, this overwhelming sense of relief, even though I had been so consumed with my life that I had not thought about them as much as I should have.

"Cher! Cher!" Jacob grabbed me tightly, squeezing me as hard as he could.

"My gosh, look at how big you've gotten in so short a time!"

My hands ran through his dark hair as I watched Shelly approach. She was a totally changed woman. Gone was the lackluster brown hair that hung around her face in straight lines. Instead was a polished woman, with perfectly styled and highlighted hair and a light layer of makeup on her face. Attired in business casual, she wore black pumps with black slacks and a red V-neck sweater. Not exactly the stuff of Neiman Marcus, but nevertheless very elegant. She looked beautiful.

"Hey there, little sister," she said in greeting.

A broad smile curved my lips. "Look at you! You look fantastic!"

"It's so good to see you," she said warmly.

"Well, let's not stand out here in the rain. Come in, come in!"

Jacob released his hold on me and went to Shelly's side. I noticed the way he held her hand tightly and felt a deep sadness. He was still so shy, so mistrusting. All of the secrecy was frightening to me, so I could only imagine how poor Jacob felt. So young and scared, afraid of the man who was supposed to be his role model. It was not right.

Before I closed the door behind them, I found myself scanning the neighborhood for anything out of the ordinary. Everything appeared normal, even the light breeze mingling with the steady rain smelled fresh and clean. There was nothing ominous. Nevertheless, I made sure I locked the door securely behind us because I wanted them both to feel safe with me, as it should be.

Shelly noticed my concern and smiled. "It's okay, Cher. He's visiting his parents in Iowa right now. He won't be back until tomorrow."

"Oh, good." Stepping forward, I reached for both of them and gave them each a big squeeze. "It's so good to see you guys. You both look so well."

She held me at arm's length and gave me a once over. "You look great, too. I guess you've moved up in the world a bit. Nice house."

"It's not mine, and I don't live here full time yet. Right now, I just spend my weekends here, but he's asked me to move in."

She scanned the interior of the house with an appraising eye. It missed little. "So it's getting that serious? That's wonderful, Cher. This is a great place, big enough for a family. Is this Sergeant Nicholson's house?"

I nodded. "Do you remember him?"

"Of course. He's the one who helped me find a place to go when I left Joe in October."

I had been filling two mugs with hot water for tea when Shelly spoke. The way she spoke, so matter-of-factly, caught me off guard. Brandon had never mentioned anything, and I knew nothing about his involvement. I turned to her with a questioning look. "When did you see Brandon?"

"He didn't tell you about it?" She waved a hand in front of her face. "Oh, gosh it was months ago... August, I think. Right after Joe was arrested. He called me to see how Jacob and I were doing. He gave me the name of a woman in the city who could help us if we needed it. He said to keep it until I was ready. I hid the paper in the hem of one of my shirts, and the day that Joe hit Jacob I called the number. It was the smartest thing I've ever done, Cher."

Somehow I was not surprised to hear about Brandon's kindness. His purpose in life was to help others, and he did it naturally. If my respect for him could have climbed any higher, I think it did at that moment.

Returning my attention to the task at hand, I warmed up the water in the microwave and dropped two tea bags in. I had not yet brought over my tea kettle to Brandon's house yet, but I suspected it would come over soon. When the microwave beeped, I took out the mugs and carried them to the kitchen table. Shelly sat with Jacob on her lap, smiling happily. Gone was the fear in her eyes; in fact, she looked more poised than ever. She seemed to exude confidence.

"I'm so glad you were able to get away, Shelly. I just wish I could have helped you more," I said.

Reaching into a cabinet, I pulled out a package of chocolate chip cookies from the grocery store deli that I had bought for Brandon and put them on a plate for Jacob and Shelly. I doubted he would mind our devouring his favorite treat, not when they were going to such a good cause.

"You helped me more than you think," she said after taking a tentative sip of the black tea. Jacob eyed the glass of milk I poured for him with caution, but after a moment of staring at the fresh cookies, he could not resist. Shelly and I exchanged glances to confirm it was okay to speak aloud with him present, but Shelly nodded.

"It's okay. We speak about things in the positive sense," Shelly whispered.

Nodding, I returned to her comment. "How so? I didn't do anything, really."

Shelly smiled. "Actually, if we hadn't gone home with you that night, I never would've gotten the police involved. I never had before. I used to put up with it and shut up. That night changed everything. It started the ball moving, and I'm tasting hope again. It's within my grasp."

I sipped at my tea and batted my eyes at Jacob. He studied me warily. It was a slow response, but soon enough my silly faces brought out a timid smile. He remained on his mother's lap, despite the two extra chairs at the table. Yes, he certainly was a shy boy.

"Besides, if you hadn't called the police that night I never would've gotten Mary's number from your sergeant. I'd still be there with Jacob, risking him every day." She reached up and tousled the boy's dark hair, earning a chocolate smeared scowl from him.

"I'm so glad Brandon did that for you. He gave me this Mary's number too, but I still haven't called her. What does she do?"

"Gosh, Cher, she's a Godsend. The woman's a saint. She's a former battered woman who broke free, went on to school, and ended up with a degree in counseling. She runs a place in Mesa now, helping other women like me get a new start. It's amazing how many of us there are out there. Did you know that almost one in four women will be battered in their lives? It's pretty scary how common it is. And Mary offers help to men also. I think that's what's so special about her. She tries to go to the root of the problem."

Now I understood why Brandon had given me the number in the first place. It was his way of trying to show me that Shelly was safe. I felt like a fool, worrying all that time, when I had the means to contact her in my book bag all along. Shaking my head, I took a bite of my cookie while Shelly continued singing Mary's praises.

"I wasn't exactly honest with you about going far away. I was in Mesa all along, but we figured that if Joe thought we left the state, everyone would be safer."

"I understand, Shelly. Really, I do. You need time to get your life in order. I just want you to know that I'll always be here when you need me." I smiled. "I'm just so happy he's out of the picture now."

When I had finished speaking, Shelly gave me a lopsided smile. Again I was taken aback at the change in her demeanor. There was anger flashing in her eyes, and I had never seen her become so hard in my life. It was refreshing. "Yes, he is. Thank God for that."

"It hasn't been easy on you, has it?"

"No, in the beginning it was very hard, and I didn't think I could survive it. I had no courage then and felt as though my life was over. He had controlled everything for so long that I didn't think I could make it on my own. The ladies at the shelter were great. I started counseling, and Jacob got some help too... I've been learning all about Joe – especially how badly he needs to talk to someone. I just fear it's not help he'll go looking for, regardless of whether it's available or not."

"But you're protected now?" I asked quickly. "He can't come near you now, right?"

"Actually, I started with an Emergency Order of Protection. That held me over until I was able to get the permanent one. The shelter's been so helpful. They were able to help me get to the court and file the petition, and luckily Joe didn't contest it. I think he thought that I'd come back."

"When was this?"

"Right around Thanksgiving."

I nodded. "Joe came to see me before we ate that day."

Shelly's face fell. "Oh, Cher. He didn't hurt you again, did he?"

Shaking my head slowly, I pursed my lips. "No, he didn't do anything but throw Ari's phone against the wall. Arianne and Mike were there."

"I'm so sorry," she said softly. "I don't know why I ever married him. I had reservations starting the day of the wedding... Do you remember? I cried for an hour."

This was something I did not know, maybe because I was still young. Being sixteen and excited to wear such a pretty dress, I had never given a thought to Shelly's emotions on the day of the wedding. I had always assumed it was natural for a bride to cry – happiness, excitement, who knew? "No, I didn't know that."

"Yeah, well, I guess I knew then. But everything seemed okay in the beginning. We had a happy year, but then he started taking away everything. First, he refused to let me work. He told me that my place was in the home. When I told him I was considering college, like you, he laughed and told me that I was too dumb to go." She stopped and glanced down at Jacob, who was still preoccupied with dipping his cookie into his glass of milk. It still felt strange to hear her speak so candidly in front of him, but I assumed he was familiar with everything that had occurred. "Then he took away the money. I was given cash only to buy things, and I had to return the change and receipts. Since he thought I was so dumb, I started hiding away nickels and dimes and let him think I wasn't given correct change. I saved up quite a bit of that money before he found it, and that's when he started hitting me."

She closed her eyes for a moment. "The first time he hit me, he was apologetic afterwards and told me if I hadn't been secretive he never would've lost it. From the first time I forgave him, it was all downhill..."

"How so?" I asked softly.

"I had a close friend down the street. He wouldn't let me see her anymore. When she moved away, he said it was my fault. Then I got pregnant." She nodded at my look of surprise. "Yes, right after Jacob was born... He wasn't happy about that, and I ended up miscarrying after ... an accident that I had. I was so afraid of him. I kept the house neat and Jacob quiet because I was afraid to set him off. And, finally, when he lost his job, his weekend drinking became daily bouts. It was hard."

"So are you going to file for divorce?"

"Yes, I plan to, once I finish the program with Jacob. I'll also be able to finish up my job training. As soon as I get a place set up for the two of us, I plan on hiring a lawyer and filing for sole custody."

"It's probably better that way."

She nodded. "Yeah, without a doubt." Glancing at the clock, she gasped and picked up her cup. "I'm going to have to cut this short. I know we just got here, but I spent so much time trying to track you down that I've got to get back. I borrowed the car and need to get it back to her. I have a mobile phone now, so I can call you. Hey, I'm even texting too. Is that okay?"

Tears threatened in the back of my eyes. I did not want her and Jacob to leave so quickly, especially since Jacob had not even spoken. There was still so much to say, so many questions left unanswered. However, I bit back my disappointment and smiled. "Absolutely, yes! That's great. Anytime you want."

She nudged Jacob off of her lap and came to her feet. Even her bearing was more confident. She held her head high, fearless and strong, and I was so happy for her. With her newfound assurance,

Shelly crossed to the sink and rinsed out her and Jacob's cups before placing them in the dishwasher. I sat and watched her, knowing that any protest would fall upon deaf ears. She had a new determination inside of her and was ready to go places.

My feet were heavy as I walked them to their car. The rain had ceased, and it left behind a cold breeze and damp air that ruffled our hair. As strands blew into our faces, we hugged awkwardly, laughing at our frustration, and I was reminded of our childhood and how different our lives turned out to be. She was escaping a relationship, and I was running headlong into one. How strange it all seemed.

As I watched them pull away, I pulled out my mobile phone and typed out a text message. It contained only two words, but that was all I needed. I sent it off to Brandon with a soft smile on my face before turning away from the wind and the departing car.

The phone message flashed upon my screen. I smiled again as I watched it being sent. "Thank you," was all I needed to say. I could explain what for when he got home.

Chapter 13

The bitter smell of hot coffee slowly awakened me, but I groaned and rolled over, pulling Brandon's pillow over my head. I heard him chuckle, and seconds later the blankets were pulled off me, leaving the cool morning air to soak my body.

"Yikes," I shrieked, pulling my legs up to my chest and wrapping his shirt around my legs. "It's cold, Brandon!"

His breath was warm on my ear, and I could feel the scruff on his chin when he nuzzled my skin. "I've been working all night, and I haven't seen you in days. Give me ten minutes," he murmured.

Because of our crazy schedules, we had developed our ten-minute rule. Like ships passing in the night, we had only a few minutes to spend together, and making love had become a challenge between our studies and work. Though in reality, our lovemaking often lasted longer than the ten minutes, it was an effective way of keeping our relationship healthy.

I rolled over and reached for him, pulling him onto the bed.

"Whoa! The coffee," he said with a laugh. He placed the mug on the night table beside the bed and then gave me a lecherous grin. "I've been thinking of you all night."

"You have?" I asked, running my fingers along his jaw.

"I was kind of hoping I'd find you dressed in that nightie we bought." He glanced down at me, his hand stroking my calf and moving up my thigh. "Instead, I find you wearing a New Hampshire tourism shirt." His lips twisted. "How romantic."

Shrugging flippantly as I grinned up at him, I blinked innocently. "I figured someone had to empty out your ratty clothes so you'd have to start wearing that closet full of nice clothes in there."

"I save those for court days," he protested.

"Besides, I'm saving it for a special occasion."

His nostrils flared slightly, and his eyes darkened. "What occasion is that?"

"Come here, I'm cold," I murmured, pulling him down on top of me.

He laughed and wrapped his arms around me, rolling over until I was on top of him. I sprawled, my legs straddling him while his hands tugged on the hem of the shirt. "What's the occasion?"

"I'm off all day tomorrow. When you get home in the morning, I'll wear it for you."

"Fair enough," he said. "I can't wait."

****

I stopped off at my apartment after another long day of work and picked up yet more of my belongings, smiling ruefully at the fact that I had almost as many clothes at his house as I did at my apartment. It was getting to the point where I wondered if I should continue to pay the rent there. I had not spoken to Arianne in almost two weeks, as she had gone home to California for the holidays and then spent the remainder of break at Mike's. I noticed that the closer I got to

Brandon, the closer she and Mike got, leaving our apartment filled with only our laughing shadows.

As I trailed my fingers over a layer of dust covering the television set, I sighed heavily. I could not just leave the place a mess, and it was long overdue for a good cleaning. Besides, Brandon would not have to wake up for another two hours. Though I was exhausted after working all day, I figured I would have at least an hour before I headed over to Brandon's house.

I set about picking up and dusting the small flat. As I did so, I realized that most of my most precious things were now nesting at Brandon's. My favorite DVDs, my nicest clothes, my favorite coffee mug, and the stuffed cat my grandmother had given to me when I was five. All those memorable belongings now had a place in Brandon's nearly empty rooms. Most importantly, it was all done at his insistence. Although subtle, Brandon had been methodically moving me in, making it harder for me to imagine an existence without him, and I began to wonder what his intentions were.

I was vacuuming when the phone rang, so it was the blinking light that later sent me back to the machine. I hesitated before pressing the button, dreading the worst. Then I laughed at my own nervousness and turned up the volume, but as I feared, it was Joe's voice that filled the apartment.

"Hi, Cher, it's me..."

I almost hit the skip button, but the then I realized that he was sobbing as he spoke.

"I still haven't heard from Shelly, and I really want her to come home. This house is so empty without her and Jacob. I can't stand it anymore. I've been having terrible thoughts, and I almost went to that nice big house you've been staying at for help. Please Cher, I need to talk to someone. Call me when you're done cleaning."

As he rambled, I shuddered uncomfortably. Though I knew he was trying to make me feel bad, I could not find any sympathy for him. He needed to get help, and I was not a psychologist able to give it to him. However, it was not until the message had finished playing that the full import of what he said sunk in. He knew I was cleaning the apartment.

That meant he was here.

Brandon's warning rang in my ears. Keep records, keep a journal, and make sure to save the messages. Reaching forward, almost blindly, I grasped the answering machine from the table and set about disconnecting it from the phone. Arianne would not mind if she missed a couple of sales calls, and I could pick up a new one the next time I was near Wal-Mart. Clinging to it as though it was a life raft, I quickly put the vacuum away and locked up the apartment.

Having the overwhelming urge to get away, I hurried to my car. I drove the short distance from my apartment to Brandon's house with one eye in my rearview mirror. Inside I was churning with emotion, but whether from fear or anger, I could not tell.

The house was dark when I entered, no surprise since I knew that Brandon preferred the dark and quiet to help him sleep when he worked nights. I switched on the hall light and stepped further inside. In my bags, I had packed up a mixture of healthy and junk food, and I paused only long enough to put it all away.

Switching the light off once more, I made my way along the textured wall in the darkness, not wanting to disturb him until absolutely necessary. What could I say to him? The lecture I knew he was going to give me made me hesitate. Still, I could not hide this from him. After Thanksgiving, I wanted to keep things out in the open. Tonight would be the test of complete honesty in our relationship.

I could hear the rustling of the sheets as I climbed the stairs. Always a light sleeper, I suspected he was aware I was home.

Home. I found more and more lately that I was referring to his house as home. He had become the world to me. My future now included him, and my problem with Joe was going to be his as well.

The door was partially open, and it swung easily on its hinges when I pushed it further. He sighed, and I saw him roll onto his side in the shadows. His arm was stretched out onto my side of the bed, reaching for me, I imagined.

"Hey, Sunshine," he murmured, his voice thick with sleep.

Sitting on the edge of the bed, I bent down and kissed his lips lightly. With my free hand, I smoothed back his closely cropped hair, easing the faint lines on his forehead and tracing the smooth skin of his face. He reached for me when I straightened, so I climbed over his hips and came to rest atop the covers. Propping up on one elbow, I stared through the gloomy darkness into his weary eyes.

"I like waking up like this," he said softly.

"I need to talk to you."

Seeming unconcerned, he pushed my hair aside and rubbed my neck. The touch was so welcome after a long day of work that I nearly purred. He chuckled, his white teeth flashing in the darkness. "What about, Sunshine?"

"I stopped at the apartment before coming home and cleaned up a bit."

"Yeah," he responded, his voice lazy and unconcerned.

"Joe called. He was crying and almost sounded suicidal, but he said something that got me nervous. He said he knows where I'm staying, and that it's a nice house."

I felt Brandon stiffen next to me immediately. He inhaled sharply through his teeth, the sound angry. "This guy is a real jerk," he muttered, "and he's really starting to piss me off."

"I saved the tape like you told me to."

"Good."

"I don't know what to do."

"Take out an order, Cher."

"I don't know if that'll help."

He rolled onto his back and covered his face with an arm. I could tell he was frustrated with me, but I needed his reassurance. He was the pro in this, not me. "He'll go to jail if he violates it. He'll go whether or not he has a good lawyer. Don't you see? The calls will have to stop, and he'd be a fool to keep following you."

"But won't that just get him angrier? I mean, he already has it out for me. I just don't want to get him mad. Shelly and Jacob are so close to this house, and she's getting ready to file for divorce. Don't you think setting him off will be worse for all of us?"

"I don't know what else to tell you, Sunshine. I can't be with you all the time, and I don't want him to hurt you to get back at her."

"I know," I grumbled.

"Would it help you to know that I care?"

I did not answer.

"Cherisse?" His hand came up to my shoulder, gentle and slightly urging. When I pulled away from him, he reached over me to switch on the light beside me. The sudden brightness caused me to squint as I hastily covered my eyes. "I'm not too pleased that Joe's still harassing you. He's obsessed. Obviously he thinks you know where Shelly and Jacob are, and he's trying to wear you down until you give her up. It's time you put your foot down. Give him the message that you're not going to put up with it." He stared down at me with his intent stare. "Please, just do it."

Sighing deeply, I nodded my head. "Fine, I'll look into it."

Sensing my continued hesitation, Brandon's eyebrows came down over his eyes. "Cher. I'm worried about this, and I don't know what I'd do if I lost you to some sort of violence."

"I know, I know."

Though I meant what I said, Brandon's tension did not ease. There was a war of emotions flickering across his face, and when he spoke, his voice shook with emotion. "I love you too much to watch another man harm you, Cher. Please, listen to me."

"That's not funny, Brandon," I whispered over the lump in my throat.

He grimaced. "Funny? I didn't imagine that my declaration of love would be considered funny. Of course, you've ruined the plans of one of the happiest men alive."

"How so?"

"I had it all planned out," he continued as though I had not spoken. "I was going to wine and dine you all evening and then bring you home to bed. Then I was going to tell you the truth."

Tears sprang in my eyes. "And what would that be?"

"That I am madly and incredibly in love with you, Cherisse. I love you so desperately that I think about you all the time."

I gasped in surprise. Though previously hinted at, this time he spoke in earnest now.

"And," he continued. "I want you with me all the time. I want to see you when I get home from work every day, not just on weekends. I like it when you make me eat healthy food, and I like it when you curl into me on cold mornings. I've gotten used to having you around all the time, and I don't want Joe to ruin that."

"I know," I whispered, the tears falling freely. "Me, too."

He reached up to cup my cheek in his palm and smiled his angelic smile at me. "When your lease is up, Sunshine, I really want you to move in full time. This time for real."

I stared up at him, my eyes wide. As long as I had waited for him to say he loved me, never had I expected him to say so much, to bare his soul so completely. "I'm speechless," I whispered.

"Well, this isn't exactly how I wanted to tell you."

"Ah, you wanted control of the situation."

"I did," he said with a nod. "You ruined my plans. But hey, at least it's out in the open. You know my weakness, and now you can take full advantage of me."

"I don't want to do that. I want you to love me as much as I love you."

He chuckled, the sound deep and rhythmic. "Oh, Sunshine, you've absolutely no idea."

"You're right. You hide it so well."

"I do love you, more than you can imagine."

"I'm glad," I whispered, drawing his head to mine. His lips were moist and soft. "I'm so glad, Brandon."

"Well, please do something for me, okay?"

"Of course. What?"

"Call Mary. If you need me to give you her number again, I have it memorized. She can help you – or at the very least tell you what to do."

Knowing that Joe would remain a wedge between us as long as I took no action, I nodded my head. "I'll call, I promise. But before I go to court, I think I might call Joe myself and ask him to back off."

I could tell he was uncomfortable with the idea in the way he frowned. "I'm not so sure that's a good idea, Sunshine."

"Let me try first, okay? I'll record it if you want. I just need to see if there's a decent man left inside him somewhere."

"Fine, but I want to be there with you when you do it."

I nodded in agreement. I knew that together we could work this issue out. If anyone could send Joe packing, it would be Brandon. Of that I was positive. And I would do him the courtesy of calling Mary, too. She had helped Shelly so much, so I knew that I could only learn more if I finally contacted her.

****

The following morning, Brandon and I had off together, so we sat down in his kitchen and planned out our strategy. The first thing Brandon suggested was making the phone call from his house number. Since it was unlisted, there was no way Joe could call back and start the harassment again.

Brandon remained cool, and his matter-of-fact suggestions made sense. I sat silently and absorbed it all, nodding occasionally to confirm his thoughts. That he could handle the situation so much better than I could was a no-brainer in my opinion, but I still felt strongly that it was something I had to do. As close as Brandon and I had become, I wanted control over my life, especially when it came to Joe and his bullying. However, in another flash of brilliance, Brandon suggested leaving the television on in the background in order to block out any sounds of the recording that he was doing in the upstairs bedroom.

With the Today Show announcing the morning headlines, I reached for the handset with a deep, determined breath. Brandon disappeared, and I could hear his footfalls as he took the stairs two at a time. There was a soft click a few moments later when he picked up the handset, so I began to dial. The moment of truth had begun.

Joe answered on the third ring, sounding slightly disoriented and not happy in the least. The sound of his voice was like a nightmare to me, but I knew that Brandon was upstairs listening in. He was my support, and I took strength in that knowledge.

"What?"

I cleared my throat, glad that I had listened to Brandon's idea of calling him when he was most likely asleep. By keeping him off-guard, I was able to keep some control of the situation. I liked Brandon's thinking.

"Joe, this is Cherisse."

The sound of my voice seemed to perk Joe up a little. I heard some rustling and imagined him sitting up in bed. "Where's my son, Cher? Where's Shelly?"

"They're not here, Joe, and that's not why I'm calling." I was surprised to hear the force in my voice. For once, it did not quiver or hesitate when dealing with him. Oh, how things had changed. I despised Joe. I regarded him with so much fury that it was hard to concentrate.

"Sweetheart, I will find her with or without your help. She needs me and can't stay away forever."

"She's doing just fine without you, Joe. You should just let go," I said as calmly as I could.

It was immediately apparent that I had made a mistake. His voice changed in pitch, becoming unnaturally calm and all-knowing. "I think you're wrong, Cher. But time will tell." He chuckled then, the sound sending shivers of unease down my spine. "So, to what do I owe this honor anyway? Are you calling to apologize now?"

"No, I'm calling to tell you that if you continue to follow me, watch me, or call me, I will go to court and take out an order of protection against you." It came out in a rush, but I sighed in relief when I finished speaking.

"You wouldn't. I know you better than that, Cher. You've always

188

thought you could tackle the world by yourself. But you're wrong, honey, dead wrong."

I bit back an angry retort, remembering Brandon's warning that he would do whatever he could to unsettle me and gain control. "This is where you're wrong, Joe. I mean it. I don't like you harassing me or my friends, and you have no business following me around like some kind of stalker. If I see or hear from you again, I'll be in court."

He laughed aloud that time. "Ooh, you sound so tough, Cher... I'm shaking."

"Good."

"Not enough to stop me from what I'm after, though, baby. Nothing will stop me... You act so tough, but you're nothing but a weak woman under that fiery show. I remember how you shook when I saw you last. You were scared, Cher. I could smell it on you."

"Joe," I interrupted quickly. "Look, I'm sorry things didn't work out between you and Shelly, but you've got to move on. She's not planning on coming back. She's starting a new life. I got your message the other day – the one where you were crying and depressed. If that's truly how you feel, it's past time you found some help. I'm sorry, but I'm not one to help you. I don't have the training or the time."

"I didn't call you for help. You're nothing to me."

"I'm going to end the conversation now. Obviously you haven't heard a word I've said."

"Are you getting scared again, Cher? I can hear it in your voice. You're not so tough now, are you? Do you remember how easy it was for me to get you on the ground? I can do that anytime. You walk around in public without paying any attention. I suggest you start watching over your shoulder, kiddo. There are beasties who could grab you at any time." I squeezed my eyes shut and struggled to keep calm, remembering Brandon's words. "Tell me, does your boyfriend know you're calling me now? Should I call him and tell him? Do you think he'd approve of your attempts to piss me off?"

"Keep him out of it."

"Oh, but he's already in it. Did you know he started calling my house after you first met him? Did you know he was seeing Shelly on the side?"

Feeling my blood pressure rise, I struggled to keep my cool. However, my temper rose and I could not manage to keep it together even though I knew Brandon was listening, too. These were his attempts to unsettle me, I knew it, but it did not stop me from saying the first words that came into my head. "Yes, he did speak to Shelly. He's the one who convinced her to leave you, Joe. And you know what? I'm proud of him for doing what I couldn't. Of course, you beating on your baby didn't help your cause. And now who's the loser? She and Jacob are happy now, and you're still the fat drunk living in a rundown house, harassing other people to get your kicks. Your parents must be so proud."

With that final dig, I jabbed the end button on the phone and slammed it down on the counter. A few moments later, strong hands came to rest on my shoulders, and I leaned against Brandon's chest with a sigh.

"I guess that didn't work out quite like I hoped."

Brandon pulled me tight and wrapped his arms around my waist. "You did great until the end. I wouldn't quite have provoked him like that, but what's done is done. We'll see if he takes your warning to heart."

Yes, I thought. We'll see. But as a shiver of cold raced down my spine, I realized that I did not believe he would.

FOREVER SUNSHINE

Chapter 14

Over the next few weeks, Shelly and I stayed in touch a little more regularly than before. She restricted her phone calls to my mobile and usually called while I was on campus. Nearing the end of her counseling sessions with Jacob, she was preparing to begin the job hunt. I mailed her a bank check to help her go shopping for professional clothes, and Brandon shipped the presents that I had purchased for Jacob for Christmas. After her visit, I had brought them over to Brandon's, and they had remained in one of his spare bedrooms upstairs, all wrapped up and ready to go. As soon as we had a good address to send them, he shipped them via UPS.

Every time I spoke to Shelly, she sounded more confident, more in control of her life. Even when I told her about my morning conversation with Joe, she remained in control. I could not help but be proud of her. We planned to meet up for lunch as soon as she was able. The beauty of Arizona State's Tempe campus was that it was so large and crowded that she could easily mingle in without anyone's knowledge. Shelly could pass through just like any other ordinary person.

With my focus back on my classes, Brandon and I spent our

evenings together studying. As I expected, he was exceptionally bright and excelled in all of his classes. He was a good, hard worker who took his studies seriously and learned things quickly. He also revered his job and loved his position on the Tactical Unit. On a couple of occasions, I heard that he had had opportunities to move on but had passed them up because he loved what he was doing.

However, he spoke of what he would do when he finished his graduate degree, and every idea always included me. Though I did not relish the idea of watching him struggle through his thesis, I refused to voice aloud my discomfort because he had always been supportive of my dreams.

Of course, they were no longer my or his dreams. The dreams we had were fast becoming our dreams. Funny how things just sort of evolved with every passing day, I thought with growing happiness. Things were turning out okay. Shelly and Jacob were safe, and I would be graduating in little more than a year. I had my whole life ahead of me, and I was feeling more certain that Brandon would play a large role in it.

Though we began preparing for my moving in with him, he did not pressure me when I told him that I wanted to tell Arianne when I thought the time was right. I chose the time one evening when we were both home with no men around to influence our discussion. These days that was a rare occurrence, and I felt badly that our friendship had suffered for it.

Arianne had books and notes spread out across the coffee table. She sat cross-legged amid the pile, her face a mask of concentration. Plopping down beside her, I picked up a flow chart of a marketing design and glanced at her work so far

"How's it going?"

Thrusting a notebook away in frustration, she scowled at me.

"Gosh, I wish I could learn as quickly as you do, Cher. This really sucks."

"Can I help you?"

"No, I guess you can't." Raising her head, she caught me with her expressive eyes. "So, how are you, Cher? We haven't seen you all that much lately. You've been so busy with that cop hunk of yours. Did I tell you I saw Paul? He's called you a couple of times, and you haven't returned the calls."

I grimaced. "I keep thinking of him, but I haven't had much time. Between classes, work, Shelly and Brandon, I've been out of the loop."

"I know how you feel... How are Shelly and Jacob anyway?"

"They're doing great, Ari. I spoke to her a few days ago, and she's got a job. She's working in Phoenix now, and Jacob is starting preschool next week."

She sighed again. There were lines of worry on her face. I could tell she was stressed about her exam. But when she spoke, I realized it was not just her exam she was worried about. "Cher, things have been busy for me, too," she began. When I nodded, she continued. Her voice was soft. Gone was her normal sassy personality. In its place, there was a somber and thoughtful woman. It was a strange change. "Mike and I have been talking a lot lately... He's graduating in May, and I'll finish in December if I take classes this summer. My parents have agreed to help me pay for those classes so I can just get it done."

"That's great, Arianne. Soon you'll be off in the business world – taking it by storm and making a ton of money."

With a distracted nod, she continued. "Anyway, it's gotten serious... He's, uh, he's asked me to marry him."

With a whoop of joy, I reached down and hugged her. "That's

great! He's a wonderful guy!" Giving her a squeeze, I pulled away and smiled down at her. "Have you gotten a ring yet?"

"No, not yet," she said slowly. There was more on her mind; I could sense her hesitation. "I'm not sure if I'm ready yet."

"Well, Ari, I wanted to talk to you about this lease." When she nodded, I continued. "Brandon asked me to move in with him."

It was Arianne's turn to shout with surprise. "Really? Are you guys getting that serious?" When I nodded, she whistled under her breath. "Wow, you don't waste any time, do you?"

"I think he's the one," I said softly. I believed it with all of my heart, too.

Arianne batted her long eye-lashes at me. "Oh, sweetie, I *know* he's the one for you. When's the wedding?"

Chuckling softly, I shook my head. "Oh gosh, it hasn't gotten that far yet. He's hasn't even asked. It's only been a few months... Besides, that's not something I'd rush into."

"You've been rushing into everything where that man is concerned," Arianne mentioned. After a moment, I realized she was right. Things were happening between us that neither of us could stop. Maybe it was just the first year of bliss, but somehow I knew that it went much deeper. Our relationship was not about just sex. There were common interests, common dreams, and a definite compatibility that helped us get along so well. After all, we never even argued – with the exception of Thanksgiving evening. And even then, the making up had been so wonderful.

"Well, if you want to stay here, I'll help you find a new roommate before I go, that way you won't lose out on our rate."

She shook her head. "I think it's more likely that you've given my nerves a swift kick in the behind. It makes no sense to stay here while Mike is down the street, and I spend most of my time there anyway. I guess I'll move in with him and give us a trial... Well, it looks as though we both have our work cut out for us. Maybe we can get this place all cleared out by spring break."

Reaching for Arianne again, I gave her another hug. "You are a great friend, Ari, and I hope you and Mike are as happy as Brandon and I."

"I'm sure we are. Here's to eternal happiness!" She raised her glass of Diet Coke and took a long sip before passing it on to me. I took a sip too, closing my eyes and allowing the bubbles to pop inside my mouth before swallowing. The two of us were growing up. We had great guys and new lives to plan for. Our school days were just about finished, leaving us with our whole lives ahead. With our degrees just months away, I felt that there was a light at the end of the tunnel.

But I was so naïve at that time. I just had no idea how quickly it could be extinguished.

****

Instead of pulling extra hours in during spring break, Arianne and I began packing up our apartment. My parents had sent me a check for my birthday, and I applied that money to my last month's rent. Though Brandon had laughed when I offered, I had been able to convince him to split the cost of his monthly mortgage payment with me. Actually, it was my all-out refusal to move in unless I contributed that finally convinced him to allow me to pay my way. To my surprise, when we added it up, the cost was less than the rent I was paying on my apartment. The idea of saving a couple of hundred dollars a month was very appealing.

So all week we packed up the place, starting first with Arianne's stuff. Brandon had Sunday off and planned to bring his truck over and move a few pieces of my furniture and belongings out then. Although his house was sparsely furnished, we had decided to save up and decorate it with new pieces so I could give my stuff to Shelly and Jacob for their new place. I grew warm all over when I thought of the implications of that suggestion. Somehow the idea of shopping for furniture together made things that much more serious.

In the meantime, I helped Arianne box up her stuff and load it all into Mike's truck for the several trips back and forth that they made during the week. By Wednesday evening, we were exhausted but excited and eager to carve out new lives with the men that we loved.

After sending the pair off with Arianne's oversized cherry dresser perched precariously in the back of Mike's Tacoma, I went back inside and began picking up the scraps of paper and dust balls that had rolled under the heavy pieces of furniture.

I was reaching for the plug to the vacuum cleaner when the phone rang. It was Ari's alarm-clock ring and it grinded on my nerves every time I heard it. "Hello?"

"Cher?"

Though she was due to come out the end of the month, I certainly had not expected to hear my mother's voice on the line. She only called on birthdays and holidays. It was a surprise to hear her voice so out of the blue. "Mom? Is that you?"

"Yeah, Cher. I'm calling because there's been some trouble."

I could hear the panic in my mother's voice and sat down hard. "What happened? Is Dad..."

"No, Cher, it's not your father. It's Shelly."

I could feel the floor slip from under my feet and was thankful that I was sitting down. My voice shook when I spoke. "What happened?"

"Joe and Shelly ... Someone from the shelter called me."

"Where? Where is she?"

"She's in the hospital, Cher." I cursed aloud, causing my mother to gasp. "Now, Cher, they say they think she's going to be okay. I was hoping you could get up there and see how she's doing. We're at the airport now. We're getting on a flight down there."

"I'm on my way, Mom, where is she?"

"She's at Maricopa Medical, Cher. Go there, honey, and let me know how she's doing."

I hung up as quickly as I could and left the apartment. In my haste, I neglected to leave Ari and Mike a note, but I did send Brandon a text as I pulled onto the Route 101 entrance ramp. As I drove into Phoenix, my mind swirled with worry. It occurred to me about half way there that I had no idea where Jacob was and whether he was okay or not. I also had no idea what had happened.

All I knew was that my sister needed me.

I don't know exactly what it was that I expected, but what I found out once I was inside the hospital came as a complete shock. A uniformed officer directed me to the Emergency Room, where I was instructed to give what information I had about Shelly and Jacob and their medical history. It was then that I found out the seriousness of the situation.

There had been an automobile accident on the Loop 202 just before the Squaw Peak Parkway exit ramp. Speed was a factor, causing the vehicle to roll. The uniformed police officer that I had seen when I entered wanted to question me. What did I know of Joe? How was I related to the occupants in the vehicle?

Scanning the faces around me, I held out my hands and pleaded with them. "Wait a minute... Please, tell me what is going on? Where's Jacob?"

I learned then that both Shelly and Joe had been rushed up to surgery, and there was no word on her condition yet. Jacob was in a room in the pediatric floor for observation and had no apparent injuries. Luckily, he had been strapped in. He was the only one who had been wearing a seatbelt, and that, with the booster seat, had most likely saved his life.

I sat down in the nearest chair, too stunned to speak. Things were happening too fast. There was so much going on around me, and I had no idea where to go or what to do next.

I felt my world slip out from under my feet.

Placing my hand to my forehead, I closed my eyes and let it all sink in. Then I was on my feet again, frantically grabbing a hold of the nearest employee. "Where's Jacob? I need to see him."

The woman smiled and led me back to the seat I had just occupied. "Wait right here, hon, and I'll see where we can put you."

She strode off, leaving me alone once again. All around me was a flurry of activity. Nurses bustled back and forth, carrying medicines and charts. Phones were ringing nonstop. No one paid me any attention. They just passed by, barely giving me a glance.

My sister was in surgery with surgeons trying desperately to save her life, and I had never felt so hopeless before in my entire life. There was nothing I could do except wait and worry. The idea was horrible to me.

Fortunately, I was not waiting long when a middle-aged woman approached me. She was dressed smartly in a black pantsuit with her long brown hair pulled back in a French braid. With a sympathetic smile, she took a seat next to me, her eyes red from tears. "Cherisse Bridwell?"

"Yes."

She reached forward and patted my knee. "My name is Mary

Phillips. I run the shelter your sister was in."

So this was the famous Mary that Brandon and Shelly had spoken so highly of. Seeing her now, I could see why people were drawn to her. Her face was kind, but her eyes were alert and strong. They studied me carefully.

"I – I've heard so much about you," I said softly. "Thank you for helping my sister. She's changed so much."

"I'd like to take all the credit, but it's your sister who's made the changes. She's quite a survivor."

I swallowed a lump that had formed in my throat and merely nodded my head.

"How are you holding up?"

I raised my head and blinked several times. My voice was unsteady. "Were you there today? Do you know how he managed to get her and Jacob into the car?"

I was surprised at how shaky my voice was. It was a shocking realization to find that I was terrified. My body had broken out into a cold sweat, and I could feel a drop slide down my spine.

Mary's timid smile faded, and she reached forward again to pat my hand reassuringly. Her long red fingernails wrapped around my moist palm. I was only slightly reassured. "She had filed for divorce and sole custody of Jacob. When he was served the papers, I'm told he broke down. He went to court today with his lawyer to contest it, claiming that he had gotten some help for his drinking and was attending AA meetings every day. She was brave, Cherisse, and she faced him in front of the judge... He approached her after the hearing and told her that he'd just spoken to you and that you had recommended he get some professional help. He said that he had looked into it and was starting counseling this week. Though I told her she shouldn't do anything without her lawyer, he asked her to discuss custody of Jacob over lunch. I told her not to, but she smiled at me and said she could handle him."

"So he wasn't acting angry or unusual?"

Mary shook her head. "No, he was charming and calm, though I did observe him during the whole hearing – he was watching her whenever he could. I think that by seeing her, the changes in her, made him really realize what he had pushed away. To see Shelly so happy and satisfied, well..."

"Do you think he did it on purpose?" I grimaced. "I mean the car. Do you think he crashed the car on purpose?"

Mary shook her head. "I really don't think so. The only one they've been able to talk to was Jacob. He said they were just talking. The police have been investigating the scene, and there's talk about debris on the roadway that may have exacerbated the wreck."

Her voice drifted off as the tears spilled over my lashes. The bright lights above me burned my eyes. I wiped at my tears with the back of my hand, and Mary reached over and handed me a tissue from the package in her pocket. Smiling my thanks, I wiped at my eyes and then blew my nose.

I hated the smell of hospitals. All that disinfectant and cleaning products made my stomach turn. I knew every time I smelled their baby wash I would remember this time in my life and cringe.

I was lonely, and I wanted Brandon. His calm strength would help. When would he be done with his shift? I wanted him here.

The minutes ticked by slowly as I waited. The employee that had promised to get back to me had vanished. One by one, people moved on. Soon the hallway sported only a few people, but Mary remained with me, sitting quietly and sipping on a cup of coffee. I refused anything. The nurse who had brought it over later steered us into a smaller, more private room with softer chairs and magazines to read, but nothing appealed to me. I could not even think about food. Instead, I continued to stare at the doorway, willing someone to come in with the answers that I sought.

The minutes ticked by slowly while I wondered where my parents were. I had spoken to my mother as they were boarding an airplane. Had it been hours yet, or just minutes? I couldn't tell. Nothing had changed in the hospital. The lights were still the same, the nurses looked alike, and the smell in the hallway still turned my stomach. I had not heard if Shelly was okay or not or whether I could see Jacob yet.

Mary Phillips was thumbing through a magazine distractedly, her intermittent sighs driving me to distraction. I wanted to speak with her, to learn more about her work, but I was unable to find a voice to put the words together.

But then a new voice reached my ears, sending all my good thoughts out the window. "Miss Bridwell?"

My head snapped up to see a tired looking man dressed in scrubs. I scrutinized his weary eyes, searching for any news. There was none forthcoming from the look on his face.

The waiting was over, and now I suddenly did not want to hear the news. A knot of fear formed in my belly, stealing my air and my ability to speak.

Mary closed the magazine with a startled flutter. She did not give it a glance as it fell to the floor. She was on her feet in an instant, her fingers knotted tightly together.

The surgeon's gaze swung to her, his eyebrows lifted questioningly. "Are you Cherisse Bridwell?"

"No, I'm Mary Phillips. That's Cherisse," she said quickly, nodding in my direction.

I nodded slowly, feeling disconnected from the scene. The doctor advanced into the small room, removing his glasses as he did so. I shrank away as he came to stand in front of me and cringed when he sank down onto his haunches.

"Are you here alone?" he asked softly.

Mary stepped forward and placed her hand on my shoulder. "I can stay with her, Dr...?"

"Doctor Anthony McGovern, I'm the attending neurosurgeon on call today."

Neurosurgeon? What had happened?

"How are they?" I asked slowly, steeling myself for the worst.

His face was grim. "I regret to inform you that your brother-in-law, Joe, was unable to make it through the surgery. He was pronounced deceased at 6:42 p.m."

Chapter 15

I heard Mary gasp behind me, but my immediate concern was for Shelly and Jacob. Ignoring the tears that streamed down my face, I spoke softly.

"How's my sister?"

"We were able to repair the fracture to her leg with no problem. That should heal without incident."

When I sighed in relief, he continued on to shatter my hopes.

"But your sister has also sustained a small skull fracture from the car accident. This brought on a very serious condition called an epidural hematoma – or a blood clot. We had to operate quickly to control the bleeding and prevent further damage. She's survived the surgery, but she'll have to remain in the intensive care unit until we can get the cranial pressure to decrease. The next forty-eight hours are crucial."

Though I heard Mary moan, my gaze remained focused on the doctor's eyes. His gaze never wavered as he began speaking, though I heard only bits and pieces through the pounding in my head. "Fracture," he said, "brain trauma."

I could not breathe; the weight in my chest was so overwhelming.

I heard him speak, though I did not feel as though I was in my own body. He continued talking, tossing out phrases that meant so little to me "lucky to be alive," and "unknown prognosis," and "next forty-eight hours crucial." All I had wanted to hear was that she would be okay and walking out with Jacob tomorrow.

I heard it all, but could do nothing but grip the arms of the chair tightly. My sister, the one I had tried to help, could die like her husband.

"When can we see her? And Jacob, too?" Mary asked for me.

I sent a silent thank you to the strong woman at my side. She had remained so calm during the surgeon's explanation, despite the obvious shock and sadness she felt as well.

"She's in recovery now. It could be some time yet. Jacob's in the pediatric ward. You can go up there and check with them."

I bit my lip until it bled as the words sunk in. Joe had died. What on earth had happened in that car? What had Jacob seen or heard?

I was vaguely aware of the doctor excusing himself from Mary's continued questions. I did not care; there was nothing he could tell me that I would understand anyway. His earlier words said it all.

"I'm so sorry, Cherisse," Mary said placing her arm around my shoulders.

"Me, too," I whispered.

"What can I do for you?"

"My parents," I murmured.

"They're on their way?"

"They don't know anything yet."

"Of course, I'll go wait for them."

With a flurry of importance, Mary slipped from the room and closed the door behind her. I was now alone.

I stared down at the floor, my grief rising. I had no idea whether

I would be able to tell Shelly that I hoped she continued to find her happiness. Also, that I was so proud to see her change before my eyes – grow into a strong and self-confident woman. Would I have that chance?

Regretting the departure of Mary, I began to feel alone and lonely. There was nothing in the solemn room to hold my attention, and my thoughts ran the gamut of planning funerals to the inevitable arrival of my parents. What would I say to them? How would they handle this latest trauma?

I was staring at a coffee stain left on Mary's vacant chair when I became aware of a hustling in the hallway. Perhaps a new trauma was arriving. After all, outside the closed door was a bustling, very busy, hospital. People came and went, and loudspeakers echoed pages incessantly.

The pounding grew louder, coming to a sudden halt outside the door. I was slow to raise my head when I heard the soft click of the door as it unlatched, assuming it was Mary returning. Instead, I found my shining angel standing just inside the doorway, his face red with exertion. Dressed in his heroic uniform, Brandon had never looked so welcome to me.

His face, usually so impassive, was creased with worry lines, and pain shone in his blue-green eyes. I saw his chest rising and falling rapidly, explaining his exertion. It seemed as though he had run the whole way in. Oddly, I found the gesture touching.

"I was tied up at a wreck on Broadway," he said softly, his voice breathless. "The car was leaking like crazy, and the road was slippery. I had to wait until it was cleaned up."

I came to my feet, an understanding smile plastered on my quivering lips. I trembled at the sight of him. In fact, my whole body was shaking. His arms opened wide, and I took another step towards him. Never had he looked so perfect.

"Joe," I whispered, unable to finish the sentence.

I drew my free hand across my forehead and then pressed it into my eyes to stop the building tears. I had to stay in control. This was not the time or the place to lose it.

"I know," he whispered.

I removed my hand from my eyes when his fingers encircled my wrist and pulled me towards him. Wrapping his arms around me tightly, he sighed heavily and pressed small kisses on the top of my head. My face pressed into his chest, and I could hear the thundering of his heart through his vest. He smelled of gasoline and sweat, so alive and solid. Again I was reminded that Shelly was in an intensive care unit, struggling for life, and a small bitter laugh escaped my lips.

"Don't do this," I protested. "Not here. Not now."

"I'm so sorry, Cherisse."

I tried to pull away, but Brandon did not budge. One hand came up to push my wayward hair away from my brow. His fingertips were soft and gentle, a caress that smoothed away my frown lines. His tenderness was killing my resolve.

"Please, Brandon, I don't want to lose it."

My voice shook and again my vision blurred. Even so, I could still see the half-smile on his lips just before they brushed against my forehead. "It's okay, Sunshine, I'm here. I'll take care of you, just let it go."

"I can't. Not here."

"Yes, you can. It's okay to let your guard down every now and then, Sunshine. I'm here."

I could feel the sob rise in my throat and tried to swallow it back. It emerged nonetheless as I reached for his uniform shirt. My fingers grasped the smooth material and bunched it into my fists. Another sob escaped when he began to rub my back, his fingers splayed wide.

"What did I do wrong?" I sobbed, my voice muffled by his shirt.

"Oh God," he breathed. "Nothing, Cherisse, you did nothing wrong."

His hands tightened around me, reminding me of his strength. He had more raw power within his muscles than Joe ever had, and yet he was always in control of it. What had made him and Joe so different?

"I should've been there. I might've been able to prevent it."

"You could never know how happy I am that you weren't there, Sunshine. Call me selfish if you want, but I can't think of what I'd do if you were in that car."

"Right now I wish I had been. Maybe I could've stopped this from happening."

Brandon's hands surrounded my upper arms, and he pulled me away from his chest. He was frowning down at me when I finally raised my face. "You can't save the world, Cherisse, no matter how badly you want to. Try to be realistic here. What could you have done? It was an accident. Things like that happen every day. Your presence would've just placed you in a hospital bed – or worse."

He pulled me close again, and I could feel the shudder run through him. When he spoke again, his voice was low and thick with emotion. "You're so tough that sometimes you don't even realize that you have limits, too. I know you're hurting, and the best thing you can do is let it out."

"I can't," I said brokenly, my lips trembling.

His lips compressed stubbornly. Leaning back to stare into my eyes, he reached up and wiped away a tear before it slipped over my cheekbone. The warmth of his hand soon spread over my whole cheek as he cupped it in his palm, and his other hand followed to my other cheek gently.

With eyes glowing with emotion, Brandon tilted my face up to his. "I love you, Cherisse," he whispered, his voice shaking with emotion. "I'll help you get through this, I promise."

His lips brushed mine, lightly and quickly. More tears spilled through my lashes, and I could taste their saltiness on our lips. When he again raised his head, he strode to my vacated chair and sat down, setting me atop his lap. "Now cry," he ordered brusquely. "I'll be here, and we'll do this together."

Curling up against him like a cat, I nodded my head slowly. My arms went around his neck, and I rested my head on his shoulder as I sobbed out all my pain and guilt. I was so thankful that I had Brandon. His soft touch and gentle words soothed my aching heart.

It seemed like an eternity before I quieted down. Brandon never flinched, or indicated that he was the slightest bit uncomfortable with my weight. He continued to hold me on his lap, his fingers combing through my hair and stroking my back until at last I settled down. What seemed like an eternity passed this way, and I was near sleep when the door opened once more and the sound of my father's tear choked voice reached my ears.

"Cher?"

I raised my head and came off Brandon's lap with a startled lunge. He came to his feet also, his hand remaining around my arm to steady me. I went forward to embrace my parents, my tears starting anew.

"Shelly's hurt badly," I whispered, hugging them both around their necks.

My mother sniffled and reached into her bag for a tissue. "Ms. Phillips told us," she answered, her voice breaking.

"Joe didn't make it." My father's voice quivered slightly, and I pulled back to look into his dark blue eyes. Tears had formed there, though none had yet escaped. He looked so old with bags under those magnificent eyes and his shoulders hunched with pain. I could feel my heart go out to them both, for they could possibly lose a child.

"Jacob's going to be fine."

He looked away, giving me a view of his handsome profile. Again I saw age there, in the sagging of the tissue around his once strong neck and the gray in his once beautiful hair. I watched him swallow several times and understood that he was biting back his emotion. Just like me, I thought.

I turned to my mother and knew she would be the weak one in this matter. Never one to be overly strong, Dolly Bridwell followed her husband in all matters. In this, too, she would do exactly what he said.

I wiped my eyes on my sleeve, ignoring the tissue in her outstretched hand. "Mom, we have to see Jacob."

She nodded wordlessly, her eyes travelling past me to Brandon. He had remained silent during our exchange, standing behind me with his hands clasped before him. I turned around and flushed guiltily. "I'm sorry... Mom and Dad, this is Brandon Nicholson, my boyfriend. Brandon, this is Dolly and John Bridwell, my parents."

Neither could hide their surprise, and Brandon was quick to notice. He shot me a curious glance, one brow raised in question, but I looked away. He had known we did not have a great relationship, totally unlike his with his parents.

"Hello, Brandon," my mother said. She politely held out her hand in greeting and offered him a tentative smile.

Brandon accepted it with a smile of his own. "I'm very sorry about Shelly, Mrs. Bridwell."

"Were you there?" my father asked gruffly.

"No, sir, I'm not a Phoenix officer."

My father nodded his head and held out his hand. "John Bridwell, Brandon, nice to meet you, although I wish it was under different circumstances."

"Likewise."

I reached for Brandon then, wrapping my arms around his bicep. He responded by covering one of my hands with his. "We need to find Jacob's room. Will you come with me?"

My parents exchanged glances before shaking their heads. "Shelly's in recovery right now. They'll let us know when she moves into the ICU. We should stay here and wait for news, and I think Jacob would feel more comfortable with you anyway. Why don't you head up, and we'll call you when we hear news."

Though I knew they made perfect sense, I wanted them to come with me. I wanted them to see Jacob.

"Come on, Sunshine, I'll go with you," he said softly.

"Thank you," my father offered.

Brandon nodded and then took my hand. With a parting nod, I allowed him to lead me away. Things were happening too fast. But one thing was for certain, I had to keep it together for Jacob, no matter what happened.

****

Jacob was sleeping soundly when I finally made it into his room. While Brandon spoke to the nurse's station in the hallway, I entered Jacob's room afraid of what I might find. Though the blinds were drawn, I could still see a glimmer of the early-evening sun setting in to the west. It cast a shadow on Jacob's peaceful face, which I studied in silence, my eyes drinking in the sight of the small boy sleeping soundly in the large bed. Remarkably, he seemed to have no injuries whatsoever, and I wondered how differently things might have turned out had they all been wearing their seatbelts. A simple click could have saved them.

I heard Brandon behind me, and I leaned toward him when he reached for my hand. His kept his voice low. "They told me that Jacob will be discharged to you in the morning. Are you going to stay here tonight?"

"I think I should," I whispered. "What if he wakes up during the night?"

He nodded. "I'll run home and pick up some things for you, and then I'll be back, okay?"

Staring into his eyes, I could see the exhaustion of having worked extra shifts all week. That, coupled with the strain of facing everything that had happened this afternoon, made Brandon appear worn out. Concern made me frown. "You look awful, Brandon. You should just go home and get some sleep."

"No. I'll come back. I can stay here with you until my next shift starts."

Knowing that he would continue to refuse, I shook my head and said the first thing that came into my head that might make him go get some sleep. "No, I don't want you here tonight. I'd rather be alone. I need some time."

No sooner had I spoken than I realized how hurtful my words were. His brows drew together as he frowned, but he did not argue. "Fine, then. Will you call me with updates?"

"Of course," I said quickly. I reached out and hugged him tight, my arms linked tightly around his neck. "You won't be much help to me if you don't get any sleep."

"I'll see if I can swap a shift. I can take some time off to be with you."

Stepping up on tiptoes, I kissed him lightly. "One thing at a time for now, okay?"

He nodded reluctantly and took a step back. "Are you sure you don't need anything?"

"It's only one night. I'll be fine."

The look he sent my way told me in no uncertain terms that he did not believe me, but he still did not argue. With a parting wave, he strode to the door and pulled it open, and I watched him go before sinking down in the chair next to the bed. The vinyl covered chair reclined, so I spread out and lay in the semi-darkness, watching Jacob sleep and waiting for news from my parents.

The hours passed slowly, and as I lay awake, I realized how cold I was in pushing Brandon away. The way I had handled his offer to stay was curt and unfair. I knew I had hurt his feelings by telling him I wanted to be alone, but I had thought and spoken quickly without thinking. I reached for my phone and considered sending him a quick text, but opted not to when I glanced at the clock. Most likely he had gone straight to bed, and it would only make matters worse if I woke him and began his worrying.

Unable to sleep and feeling stiff from the awkward chair, I shifted once more and sighed. The thin sheet that covered me had bunched up around my neck, leaving me uncomfortably warm. The activity in the hallway had calmed down once visiting hours ended, and all I could hear was the occasional laughter shared by the nurses at the station down the hall. One had visited earlier and offered me a heavier blanket, but I had sent her off with a lie that I was fine.

My father had come upstairs little more than an hour before to tell me that Shelly was in a room now and doing as expected. They had found a hotel on 44th and McDowell to spend the night, a mere ten minutes away. After giving me a warm hug and a box of tissues, he said his goodnights and promised to call in the morning. Alone then, I allowed myself a few moments of self-pity. I had gone from the highs of extreme happiness to the lows of dealing with trauma and death all in the space of a day. Though I knew nothing had been set yet, as I finally drifted into fitful sleep I wondered what life would throw at me next and whether I would have the courage to face it.

Chapter 16

After spending a night of sporadic sleep at best, I woke with a splitting headache and stiff as a board. Jacob had awoken early, waking me with his fearful calling, but when he saw me approach the bed, he had calmed down enough to ask when we could go home. I was able to convince him to wait until after breakfast, giving me time to hurry downstairs and meet my parents outside the unit where Shelly's bed was.

Earlier that morning, Shelly had appeared awake for a few moments. Her eyes had opened, but she stared off into space, seeming like she was a million miles away. No one was able to get a response before her eyes closed again. My parents had warned me that even though they caught the hematoma quickly, Shelly would not recover immediately. Since she had not regained full consciousness, she remained intubated and the doctors had no plans to remove some of the tubes until they were more confident that she could breathe on her own.

Through all of this, no one knew yet if Shelly would regain full mental abilities when – and if – they got her under control. The first few days were the most critical, they had told us, and I just hoped she would come back soon.

Having never visited an ICU before, I was shocked at the wires and tubes attached to my sister. They had tied her hands down to the bed, and her head was wrapped in white bandages. The things you see on the television never prepare you for the truth. Even though she appeared to be sleeping through all the wires and tubes, I could not help but wonder how badly she was hurting inside.

It was hard to be in that room, looking at my sister through a maze of medical equipment. Calling myself a coward, I spoke quickly to Shelly. Leaning in close to her ear, I spoke softly, telling her that I would take care of Jacob for as long as she needed me to. I also told her to fight on, that she had come so far already, and not to give up. By the time I pulled away, tears were once again rolling down my face.

Feeling the urge to escape, I hurried from the room and down the hallway, back to the double doors that sealed off the ICU. My parents were still hovering outside, waiting for me, and my father offered me a cup of hot coffee which I took gratefully.

"Thanks, Dad."

My mother leaned forward and gave me a tight hug. "Did she respond to you at all?"

Shaking my head, I stared down at the Styrofoam cup. "She didn't even twitch."

"We have to give her time," my father said softly. His hand came down on my shoulder and gave me a light squeeze. "You've held up really well, Cher. I'm so proud of you, little girl."

Ignoring the compliment, I nodded towards the elevators. "I have to get Jacob out of here before he tries for the door without me. I'm going back to my place to shower and get him cleaned up. Maybe I'll hit a store and pick up some stuff for him until we can gather his things at Shelly's. I'll have my mobile with me if anything changes before I get back here."

"Oh, honey, but you've barely gotten any sleep," my mother said.

"There's no rest for the weary, I guess."

"Too true," my father said gruffly. He put his arm around my mother's shoulders and tucked her up against his side. "Come on, Dolly, it is past eight. We should head back in, and Cher should get going."

****

Jacob really was unharmed, with the exception of a slight bruising from the seatbelt. I noticed this as soon as he was released from the wheelchair that gave him a ride out the doors. No sooner had he been given the okay to get up than he was running for my Kia. Since he was feeling so well I decided to take him clothes shopping. While not the most enthusiastic of shoppers, he did well enough, so we made another stop to find him necessities like a toothbrush, toothpaste, and enough groceries to feed a finicky five-year-old for a week. Though we drove past Brandon's exit on the highway, I did not bring him there.

Despite the fact that I knew I was not being fair, that I was deliberately pushing him away and most likely hurting the man I cared most for, I still ignored the twinge of guilt and headed for my apartment. After all, Brandon and I had not spoken about bringing Jacob home there, and I felt insecure enough at the moment to not take his agreement for granted. Instead I drove up McClintock, making a stop at Blockbuster to pick up some movies, and unloaded the stuff at my nearly empty apartment.

During a quick phone call to the hospital, I was informed by my father that the doctors thought it best that Jacob not see Shelly until she was more alert. After seeing her that morning I was in full agreement, but I felt useless just staying home. The apartment had been cleared of the rest of Arianne's belongings leaving only my sofa, and the items in the bedroom. It echoed with our voices, and Jacob did not like the changes. The idea of sitting there the entire day appealed to neither of us.

With wary eyes, he scanned the apartment from the doorway before he took a few cautious steps inside. However, by the time I had showered and he had enjoyed a hot bubble bath, the invitation of climbing under my duvet in front of my 21" television with a large bowl of popcorn and a few animated movies was sufficient enough to settle him down.

That was how Brandon found us when he arrived late in the afternoon.

We were midway through *Despicable Me* when a firm knock roused us from our sleepy stupor. Jacob sat up quickly, but I patted his hand and told him to stay put. "I'll be right back."

When I pulled open the door, I could not deny the rush of happiness I felt. Brandon stood leaning against the door jam with a bouquet of red and pink roses in his hand. Knowing that I had been abrupt the night before, I eased the door open with a hesitant smile.

He looked as tired as I felt, and my smile went unanswered. "Here you are," he said softly.

"Yeah, they didn't want me to bring Jacob to Shelly. We're watching movies," I said stupidly, indicating behind me with a thumb over my shoulder. "What are you doing here?"

"Picking you up."

"Picking me up? What's going on?"

He stepped deeper into the apartment and closed the door

behind him before placing the roses down on the sofa. "This place is empty," he commented as he wandered deeper into the apartment.

"Arianne must've finished up last night."

"Why are you here?"

"Where else should I be?"

He glanced over his shoulder at me, one eyebrow raised. "You serious?" Before I could answer, Brandon was in front of me and taking hold of my face in his hands. "I'm not going to let you push me away, Cherisse."

Though I wanted to protest, I knew that I could not. So much had happened in the last twenty-four hours that I knew I was not behaving in the most rational way. "I'm not trying to push you away, Brandon. I'm just so scared, that's all. I've been thinking and I just – well, things have been crazy and I didn't know where you stood..."

"Let's go home now and talk about it like adults. I made up the spare bed for Jacob, and I was able to swap out of work. Come home and stop thinking."

Nodding slowly, I wrapped my arms around his waist and snuggled up close. "I love you, Brandon."

****

The house was dark when Brandon pulled into the garage. Gathering up the new stuff we had bought in one hand, I reached for Jacob with the other. We had barely gotten out of the car before he sidled up to my side and gripped me tight.

Seeing his weariness, Brandon backed up a step. "Why don't you show him around and get him into bed? I'll meet you down here when you're done."

Giving Jacob's hand a little tug, I smiled down at him. "Do you want to look around again? This is a really big house, and it has stairs, too. Do you remember?"

Jacob nodded, though I could see the exhaustion in his lackluster eyes. After an afternoon of lounging in bed, he looked as bone weary as I felt. With a quick glance of thanks to Brandon, I wandered off. Allowing Jacob to lead the way, we headed for the stairs. He scrambled up them, thoroughly enjoying the physical challenge, and waited at the top for me to join him.

"Your room's right here," I said, pointing to the doorway directly in front of him. "That room is Brandon's." I pointed over to the master suite. The doors were open and inviting, and Jacob nodded slowly.

"Where will you be?"

I almost said 'hopefully', but I caught myself in time. "I'll be in the big bedroom, too."

Again he nodded.

Hefting his bag onto my shoulder, I reached for his hand and brought him down the hall to the bathroom. "This is your bathroom, Jake."

Luckily, there were towels in place, and the bar of soap I had put on the tray the week before was still there. I waited as Jacob went to the bathroom and washed up. Then I unpacked his belongings and lined them up on the marble counter next to the sink. The stark white walls now had a lived in feeling. For however long it lasted, I considered it a definite improvement.

Moving into the bedroom, I flicked on the light to find that Brandon had indeed made up the spare bed. A pale blue comforter covered the queen-sized bed and white sheets lined the mattress. As Jacob changed into his nightclothes, I set about plugging in the nightlight and searching through his bag for a book to read before bed. I could hear Brandon on the stairs and wondered if he was coming in to say goodnight. When he did not appear, I settled into bed next to Jacob and began reading. Soon after, I heard the sound of a shower running.

By page twenty he had fallen fast asleep, and I admired his ability to relax so quickly, a skill I wished I shared. For a few moments, I lay beside him, watching him sleep and studying his face. He had seen so much, and yet his face still bore the markings of a young child. It was his eyes that demonstrated his wisdom. The wariness and mistrust aged him beyond his years. He needed stability, and it appeared that he would have to find it with me. That meant that I would have to find it first myself.

The scent of cinnamon caught my attention as soon as I opened his bedroom door. It was the smell of candles, and my eyes widened when I saw the small, glass-enshrouded tea lights placed strategically along the stairs. Stepping by them carefully, I blew them out on the way down.

The flaming trail led around the corner to the kitchen, and when I entered Brandon was just setting a bottle of wine on the table. His hair was damp from his shower, and he had dressed in black slacks and a cream-colored dress shirt. Pausing in the doorway, I stared at him and wondered why he had dressed so nice. "What's going on?"

"There you are," he said.

In his hand, he held two wine glasses by their stem. I stared at the table in surprise. He had set out two places on his finest plates, with place mats and more candles. "A candlelit dinner?"

He gave me a sheepish grin. "Once again, I have you to thank for ruining my plans."

I pursed my lips and stared down at my place mat. My fingers trailed along the kitchen table, feeling the smoothness of the glass under my fingertips. I was growing more nervous by the minute. What was on his mind? "Plans?"

"Well, yeah. I had expected to do this at a more convenient time."

"Do what, exactly?"

"How about we eat first, and then we'll talk. Are you hungry?" His eyebrows lifted questioningly.

I shook my head. "Not really."

He looked disappointed. "I see. I have a steak out on the grill and was hoping to have a nice dinner. Will you at least have a glass of wine?"

"Why in here? Why not in the dining room?"

"I wanted to be close to you."

My breath caught. Across the kitchen our gazes met, and he came forward quickly to pull out a chair for me to sit. As soon as I did, he took his place across from me and busied himself with the wine bottle. Once the cork popped, he returned his attention to me. "Why didn't you come over today?"

"I assumed you'd be working. I didn't want to bother you."

"Bother me? What bothers me is that you pushed me away last night. You don't have to face this alone, you know. Your sister's hurt, you are taking care of her son – yes, I understand that you're a little stressed out. But Cherisse, I'm here, and I want to help you get through this. You don't always have to be so damned independent."

Unable to view the wounded look in his eyes, I turned my gaze to the patio doors. Smoke from the grill was rising outside, casting gray shadows in the darkness. "I'm sorry I hurt you. I knew I did as soon as I said it, but I didn't mean to. You're so special to me."

"I love you, Cherisse," he said softly. "I'm still here for you. Like I said yesterday, together we can tackle things, for better or worse."

Almost instantaneously my eyes filled with tears. I stared down at my plate sightlessly, feeling my fears ebb away slightly. "I'm sorry, Brandon. You're right. You deserved better than that."

"I'm sorry, too. I shouldn't have let you push me out the door so that I could sleep. You know, it did no good. I barely got any last night. I should've just stayed with you." He spoke quickly, the words tumbling out. "You mean the world to me, you know? You'll never know how much I love you..."

"I know."

"Then why are you trying to push me away?"

I pulled free from his grasp and put my head in my hands. "I don't know. I'm so confused. Things are happening so fast... Things changed so fast. I'm suddenly responsible for a five-year-old child, and I'm not prepared for that. My schedule's full already. I might have to drop my classes to take care of him."

A single tear ran slowly down my face. I watched it land on the side of the plate Brandon had laid out and wiped at it absently. He was silent, but when he saw the tear he rose from his seat and crouched beside me. "Why do you need to quit this semester? Why do you need to stop your entire life? Why has Jacob's presence changed things?"

"Everything's changed."

"You keep saying that, but I don't see how."

"It just has."

He sighed. "I don't know what exactly led me to you, but I do know that we have something special."

I nodded. "It's all you. You're special."

"It's us." He corrected. "I knew it right from the start, and I've done everything I could to make sure I didn't mess it up. I don't want to lose this chance to be with you. You make me so happy... I don't want to be without you."

"But I..." My voice trailed off, leaving him to stare at me hard.

"No buts, Sunshine. I want to be with you. Having Jacob won't change things too much. You work too much anyway. If you cut back on your hours, he'll have a mother figure around until Shelly gets well. It'll be good for him."

"What about school?"

"I can keep taking classes, just like you can. We can work out a schedule with Jacob. You've come too far to consider dropping back. I'm almost done, and my workload isn't as full. I'll take a couple of morning classes while Jacob's in school."

"No," I said, shaking my head. "That's not fair to you. You're talking about supporting me and my nephew. I can't take advantage of you like that."

"How would that be taking advantage of me? Wouldn't it be my responsibility to take care of my wife and her family?"

My eyes went wide. No matter what I had expected this evening to bring, it certainly was not a proposal. "Your what?"

Mesmerized, I watched as he reached for the bouquet of flowers in the center of the table. It was the same bouquet he had carried into my apartment. On the top of the mass of pink and red roses was an envelope.

"These were for you, but you didn't seem too interested earlier, so I set them up down here." He handed me the vase, and I reached for the bouquet with a trembling hand. It was a small card, addressed to me in Brandon's neat block-style writing.

Sticking my index finger under the sealed flap, I began to pry it open. "I'm so dreadful," I said softly. "Thank you for the flowers. They really are beautiful."

"Open it, Cherisse."

I took a deep breath and held it. The last of the envelope opened

224

with a slight tear, and I pulled the card out before I lost my nerve. All of the air in my lungs came out in a rush as it emerged, and my squeak of disbelief echoed in the silence around us.

Attached to the card was a ring, an engagement ring, and just two words were scrawled upon the blank note card. "Marry me."

The rushing in my ears grew louder as I studied the ring. It was a beautiful channel-set round solitaire, with three sidestones on either side set in a thick platinum band. I placed the heavy ring on the table and took a shuddering breath.

When I raised my head, Brandon was smiling at me. "Will you?"

I shook my head. "We can't get married. We barely know each other. It's only been – what? Eight months?"

"I won't accept no for an answer," he warned. "Besides, we don't have to get married tomorrow. We have a lot on our plates right now. We'll just have to stick one foot out in front of the other and take things as they come. You should know by now that things always have a way of working themselves out. We can marry once everything settles down. It'll work, Cherisse, you and I both know that. Trust me?"

The way he said it brought me back to our argument on Thanksgiving evening. It was the one thing that Brandon asked for from me – trust. With Brandon there by my side, I knew I could attain any goal.

I swallowed hard, knowing in my heart that I should say no, but unable to speak the words. I wanted to – boy, did I want to so desperately. Still there was the selfish part of me that took control and told me to nod my head. With a whoop of triumph, he pulled me to my feet and held me close. "I don't know what I did to deserve you, Brandon, but I love you so much," I whispered against his lips. "Of course I will."

"You are my Sunshine, Cherisse, and I love you." Raising his head, one hand released me as he reached for the ring on the table. He pulled it from the card and held it out to me. "I'd like to put this on you."

I held out my hand to him, noticing that my fingers quivered. As I watched, he pressed the ring against his lips and then held it out. It hovered between our hands for a moment, and we both stared at it with wonder. We would be sealed forever, I thought. A small smile curled my lips, and Brandon closed the distance and slipped the ring on my finger. It was heavy yet secure, and I now officially belonged to Brandon Nicholson.

Once in place, he raised my hand and placed a warm kiss on the ring again. I trembled at the feel of his soft lips teasing my skin and reached up to cup his cheek. "You're so special," I said brokenly. "And you are far too good for me."

When he smiled at me, the tears spilled over my lashes. "Why are you crying again?"

"I'm so happy that I've still got you, even though I know I'm not being fair."

"Cherisse, you are making me the happiest man alive by marrying me. How can that be wrong?"

"I have a lot of baggage now."

"It's mine, too."

"It doesn't have to be."

"I'd rather have you and your baggage than live without you, Cherisse."

"You may regret this, you know."

Brandon threw back his head and laughed. "You're so wrong. I have no regrets when I'm with you."

Before I could answer, his hand slipped around my back and

scooped my legs out from under me. He lifted me high, and I was suddenly cradled against his chest. Squealing in surprise, my hands locked around his neck. "What are you doing?"

"It's late. Neither one of us has slept much in the last couple of days, so I'm putting you to bed.

"What about the steak?"

"Damn," he muttered, putting me back down. "Let me just shut off the grill."

For the first time in the last twenty-four hours, I giggled, and the sound brought a smile to his face. He stepped outside briefly, returning with his lovely steak on a platter. The purposeful look he sent in my direction as he wrapped it up spoke volumes. Once again, I had ruined his plans. Yep, Brandon might still regret his decisions, for I was always wrecking his best laid plans.

Chapter 17

A new cluster of flowers rested on the table next to the balloons and bouquets that filled up Shelly's room. Now that she was out of the ICU, she was able to receive both, and the women from the shelter had pitched in what little money they had to buy her the biggest bouquet of get-well flowers that they could. Those, coupled with some from me and Jacob, Brandon, and my parents, made Shelly's room appear more like a florist's shop than a hospital room.

I shook my head as I entered the room, realizing that yet another bouquet had arrived. This one was from her new job at a bank in Phoenix. It was just as large as the one Brandon had sent. Brandon's was still the best, though, because his had a giant stuffed Teddy bear with the lovely arrangement that Jacob could not wait to get his hands on.

In addition to the flowers, someone had found a small spot on Shelly's leg to sign their name. Apparently she had some visitors.

Eight days had passed since Shelly woke up. Jacob was still living with me, and accompanying me everywhere I went. Despite some initial soreness, Jacob had been remarkably unharmed in the accident, and the only one in the vehicle to escape injury. He had confirmed to me what he had told the police officers – that his mommy and daddy had been talking when they suddenly went off the road, and as of yesterday, no one had told Shelly that Joe had passed away.

She was dozing when I shut the door a crack behind Jacob, and I signaled to him to be quiet. My mother came to her feet immediately and hurried over to Jacob, and my eyes squinted as I took in her bright pink slacks and turquoise blue top. She reminded me of a peacock with her colors. Still, I managed to smile in greeting.

"Hi, honey," she whispered loudly.

"Hi, Grandma," he answered softly.

Making our way to the bedside, we pulled out our usual chairs and waited for Shelly to become aware of our presence. Within moments, her eyelids began to flutter.

"Why don't you and I go and find something to eat in the cafeteria. I don't know if Aunty Cher has been feeding you, but I haven't had anything to eat all afternoon."

I continued to listen to my mother chatter away as she led Jacob from the room. When her bubbly voice receded, I turned my attention to Shelly. "Hey there," I said cheerfully. "How are you feeling today?"

A lopsided smile appeared on Shelly's face. We had been warned about this, the fact that her brain could take months to heal and physical therapy would most likely be necessary.

We were thankful to realize that Shelly was able to speak, though her speech appeared slurred – almost like she was drunk. It had been frightening when Jacob first heard her, but he had adapted quickly. In fact, he had adjusted to everything rapidly over the last few days. I just hoped that he was not just covering up his feelings.

"I heard about Joe," she said softly.

Slowly nodding my head, I compressed my lips. "I'm so sorry, Shelly. I can't even imagine how you must feel right now."

Her eyes seemed to fill with tears, even though none spilled over her long lashes. I was ready with a tissue in my hand in case she needed it. "He's gone."

"Yes, he's gone... I'm sorry that things ended up this way."

She nodded, knowing even through her injuries that my words were shallow. "He was changing."

"He would've had a long way to go. At least now you can really move on with your life without having to look over your shoulder all the time."

She grimaced. "You sound relieved."

The somewhat accusatory way she spoke made me instantly contrite. Arrangements had been made for Joe already, and no one from my family had gone. My parents had taken the high road and sent off a card to his family, but they had not responded. Nor did they check in or visit Shelly. I felt it was just as well that he was out of all of our lives once and for all, even though in private I had shed some tears over the tragedy of it all, and the repercussions for Jacob.

Pasting a smile on my face, I tried my best to hide all this from Shelly. "I'm not relieved, Shelly, not in the way you think. This is something that never should've happened. It was an accident. But now you can move on and never have to fear again. It's going to be hard for you, but now you can make your life what you want it to be."

Her right hand rose from the bed and waved at me in dismissal. Her face screwed up in frustration as she tried to articulate her words. "You make it sound so easy."

Reaching forward, I grasped her limp left hand and gave it a little squeeze. "I never thought it would be easy, Shelly, but I know that you can do it. You've come so far already; you'll have no trouble making it through. You're so strong."

One tear escaped through her heavy lids. I reached out and wiped it away. "Keep reminding me, Cher, because I don't remember anything anymore."

The doctors had told us that this was not uncommon, but I still grew afraid for Shelly. I could not imagine life with no memories, and as I squeezed her hand I wished with all my heart that it would come back soon.

Trying to ignore the bite of tears that stung the back of my eyes, I pasted a new smile on my face. "Not a problem. Just think... you can start all over again with just your family. A new life, Shelly. No strings attached. Take it and run with it... But first you have to get better for Jacob. He needs you now more than ever before. I mean, I was able to get him dressed, and I even gave him a bath last night, but I really don't compare to you, Shelly. He misses you so much."

No sooner had I spoke than the door swung open, and Jacob and my mother came in followed closely by Brandon. He had taken the time to dress in khaki casual slacks and a chest-hugging, short-sleeved, navy blue pullover shirt. We had barely spoken since he had brought me home the first night because things had been so hectic, and I longed for our private little world again.

With a shy smile of greeting, I stared past my mother and met his gaze. The weariness in his face matched my own. It had been a difficult ten days.

"Here he is – my future son-in-law!" My mother announced cheerfully.

Coming to my side, he placed a warm hand on my shoulder and gave me a reassuring squeeze. Then he reached out to Jacob and tousled his hair. "Hey there, Jake. How are you, ladies?"

My mother continued to beam at him. "We're doing better

today," she announced cheerily. "Every morning it's something new. This afternoon Shelly's boss came to visit. He brought that nice bouquet there and told us not to worry about coming back to work yet. She can take all the time she needs."

I hated that she had taken to referring to Shelly as 'we' as though she knew exactly how Shelly was feeling at any moment. With an exasperated glance at Brandon, I rolled my eyes. Biting back a grin, Brandon reached for Shelly's weak hand and picked it up. "How are you doing today, Shelly?"

"I can almost smile," she said.

"Hey, that's great. Every day will bring you closer to getting out of here." He cleared his throat. "I spoke to a friend of mine yesterday, and his sister runs a great rehab nearby. He just got back to me today, but the news was good. Once you're discharged, I can get you set up in this place with no problems. But you have to focus on getting out of here first. Can you do that for me?"

"Oh, Brandon, that was very kind of you," my mother gushed. "The doctor was just saying that we needed to make plans for her discharge. This is great news. Will they have a bed ready?"

"Yes, absolutely. Whenever she's ready to go."

I turned my attention to Jacob, wondering how much longer I could take my mother's false happiness. While I understood why she was trying to put on a happy front, I knew that even Shelly could see right through it. However, it was not my place to be critical. She was, after all, my mother and was dealing with the situation in the best way she could.

Jacob sat by my side, half on my lap, watching the exchange with Brandon with a gaze full of worship. I felt a twinge of jealousy at how easily Brandon had won over the wary child. It did not seem fair that I had to earn his trust while Brandon had it from the beginning.

Though he continued to avoid my gaze, I reached for Brandon's hand and squeezed it in thanks. That he would have gone to the trouble for us was moving, and I was aware of the sting of tears again.

There was some more stilted conversation before I noticed that Jacob was beginning to fall asleep against my shoulder. "Listen, I'm going to run Jacob back home. He's exhausted."

Shelly's gaze shifted to her son, and she pointed with her right hand. "Yes."

"I'll come with you," Brandon said quickly, rising to his feet.

My mother came to her feet also. "I think I'll wait here for your father. He went to play golf this afternoon, and he hasn't called yet. I would've thought he'd be done by now."

I bit back a smile, but Brandon saw my humor and gave me a wink. He bent and reached for Jacob, lifting him into his arms. Jacob smiled wearily and then rested his head on Brandon's shoulder. At that moment, I wished I could do the same. Instead I turned to my mother and Shelly and kissed them both on the cheeks. "I'll call you tomorrow."

"That's fine, honey. Drive safely."

Following Brandon out the door, I fell in step behind him as he made his way to the elevator. By the time the doors opened in front of us, Jacob was sleeping soundly. The elevator was empty, too, leaving us alone for the first time in days. After an awkward silence, Brandon cleared his throat. "I spoke to Mary today. She had tried to reach your mobile and ended up calling me. She said that she got your message about swinging in and will wait for you on Monday. What's going on?"

"We thought it might be good for Jacob to go back into counseling there for a little bit, while Shelly's getting better."

"She's getting better every day."

I nodded. "She's made it through the worst, I think. The question now will be whether she can regain all of her brain functions."

"She's in for a long haul, Cherisse."

I nodded. "Aren't we all?"

My words seemed to affect him. For the rest of the ride in the elevator, he remained silent, and I focused on just putting one foot in front of the other, just like he had said. The past week had been rough on all of us. No one, including Brandon, appeared to have gotten much sleep. But Shelly was a fighter, and I knew that she would pull through. With Brandon's help, I knew I could pull through too.

****

To say that the next months were not an adjustment for all of us would not be the truth. After catching up my missed work in school, I cut back my work hours while keeping close tabs on Shelly. My sister's recovery was slow, but recover she did with a determination I would never have thought she possessed. However, while she focused on getting better, I took on her responsibilities. To become the acting mother of a little boy that I hardly knew proved daunting, but with Brandon's calm determination and kind support we managed to get by. He insisted on doing everything as a team, which was a new learning experience for me. Suddenly all our previous talk of mutual goals was not just talk. We were taking action together.

Moving in to Brandon's house and taking on the role of mother caused profound changes in my lifestyle. I was suddenly thinking of others on a daily basis – not just of my own needs. All of Shelly's carefully laid out plans had to be cancelled, with the exception of

Jacob's daycare and her newly acquired apartment. Until further notice, my parents moved into the apartment for her, paying her rent and utilities while being able to stay nearby to help her with her care. They were officially Snowbirds now. Brandon found a great preschool to place Jacob and registered him for Kindergarten in the fall. Throughout the summer, he became a master at structured living, and the socialization skills he learned were wonderful in preparing him for school.

With Brandon's connections, my parents were able to handle the transfer from the hospital to the rehabilitation clinic for Shelly. She remained inpatient for what seemed an eternity, going through physical therapy, speech therapy, occupational therapy, and cognitive treatment to instruct her on how to live a normal life again. Her long-term memory began to return in the hospital, but her short-term memory was slower to recover. That, coupled with some changes in her behavior, made the path to healing less than ideal for my impatient family.

In the weeks following the car accident, I found myself speaking to Mary Phillips more frequently. She was a great listener and was able to bring a smile to Jacob's face with just a look. Within a month, I found myself wandering into Mary's facility for battered women, "A Better Place." What started out as a visit to thank her for her help ended up becoming a position as a volunteer, and by the end of summer, I had given up food service forever and taken a part-time job on the evenings that Brandon did not work.

Though I thought that I had first-hand experience with domestic violence, I was quick to realize that I really knew little about it. Seeing these frightened women and children enter the shelter, sometimes in the middle of the night dressed only in pajamas and bruises, were a stark reminder of how good I really had it and how little I knew about the silent and hidden violence that occurred behind closed doors. The courage these women showed when they finally left their batterers at times brought tears to my eyes.

"Inner strength is taken for granted by many," Mary told me one afternoon after a busy evening.

"And it's scary to see how quickly it can be stolen away from someone," I muttered in response.

She nodded her head in solemn agreement. "There are those few who do take advantage of our help and do their best to reform. But for every man who finds peace, there's another who has just begun."

"A cycle."

"That's right."

My new position in Mary's shelter was as an advocate for the women who sought help. In addition to assessment, I performed intervention, and there were a few episodes where I had completed work and gone home to cry. It was an emotionally draining job at times, though there were also instances when we would see women like Shelly finally reach their limit and refuse to go home. After viewing close up women like my sister on a daily basis, I regretted ever thinking of Shelly as weak. Deep down inside of her, there was a lioness ready to roar. Though she was the timid one, once she had her mind set on something, she was able to accomplish it.

Seeing my smile, Mary raised a neatly manicured eyebrow. "So what are you smiling about?"

"I was thinking of how far Shelly has come. She has more inner strength than I ever thought possible."

"Your sister has suffered more than she should have. She's come a very long way, and you're right: she is a strong woman."

Gathering up my purse, I reached for my keys. "She's having six sessions a day, and it's been hard on her, but she's getting there. I think she'll be sent home next week, and my parents have offered to stay with her until they're sure she can handle Jacob alone."

"I saw her last weekend," Mary said. "She seemed to have gotten both her long-term and short-term memory now. That's great."

"But thankfully she doesn't remember what happened that day."

"It's just as well."

"She can't wait to get home and be with Jacob. I've been bringing him up to see her, but he still doesn't understand."

"You've been bringing him to see Doctor Stansfield, right?"

"Oh, yes," I said quickly.

The on-staff counselors were wonderful, but with all the terrible things that had happened, Mary advised a psychiatrist for Jacob. It had been a good help, and Doctor Stansfield was a very nice man. Jacob liked talking to him.

"Soon things will be back to normal." I spoke more forcefully than I felt.

Mary winked. "Then you can get yourself married and have those babies I see you wanting more and more every day."

I grinned. There was no point in hiding the obvious. Coming into contact with children of all ages, as well as having Jacob at home with us, had started my biological clock ticking. It was a strange feeling – to desire the added responsibility of a child of my own – but I could not stop it. Though we had never spoken aloud about having children, Brandon's eagerness to marry gave me the sense that it was a future he would look forward to also.

Therefore, after months of making slow plans, we had decided enough was enough. We were marrying during Christmas Break. It was a holiday weekend, and both our families would be available to attend. Plans were already just about complete.

"Yep, we're finally doing it."

"I want an invitation."

"Yours is already addressed."

"I'll be there, hon. Don't you worry. I just love to see happy people every now and then, and you and Brandon seem to be the happiest people in my life right now."

I smiled. Yes, I was happy, happier than I had ever been in my entire life. Things were finally going my way.

Chapter 18

"Has anyone seen Jacob's pillow?"

I lifted the voluminous skirt of my ivory matte-satin wedding dress and stepped around the kitchen table. I bent low to look under it, panic welling in my breast.

"No, Cher," Arianne called from upstairs.

I grimaced and dropped the skirt, not heeding the re-embroidered lace appliques that curled under my feet and threatened to trip me. "This is just great. Has anyone seen the pillow?"

"What pillow, honey?"

My mother strode into the kitchen, her voice breezy. I swung around to face her and felt my scowl fade into a smile. She looked lovely with her brown hair swept up on the crown of her head. She wore a luminescent lavender dress that accentuated her narrow waist and full bosom to perfection. The sweetheart neckline mimicked my own, and I stared at her in appreciation.

"Mom, you look stunning," I gasped.

"You too, dear, though I doubt you should be crawling around the floor in your wedding dress. You're going to rip your train."

I grimaced. "We have to leave in less than a half-hour, and I can't find Jacob's pillow."

"Is this it?"

I spun on my heel and saw my father standing in the doorway, holding Jacob's ivory silk-edged pillow. Sighing in relief, I grabbed it from his hand and hugged him. "Thanks Dad, you're a life saver."

"Nonsense," he said with a smile. "You look beautiful, little girl."

I smiled up at him, my eyes brimming with joy. "I can't believe it's time already."

"Cher, you know, I wanted to mention that to you," my mother said softly.

"What?"

"Are you sure you're doing the right thing? I mean, this is all so sudden."

I smiled at my mother. "All I know is that I feel so special when Brandon looks at me, and when I'm with him, I feel complete. I know nine months isn't a long time to be engaged, but we've been seeing each other over a year. I think I'm wise enough to make good choices."

Tears welled up in her eyes. "I know you're a smart girl, Cher, but I just remember your sister, that's all."

Nodding slowly, I patted my mother's arm. "I know how you feel, but Brandon would never hurt me. He's such a special person. I'm lucky to have found him."

I remembered Shelly's confession to me that day she visited me in Brandon's kitchen. She had admitted to having reservations on her wedding day. Though Brandon had put up quite a fight in trying to tame my freedom-loving spirit, I could say confidently that I was going into my marriage without any hesitations at all. At that moment, there was nothing that I wanted more than to become Mrs.

Brandon Nicholson.

My father came up behind my mother and put his hands on her shoulders. "Come on, Dolly, leave her alone. She's always had a good head on her shoulders. It was a sight better than Shelly's anyway."

"Shut up, John," my mother answered cheerfully, though I saw the flicker of pain in her eyes. Shelly should have been my maid of honor today, but she had refused. Instead she offered to go as Mary's date. She was still having trouble walking and preferred to just sit up front with my parents. She told them that Jacob was representing them both.

"Mom, Dad, just be happy for me, okay? I know Brandon's a good man. That's the most important."

"I agree," my dad said. "I like Brandon. I think he's a good young man. The military does that to a person. Teaches them respect."

"I don't think anyone needed to teach him anything," Arianne said as she entered the room.

We all turned to look at her and sighed at her beauty. She was dressed in an off-the-shoulder gown of dusky rose with a rounded neckline and tight sleeves. It tapered in at her waist and flared out to mid-calf. Matching two-inch heels were trimmed in small pearls that were also woven into her blond hair.

"You look fabulous, Arianne," my father said appreciatively.

I scowled at him, but Arianne gave him one of her best smiles. "Thanks, John. You look pretty good in a tux, you know."

"I don't look so old anymore, do I?"

"You look old enough," my mother snapped.

"Where's Jacob now?" I asked, trying to change the subject.

My mother had never cared for John's open flirting, even though to the best of my knowledge he had never acted on it. Unwilling to take the chance of a heated argument, I figured the safest route would be to get their attention away from Arianne and her full bosom.

"He's upstairs with the girls."

Arianne tugged on her neckline, setting herself more comfortably. I gritted my teeth with irritation. "Ari," I warned.

She raised innocent eyes to me and winked. "I love you, Cher."

Rolling my eyes, I strode past her to the base of the stairs. "Jacob? Come down here so I can look at you."

I heard the voices of Kerri and Brandon's sisters, Gina and Lori, laughing and teasing my nephew. With a flash of gray, the small whirlwind hurried down the stairs, his hair falling into his face as he took the steps two at a time. He stopped two steps up and stared at me, his eyes wide. He had not looked so stunned since Brandon had brought home the fourteen-foot Douglas fir Christmas tree. It was lit up, all eight hundred lights, in the living room behind me.

Santa had not forgotten Jacob this year, for his new family members had arrived bearing all kinds of gifts for a five-year-old boy to enjoy when Brandon and I went away. He held a new Matchbox car in his hand tightly as he gaped up at me.

"Aunt Cher, you look nice," he said in awe.

"Thank you," I said, smoothing back his unruly hair. "Are you ready to go? Have you gone to the bathroom?"

He nodded.

"Let me fix your suit."

He groaned impatiently as I reached forward and straightened his vest. After ensuring that his shirt was tucked in properly, I buttoned up his jacket and graced him with my widest smile. "Are you excited to go visit Grandma and Grandpa's?"

He nodded. "Will I come back here?"

"Of course, as soon as Brandon and I come home."

"Will I be gone a long time?"

"No, just two weeks."

"Two weeks?"

I nodded my head, feeling some strands fall free from my knot. Bending over at the waist, I reached forward and hugged him close, not caring that he crushed the front of my gown. "Yes, Jake, just two weeks. Now run to Grandpa and get your pillow. The car's going to be here any minute."

As he ran off, more footsteps sounded on the stairs. I glanced up to see Brandon's two sisters, Gina and Lori, making their way down. Like a pair of runway models, the two statuesque blondes moved slowly and gracefully in their dusky rose gowns. Their heads were bowed together, and their blond hair was swept elegantly in twists entwined with pearls high upon the back of their heads. When they saw me, they stopped mid-way down the stairs and smiled widely.

"Cherisse, you look dazzling," Gina said, holding her hands against her breast.

"Ravishing," Lori agreed.

"I knew you were beautiful before, but now I can really see it," Kerri said from the top of the stairs.

"Well, I think you all look wonderful," I said quickly, feeling an uncomfortable flush rise on my cheeks.

"She's blushing," Gina said with a sigh.

"Brandon's going to flip when he sees you," Kerri said authoritatively.

The two sisters looked up at her, their smiles knowing. Lori put her hand to the side of her face, as though hiding her words from me. Her whisper was loud enough for me to hear, as she expected. "Did you see how upset he was that he had to go to my parents' hotel room? He was beside himself. They haven't been apart since they moved in together."

"You guys – stop," I pleaded, pressing my hands to my flushed face.

Barely giving me a glance, Kerri smiled back. "Girls, you don't know the half of it. He's been head over heels since he met her."

"I believe it," Gina agreed.

Thankfully the doorbell rang, and Arianne appeared to admit the driver. She turned to me then and winked, her eyes suddenly glistening with tears. "It's time to go."

I patted my hair, panic growing inside my breast. "Quick, fix my headpiece."

"I've got it," Lori said, hurrying down the stairs.

Her fingers were skilled and gentle as she made the adjustments, but she did not release me when it was done. Almost as tall as Brandon, I had to look up at her when she spoke. But her eyes were as gentle as his, and I knew that their similarities were what made them so close. "Cherisse, I just wanted to say that I'm glad you're marrying my brother. I've never seen him so happy, and I'll be proud to call you my sister."

She bent and air kissed my cheek lightly, so as not to smear our makeup. Through tear-blurred eyes, I smiled my thanks and squeezed her hands. "Thank you so much," I whispered.

I turned and faced the door, my blood rushing with excitement. No second thoughts clouded my mind, no doubts whatsoever. I knew I was fulfilling my destiny, and my feet never hesitated as I strode to the door. My future was out there, and I wanted to embrace it.

****

The strains of Pachelbel's "Canon in D Major" reached my ears from the doorway of the limo. Hearing the organ now warmed my heart. Brandon had requested that one specifically. It was one of his favorites.

I glanced out the window and smiled. We had been blessed with another beautiful day. The winter day was heavenly, and the dry desert air kept the sky a deep blue.

"Jacob and Savannah, stop fidgeting," Lori scolded gently.

"Look at how handsome Brandon is," Gina whispered to Lori.

"He makes Adam look so old," Lori whispered back, stifling a giggle.

My eyes strayed to Brandon's brother, Adam. Now forty, Adam was married and had two children back in Connecticut. His wife and children had elected to stay home for fear of flying, and I heard that Brandon's parents were very upset about it. No family was ever perfect, even though I thought Brandon's was pretty darned close.

Brandon was the better looking of the two sons. Adam's jaw was not quite as strong, and instead of the Nicholson aquamarine eyes, Adam had his mother's brown. Even so, he was still a handsome man and had proven to be very friendly. The previous afternoon, he and Jacob had disappeared down to the community playground under the pretense of getting to know the newest family member better. I had concluded that Brandon's parents had taught all of their children the same kindness and thoughtfulness that Brandon exuded so well.

At that moment, Adam bent his head towards his brother and whispered something low. I saw a smile curve Brandon's lips, but it faded quickly when the music changed. The high ceilings echoed with the sound of the organ and violins. In front of me, the last flurry of adjusting bouquets and smoothing skirts took place as the ladies lined up.

"Are you ready?"

I glanced up at my father and smiled. "I'd run if I thought I could, Dad."

He chuckled, his lovely eyes gleaming. "Don't do anything stupid, Cher. This is your big day."

"I know."

I watched as the procession started down the velvet-covered aisle. Along the flower studded pews to the front of the church they went, their steps measured and timed perfectly. Candles lit the altar with a soft glow, and two large bouquets of fragrant roses stood on either side of the candelabras. The setting was ethereal, the music was powerful and moving, and the church was filled with the gentle scent of our roses.

The guests watched, smiling their support, and my heart was singing as I took it all in. Although hurried, I knew that Brandon and I had planned the perfect wedding, and the stamp of approval on the guests' faces sent the message home.

Though not altogether thrilled with having to dress up, Jacob took his steps easily with his pillow balanced carefully between his two hands. I saw him send a happy smile to Shelly and her answering wave. Behind him strode our flower girl, Gina's five-year-old daughter, Savannah. Dressed in the same shade of rose as the maids and maid of honor, Savannah stepped proudly in her flounced skirts, dropping rose petals with every small step.

The music paused for a moment, and then began in earnest. The high ceilings echoed with the sound of the one hundred people coming to their feet. Though brief, the hush was loud in the silence. With a slight tug, my father urged me forward.

The sea of smiling faces appeared before me, and I scanned them all with my own happy smile. There was Paul and his new girlfriend,

Stacey. I saw my friends from work, all grinning from ear to ear with excitement and jealousy. Was there anyone alive that was not halfway in love with Brandon? On Brandon's side, I saw Chuck's wife, Tina, her big blue eyes glistening with tears of happiness.

The members of his team were smiling at me encouragingly, like the proud family members they almost were. Then there were his parents, Ken and Brigid, nodding approvingly and crying openly. I swallowed hard to keep the rising emotion at bay and quickly looked away.

Then I saw him.

Brandon stood at the end of the red velvet carpet, the end of my journey. The music, the people, and even the sight of the pastor all seemed to melt away, leaving only Brandon and I in the whole church.

My smile grew wider.

His eyes were round with pleasure and surprise. They burned with a mixture of desire and pride, and he glowed with happiness. How proud I was to be the recipient of his love. How lucky I was. I felt as though I were floating in a sea of matte satin to an island paradise called my husband-to-be.

As we grew closer, my father squeezed my hand. "Now that's one happy man," he whispered out of the corner of his mouth.

Sudden tears of emotion pricked at my eyelids, threatening to spill over. I blinked rapidly, trying to force them in. I could not cry now; I had to stop being so weepy. But they were tears of such happiness that I thought I would die.

What a way to go it would be.

My father's steadying hand helped to keep my wits about me. Just a few more steps and I'd be with Brandon. I had to remind myself to keep them measured and slow. It would be so easy to run, but I didn't. My father made sure of that.

Brandon took the last steps to meet us. My father's smile widened at his eagerness, and his eyes twinkled. "I hope you kids can make it through the ceremony."

Brandon's chiseled lips curved at him, bestowing one of his breathtaking grins. Then he reached for my hand and took it from my father's arm possessively. Taking the cue, my father turned to me and kissed my cheek. "Good luck... I love you."

"Thanks, Dad."

Brandon's eyes never left me even when we moved forward. His eyes spoke volumes, and his voice was deep with emotion. "You are... magnificent."

"Thank you," I whispered. "You are, too."

Squeezing my hand, Brandon led me forward. I went willingly, eagerly. We stopped in front of the gray haired pastor, who gave us a broad fatherly smile. Pastor Mendoza was one of the nicest men I had ever met. With laughing brown eyes and a soft heart, he embraced the future with open arms and was very lenient in his convictions. He had a strong voice that carried throughout the church as he began the sermon.

I could feel Brandon's presence beside me, and it gave me the strength to commit myself during our vows. My voice wobbled only a slight bit as I promised to love and cherish the wonderful man across from me. His thumbs caressed my wrists as I spoke, and his touch was gentle and reassuring.

When it was Brandon's turn, his voice was clear and strong. I continued to blink rapidly to clear my eyes, but Brandon's face grew blurred as we spoke of our undying love for each other.

When our matching bands appeared, I took a deep breath and reached for Brandon's long-fingered hand. The heavy, platinum band slipped over his knuckle with ease, despite my shaking fingers.

All too soon it was over, and Brandon was stepping forward to take my face in his hands. They were so large that his fingers covered my ears, leaving me with only the sound of my blood rushing through my veins. He smelled of soap, and his rough thumbs briefly caressed my lips until they parted. I lifted my face to meet him as he bent his head.

A gentle sigh settled over the congregation as he wrapped both arms around me and pulled me close. They changed to chuckles when he pressed further, bending me back over his arm. I gripped his shoulders for balance, my breath stolen by the firm and insistent pressure of his mouth.

Not done yet, Brandon raised his head and glanced at the pastor. "Are we done?"

The pastor nodded indulgently, his eyes twinkling. "I think I can finish up."

As he spoke, Brandon kept me close in his arms. As soon as the pastor stopped, Brandon smiled down at me. His eyes glowed with delight. "I love you, Cherisse Nicholson," he said softly.

"And I you, Mr. Nicholson."

Laughing, he bent over and lifted me into his arms, ignoring the surprised gasps of the congregation. After a brief silence, a roar of applause rose throughout the building. Laughter, too, echoed in our ears and our hearts.

With a wide smile, he began his journey down the aisle. Multiple flashes exploded in our faces as the photographers scrambled to take our pictures. My smile was not forced. I was so happy that I barely noticed that my feet never touched the floor.

Chapter 19

"That was so beautiful, Cher. I can't believe you let him carry you out of the church! I bet your guests will be talking about this for ages."

Placing a hand to my racing heart, I grinned at Arianne. "He grabbed me before I realized what he was doing. It happened so fast."

Shelly was the focus of everyone's attention at the moment, and I was rewarded with her tears of happiness when Brandon collected her for a slow dance. Not to be undone, Chuck appeared and claimed me, swirling me way too fast for the slow music, so I escaped as soon as was humanly possible to hide in the bathroom and collect myself. Ever attentive, Arianne deftly repaired my loose hair. The expert twist she had put in my hair was now coming undone, no doubt from Chuck's unbridled maneuvers.

"He looks so happy, Cher. I'm so thrilled for you both."

Nodding my head, I grimaced when Ari pulled my hair. "Sorry."

"Stop moving." She gave me another tug for good measure.

Wincing, I scowled at her, my eyes narrowing. "Be nice," I warned.

Grinning, she secured the last of the pins and then sprayed my hair. "I spoke to Jacob a little while ago. He seems to really like Brandon."

"He idolizes him. Every day he tells me he wants to be a police officer, just like him. I just hope everything that has happened to him lately won't affect him."

"Jacob will be fine. Look at how different he is already. He's just turning six, Cher. He'll forget all about his father in time."

"I can only hope," I whispered, a sudden pang of pain piercing my heart. "And I have Brandon to thank for most of it."

"Well, he has you now. That should be thanks enough."

"Or punishment."

We both burst into laughter that stayed with us until we made our way back into the ballroom. Everyone was out on the floor. I could see Kerri and Jeff letting loose to a pop song, and Chuck dancing with his wife, Tina, for a change. I grinned as they scrambled past. Tina's eyes were closed tightly, and she hung onto her husband for dear life. Having danced with him on two occasions, I knew exactly how she felt.

"That man is a trip," Ari said into my ear.

"Try dancing with him. You can't help but have fun."

"You know, I think I might just cut in."

"Go for it. Tina'll probably thank you."

Arianne wandered off, leaving me alone by the entrance of the ballroom, my ears echoing with the disc jockey's latest choice. Scanning the crowded room for my husband, I spied him sitting at the table with his parents. His head was bent towards his father, but when he raised his head and saw me, he lifted his wineglass in a silent toast.

I remained by the door, caught up in the crowd of friends that passed by and commented on the fine party. After watching me for a few minutes, Brandon slowly pushed his chair back and placed a hand on his father's shoulder. Smiling in my direction, Kenneth laughed at something Brandon said and then nodded his head.

I watched as Brandon made his way through the crowds towards me. His steps were deliberate, though he stopped a couple of times to speak to some of the guests. When he finally reached me, he leaned in close. "Hi there, Mrs. Nicholson," he murmured in my ear.

"Hi. I haven't seen you in ages."

"Ah, but I've seen you. Did you have fun dancing with Chuck?"

"I don't know why I keep torturing myself," I said with a laugh.

"You looked good up there. You've planned a good party."

Wrapping an arm around my shoulder, he allowed his hand to dip and cover one of my breasts. "Stop it," I warned. "What if people are looking?"

"So what? You're my wife now."

"Wife. I like that."

"Me, too."

He pulled me closer, and I readily leaned against him. Closing my eyes briefly, I took a deep breath and let it out on a sigh. "I see Shelly sitting with my mom, but I have yet to see Jacob. Have you seen him lately?"

"He was with Savannah under my father's table."

"Under the table?"

"Yes, they're playing with something under there."

"Should I go fish him out?"

"Nah, he's having a good time." He gave me a slight tug. "Come with me. You've got to meet the Chief before he leaves."

I allowed Brandon to lead me to a solemn pair of men standing near the exit. It was the same men that I had seen Brandon seclude himself with in the corner of the room some time ago. Though dressed in suits, the pair stood erect and alert to their surroundings, and I was immediately reminded of the guards posted in front of a bank. Pasting a smile on my face, I studied the pair, taking note of the friendliness in the older, gray haired man's swarthy face and his deceptively muscular build.

"Chief Ortiz, Jose, this is my wife, Cherisse Nicholson."

"It's very nice to meet you, Chief," I said genuinely. "Thank you for coming."

"Manny, please. And I wouldn't have missed it for the world."

"Very well, Manny. It's still nice to meet you."

Reaching out, I shook the older man's hand. Brandon stood erect beside me. It was a side of him I had seen a long time ago, one he had long tucked away for strangers.

Turning my attention to his companion, I felt my smile falter just a bit. It was Brandon's continued introduction that kept me on course, yet I remained startled by the man, Jose, and his fixed, almost lifeless, stare.

The tall, dark-haired man was sizing me up as though weighing me or my worth. His pale-gray eyes were so light in his dark face that they seemed almost surreal. I shivered slightly under his scrutiny and leaned closer to Brandon.

"Cherisse, this is Lieutenant Jose Fierro. He's the team lead on the unit."

"Nice to meet you, Lieutenant," I murmured.

He squeezed my hand in his large, long fingered grasp. As soon as it was possible to do so, I pulled my hand away and wrapped it around Brandon's cool fingers.

"So that was quite a stunt you pulled in the church, Brandon," Jose commented. His deep voice held a slightly amused tone.

"I agree. That was unlike you."

Grinning broadly, Brandon squeezed my waist. "I just couldn't help myself."

"Seeing your lovely wife now, I can't say I blame you," Chief Ortiz said gallantly.

"Stop," I pleaded, pressing my hands against my cheeks.

"She never can accept a compliment," Brandon explained.

"Well, you'll just have to remedy that," Jose said.

"Give me time," he returned quickly. "I just got married."

"Yes, so you have. I hear you're off to Fiji? Why Fiji?"

I grinned at the Chief. "Brandon loves far-off places. Anything weird, actually. This was one place he wanted to visit while he was in the service. Now he has the chance to show it to me."

The Chief's brows rose with interest, and he smiled. "I'm learning more about you now than in the six years I've known you."

I glanced up at Brandon with a happy smile. "That's okay. I like to know all his secrets."

"Secrets? With you around, woman, I'll have none."

I laughed. "And that's a bad thing?"

He grinned down at me, his eyes crinkling with mirth. Releasing my hand, he slipped behind me and placed his hands on my hips. With a playful smirk and bent on retaliation, I discreetly pressed against him. Neither of our companions seemed to notice my slight movement, but Brandon did. His hands tightened slightly and then more forcefully when I answered with a minute wiggle.

"Ah, to be young again," Chief Ortiz said, elbowing the lieutenant in the ribs.

Out of the corner of my eye, I spotted my mother waving at me. She and Shelly were seated at the head table with Kerri, and the way the three of them were staring at me, I assumed it was something important. "Will you gentlemen excuse me? I'm being summoned."

Chief Ortiz nodded politely. "Of course, of course. You must have a lot of guests to see to. It was a pleasure to meet you."

"The pleasure was mine. Thank you again for joining us today."

I shook the Chief's hand again, and then turned to Lieutenant Fierro. My smile felt forced as I quickly shook his hand. "Have a nice evening, Lieutenant Fierro."

"And you as well. Congratulations on your nuptials."

"Thank you."

With a parting smile, I eased between the men, and they all stepped back to let me pass. Brandon remained behind to chat with the men, but I could feel his stare on me as I made my way to the head table. I felt as though I was floating on clouds.

"You look so darned happy, Cher," Shelly said in greeting.

I reached forward and wrapped my arms around her shoulders. She looked great in her sapphire-blue cowl-neck, curve hugging silk dress. Her initial baldness had grown into a short, modern style that suited her large brown eyes and high cheekbones perfectly. In fact, she looked healthier now than even before her accident.

"I am happy, Shelly. You're getting better, Mom and Dad are taking Jacob for two weeks to spend some quality time with him, and I'm marrying the man of my dreams. What could be better?"

She hugged me back, but when we pulled away I saw tears in her eyes. "I'm so happy for you, Cher, and I'm so glad that I have the opportunity to be here with you today."

"Me, too," I said, squeezing her hands with my own. "You have no idea."

"Now, you two, stop it before you make us all cry," Kerri interrupted.

My mother stepped forward. "And I'm so happy that I have my

family safe and sound here today. My new son-in-law is a great addition to our family."

"My son is a wonderful addition to anyone's family," Brigid Nicholson announced with a broad smile. Taking a chair from the nearest table, she plopped down across from us. "Although my new daughter-in-law is quite the asset, too."

"That's right," Shelly announced.

Sneaking up behind me, Brandon wrapped his arms around my shoulders and kissed the side of my neck. "Hi there," he whispered in my ear.

"Brandon, really," his mother said teasingly, her brown eyes twinkling.

Throwing his mother an exasperated look, Brandon pulled me to my feet. "Come here."

"What?"

He took my seat and pulled me down on his lap. I tottered for a moment with indecision, but his hands settled around my waist and held me firm.

Sliding an untouched glass of wine towards Brandon, Ken Nicholson nodded his head in the direction of the dance floor. "So things are winding down now. We were just deciding on leaving. Are you two heading out?"

Brandon twisted slightly to glance around. I did so as well and noticed that people were heading back to their tables to collect their belongings. A sudden ripple of excitement raced through me. "I'm ready," I whispered, my tongue sneaking out to gently trace the curve of his ear.

His head swung back in my direction, and I caught the knowing look deep in his eyes. "You've been ready for a while now, haven't you?"

Once more a slight blush heated my face as I remembered my teasing. "Sorry about that. Did they notice?"

A dry look appeared on Brandon's face, and his lips came together in a wry smile. "There's not much they miss, especially Lieutenant Fierro. That's why he's good at what he does."

"Who's good?" Brigid asked.

"It's nothing, Mom," he answered quickly, sending me a smile. "So, are you ready to go, Mrs. Nicholson?"

My hips wiggled again. "I'm ready."

"Tease." Shaking his head, Brandon lifted me off his lap, and quickly stood behind me until his jacket was safely buttoned. "Well then, I guess we'll say our good-byes now. Shelly, Kerri, Dolly, John, and Mom and Dad, thank you for everything. I'll call you when we get home."

Sudden tears filled my mother's eyes. "You two look so happy. I wish you all the best."

"Thank you so much," I said, bending down to kiss her cheek.

I reached for Jacob under the table and pulled him out. Wrapping him in my arms, I promised to get him a really cool surprise when we returned. He hugged me back, a little desperately, and then ran to his mother's side. I was just glad that he had not shed one tear.

Before I knew it, Brandon was tugging on my arm. He guided me around the room, sending our thanks and farewells in a hasty gush. Then he was leading me away to the waiting car, and I welcomed the cool night air on my heated skin. I was beginning my new life now, and I could not wait to do it. We were moving on to bigger and better things. We had the world in front of us to conquer.

****

I was floating high on the strength of Brandon's caring. Never in my life had I felt so complete, so utterly cherished. Like a lost soul finally found, I clung to every day of our honeymoon and wished they would never end. They were happy and carefree days, so far away from home and our day to day responsibilities.

In all the many months I had known Brandon, we had never shared so much time together alone. Instead of ten minutes between hurrying to work or class, we had twelve long, leisurely days to just be together. Adding to that the cramped sixteen hour flight to Nadi where I curled into him like a cat, we were all alone for two whole weeks.

In addition to a romantically secluded beachfront suite with magnificent views of the deep blue oceans, we shared time together fishing and scuba diving. Brandon even booked us for a couple's treatment one afternoon after sunning all day. The lazy activity and then the massage left me totally pliant to his every whim. When I was finished, he brought me back to our room and then took advantage of my serene state.

We explored the island and made some friends at the resort. Evenings were spent in the lounge with our new friends, and I found myself wishing it would never end. Even though I had not thought it possible, I returned home even more in love with my new husband.

Reluctantly, we returned to the real world: a world that included our jobs, our schooling, Shelly's recovery, and Jacob, too. Jacob had spent the time with my parents, but we could see immediately that he had missed us very much and was happy that we were home.

Brandon was quick to lift him high onto his shoulders and carry him out of Sky Harbor Airport to our car. The whole ride home, we listened to his adventures and updates from his mom, and when we finally got him into bed we were just as exhausted as he. A combination of jet lag and time changes did a number on us both, and Brandon was relieved that Jacob was ready for bed early, too.

Still trying to finish the book I had brought with us on our trip, I scanned the pages half-heartedly while I waited for Brandon to come to bed. My lids were heavy, and the silence in the room coupled with the soft glow of my reading lamp was quick to lull me to a drowsy state.

When he arrived in the bedroom doorway, I glanced over the book and smiled. There he was – my glorious angel of a husband. He stood just inside the room, a mysterious smile on his tanned face. Even disheveled, he was a handsome man. With his shirt un-tucked, top buttons unbuttoned, and hanging loosely around his narrow, jean-clad hips he posed the picture of a sullen model.

"Jacob tucked in?" I asked, returning my attention to the forgotten book.

"Yep," he said, his voice muffled as he pulled his shirt over his head.

I could not stop myself from peeking over the book to get a glimpse of his tanned chest. His muscles appeared even more defined with the color he had obtained under the Fijian sun.

Rolling the shirt into a ball and throwing it across the room, Brandon suddenly jumped onto the bed and stood above me. With a startled yelp, I raised the book over my face and squeezed my eyes shut, only to open them seconds later to see what he was doing.

He stepped forward, his long legs on either side of me. This playfulness made me suspicious, so I placed the bookmark in my book and set it aside before scooting up the bed. "What are you doing?"

He threw himself forward but caught himself on his extended

arms. Nevertheless, I squealed in alarm and frowned fiercely at him as he settled between my legs. Coming to rest on his forearms, Brandon lowered his face to nuzzle my neck. "Ssh. Don't wake up Jacob," he said softly.

"Don't scare me like that, then." I tried to ignore his teasing lips to no avail. "Mm," I murmured. "That's nice."

Rolling over with a soft sigh, his hand slowly pulled back the covers and exposed me dressed once more in one of his shirts. His smile was tender as he stared down at me, and once more my brows drew together with suspicion.

"Nothing excites me more than seeing you in one of my shirts," he murmured dryly.

"Really?"

"Oh, yeah."

His palm came to rest on my abdomen, and his long fingers gently kneaded the soft flesh there. My eyes drifted closed, though I could hear him breathing next to my ear. Even though we had been busy all day, with airports, customs and luggage, I could still smell his after-shave. It was the same familiar scent I had always loved.

"I've been thinking," he continued softly.

"About what?"

Instead of answering right away, his fingers slipped under the ends of my borrowed shirt where it rested at my thighs. Gently and slowly, he pulled it over my hips to expose my midsection. I opened my eyes and stared down at his hand. It looked so large against my small belly. He was darker than I was, even though I had also tanned from all the hours we had spent under the hot sun too.

His fingers splayed wide, gently stroking me until I spotted gooseflesh. "Your skin is so beautiful. It's soft and smooth."

Dipping his head, he pressed a soft kiss right above my navel.

261

Unwillingly, the muscles there contracted, and I inhaled sharply. My fingers were trembling when I reached up to entwine them in his close-cropped hair. It felt soft and silky under my eager hand.

"Your skin is like silk there," he whispered.

I bit my lip as his lips proceeded after his rising hands, the moist and wet trail feeling cool in the evening air. Stopping at the underside of my breasts, Brandon raised his head and smiled. "You are my Sunshine"

"Are you trying to seduce me with words?" I asked lazily. I could hear the heaviness in my voice and smiled. "Whatever you're up to is working."

"Good."

My hand dropped away as he straightened, and I watched him with growing curiosity. He reached into his pocket and pulled out my birth control pills. My eyes widened. "Where did you get those?"

Holding them in front of my face, Brandon returned his free hand to my belly, and once more the soothing caress began. "You're going to graduate next semester."

"Yes," I said slowly.

"That's only a few months away."

"Yes."

He pressed his lips together as though thinking, yet I knew he had planned what he was going to say already. "You've been on the pill for a year or so, right?"

"Right."

"So it would take a few months for the effects to wear off."

"What are you getting at?" I asked, fearing the hopeful racing of my heart. It couldn't be. He wasn't!

His fingers stopped moving and once more spread out. Leaning over me, Brandon lowered his face until our noses touched. "You've been mentioning babies for a few months now, but you've never asked me how I felt. Well, I'm ready, too. If you want to stop taking the pill," he said softly. "I want you to have my baby. I want to see your belly grow with our child."

I blinked. "Are you serious?"

His face dipped down to press his lips against mine. When he once more raised his head I knew he was dead serious.

"But we just got married."

"So now it's legal in the eyes of our families."

Reaching up, I linked my arms around his neck. "But can we afford it? I mean, I'd have to take time off from work and all those baby things – it gets expensive."

"Don't worry about money, Sunshine. I can take care of the working for a while. Besides, it really wouldn't be that different. I can just pick up a couple of extra details every now and then to cover the loss of your salary."

"But when will you sleep?"

"I'll find the time. It might be a little hard at first, but we'll manage.

"Are you sure?" I asked, my eyes shining. "What about Jacob? I'm still not sure when Shelly will be well enough to handle him on her own."

"I just spoke to him right now. He's thrilled with the idea."

"Wow," I murmured.

"So does that mean you'll think about it?"

"Think about it? I've been thinking about it forever!"

With a triumphant smile, Brandon lifted the shirt the rest of the way over my head. His hand covered one breast, kneading it tenderly. "I can't wait to see a baby at these beautiful works of art, Cherisse. Although... I hate to admit I don't want to share."

I laughed. "Come to bed, Brandon. With your high expectations we'll need to practice."

He needed no further encouragement. Raising himself off me, he reached over and shut off the light. Then he was back, covering me in the darkness and demonstrating his love.

Chapter 20

My parents moved back to Montana the following month, so Brandon and I moved Shelly and Jacob into a small apartment near our house in Tempe. Taking the new role as brother-in-law seriously, Brandon, with the help of Mary, helped her arrange a transfer from her bank job in Phoenix to a branch in Tempe. Ease of commute was a deciding factor in moving her job closer to home. She rode the bus since no one knew for sure if she would be able to drive again. Whenever possible, I shuttled her and Jacob around, but Shelly never asked. She had so much happiness for life now that she had come so close to losing it that she never complained. Apparently, when I had mentioned to her that she could start life all over again, she took me more seriously than I ever could have imagined.

From the moment Brandon and I returned from our honeymoon, life was again caught up in a giant whirlwind of activity. However, we were happy with our roles. We worked as a team and tackled our mutual goals one step at a time. I was able to graduate in mid-May, with Brandon's full support through student teaching and night classes.

Not only did I graduate with honor, but I also completed my

program two months pregnant. Though not yet showing, our friends and family knew straight away, mostly from Brandon's proud ramblings. His joy was hard to contain, and his enthusiasm filled me with even more awe for the man who I was proud to call my husband.

With a glimmer of sadness and a few tears, I said my final good-byes to my closest friends. After a knee injury, Paul quit football and went off to New York City in the hopes of hitting it big in the publishing world. After working a few months for the Arizona Republic, Mike decided to try his hand at screenwriting and returned to California with Arianne. And dear Arianne, my roommate for years and my best friend, packed up their apartment into their cars and returned to her family in Los Angeles to pursue a career in marketing.

Although I knew it was bound to happen, I hated to see my friends move on with their lives. It just served to remind me that I had a full life already. It was so different from theirs, so much farther along in the scheme of things. I had changed so much in the nineteen months since Shelly had come over that hot night in August. Where marriage and children were still far off for Arianne and Mike, I had already tackled both. They had decided to go slower, to move their careers along, get settled in life, and have a lot of fun at the same time.

Not me. I had settled down with Brandon with ease. I had taken life by the horns and accepted everything it sent my way. While certainly not the standard path of a recent college grad, I had my job at A Better Place with Mary and the numerous ladies who went to her for help, as well as a full-time offer in the Scottsdale School District for when I was ready to return to work. Domestic bliss was my current route.

In the meantime, Mary had added to my duties the job of handling the newsletter and website, so my time there was full of hard work. I was exactly where I wanted to be at twenty-five, though. I had a man who loved me, a growing family, and plenty of friends who needed my help. How could it get any better? I loved my life.

As my belly grew rounder and my temper shorter, my husband was by my side. Being Brandon, he was completely understanding of my discomfort and strove to make me feel better. After every shift, he would stop somewhere and bring me home some silly trinket, from a card professing his love to a bag of Hershey Kisses. Though I whined at times, later I would admit that I did appreciate his thoughtfulness. I also laughed when Brandon complained teasingly that I ruined a perfectly good surprise. Wasn't I always the one to mess up his best-laid plans?

Our son, Tyler Brandon Nicholson, entered the world on December 19 at six in the morning. Labor was not easy for me. Struggling with long hours of painful back labor and giving birth to a large baby over eight pounds left me exhausted and relieved at the same time. However, I felt it was all worth it when I watched my husband gingerly hold his first child. My heart leapt in my chest every time I saw him gaze at the small miracle we had made, and tears would blur my vision when he spoke softly to him.

Although I knew that Brandon enjoyed children, having seen him bond with Jacob and interact with his niece and nephews, his infatuation with his son still came as a surprise. I could not believe how easily he had fallen for the red-faced, chubby baby. The way he watched me when I nursed in bed, and the way he jumped up every three hours to change Tyler's diaper, served only to deepen my love for my husband.

Shelly and Jacob came to visit as often as possible to offer their help. My sister was a natural with the baby, easily able to soothe him when he had his afternoon crankiness, and she gave me more tips than I ever thought possible. My nephew was a bundle of excitement, though he approached the child with the same wariness that always showed in his eyes. He would hold Tyler's small hand and smile shyly when the little fingers clasped tightly around his own. Shelly and I would watch on with tears in our eyes, and I often wondered how she felt seeing her son interact so well with a new baby. In just a short time, Tyler would be crawling along after his older cousin, and I hoped that they would be able to forge a solid friendship.

After two weeks of support, Brandon had to return to work. Now that I had completed my degree, he focused more on finishing up his classes and beginning his six hours of thesis. Deep down, I was just as eager to see him finish his program and work on his next career move. I still carried that deep-seated fear – the fear that I could lose him – and I had long passed the point where I could not bear anything happening to him.

I had no idea how real those fears were to become.

****

Although Brandon had the scanners in the house, programmed at that, I was never one to listen since he showed little interest in them as well, unless his pager went off on those rare occasions that he was called in for the unit.

Since I did not keep track, I never heard about Chuck's accident. It was the phone call from Ethan Schor's wife, Sandy, that first alerted me to trouble. In her panic-stricken voice, she told me that Chuck was in intensive care, and I should turn on the television right away.

Shelly and Jacob were visiting, so I transferred six-month-old Tyler from my breast to my sister and reached for the remote.

"Hey, that's Poppy," Jacob said once I had found the channel.

It had pleased me when Jacob had started calling Brandon 'Poppy', telling me that he had accepted his uncle as some sort of a father figure. Of course, he also called me 'Sunshine' instead of Aunt Cher or Cherisse. Brandon had gotten a kick out of that, and together the pair of them would sing to me all the time.

Shelly frowned, drawing me back to the television. "Cher, what's happened?"

"There's been an accident. Chuck, the crazy dancer from my wedding, has been hurt."

Shelly put Tyler over her shoulder and patted his back gently. Taking a seat on the new leather loveseat we had bought ourselves for Christmas after Tyler was born, Shelly placed him face-down over her knees and continued patting. "Is he okay?"

"I don't know? Let's watch..."

There was my handsome husband in the background, talking animatedly to one of the other officers behind the tragic yellow police tape. The camera briefly zoomed in on the pair, and I saw the distress on Brandon's face. A piercing feeling entered my heart. He needed me for a change, and there was nothing I could do until he came home.

The news reported that Chuck had been struck by a car while on the side of the road with a broken-down vehicle. According to the driver of the vehicle that hit him, he had been deliberately forced off the road by a small red import with dark-tinted windows. The mysterious car then sped off, leaving the repercussions of their carelessness behind.

Chuck was in the hospital with bilateral femur fractures and a shattered pelvis. The news reporter did not know if he was going to make it.

"Oh no," I whispered.

"What's wrong?" Jacob asked, sending me a worried look over his shoulder.

"Chuck's hurt," I whispered.

"Chuck?" Jacob asked, frowning.

"Yes, baby," Shelly said softly. "Chuck was hit by a car."

"Is Poppy okay?"

"Oh, yes, don't you worry. Poppy's fine. He's on the television right now."

I watched and I waited. I waited all evening, preparing dinner for Shelly and Jacob before sending them home to bed. By the time I laid Tyler down to bed in his crib across from Jacob's old room, I managed to get Chuck's wife, Tina, on the phone. Having stopped home from the hospital to ensure their son was all set with a sitter, Tina took the few minutes to update me on Chuck's condition. "He's had surgery to repair his legs and pelvis. They're optimistic about his survival, but he lost a lot of blood. They had to give him so many units; I'm not even sure how much." Her voice quivered just a little. "They don't know if he'll walk ever again if he makes it. They don't know what kind of nerve damage he's suffered. Goodness, Cher, how could this have happened?"

I inhaled deeply and let it out on a sigh. Cradling the phone against my neck, I could feel the tears flood my eyes. "I'm so sorry, Tina. Is there anything I can do for you? Anything at all?"

"Cher, you're so sweet."

I snorted. "That's not sweet, Tina. It's worry."

"I'm fine, really. I just wanted to check in on CJ. He's really upset, even though he doesn't understand completely yet."

"I know what you mean. It's always hard on the kids."

"I'll call you later. CJ's in bed. I want to get back to the hospital, you know, just to be near."

"Well, if you need anything for CJ or if you need to bring any of the kids here, you just call me. Anytime, Tina. I don't care if it's 3 a.m., okay?"

"Thanks, Cher. I really appreciate it."

"I just wish I could do more."

"Me, too," she whispered.

Hanging up the phone, I crawled into bed and sat and waited. I waited with the phone by my side, easily within reach. Brandon never called, not that I really expected him to. There had been nights before when he was tied up for hours doing paperwork at the end of his shift, and I knew tonight would be no different.

Still, I waited. I waited just in case he needed to hear my voice before he came home for the night. I waited with bated breath to see him with my own eyes, to make sure that it was not my husband sedated in the intensive care unit, not knowing whether he would make it through the night, and if he did, if he would ever use his legs again.

Squeezing my eyes shut against the threat of my tears, I bit my lip with the memory. Maybe Chuck would never dance again. If he made it at all, he might never swing another laughing young woman around the dance floor. I drifted off to sleep with that thought in mind.

Brandon did not come home at all that night. When Tyler woke up for his 5 a.m. feeding, I brought him back into our bed and nursed him there, my fingers smoothing back the fleecy soft blond hair.

With every passing day, Tyler looked more like his father. They shared the same serious eyes and the same devastating smile. I held his little body close to my heart, thanking whoever or whatever it was that brought me to Brandon.

Once Tyler was burped and back in his crib, I found myself pacing about the bedroom, from one end to the other, casting covert glances out into the early morning gray sky in the hopes of seeing his familiar Frontier drive down the street.

At seven, I'd had enough and made my way downstairs for a cup of coffee. Settling in the living room with a steaming mug cupped between my hands, I sat and sipped with my mind running in all directions of thought. They came to an abrupt end a short time later when he strode in through the front door, coming to a surprised halt when he saw me. He looked haggard, distressed, and worried all at once.

"Did you sleep?" His eyes never left mine as he closed and locked the door behind him.

"For a little while."

"I tried to call the house last night, but the line was busy. My mobile battery was dead, so I couldn't send you a text."

My eyebrows lifted in surprise. "What time?"

"Around nine."

Of course, I would have been on the phone with Tina then. I grimaced. "I called Tina."

He nodded curtly. "She's at the hospital. I saw her."

"How's Chuck?"

"Still critical."

"Did you find the other car?"

A fleeting look of surprise crossed his features. "How'd you know?"

"It was on the news."

"No. Nothing yet."

Not knowing what else to do, I held my arms open. Suddenly he was on his knees in front of me with a muffled curse, his arms wrapping around my waist and his face in my abdomen. "God, Cherisse, you are a sight for sore eyes."

"Oh, Brandon."

My hands went to his back. I kneaded the taut skin there underneath his T-shirt, trying to smooth away the tension in his bunched muscles. I could feel a lump in my throat and swallowed convulsively. I could not cry now. He needed me to be strong, and I would not disappoint him. "Come upstairs. Tyler will be up soon."

I felt the stubble on his chin brush roughly against my thigh when he nodded. As he released me and sat back, I came to my feet and grasped his hand to help him back up. Leaving the coffee mug on the table, I led my exhausted husband upstairs. His feet were heavy on the stairs, more proof of just how tired he was. "I'm sorry you were worried," he mumbled as we went. "It was nuts at the station, and mountains of paperwork had to be filled out."

Closing the bedroom door behind us, I led Brandon to the bed and pushed him down. He sat with a long sigh and allowed me to remove his boots. "I understand."

"Do you? Really?"

My smile was fleeting. "Actually, while I sat up and waited, I thought that perhaps all those late nights at the computer were actually chat room visits, and that you were off visiting some broad last night."

As I spoke my fingers wove through the short strands of his hair and my nails gently massaged his scalp. Though hoping for some sort of smile, it did not appear. His face remained serious when he spoke. "You couldn't be any farther from the truth."

"So you're not seeing someone else, then?" I asked flippantly.

"Not a chance."

"You say that so authoritatively."

He paused for a moment, his lips twisting in a wry smile. "Because I love you too much, Cherisse, and I need you right now more than you can imagine."

"Oh, honey," I whispered.

My fingers went to his cheekbone and stroked slightly. Grasping my hand, he placed a warm kiss on my palm before pulling me down next to him on the bed. He rolled with me, and I took his weight with a sense of glory. He groaned softly and buried his face in my hair, and I knew that I was what he wanted. What he always wanted. There was no way there could be another woman, not now, not anytime soon. Nothing could compete with what we shared.

With rough and urgent hands, he pulled my shirt over my head and thrust it across the room. His white undershirt soon followed, leaving our chests bare. Staring down at me with appreciative eyes, Brandon's moist lips curved ever so slightly. "I never thought it possible that you could become even more beautiful... Cherisse, don't ever leave me. I love you and Tyler so much I couldn't bear it if you did."

"Don't worry, I'm not going anywhere," I whispered.

"And if something happens to me, Sunshine, know that I love you more than life itself."

"I know," I whispered. "I love you too, Brandon, so very much."

He had become so special to me that I could not say the words emphatically enough.

Chapter 21

Afterwards, we lay entangled with me stroking Brandon's back until I felt him slowly relax and give in to the urge to sleep. As I waited, I thought with some amusement that we had not used protection in our heated haste. While a second child had not even crossed my mind this soon, I felt little flutters of excitement in my belly just thinking about how happy Brandon would be if I did become pregnant again. My husband was exhausted and stressed, and now I understood how he felt all those months ago when the stress was on me. I wanted to help him. I wanted to ease his mind in any way I could. But first, he needed to rest.

He was breathing evenly and deeply for some time before I slowly disentangled my limbs from his and slipped from the bed. Gathering up our clothes, I stepped silently from the room with Tyler's monitor. It would not do Brandon any good if the baby woke up while I was in the shower, and he had to get him. I could take a load off Brandon's shoulders today by making sure he relaxed. A good meal, strong coffee, and maybe a nice afternoon spent on the sofa would do him good.

Luckily, Tyler stayed down until I had showered and dressed, so

Brandon was able to sleep until close to noon. When I heard him stir upstairs, I prepared a meal and pot of coffee for him, all the while planning out my surprise for him.

When he at last came downstairs again, he was freshly showered and again dressed for work. He was as unsmiling as I was when our gazes locked, and I felt a slight twinge of hurt that I would be unable to help him relax. "You're leaving again?"

Striding to the coffeemaker, he poured himself a cup and began rummaging through the cabinets for something to eat, not even glancing at the plate of scrambled eggs, turkey bacon and blueberry muffins I had laid out for him earlier.

When I spoke, he raised his head and nodded briskly, avoiding my penetrating stare. "I have to check in and finish up some things."

"On your day off?"

Although I tried, I could not keep the hurt out of my voice. He caught it and raised a single brow. "Yes, on my day off. Chuck is not just any other accident, Cherisse. He's a cop."

"And cops get better treatment?"

I saw the dismay in his eyes. "They do when we he's in intensive care, and we still haven't caught the guy who put him there."

My surprised gasp reminded him that he spoke sharply, and he slammed the cabinet door hard as he straightened. Tyler fell over with the shock of the sudden surprise, letting out a cry of frustration as he rolled onto his belly. Striding to his side, I picked up the baby and then crossed to the window to look outside. It was hot, and the desert sun warmed us through the glass.

"Look," Brandon snapped. "I'll call you later, okay?"

Reminding myself that I would have other opportunities, I sighed with agreement. "All right."

His boots barely made a sound on the tile floor as he came up behind me and pulled me close. I closed my eyes and leaned against his broad chest, listening to the sound of Brandon's breathing mingled with the cooing of the baby against my shoulder.

One of Brandon's hands lifted to cup little Tyler's head. I felt rather than heard his soft murmuring to his son and could not hold back my small smile.

"Cherisse," he said, spinning me around. His touch was as gentle as ever.

I leaned back and stared up at him solemnly. "Yes."

"Sunshine, please," he said softly, his voice coaxing.

"Please what?"

"Aw hell, I don't know."

Released abruptly, I took a step back. "What is it really, Brandon? Are you okay enough to go to work?"

"Nothing...I'm fine. Don't worry about it." He turned around on his heel and picked up his coffee mug, downing the contents in a single gulp.

I watched on as he rinsed out the mug and placed it in the sink. His movements were jerky and harsh, belying his stress, and I fought the urge to approach and instead continued to observe him, my heart aching in my chest. There was something troubling him, and it was somehow related to what happened to Chuck. I remembered his words as we were making love, "If something ever happens to me..."

"Brandon?"

He glanced at me, his brow raised in question.

"Come home soon, okay?"

The hint of a smile appeared upon his lips. "I will."

Then he was gone, striding out the front door and leaving Tyler and me alone.

****

Several weeks passed of late nights and more extra shifts while Chuck worked on his recovery. Though our small argument never went any further, I was still frustrated by Brandon's stress levels and reluctance to share with me. All of my attempts to help seemed to go nowhere. Therefore, I was surprised when Brandon arrived home late in the night one evening and woke me up. The most recent routine he had settled into had comprised of him removing his boots downstairs and sneaking into the bedroom as quietly as a mouse, so I would not be disturbed. So when he climbed into bed and awakened me with soft kisses pressed along my jaw and temple, I was both surprised and suspicious.

Soothed by the steady hum of the air conditioning and the silence from the baby monitor, I groaned and rolled over since I had just gotten to bed myself. With Tyler teething, peaceful sleep was a thing of the past.

"Come on, Sunshine, I need you," he murmured.

"Go away, Brandon."

I heard him chuckle. "No way, this is too important. The baby's out cold. Come on."

His fingers encircled my wrist. Planting his feet on the ground, he easily pulled me up to a seated position. Then he bent over and scooped me up into his arms. I realized then that his chest was bare. He had removed his uniform and was dressed only in his swim trunks. If he had thought that I would join him for a midnight swim in our new pool, he was sadly mistaken.

"Brandon," I gasped. "What are you doing?"

"I want to show you something," he replied.

"How do you get around without making any noise?"

"You were dead to the world, babe. I made plenty of noise. But you were snoring, and it was so cute." He laughed at my struggles. "Come on, join me."

"Fine," I said reluctantly. "Put me down before you pull a muscle."

"With you?" he scoffed. "You barely weigh anything."

Wrapping my arms around his neck, I rested my tired head on his shoulder. In the dim light, I could see the beating pulse in his neck. It was steady despite the extra weight he carried down the stairs, making me feel like a feather in his arms.

Stopping in the kitchen, Brandon released my legs and lowered me carefully to the floor. The tile was cool under my feet, and the darkness surrounded us like a cool blanket. Without a word, he turned me around and covered my eyes from behind. Then he led me cautiously outside, chuckling as I stumbled and reached for his wrists to keep my balance.

The first thing that hit me was the heat of the night air. Once again the monsoon season was approaching, and it was humid and hot outside, still over ninety degrees. It was the kind of heat that slapped you across the face, and I wanted to run back inside and go back to bed.

"What are you up to?"

"Just wait a minute," he murmured. Guiding me to the center of the patio, he pulled his hands away with a dramatic, "Tah-dah!"

The lights were dim, but I could still see the bottle of wine and dish of pastries on the patio table. Two chairs were set out, side by side, and on one place mat there sat a small, brightly wrapped box with a single red rose set out beside the Waterford crystal glass.

"Is this some sort of anniversary?" I asked, pressing my hands against my breast.

Sending me one of his heart-stopping grins, he shook his head. "No, I just wanted to show you how much I appreciate you."

"Show me? Don't you show me all the time?"

"Not lately." He sauntered up to me, resplendent in his navy swim trunks. I admired his broad chest and narrow hips. He was lean and muscular, tall and lanky. Watching the direction of my thoughts, his grin widened. "Sit down," he said, pulling out the chair. "I have something else for you."

"More?"

I sat down sideways and crossed my legs. Under my watchful gaze, Brandon strode over to a darkened corner of the patio, next to Jacob's small picnic table.

"What's over there?" I asked, hearing a scuffling sound.

"Hold on," he called over his shoulder. "I'll be right – hey!"

"What's wrong?" Not waiting for his answer, I came to my feet and hurried to the spot I had last seen him.

"Hold on, Cherisse, I've got him."

"Got who?"

I peered over his shoulder, but it was too dark to see what he was doing. The clanging of a metal door against plastic raised my suspicions, and they were well founded when the bundle of warm fur was placed in my arms.

"Here you go," Brandon said, straightening. "I just woke him up."

He smiled down at me as I gasped in surprise. "What is this?" I need not have asked. Suddenly a wet tongue appeared and lathered my cheek and chin. Laughing, I held the puppy away from me and wiped at my face. "Where did you get a puppy this late at night?"

He beamed down at me, his eyes crinkling with mirth. "He was left on the side of road in a garbage bag. A motorist called in a wiggling bag on the side of the road, and there he was. We managed to wash him off a little, but he'll have to go to the vet first thing tomorrow."

Hurrying back to the light, I held him up to get a good look at him. It was a small, soft German Shepherd looking pup, with warm brown eyes and a fiercely wagging tail.

"He's thin," I commented.

"Yeah, I doubt the previous owner took the time to feed him when they just dumped him on the road."

"Can we keep him?"

"I don't know yet. We'll have to see if anyone claims him. Also, if he's unhealthy I don't think I'd want him near the baby."

"Then why'd you bring him home?"

He cocked his head to the side in thought. "I dunno. I just saw him and thought it was the thing to do. He's awful cute... besides, every boy needs a dog."

"Yes," I murmured, pressing my nose into his soft fur. He smelled of shampoo, most likely borrowed from one of the officers at the station.

Brandon came up behind me and placed his hands on my shoulders. "Come and sit down. I've got more to show you."

"I saw the rose, thank you."

He placed a warm kiss upon my neck. "There's more."

"Wouldn't be the small box would it?"

"As a matter of fact..." His grin appeared again as he tucked in the chair behind me. I watched as he seated himself next to me and tucked in his own chair. The puppy was wagging his tail again, his inquisitive nose sending him up onto the table to sniff the dish of chocolate.

Reaching for the dish of Hershey Kisses, I sent a slow smile in Brandon's direction. "Kisses, eh? My favorite."

"I know." He gripped the wine in both hands and opened it with a subtle pop, reaching out to pick up my glass in a two-fingered grasp. He poured a small amount into my glass and a more liberal amount in his.

"Don't want to get Tyler drunk," he said smoothly.

I sipped at the drink idly, watching Brandon out of the corner of my eye. Inside I was bursting with curiosity and excitement, yet I maintained my composure long enough for Brandon to reach over and hand me the box. "Are you going to open this?"

Hearing the suspense in his voice, I gave him a sidelong glance. "Well, you know, those pastries look awful good."

"There's plenty of time for them later."

He placed the box in my hand pointedly and wrapped my fingers around it. With my hand trapped between both of his, I was left with no choice. Nodding my head briefly, I pulled free and stared down at the red paper. "Why did you buy me something?"

"I wanted to."

"That's it? No other reason?"

"I wanted tonight to be special. I have some revelations to make."

My eyebrows shot up in surprise. "Revelations?"

"Open your box first, and then we'll talk."

I stared down at the box for a moment, my mind whirling with possibilities. Though he usually kept me on my toes with his romantic ways, this was a highly unusual moment in our relationship. He had never awakened me in the middle of the night before with a puppy, box and food and drink, and I had to admit I was suspicious.

"Go ahead," he urged again.

I pulled the bow off the box and then slipped my fingers under the tape securing the paper. It came away easily, revealing a black jewelers box. "Jewelry?"

His smile widened.

The lid slid off easily, and I stared down at the contents with wide eyes. "You bought these?" I asked, pulling out a pair of one-carat diamond earrings.

He sat back with wineglass in his hand, looking sublimely pleased with himself. "I did."

"But why?"

As though pondering my question, he took a drink of his wine and reached for an éclair. Taking a bite and chewing it slowly, he studied me with avid interest until I was squirming in my seat. "I haven't been entirely honest with you, Cherisse."

"Is it another woman?" I asked, fighting back the sudden pain in my heart.

"No, no," he scoffed. "Like that would ever happen."

"What then?"

"Chuck."

"How is Chuck?"

He smiled faintly. "Ready to come back to work. Ready emotionally but not physically."

"Oh."

"Anyway," he continued. "We think that Chuck was hit by a group of men the detectives are building a case against. These coyotes, you know? The men that smuggle people across the border for money? Well, two of them are the main suspects, and the case hasn't been going well."

My eyes widened. "Are you serious?" When he nodded, I laughed. "No, not really? I mean, that's the stuff they make movies about."

"Well, it's happening."

"What exactly?"

He stared down into the red wine in his glass. "We've been having a problem with safe houses downtown. There are allegations of drug production, smuggling, and prostitution. I don't want to get into it too much, Cherisse. The less you know the better, and I don't want to jeopardize their case."

"Was Chuck doing something illegal?"

"No."

"Are you being careful?"

My final question hung in the air between us like a heavy smoke. I was concerned, or rather – scared – and I was sure it showed on my face.

There was a long pause before he answered. "Of course I am."

"Then why tell me anything?"

"Well, I remember how I felt when Shelly had her accident and you sank into your shell. I know that I've been doing that myself. It bothered me that you've been so unhappy, and it feels better clearing the air between us."

"Do you feel better?"

"For now, yes."

"Then I'll accept that." I glanced at the earrings again. "But you didn't need to buy me earrings and bring home a puppy to say that."

"You're right. I wanted to spoil you a little bit." He chuckled. "Besides, this was one plan that I was able to pull off... of course, I had to wake you out of a dead sleep in order to do it, but it's worth it."

"I love you," I said softly.

Brandon smiled at me. "You are the world to me, Cherisse. No matter what happens at work or at home, I want you to know that I love you more than anything in this world." His voice grew softer, huskier. "That baby sleeping upstairs is the greatest gift you could ever have given to me, and I thank your sister every day for bringing us together, as selfish as that is."

"That's not selfish. I'm sure she loves seeing us so happy together. It would make her feel as though all of her troubles weren't in vain."

"Oh, Sunshine," he groaned, rising up before me. His arms went to the arms of the chair on either side of me, and he hovered above me. "You're really something else."

"I know."

He angled his face over mine and kissed me with all the love in his soul, and I returned his kiss with just as much passion. Our breath mingled in the arid air around us, filling our nostrils with the scent of wine and sweat. Our skin was damp where we touched, heated in places we wanted to be touched.

The puppy on my lap whined, drawing Brandon away. He stared down at me, pinning me with his blue-green gaze. They were almost black in the darkness with desire, and the promise they held sent my heart fluttering.

"Let's go upstairs," he said, reaching for the pup. "I'll put him back in the cage once he goes to the bathroom."

I came to my feet feeling a little dazed. With wobbling knees, I picked up the earrings and our wineglasses and carried them inside. I could hear Brandon outside, coaxing the puppy to do his business. A small smile curved my lips as I watched him in the darkness, cloaked from the dim light by the shadows.

As I carried the rest of his things inside, it occurred to me that he never had taken a swim. But the glow in his eyes told me he did not mind in the least. He had other things on his mind.

****

The ringing of the phone just a few hours later awoke me from a deep sleep. Not completely awake, I reached for it on my side of the bed, ready to hang up on the rude caller, but Brandon was faster than I was. The arm that had cradled me against his broad chest snaked out and grasped the receiver, and I could hear his sleep-heavy voice answer gruffly. "Nixs."

I could hear the male voice on the other end, serious and deep, though I could not understand what he was saying. Glancing down at me, Brandon told the caller to hold on and slipped from the bed. As I watched through blurry eyes, he reached for his shorts and pulled them over his narrow hips. Adjusting the phone against his shoulder, Brandon held it there with his chin as he dressed. Then he was gone, gliding from the room like a ghost in the night.

I lifted my head and glanced at the clock as I heard him go downstairs. It read 4 a.m. We had gone to sleep not an hour ago. Groaning softly into my pillow, I closed my eyes but sleep eluded me. Ten minutes passed without his return. Sighing impatiently, I threw back the covers and came to my feet. Whether I knew I was sneaking or not, I was on tiptoes as I made my way to the stairs. I could hear his voice, muffled and soft, in the kitchen. His words were forceful, but I could not hear what he was saying. I made my way down to the last step and huddled, waiting for him to speak again.

"Jose, no. Tomorrow's no good. I'm home with my family."

Jose. My mind went back to our wedding, the day I was introduced to Lieutenant Fierro. He was the man who had stared down at me so knowingly. I had not liked him on the spot, and finding out now that he was behind the late-night phone call only worsened my dislike.

I had heard enough. Brandon was finishing up, and I could hear him tell Jose to call him back with an answer. Then he was saying good-bye, so I came to my feet and stumbled into the kitchen to meet him just as he hung up the phone. Placing the cordless on the counter, Brandon turned to face me with his hands crossed over his chest. "Sorry about that."

I smiled sympathetically. "I don't suppose you'll tell me what that was all about."

"No."

"Okay... Well, are you coming back to bed, or are you running into work?"

He smiled at me, his eyes glowing. "Dressed like that, how could I resist coming back to bed with you?"

His eyebrows wiggled with insinuation, melting any irritation away. He lunged for me, sending me running back towards the stairs, laughter ringing in our ears. Grasping the railing, I bounded up the stairs, fully aware that he was right behind me. He caught me at the top, his hands encircling me from behind, and his fingers quickly untied the knot, causing the robe to fall in a heap on the floor before I could stop him.

Laughing, I slapped his hands away and jumped onto the bed, quickly burrowing under the covers. He landed atop me and stared. My laughter faded as I met his gaze. He was so special to me, the love of my life. The idea of him in danger sent my blood cold, even though his smile was warm and full of happiness.

"Brandon," I whispered.

"What's wrong?"

"If you don't want to get into the specifics of this investigation, that's fine. But promise me this: if you get into trouble or danger, please tell me. I don't want to lose you, Brandon. I don't think I

287

could function without you."

"You could and you would," he said softly. "I've seen you in the worst of situations, and you've survived every one. You're one helluva strong woman, Cherisse Nicholson."

When my eyes pleaded with him, Brandon nodded slowly. "The investigation has nothing to do with me right now. The detectives are handling it. But I don't expect anything to happen. Really..." He grinned down at me, his tone turning light and teasing. "Besides, I'm a careful kind of guy, you know. I have a great family, a beautiful wife, and the best baby around. I don't want to lose that either."

"Then come here," I ordered, pulling his head down to mine.

He needed no further invitation. I held him close, savoring him, fearing that I could very well lose him.

Chapter 22

The phone was ringing. Over and over again it sounded, but I was up to my elbows in soapy water and Jacob was sitting in the tub with shampoo in his hair. Tyler had just slipped and bumped his head, sending out wails of pain and fear into the small enclosure.

I still had dishes to load in the dishwasher and leftovers to put away. The toilet downstairs had clogged after Jacob inadvertently flushed something – I did not know what – down that afternoon. And to top it all off, it was already an hour past the baby's bedtime. Jacob was spending the night with us while Shelly went to speak at a conference in Tucson about battered woman's syndrome, so I was on my own in trying to get the two to settle down.

"Where is my phone?" I snarled, reaching for the closest towel.

I managed to pick up a towel that I had mopped up spilled juice with earlier. Thrusting it down in disgust, I growled with anger and stood up. "Where is the clean towel?"

With growing frustration, I spun around frantically trying to find the towel.

"Right behind you, Sunshine," Jacob offered.

Sure enough, there was the clean towel, resting haphazardly on the toilet seat. I hurried to it and wiped off my hands, and then scooped the baby into my arms.

I hurried out the door, conscious of the fact that my mobile had stopped ringing and now it was the house phone. Muttering a string of curses behind me, I dove on the bed and reached for it, swearing that if they hung up now I would flip my lid. "Hello."

At first, all I could hear was beeping and computer printers in the background. Voices mingled to a rough blur, coupled with the ringing of telephones. There was a long pause before he answered. "Hi, it's me."

"Oh Brandon," I gasped. "I'm sorry about that."

"Is everything okay?"

"Oh, yeah. I had the baby in the tub and didn't have my phone. Hold on while I get the cordless." Balancing Tyler on my shoulder, I reached for the cordless phone and hurriedly hung up the extension. When I at last placed the handset against my ear, my anger had diminished to a frustrated hum, and the sound of Brandon's voice was just what I needed. Tyler reached for my hair, so I lowered him to my hip and reached for his diaper and nightclothes.

"Everything okay now?"

"What a night," I grumbled. "Everything that can go wrong has."

"Well, that's why I'm calling..."

"Don't tell me – you're going to be late again."

"I'm sorry, babe, but I just got a call for the Unit. I'm on my way to briefing now. I'll be home as soon as I finish up there, okay?"

That was not what I wanted to hear. "What kind of a call?"

"Warrant."

My worst. "Will you be okay?"

I heard his laughter, and it sounded lighthearted and cheerful. In fact, there was relief in his tone, a carefree happiness that I had not heard from him in a while. "I'm fine, Sunshine. I love you."

That he had broached those treasured words while in the middle of the station filled me with warmth. I smiled against the phone, my lips parting with the memory of the night before.

"I love you, too" I said, hearing the huskiness in my voice.

"Wow," he said, lowering his voice. "You sound like Heaven. What are you thinking about?"

"You."

He laughed again. "At least it wasn't dirty diapers down the toilet."

"Speaking of which..."

"I'll tell you what. When I get home we'll repeat last night, okay? Go find those pink silk things from Valentine's Day and put them on. If you do, I promise you that Tyler and Jacob *will* wake up when they hear you scream."

"Oh, Brandon," I said with a sigh. "I wish you were here."

"I wish I were there too. But, alas! I have bad guys to catch and fair maidens to save."

"What about me?"

"The fairest maiden always has to wait. That's part of her appeal."

"Thanks a lot," I said, laughing.

He returned that laugh. "I'll see you in a little while."

"Fine." He was about to hang up when I suddenly called him back. "Please be careful."

Laughing aloud, he took on a saucy edge to his voice. "Sunshine, I'm always careful."

With that he hung up.

It was the last time I heard his treasured voice.

****

Tyler woke up screaming around the time of the shoot-out, and I never did figure out why he was so upset. As I stumbled into his room, I contributed it to his teething, dosed him with Tylenol, and rocked him back to sleep. Once he was down, I checked in on Jacob, who was sleeping soundly on his belly with one hand hanging over the mattress. I approached the bed and smoothed back his hair before closing the door and returning to the bedroom.

With just a little while left before Brandon was due home, I decided it would be useless to go back to bed. Instead, I filled up the bathtub, dropping in the seldom-used bath crystals that Brandon's mother had given me after Tyler was born, and settled in for a warm bath.

No sooner had I climbed under the covers in the middle of the bed when the doorbell rang. It was followed closely by a solid knock. The puppy growled in his crate and followed up with a sharp bark of excitement. Thinking Brandon was once again up to something, I bounded off the bed and hurried downstairs, not bothering to put on my robe. I pulled open the door with an inviting smile on my face which quickly faded.

It was not Brandon at the front door.

"Cherisse?"

Two shadowed forms stood in the entrance, their faces hidden by the glare of the light behind them. They were dressed in dark suits, and the car in the driveway I recognized as a Detective Kellerman's. Glancing back at the two, I saw their eyes, bloodshot and swollen, and knew something was wrong.

Though they say it is impossible, I felt my heart come to a complete stop. It hovered for seconds, sending me stumbling back from the door with a hand pressed against my chest. Seconds or an eternity later, it began to beat violently, sending blood rushing through my ears and down to my toes.

Forgetting that I was dressed in the pink silk things that Brandon had requested earlier, I merely stared at them, fear and mistrust shining in my eyes. Averting their eyes modestly, the taller one stepped forward and spoke. "Can we come in, Cher? We need to talk."

I shook my head. "No."

They exchanged glances. Then he spoke again. "Cher, we need to talk."

"No," I repeated.

I took another step back into the house, intending to flee before I heard those dreaded words.

"I'm sorry, Cher, there's been an accident."

How many times had I feared hearing those words? I knew what they meant. The weight of denial closed around my chest, making it impossible to breathe.

I knew.

I felt it down deep in my bones. Like a sharp knife, the pain in my chest grew, prying my chest apart and exposing all within.

Still my mind screamed that it could not be. I had just spoken to him. How could they be here so fast? Backing away from them with more desperation, I shook my head violently.

"Don't play games with me," I snarled, preparing to slam the doors in their faces.

"Cher, wait!"

I recognized him as he stepped into the light. As I suspected, it was Detective Kellerman. He placed his hand on the door, refusing to allow me to close it.

"There was an accident," he said quickly. "Brandon was first in line. There was an explosion..."

There it was, revealed plainly in his eyes. Dear old, fatherly Kellerman would never lie to me. Brandon had told me that once. He said that he had requested Kellerman to be the one to notify next of kin in case of an accident. They sent him to break it to me gently.

It was the shock and despair on his face and in his swollen eyes that said it all.

This was no joke.

Shut the door. Shut the door. *Shut the door*.

I tried to force it closed against the strength in his hand, but his foot came to block my feeble attempts to slam it.

My mind was working frantically, absurd thoughts that perhaps if I could get them to go away, it would all go away. I could go back upstairs and wait, wait for Brandon to come home.

"I just spoke to him," I said, shaking my head. "You're wrong... you're just wrong. No."

Chest heaving, I backed away, turning and running away from them, despite their protests for me to stop. I made it three quarters of the way up the stairs before Kellerman caught me around the waist, his arm scooping me up and pulling me against his chest.

"It's not true! Tell me it's not true."

I kicked at him, kicked hard, despite his attempts to control me. His resulting grunt did nothing to slow me. I began to howl, denials pouring forth like a tirade of bitter stones.

"I'm sorry, Cher, I'm so sorry."

I bit my lips hard to keep the wail inside, but it bubbled in my chest as I shook my head violently. He sank down on the carpeted stairs, following me as I collapsed.

"No! You're wrong. I just spoke to him. He called here just a few hours ago. He was on his way home. You're just wrong!"

My voice escalated to a high-pitched cry.

"Mike, get someone over here." The arms tightened around me as I finally went limp with disbelief, anger and denial.

"Who?" Detective Kaplan asked, standing helplessly a couple of stairs away.

"I don't know. Kerri – get Kerri over here." I did not look at him. His voice cracked as he spoke, and suddenly I knew for certain that it was true.

Something terrible had happened.

"No, no! It can't be," I moaned, squeezing my eyes tight against the truth. Tears slipped through my clenched lashes, dripping down my cheeks and splashing down onto thighs. I was sobbing, and the sounds that reached my ears were like nothing I had ever heard before. This was not happening. There had to be some sort of mistake. There just had to be! "I just spoke to him. He'll be home soon."

"It's all right, Cher," Kellerman said softly, his hands awkwardly patting my back. "Just let go, Cher, it's okay."

"Oh, God!" I gasped, looking up at the white face above me. "Tell me it's not true."

I watched him swallow, his Adam's apple bobbing uncomfortably. Unable to meet my stare, he turned his face away. "I wish I could, Cher. You've no idea how badly I wish I could."

I could not breathe, and I was repeating the word "no" over and over again in my refusal to accept their words. Everything was wrong. This was all a terrible mistake.

I heard Kaplan speaking on his mobile. His words were indecipherable over the rushing in my ears, but I heard him hang up and approach us.

Placing his hand tentatively on my knee, Kaplan leaned over and spoke softly. "I've got Kerri Moore coming over, Cherisse. She'll be here in about ten minutes."

I did not respond. I could hear the puppy barking in earnest now. His oversized paws scratched at the inside of his crate eagerly.

"Sunshine?" I glanced up and saw Jacob standing at the top of the stairs, rubbing his eyes wearily. "Sunshine, what's wrong?"

It was the sound of Brandon's pet name for me. That one word.

"Please God, please. Please, please, please don't do this to me," I whispered.

Jacob was staring at me in fear, but I did not know how to respond. He shook his head and backed away. He knew.

With a sharp cry, I felt myself curl into a ball with a wail. Flashes of Brandon singing off-key with his beautiful smile appeared before my eyes. Flashes of his face, smiling and laughing exploded in my mind with such finality that a crushing pain filled my chest. Tears streamed down my face unchecked.

I inhaled raggedly, my lungs trying to expand over the uncontrollable sobs that kept rising from deep within my broken heart.

"She's hyperventilating," I heard Kaplan comment.

Dizziness washed over me, and I clung to Kellerman's shirt, balling it into my fingers so tightly that my nails complained bitterly. From behind me the sound of the baby's cries reached my ears.

"Jacob! Oh God, Jacob. The baby!"

Kaplan climbed past Kellerman and I on the stairs and approached the closed door to the baby's room. He reappeared a few seconds later, holding him close against his chest and reached for Jacob.

The boy stared at the middle-aged detective with fear and

continued backing away. "Sunshine. What's wrong?"

Kaplan exchanged a glance with Kellerman and then went down on his haunches before Jacob. "Jacob... I'm sorry, son. We're here about your Uncle Brandon. I'm afraid he's been in an accident. He won't be coming home."

"That's not true, sir," he said bravely. "Poppy said he'd always come home. He promised. He said we'd always be together."

"And I know he meant it," Kaplan said hastily. "But sometimes accidents happen."

"No," Jacob said quickly. "You're wrong. Poppy wouldn't do that."

Raising my head, I pulled away from Kellerman and held out my arms to Jacob – the boy who had seen too much for his young years. "I'm so sorry."

Trying to smile, my lips trembled uncontrollably. My smile appeared more like a grimace, and Jacob took a step away. "No, Sunshine, you're wrong! Poppy will come home. He will!"

I prayed like I had never prayed before how I wished he was right.

Jacob ran away, leaving us with just the sound of the slamming door behind him. I watched as Kaplan came slowly to his feet, still balancing Tyler on his shoulder, and plodded down the hall to Jacob's room. The door closed behind them with a soft click.

It happened so fast. Kellerman held me in his arms on the stairs while I sobbed uncontrollably. There we remained until my muscles tensed up so much that I began to shake. Trembling all over, I clung to Kellerman as though my life depended on it. At that moment, I felt it did.

More people arrived, just striding through the door as though they owned the place. Someone climbed the stairs and wrapped me in the blanket from the den. Then Kerri was there, her arms going around me tightly, and her voice, soft and soothing, in my ear.

"Come here, Cher... God, sweetie, you look awful."

With her cleverly disguised strength, she pulled me away from Kellerman and guided me down the stairs to the sofa in the living room. There she enfolded me in her arms and smoothed my tear-soaked hair away from my face. "I'm so sorry, Cher. I'm so, so sorry," she whispered.

I glanced up at her, seeing her tear-stained face through blurred vision. She smiled tremulously at me, her lips quivering as well. She had loved Brandon, had held that deep friendship bond. Apparently she ached, too.

"He loved you so much, do you hear?" she asked in a determined voice while her hands continued to smooth my hair. "You meant the world to him."

I nodded, numb.

"And he was so lucky to have you," she continued brokenly. "From the first moment he met you, he was hooked. I had never seen him so complete, so content. He was happy and let everyone know it. How wonderful you were. How wonderful Jacob was. And when Tyler was born – wow! We thought even the bad guys would get a cigar."

I nodded again. Hearing her soft voice was soothing me, relaxing me slightly. I wanted to hear about Brandon; I wanted to hear the stories now like I never had before. This was his other family, his law enforcement family. They stayed together like the closest of siblings.

"You were the best thing that ever happened to him, Cher," she whispered, pressing her lips against my ear. "God knows we tried, he and I, but we never had that magic that you had. He was so happy with you."

Raising my head, I pulled away from her and stared hard. "Then why did this have to happen?"

She crumbled. "I don't know."

"What happened?"

"They're still investigating the scene."

"What about his, uh," I stumbled, unable to say the words. "Where is he?"

She shook her head. "Try not to think about that right now."

Her voice trailed off, leaving me to scowl at her. "What do you mean? Of course I want to see him. I mean, doesn't someone have to identify the body?"

"Don't, Cher, please," she whispered. Reaching for my hands, she gripped them tightly between her own. "Lieutenant Fierro was with him the whole time. He took care of it... I heard that there was some kind of explosion. He was right there."

"But didn't he have protection?"

"Yes, he was wearing body armor." She shrugged, and I noticed that the words rising on her lips were painful. They struck me to the bone. "It was an explosion, Cher. They didn't see it coming."

I shuddered fiercely as flashes of Brandon being torn apart struck me like a blow to the head. I shook it and placed my hands against my ears, willing the visions to go away. But they were there. I would never hear Brandon whistle again; I would never feel his arms around me, supporting me and loving me so gently.

The panic that filled me took my breath away. "I can't −"

"I know," Kerri said softly. "Believe me, I know."

She pulled the blanket around me, securing me in its artificial warmth. I huddled deeper within it, swallowing back the scream that threatened to explode from deep within me.

A new sound from the doorway caught Kerri's attention, and she raised her head and stared past me to the front door. With her sharp inhale, I followed her gaze, hoping that it was all a mistake and Brandon would be standing right there.

It was not Brandon.

"Where is she? Where's my baby?"

Chuck, wheelchair bound and dressed only in sweats over his injured legs, was struggling to get in the doorway. His wife, Tina was by his side, her face a mask of shock. Seeing me, Chuck cursed under his breath and heaved once mightily, sending his wheelchair over the last hump into the foyer. He rolled forward as fast as his arms could wheel him and then stopped a few feet away.

"Cher, baby, come here," he ordered softly, opening his arms wide.

I went off the sofa and lunged at him, heartfelt sobs shaking my whole body as I poured out all my grief onto his expansive girth. I could feel Tina's hand stroking my back, her fingers trembling as they patted my hair. "Where are the kids, Cher?"

"They're upstairs," Kerri volunteered. "I think Kaplan's still with Jacob, and the baby went back to sleep."

"Asleep, wow, with all this commotion?"

"I guess so."

"Well, I'll go check on the cherub," she said.

Blocking out the visions of Brandon's body in a mangled pile of blood, I envisioned Tina instead with her chest filling with importance, striding up the stairs to pick up Tyler. She loved that baby; in fact, everyone did. He was so like his father in looks, lending him an angelic face, and the new solid foods I had been integrating into his diet had plumped him up quite a bit. Cherub was an apt nickname.

"What can I do?" Chuck asked softly. "I'm here for you, baby. You tell me what you need, and I'll take care of it."

"I want him home! Tell me this is all a mistake. Please, Chuck, please," I whimpered.

When I raised my head I saw his lips trembling. His eyes were full of tears. "I can't do that for you," he whispered. "I'm so sorry."

"What – what happened tonight? They keep telling me I don't want to know, but I do."

He sighed heavily. I could tell by the slight tensing of his muscles that he had already heard. "They were briefed to serve a hazardous warrant. It was a suspected meth lab, so they were cautious. When they went in, they found forty illegals in various stages of malnutrition and dehydration. During the evacuation, one of the suspects mingled in and took two hostages, a woman and child. Brandon's team had just finished evacuating everyone when the man broke free and shot at them. They tried to fall back, but they didn't have enough time. The shots he fired smashed the chemicals. Some acetone and phosphorus ignited, and the chemicals ...exploded." He took a deep breath. "That's all I know right now. The investigation is still ongoing. But Cher, baby, Nixs died doing the right thing. He was trying to save the people in the house."

My hands went over my ears again. I did not want to hear any more. Every word was like a knife in my chest; the pain was overwhelming. There was no doubt in my mind that Brandon had been doing the right thing. Didn't he always?

I sat up and looked around. Two uniformed officers had joined Kerri and Chuck, replacing Kellerman and Kaplan, who had returned to the scene. The new arrivals already bore black bands over their badges. It was horrible. I could smell their coffee, and I could hear their solemn voices. Disbelief seemed to be the collective emotion, though I heard some commenting about the accident with a sort of fear. Kerri was in there as well. I could hear her asking one of the guys to get out of the way so she could get the milk.

"What is it, Cher?"

"Nothing."

"No, really. What is it? What do you need?"

I looked around again, seeing Brandon's face everywhere. There he was on the coffee table, us smiling as we held Tyler between us. Then there was our wedding photo, with Jacob between us. He was everywhere and nowhere. Not where I wanted him to be.

"I don't know," I said, shaking my head. "All these people..."

"Do you want me to get them to leave? They're just here to make sure you're okay. Tina and I can stay, and I'm sure Kerri will, too."

"I don't want anyone, do you understand? All I want is Brandon."

I watched his eyes fill again, and his voice was rough when he answered. "But Brandon is not coming back, Cher. I'm sorry."

Brandon. Not coming back.

Not coming back.

Not. Coming. Back.

I heard the words over and over again.

My head began to spin uncontrollably as I came to my feet, and I reached out blindly to regain my balance. Chuck's concerned features swam in front of me, but I could not focus. Everything was spinning around me, and I felt lightheaded. It was with thankfulness that the blackness came and swallowed me, sending me to oblivion.

Brandon.

Not coming back.

Chapter 23

"I think everyone's been very kind. Their help setting up the funeral really says a lot. He's going to be buried with a grand ceremony, Cher. Isn't that nice?"

"Nice?" I sneered.

My mother's eyes filled with tears. "I'm sorry, Cher. You know that wasn't what I meant."

When I continued to glare at her, she pressed her hand to her lips and stood up, a muffled sob escaping as she hurried away. For the second time in my adult life, my parents had dropped everything and hopped on a plane to Arizona. They were the first of our growing family to arrive, within hours of the early morning phone call actually, and it was harder than I thought watching everyone gather in Brandon's house.

"Cher, that wasn't very nice," my father said softly.

"Well, I'm not feeling very nice right now, okay?" I snapped.

I was aware that Kerri and Jacob had watched the exchange from their seats in the den, and grimaced. Jacob should not see me so emotional. I knew I needed to be strong for him, but at that moment I just couldn't. Unfortunately, every television had been removed from the house immediately so no one would mistakenly flip on the news, so I could not set Jacob in front of a movie in order to preoccupy him.

He needed his mother. Shelly would be better able to deal with him than me. I just wished she'd hurry up and get here. Mary had said that she was driving as fast as she could.

Brandon still had not come home.

With only five hours of sleep over the past two days, facing Brandon's sudden death was all the harder. Bags had long ago formed under my eyes, despite the gallons of coffee I had consumed in the past eighteen hours.

Oh, God, I raged, only eighteen hours had passed. If I couldn't handle eighteen miserable hours, how could I face the rest of my life without him?

The phone rang again. I had been tempted to pull it from the wall but knew it would be useless. Kerri leaped to pick it up, grabbing the cordless and going down the hall to the spare bedroom. She had taken up residence there earlier, promising not to leave me until I asked her to.

We were silent until Kerri returned, and I placed my chin on my cupped hands and stared at her blankly. "That was Gina. She's on her way from Colorado Springs. I'll see if one of the guys can get her and her family at the airport. She also said that Brandon's parents left Payson an hour ago. They should be here within an hour."

I nodded emotionlessly. My eyes could not focus, and I turned away to look outside. The pool was empty, with no giggles as Brandon held Jacob over his head and tossed him into the crystal blue water. I hastily looked away with a low moan escaping my tightly clenched lips.

"Cher. I think you need something. Hold on a minute." Kerri

went back to her room, reappearing a few minutes later with a prescription bottle in her hand. She set it before me and placed her hands on her hips. "Take one and go upstairs."

"What is it?"

"Something to help you sleep. You need to rest. We'll watch Tyler and Jacob until Shelly gets here. Take one."

"Take one," my father agreed.

Reaching for the bottle, I struggled to read the contents, but my eyesight was so blurred I couldn't focus. At that point, I didn't care either way. So what if I overdosed or had a reaction? At least I would be with Brandon again.

I swallowed the pill with a swig of my cold coffee, thanking Tyler for insisting on weaning off the breast the week before. With Kerri's assistance, I stumbled upstairs a little while later, falling into our bed without a thought of how empty it was. Once again, I fell into sweet oblivion, embracing the blackness with a sigh of relief.

****

Lieutenant Fierro came to see me the day before the funeral. Although I wanted to tell him to go away, Kerri felt it was important for me to at least hear him out. Therefore, when he appeared at my door, looking dazzling in his tailored black suit, I made sure that Brandon's whole family was with me.

I remained seated in the living room, with Tyler on my lap, while Brandon's father, Ken, opened the door and admitted him. After a few brief exchanges, Fierro's gaze swung over to me, and I shuddered with distaste.

There was something about him that I just did not like, and the way he studied me, missing nothing, brought a lump to my throat. I wanted to come to my feet and scream at him that yes, I was falling apart, and yes, I could not face life without Brandon by my side. It was true. I was helpless. I was so much weaker than Shelly ever was. All that time I had thought that I was the strong one, when in fact I was weak. Everything was false about me. I needed Brandon in order to survive.

Nevertheless, I held my tongue. Instead of shouting at him, I gave him a view of my profile as I stared outside. I remained thus as he approached me and crouched down. His hand, I noticed out the corner of my eye, was shaking slightly as he reached out to touch the peachy-soft fuzz of Tyler's fair hair. Tyler reached for Fierro's hand, pulling one of his long fingers to his mouth and clamping down. Instead of pulling away, a small smile curved the corner of his lips, and a gleam that looked a little like envy appeared in his eyes.

"Cherisse, I just wanted to come over and give you my condolences —"

"Thank you, Lieutenant," I said hastily. I still could not look at him.

He continued, ignoring my rudeness. "Is there somewhere we can speak privately?"

I did turn to look at him then, a frown marring my pale face. "Why? Can't you say it in front of his family?"

I heard my mother gasp at my uncustomary rudeness, but I didn't care. Nothing mattered to me anymore.

Fierro shrugged, but his face spoke volumes. I saw the jumbling of emotions come and go on his face, finally settling on concern. "I'd heard that you had questions about the accident — about what happened."

"Yes."

"I wanted to tell you what happened, that is, if you're up to it."

The unspoken challenge hung heavily in the air between us. Coming to my feet, I placed Tyler on my hip and nodded in the direction of the patio outside. "Is it too hot to sit out there?" I asked mechanically.

"No, not at all."

He stepped before me and slid the patio door open, stepping aside so I could pass. The others in the living room watched on, and Kerri came to stand in the kitchen with a tearful Lori by her side. Seeing me stare, Kerri gave me a subtle nod of encouragement.

After closing the door behind him, Jose pulled out a chair for me to sit and then sat modestly across from me. I again noticed the nervousness around him, appearing mostly in the covert glances he gave me under his lashes.

"I was present at the call," he began, his voice even. "He was the first to go in." I nodded expectantly, urging him to continue. For a moment, it appeared as though Fierro might break down, but he took a deep breath and plowed forward. "Anyway, you know all that, and I can't really give out any more details... After the...explosion, he was conscious. I took off his helmet. There was so much blood, and he was burned, but he was breathing. He said to me –" He took a deep breath that quivered. Tears filled his eyes. "He said to me... 'My wife's going to be furious. I told her I would be careful' and then he said, 'make sure you tell her and my son that I love them.' He smiled."

I bit my lip to keep from crying out as the hot tears again filled my eyes. His final words. Pressing my fingers to my compressed lips, I tasted blood. I looked away from the sympathy in Fierro's eyes.

"I stayed with him until the ambulance came, Cherisse. I couldn't leave him alone. He was losing so much blood. I did everything that I could to stop it, but it just kept coming. I'm sorry –" He broke off with a soft curse and pressed his hands to his eyes. The tears poured out of my eyes now, like silent streams, they forged their way down my cheeks to the top of Tyler's head. He continued gurgling and chewing on my fingers, taking a break every now and then to wave my hand in his small fist. "I'm sorry... When we got him into the ambulance, he was suffering from head trauma... and other problems. He lost consciousness soon after. They lost him at the hospital."

The silence was heavy between us for several minutes as I cried silently into Tyler's neck. Fierro just watched me, but his eyes remained damp. When I had at last regained some sort of composure, he came to his feet and held out a hand. When I did not immediately accept it, he reached forward and grasped my fingers. Despite the heat outside his hand was cool, dry, and strong as he helped me to my feet.

"I wanted you to know that he was thinking of you in the end, and that I was proud to have him on my team. I've never seen another officer give himself so easily to the dangers on the force. He was a brave man, Cherisse, and I hope you know that."

"I do," I whispered, my voice cracking.

"If you need anything, please call me."

I nodded reluctantly, and then he was gone.

****

Brandon's death was everywhere. From the people coming and going in our home, to the newscasts on in the morning, noon, and night, I could not escape the harsh reality even though the house was still television-free. When Ken and Brigid arrived, they brought the latest and a current newspaper. From them, we heard about the two coyotes arrested in connection with the smuggling of immigrants and production and distribution of crystal methamphetamine two days before. I sat stunned, anger flashing in my eyes. Glaring at Kerri, I narrowed my eyes at her. "They're still alive? Why didn't you tell me?"

"The one who took the hostages is dead, Cher. I didn't want to upset you anymore."

I turned away in disgust. "There will be a trial."

"Yes. Maybe you shouldn't hear all this right now," she said softly.

The photo on the front page of the newspaper was a view of the outside of the house they had raided. It was focused on the spot where the coyote, woman, baby, and Brandon had died. A bundle of flowers had already begun the make-shift shrine to the dead.

In the process of delivering the news, I knew that the reporters had no idea what they did to the families who suffered. That seeing how terribly their loved ones died was painful enough without having to rehash it everywhere they looked.

I cried.

****

Tomorrow was the funeral. It would be televised, much to my chagrin. The idea of thousands of people viewing my grief was extremely distasteful. However, I had been promised that the cameras would not zoom in on the immediate family, especially me.

There was a public outcry about the circumstances of Brandon and the two immigrants' death. Questions about the department as well as their safety measures were raised, and even I felt horribly. I had met the men on the force, and never had I met such a dedicated group of men and women. They worked hard and risked their lives on a daily basis, and there was no doubt in my mind that they had all done their jobs as they were trained to do that night with the time that they had. Everything happened so fast.

Hearing this without being able to turn to Brandon and confirm my thoughts reminded me again of his loss. I silently watched the discussion with a touch of loneliness. Moving through life with the help of sleeping pills and routine, I had made it through the day denying the pain in my breast. Bedtime, however, was the only time when I was completely alone. I could not hide from the pain or the truth there. Never had a bed seemed so huge, so empty – so unwelcome.

The night before I had stripped it down to the bare mattress and slept on the floor, hating the sight of Brandon's pillow which was still enmeshed with his scent. I was not ready yet to deal with it all.

All those long nights ahead without Brandon next to me.

I awoke the next morning and showered in the bathroom downstairs. It was difficult to escape all the memories. There was the bathtub, where Brandon had lovingly washed my hair after our first night together. Then there was the other upstairs bathroom, where Brandon had called to tell me he would be late. The night he never came home... Oh, God, had I known!

With a sense of numbness, I dressed in a black dress that my mother had bought for me at the mall the day before, smoothing the material over my hips and slipping on my black shoes with uneasy reluctance. Today was the day I would bury my beloved husband.

That was the last place in the world I wanted to be.

The press had called the house twice over the past two days, looking for a statement about the arrests. My father stepped up to the plate and had held them at bay, saying we were mourning and not ready to discuss Brandon's loss, but that we supported the department in every way. Brandon's parents, a shallow shell of their usual liveliness, watched and nodded their agreement. Even as I ached inside, I knew that they too were suffering. They had lost their child.

With heavy hearts, we all loaded into the car and made our way to the funeral home.

I stared at the shiny walnut coffin with revulsion. Inside it, sealed from my eyes, my husband lay. Someone – I think it was Jose – had taken his best uniform from the closet in my bedroom. It was gone in a flash, delivered to the unseen hands that had sealed my husband into the pitch black, airless block of polished wood. All along, I wanted to say that he would have been more comfortable in his sweats, but I doubted anyone would listen to me.

Flowers were draped over the coffin, as well as a United States Flag. It looked so final that I had to turn away as they loaded it in the hearse. Shelly wrapped her arm around my shoulders and squeezed me tight. "Are you okay, Cher?"

"We could've met them at the church," Gina said in my ear, placing her hand on my other shoulder.

"No, I wanted to see this. This is probably the closest I'll ever be to him again."

She nodded, though I could see that she still did not understand. He was her younger brother – nothing more. She had not lived with him in years; she didn't know him the way I did.

"Are you ready?" Adam asked.

I nodded, allowing Brandon's older brother to guide me to the waiting limousine. Shelly, Ken and Brigid were inside already, holding Tyler and Jacob closely to their sides. Jacob was gray-faced and sullen, his eyes bloodshot from early morning tears. I reached out and smoothed down his unruly hair, my eyes curiously dry when Shelly hugged him tight.

The cars proceeded to the church with a police escort, and again we waited while the coffin was brought in and set up. People were milling about, with news crews filming everything, including helicopters hovering over our heads. Uniformed officers lined the way to the doorway of the church where we were married, and the parking lot was filled with cruisers from all over the state. I was amazed and would have been touched if I had any feeling left in me.

Uniforms of all different colors saluted us as we passed. It was touching in a macabre sort of way. Although I had once been a part of that brotherhood, I never understood the mass of feeling when an officer was lost.

Off in the distance, I saw a small group of bystanders waving flowers in our direction. Ken broke away and approached them, clasping their hands and thanking them for the effort. When he returned, his eyes glistened with tears from their kindness.

I avoided him lest I should lose my own tenuous control. It took all of my strength to remain dry-eyed when inside I was burning up with agony. I felt helpless and alone, even though our friends and family milled around me, eager to do anything I asked.

Somehow I was inside the church, and the very same pastor who had married us approached me and took my hands. They were dry against my clammy skin, but his gentle eyes shone with sadness in addition to sympathy. I remembered how much Pastor Mendoza had enjoyed being with Brandon, and my heart went out to him as well.

"Cherisse, how are you?"

I managed a weak smile. "As much as I hate to admit it, I'm actually hanging in."

"She's been very strong," Shelly said, squeezing my shoulder.

"That's the best you can do," he said softly. "Time will heal."

"I hope you're right," I said hoarsely.

"Sit down, right here," he said, guiding me to the front row. "And who has the baby? Ah, here you are. Stay with your Mama. That's right. Good."

He stepped back and cupped his chin in his hand, so I glanced down the row. Shelly and Jacob were now to my left, and Brandon's parents with Tyler and Lori sat to my right. Tyler was sucking his fist and babbling happily, and I prayed that he would hold out until the ceremony was over.

Behind us sat Brandon's older brother and sister and their families. While Jacob had wanted to sit with Savannah, my mother begged him to sit with her, and he reluctantly agreed. Sullen and angry, Jacob still denied that Brandon's body was in the flag-draped coffin set on the stand before us, surrounded by sweet-smelling flowers. He continued to believe that Brandon was coming home.

Mary suggested that he go back to counseling yet again with Doctor Stansfield, and she and Shelly both agreed that I should go, too. It was too much to think about at the time, so I merely nodded my head. The police chaplain had visited the day before and spoke to me for hours, but I could barely remember what she said. It all seemed superficial and useless.

As my thoughts ran the gamut, I missed the arrival of the other mourners. I had no idea who was coming, and I didn't really care. Pastor Mendoza was standing upon the dais with the same police chaplain I had met before. They waited patiently for everyone to sit.

The music droned on, rubbing my nerves raw. I adjusted on the hard wooden bench, crossing my legs and reaching blindly into my small bag for the tissues. I suspected I would need them today.

As my mind continued its aimless wanderings, the music

changed and the ceremony began. I tried to block out the sound of Pastor Mendoza's words, but then there was Chuck in his wheelchair, his eyes red-rimmed as he read off the white-lined piece of paper. "I remember when Brandon came to me, fresh out of the military. He was so full of himself, a typical rookie, with one exception: he took his job seriously and never behaved foolishly..."

And Ethan Schor appeared: "I remember when I began training to get on the Unit. Brandon was lecturing that day, and when he saw me he sort of, you know, smiled that big smile of his. I should've known he was up to something. Well, he got me good. I nearly wet my pants when I was the bad guy and they were all hunting me. The joke was on me, you know?"

I did not understand, but the small, short chuckles from around me told me that the officers knew exactly what he was talking about.

Lori was up next, speaking on behalf of her family. I watched her move slowly, almost painfully to the dais, her tissues clutched in one hand and the paper in the other. She took a moment to stare at the massive crowd as it extended out into the daylight before glancing down at her speech. Smoothing it out carefully over the podium, she began to read. "Brandon was my brother. He was not the eldest, but he was my closest sibling and my best friend growing up. Sure, we had our fights and squabbles just like any other family, but Brandon was always there for me. He would walk me home from school and protect me from the other kids. He even took the time once to bring me on one of his dates once when I was stood up. I'll never forget that about him. He was always there when you needed him.

"But I knew early on that there was something missing in his life. Sure, he moved on and made a good career for himself, but no one in my family could say that he was truly happy until he met his wife, Cherisse." She stopped and looked at me, a small smile appearing as

I wiped my eyes. Her hands made rapid movements as she continued to speak, and the pleading quality brought tears to many more eyes. Her voice trembled uncontrollably. "She's a strong woman, his wife. He would glow when he spoke of her, Jacob, and Tyler. And when he called me to tell me he was marrying Cher, I thought he was going to burst at the seams. 'Lori,' he said, 'I have never met another woman like her. She's amazing. She's the best thing that ever happened to me. I want her to have my children. I want to get old with her. She's the one.'" She paused again to regain control. "And I'm so glad that he had her when he died, that he was able to have that happiness in his life. Thank you."

Brigid's arm went around my quaking shoulders. I needed to fight the urge to get up and run away, but I couldn't. Chief Ortiz's voice was filling the high ceilings with his deep monologue, speaking of Brandon's many achievements and his bravery. I had heard enough. I wanted to escape.

The fingers around my shoulder tightened as I made the move to run. Glancing over, I saw the tears on Brigid's face and shook my head. "I can't take this," I whispered. "Everyone's saying how strong I am, but I'm not."

"Ssh," she admonished softly.

"I'm not strong enough, Brigid. I need to get out of here."

"Ssh, baby, it's almost over," my mother said, bending toward me. Her arm joined Brigid's around me, holding me down. "You can do this, Cher, they're not wrong. You can go on."

"I don't want to."

The weight of someone's stare compelled me to look up. Fierro had just spread out his notes, but he was staring at me and the commotion in the front row. I stiffened immediately, raising my head with pride. I needed to honor my husband in front of his superior officer. He deserved my respect.

I returned my attention to the podium even though I barely listened to him praise Brandon's accomplishments. Then he moved on to more personal words, and the weight of his guilt caused his voice to break. It was then that I gave him my full attention, and my eyes never wavered from his chiseled profile.

"The hardest thing I had to do was clean out Brandon's locker. He kept his private life private, and he told me once that he kept his work life at work. But when I opened up his locker I saw that even though he didn't talk about it, he still kept his family close to his heart while he was with us." He paused and took a deep breath. "There were pictures everywhere. Pictures of his wife, his son and his nephew. They were happy shots; everyone was smiling. And for a moment, I felt real jealousy. It was the kind of jealousy that you feel when someone has something you would want for yourself. He had such a loving family and was so happy with them that there was nowhere else in life that he'd rather be.

"It was a pleasure to know and work with such a fine officer. I know he'll be leaving behind a lot of good friends and a lovely family, but at least we can all say that we were rewarded to have known him and worked with him. I, myself, will certainly appreciate the memories he's given me."

Nodding his head in thanks, Fierro stepped down, not glancing our way. I watched him go, watched him as he pressed his palms into his eyes and began to understand. Brandon had liked him for a reason. There was a reason Fierro appeared so tormented, and that reason had to be his guilt at not being able to prevent the tragedy.

I was so proud of Brandon. I was proud that I had been the woman who had captured his heart.

But I was also the woman who lost that wonderful man. And the knowledge cut deeply into my bones.

I put my face in my hands and cried.

****

The cemetery was awash with blue lights. A long procession of police cars, all ablaze, had followed us from the church. They closed Route 60 for a six-mile stretch to allow for the lengthy procession. People lined the way, some holding signs, and others tossing flowers. Two ladder fire trucks were parked at the entrance to the cemetery with their ladders extended, and an American flag was hung between them. When we arrived, I noticed in the crowd stood uniformed military officers as well as the policemen. Firefighters and EMS personnel also stood at attention. There were so many men and women there that I could barely see the street just beyond. Such a strong and loyal show of support reminded me again of the brotherhood Brandon had adopted.

Despite the massive crowd, it was eerily silent. An occasional cough or the mumblings of one of the children was the only thing disturbing the heavy silence.

Pastor Mendoza bent to speak to my mother. I listened half-heartedly.

Were we ready to continue? No, I wanted to scream.

I was not ready to say good-bye.

Then he was speaking. Thanking everyone for their support of us. Thanking the department for honoring Brandon so highly. He was doing it all for me, I thought dryly. Of course, I was in no state to do it myself. Not yet.

When the 21-gun salute sounded, Tyler began to cry. I was vaguely aware of Lori reaching for her nephew and soothing him in soft, crooning voice. As so many had before me, I jumped at the sound, wishing I could block them out with my hands.

My tears overflowed when the police helicopters flew by in the missing man formation. Adam stood behind me, one hand on my shoulder and the other around his wife's waist. He squeezed gently when the doleful notes of "Amazing Grace" sounded from the bagpipers. And then there was the slightly off-key sound of "Taps". Throughout it all I wished I could escape. I did not want to be there, sharing this spectacle with all these people.

I thought how uncomfortable Brandon would have been with all the trouble they went to. He would have shaken his head and smiled one of his angelic smiles.

The rustling around me caught my attention once more. The men and women dressed in their finest were reaching to their belts and turning on their radios. The air crackled with the sound of their portables, all tuned in to the same frequency.

The woman on the other end sounded tearful, despite her professional words. She called his cruiser. Three times. Over and over again I heard his number called.

Answer!   I wanted to scream. Please, Brandon, please. Oh, please, answer.

But he didn't.

"This is the final call for Sergeant Brandon Michael Nicholson, may you rest in peace, sir."

Rest in peace.

I stared at the coffin.

I would never see his smile again.

He really was gone.

It was over.

Epilogue

I went to the cemetery again this morning, having just finished my story. I have come full circle. Two months have passed, and I'm still trying to move on with my life, but things have been difficult.

I went to the cemetery to talk to Brandon. Doctor Stansfield told me there was nothing wrong with doing that, at least not at first. In some small corner of my mind, I knew I would have to move on, but the time did not feel right yet. I still wanted to share with him the things that had occurred since I last heard his voice.

Staring down at the flower-lined gravestone, I pressed my cheek against the cool stone and spoke softly. "I'm still sleeping with your clothes beside me. They still hold a little of your scent. It helps me to avoid reality."

I laughed at that, thinking that if someone had walked by and heard me I would be locked up. "Everyone's been so nice. Mary and some of the ladies at A Better Place had been bringing me meals every night, but that's eased up a bit since I went back to work there. A couple of weeks ago, a few of the ladies stayed over for a mini-session, and I sat in on a few counseling sessions there. I just couldn't understand any of it. How can these women allow their spouses or partners hurt them and then hold their own once they get away? I mean, some of these women have been hurt so badly that it's horrible to think about, and yet they survive.

"I was thinking about how I just didn't think I could without you. But then something happened. There was an incident at the shelter yesterday. One of the ladies locked herself in an office and wouldn't come out. She had given up. I went to the door and thought of you. I told her that life was too short, and that we needed to treasure every day as though it was our last. I told her that the people that we love count on us to be strong. You taught me that, Brandon.

"I also told her something that you said to me that first time we shared coffee. You said that 'life is what we make of it. We can either let it pass us by or take advantage of what is handed to us.' I've been thinking about those words a lot lately. You were so right. Gosh, I wish I had told you when I had the chance that you've taught me so much."

Sighing shakily, I brushed at my watery eyes. "Shelly and Jacob moved in today, although I'm not sure how long we'll be there. First of all, Shelly is driving again, and she's got a new boyfriend. It's a guy that she met in rehab, another brain injury patient, and he's really nice. He lets her come and go as she pleases, none of this possessive stuff. Oh, and I also put the house on the market. One of Mary's gals got her real estate license and she's selling it for us. I think I'll downsize a bit."

I laughed a little, remembering Brandon's quip about how he would have to find a new wife if the woman he married did not like his house. "It's not that I don't like it. It was just your house and the memories... Well, enough of that. Besides, I took a teaching job in Phoenix starting later this month. High school English, Brandon, just like I hoped. I'll be working with lower income kids, and I'm really looking forward to it.

"Oh, so once everything settled down again around home, Shelly and I had a long chat about how strong she really was. I think that she liked hearing it from me." I snorted. "You always told me that I was the strong one, but you know what? I think it was her. I don't know how I could've managed these last two months without you if she hadn't stuck around."

"Also, Arianne came out with Mike. She was very upset when she heard about it on the news, but then, I always knew that she loved you, too. It wouldn't surprise me if you knew it all along."

Sighing, I reached for a daisy that some kind person had dropped off. It sat alone on top of the gravestone, all by itself. I wondered who had been there, thinking it was most likely Kerri as I twirled it around in my palms. "Paul called me yesterday. Arianne had called to tell him about my writing, and he wants me to send it to him. He's in New York, you know, working as an editorial assistant at one of the big publishing houses. I was thrilled he wanted to read it. He said I always knew my way around words, and anything I wrote would be good by his standards. Ha! Imagine that. My blubbering sounding good?"

My voice sounded loud in the slight breeze blowing around me. I stopped speaking and glanced out towards the car. It was alone there, with no one else in sight. I liked it best this way. I had privacy.

Gulping back a sob, I reached out to stroke Brandon's gravestone. It was still so difficult to imagine him lying in the darkness, with only cold, damp earth around him. A single tear careened down my cheek and landed upon my top. I swiped at it, but it seeped into the pink cotton. It was hot outside and my bare legs were sweating at the knees where they crossed.

I came to my feet and stared down at the gravestone. "Sometimes I still wish I could leave it all and join you. But then I think of what you said after Shelly's accident – you just keep putting one foot in front of another and things will work themselves out. Gosh, Brandon, we had so short a time together, but you made such an impact in my life. I miss you desperately..."

My voice trailed off as a gust of wind blew my hair into my face. Off in the distance, towards the Santan Mountains, a large wall of dust was approaching. One of Phoenix's monsoon storms was coming, and it brought another gust of wind with it. I froze when I heard it.

"Sunshine..."

It was so soft that I felt I must have imagined it. I glanced around, spinning on my heel, looking everywhere for the source of that cherished word. There was no one about.

A movement caught my eye. Another car had arrived, and three figures emerged. It was Shelly and Jacob with Tyler. They waved at me, and I had to laugh as Tyler's chubby fist waved dramatically up and down.

Wiping at my face to clear the tears, I stared down at the gravestone and smiled. "I should've known you'd never leave me. You'll always be up there watching over me, talking to me when I can barely hear you, won't you...? I promise I won't give up, Brandon, my darling, I will always taste hope," I said softly, my fingers caressing the smooth stone. "And like I said to that poor woman at the shelter yesterday, the people who love us count on us to keep going. Well, you've given me a new reason to keep going, too."

Shelly set down Tyler in the grass, and the chubby baby began to instantly explore his surroundings. Putting his hands down in the prickly grass cautiously, he pushed himself up to a wobbly upright position. Holding up my finger to signal her to wait, I allowed my other hand to go to my smooth abdomen. "I went to the doctor today. Yes, that last night we were together you gave me another baby. I was worried that I had taken all those pills to help me sleep in the beginning, but he told me that our bodies have a way of protecting those tiny cells early on. He said everything looked fine. So, while I may not have you here by my side, at least I'll always have your likeness in our children."

I bent and kissed the gravestone. It was cool under my lips. Like death. Straightening, I saw Tyler fall face first into the grass. He pushed himself up with a hesitant cry. Smiling, I walked forward with my arms open to embrace him.

Here was my future: Tyler and now my unborn child. They were my reason to keep going and face the days ahead. Just like Shelly and all those other women who found the strength to move on, I knew that it was possible. We would all continue tasting hope on our tongues, reaching out to grasp it, and feeling it in our hands. And I, for one, knew that Brandon would still be there, his voice on the wind, saying just one simple word.

Sunshine.

The End

Author's Note

●▼●

Domestic abuse is a serious situation that no man, woman or child should have to endure alone. The Internet has many resources (too many to list) for those who suffer from or know someone who suffers from abuse. Please help those who cannot help themselves, as our fine officers on the police force and in EMS around us do every day. We should all grant the men and women who uphold the law the respect they deserve, as well as those men, women and children that survive domestic abuse.

All of you are my heroes.

About the Author

•▼•

Always composing stories in her head, Collette began her first novel at the age of eight. Since then, she has obtained her bachelor's degree in literature and master's degree in education while squeezing in her writing whenever she can. The best-selling New England native now resides in Arizona with her three children and multiple family pets.

Connect with me online at: http://www.collettescott.com